I0819674

Light Wielder

ALSO BY RACHEL SCHNEIDER

Metal Slinger: Fire & Metal: Book One

Light Wielder

FIRE & METAL

BOOK TWO

RACHEL SCHNEIDER

SATURDAY BOOKS
NEW YORK

First published in the United States by Saturday Books, an imprint of St. Martin's Publishing Group

EU Representative: Macmillan Publishers Ireland Ltd, 1st Floor, The Liffey Trust Centre, 117–126 Sheriff Street Upper, Dublin 1, D01 YC43

For information, address St. Martin's Publishing Group, 120 Broadway, New York, NY 10271.

www.saturdaybooks.com

Endpapers and case by Lía Ramírez

The Library of Congress Cataloging-in-Publication Data is available upon request.

ISBN 978-1-250-41910-1 (hardcover)
ISBN 978-1-250-41911-8 (ebook)

First U.S. Edition: 2026

10 9 8 7 6 5 4 3 2 1

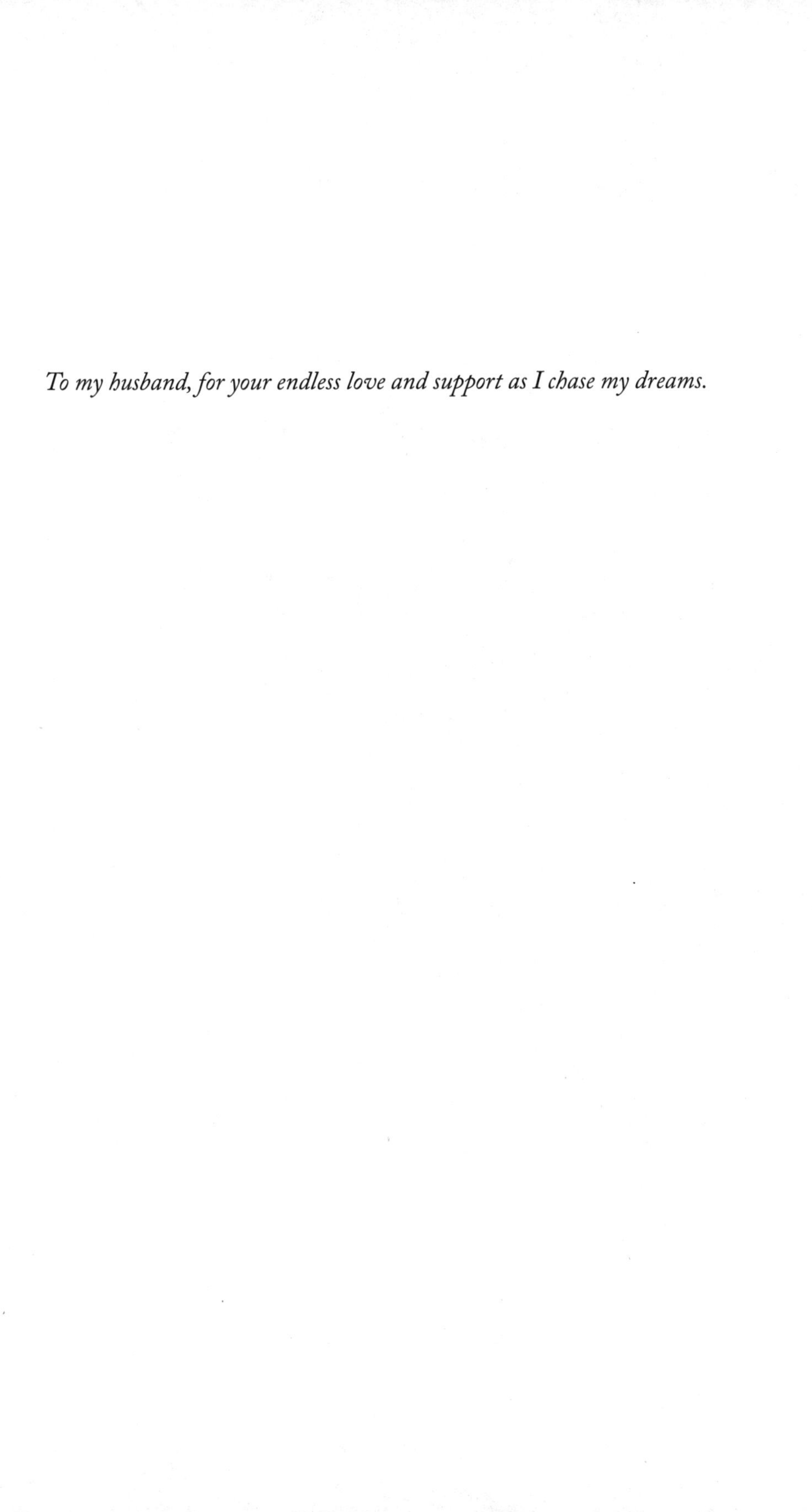

To my husband, for your endless love and support as I chase my dreams.

Light Wielder

Acker,

While you've been fending off Roison's forces to the east, I've just received word that Kai and his father, along with all of the Alaha, have reached the black sand beaches of their shores. Your army is soon going to be outnumbered. You know it as well as I do. And you're going to call upon your closest and only allies, the Strou to the north of both of our territories across the gulf if you haven't already.

This is my letter asking you not to.

I cannot allow the Strou to reach your land, and my people have done nothing to incite any harm onto them. I understand this is a significant request considering our fraught relationship, but I'd be remiss to not advocate for my people. I believe, if faced with the same dilemma, you would do the same.

Gods, I'm still confused on how we got here.

The last two years have felt endless. Yet, life continues to move forward anyway. Sometimes I think of removing the mangi stones on the off chance you've done the same just so I can get a glimpse inside your head. But then I remember what happened the last time I did, and I convince myself I'm better off not knowing.

If you can't seem to see that your father is tyrannical in his rule, then I was wrong, and you don't deserve the crown any more than your father does. I'll consider any attack on my people as a direct attack from you, and I'll send the Maile army for both of your heads.

-Jovie

I lift the quill from the parchment and let out a breath of frustration. I'm wasting my time. There's no reason for Acker to ever consider sparing Maile when his people are in tatters due to my betrayal. All this letter will serve to do is humiliate me.

Opening the door to the lamp on my desk, I touch the corner of the parchment to the flame, watching as it slowly works its way up the parchment.

A better leader would send it. Saving her people by any means necessary, including her pride.

But I'm going to need what little pride I have left to lead an army to defend my territory, and I can't do it with Acker snapping the last thread of hope holding my heart together by denying me.

I'd rather face death instead.

Chapter 1

ACKER

"Where the fuck is he going?"

Hallis pivots from his watch point at the top of the stairs outside the palace's front doors, eyes roving over my half-dressed state, brow raised. "Rumor has it he has female company awaiting him at the southern cottage."

I finish buttoning my shirt as I descend the rest of the steps toward the carriage. "Father," I announce.

He turns, fixing the gloves at his wrists, grin firmly in place despite my obvious displeasure. "Son, where are your shoes?"

"Tyreek called an urgent meeting. The entire council is waiting as we speak."

"I have something important to attend to. I'm sure it's nothing you can't handle without me," my father says.

"They won't see it that way," I argue.

My father's calm expression doesn't wane. "Then you make them."

He taps me on the cheek. The gesture is meant to be placating, something he's done ever since I was a child, and it's condescending as fuck. Harold, the driver, holds the door open as my father slides into the carriage. He, at least, has the wherewithal to appear repentant.

I, along with the trainees in the courtyard, watch as the dark stallions parade the carriage toward the palace gates.

Unbelievable.

Hallis's footsteps draw near and his gaze turns toward the sky. "Still odd to see the wall free of buzzards."

My eyes shift to the parapets where the birds used to rest.

When Jovie and her pet shifter, Messer, fled from the palace after killing every last member of my father's council, they stopped just long enough to disarm the soldiers at the gate, and as the birds above scattered into the night sky, Jovie stood under that iron fence and unleashed her magic. A bolt of burning light so bright I had to shield my eyes from my place on the balcony. She broke through the iron chains holding the cages aloft, sending the enclosures holding the bodies of the king's prisoners to the ground in a clash of defiance.

It was the least of her transgressions, considering the blood-soaked floors of the dining hall, but somehow the most damning to my father's crown. It sent a message to the people: the princess of Maile does not condone the oppression of anyone born of magic.

Since that day nearly four years ago, Jovinnia's name has been whispered in dark alleys and back rooms of taverns. The once-feared light wielder became a beacon of hope in the city for those with magic. Apparently, a hidden seed of rebellion has been festering in my father's city, and Jovie's actions gave it the water it needed to grow. It didn't take long for people to grow brazen. Protests erupted; mangi stones from the collars that magic wielders had been forced to wear littered the streets or were ground to dust under the hordes of marching feet. They began calling for change; for release from oppression. The image of my father's hanging body painted on the outside of the palace walls is vivid in my mind. The rope around his neck the same mottled orange as mangi stones.

The cages never went back up.

Hallis's voice calls out to the trainee soldiers still lingering in the courtyard. "Quit your gawking! Back to work."

The young faces of the boys make my stomach roil.

"Have Imen take over training and report to the war room," I tell Hallis, brushing past him. "Have a maidservant send in the best wine they can find in the cellars. And something to eat. Maybe it'll help smooth over my father's absence."

"Doubtful," Hallis mutters under his breath as he turns to comply.

Taking the stairs two at a time, I reenter the palace and head upstairs to the spare bedchamber and quickly straighten the unkempt bedding to hide any evidence of my presence in the space. The last thing I need is the maidservants gossiping about me not staying in my own bedchamber. I retrieve the string of mangi stones from the bedside table. In my haste to try and stop my father from leaving the city, I'd forgotten the necklace. A careless mistake.

As much as I despise the speckled stones, they serve a vital purpose in bringing comfort to the appointed council lords, buffering my magic in their presence. A few of them have gifts, but none that can rival the lethality of mine, and that makes them nervous. More importantly, however, the stones prevent my Match from eavesdropping.

Wrapping them around my neck, I let the ends hang across my lapels. They're heavy and the way they smother my magic is exhausting. A constant reminder of *her* betrayal.

Not that I expect Jovie to bridge the gap of the Bond to spy on me. She's only done it once since her departure that I'm aware of . . . and I'm positive she learned her lesson the first time. I made sure of it.

I put on shoes and make my way down to the war room, taking a deep breath before I enter. I'd rather face down an army of men twice my size before dealing with the council, but, alas, here I am. My father's *substitute*.

Conversation comes to a halt as I enter, all heads swiveling in my direction. The chandelier overhead shines down over the war map in the center of the room, kept lit at all hours during times of war in case of urgent business. Although bright on the map's topography, the light never quite reaches the walls of the chamber, keeping shadows lurking in the corners.

Lord Draken speaks first. "Where's the king?"

"He won't be attending," I say, addressing the other fourteen men. I nod to Hallis. "Let's go ahead and begin."

Tyreek, the last to agree to take a seat on my father's newly appointed council, leans forward, hands gripping the side of the table. "I stressed the importance of your father being here when I requested this meeting," he says.

The formidable man is not one to be easily rattled. After he served in my grandfather's military as a boy, he returned to his life manning his family's farm on the outskirts of Kenta. He's weathered droughts and dealt with the occasional troll trespassing his lands before I convinced him to sit on my father's council, so the pinched frustration lining his features has my hair standing on end.

"What is it?" I inquire.

"We've been forced to retreat from the front line."

I stalk around the table to his position. "Where?"

He points to the northern outskirts of his land where the planes of farmland turn into a rocky hillside. "Roison has pushed my men into the valley."

It's not ideal, but it could be worse. The land bottlenecks, making it difficult for any sized battalion to maneuver through it. My real concern is the crop of wheat beyond the small fjord. With the help of Alaha's forces, they could demolish our food supply, starving the battalion out.

I look at Hallis. "How many men can we spare from nearby posts?"

He's already shaking his head. "We're spread thin across the front lines covering the increase in Roison troop movement. It'd be a waste to take men from more vulnerable areas just to save one battalion."

I turn my gaze back to Tyreek. "Numbers?"

"We have five thousand to Roison's thirty." He drags his hand across the board. "If they take the valley, they can be at the palace walls within a few weeks' time."

Hallis shifts on his feet. "It would take weeks just for Roison's thirty thousand men to move through the narrow passage. Months if the end of summer storms come early." His tone is apologetic, clearly hating to vote against Tyreek.

"They're more likely to die trying than actually succeed in breaking through," I concur.

By the looks on the men's faces, they're not happy about our conclusion. They're worried. If Roison is successful in pushing their forces through the fjord, it would set a terrible precedent. Being the first to lose ground is never a good sign.

"This is bullshit!" Lord Paul slams a closed fist on the table, rattling the pieces on the map. He's one of the few in the room with noble blood, and he sure as hell acts as though it gives his opinion more weight than the lower-born lords sitting on the council. "I didn't accept this council position only to take orders from two boys a fraction of my age. It's insulting."

"It'd be less disrespectful if the king spat directly in our faces," another agrees.

This is what I'm not good at. Pacifying old men, playing babysitter in my father's absence. I'm better suited for the battlefield where I can actually see the differences I make in this war.

Then you make them.

"Have you all forgotten?" My eyes land on each of their insolent faces in turn as I march around the table. "I've fought for my land. Bled for it. My people. As has Hallis." I point to my friend, less his left hand from the battle we fought as children, and hence giftless. "No one has sacrificed more than he has; the youngest in this room. How dare you question our authority? Our understanding of what it's like to be outnumbered?"

The silence that follows allows the last of my words to hang over the room. They know the story of our survival, the tales of my lethality on the battlefield. They may be able to question my authority in my father's absence, but they cannot question my experience. But the bitter truth is . . . they question my judgment because I'm the one who brought death and betrayal to Kenta. It may have been my Match's actions to cripple my father's court, along with my sister's, but in their eyes it may as well have been mine.

As anticipated, Paul is the first to dare a response. "And where are you now?" he slurs, rattling more pieces. "Standing in this room, far, *far* away from any battle of this war."

"As are you," Hallis drawls. "Go ahead and have another bottle, Paul. What an honor to your people."

The drunkard opens his mouth, face belligerently red, but Tyreek effectively shuts him up with a hand on his shoulder. "I am not questioning your leadership, Ace," he says, using the nickname my comrades gave me. "I'm only asking for a few bodies to even the playing field. Zion is down there."

His son. A brother to myself and Hallis. One of the five who shares the same scar.

Like half the men in this room, Tyreek was unprepared to replace the previous lord. Unlike them, he didn't want this position, but I knew his military knowledge and genuineness would be valuable to the council. It took a lot of convincing and many trips to his region to finally sway him. The very last thing I want is for him to feel as if I'm abandoning the promises I made to him and his family. I swore to Tyreek that I would provide for his family as well as his entire region if he agreed to take on the title of lord. Made up of mostly farmers, his community already felt disregarded by my father after a bout of harsh winters, and leaving Zion's battalion defenseless will only look as though I'm doing exactly that.

"Tell Zion to disperse his men to higher ground," I say, running my fingers along the hillside. "The passage won't allow more than a few hundred men to funnel through at a time. They should be able to pick them off from above. We will divert the next batch of troops as soon as they're ready."

Tyreek accepts the plan of action with a tilt of his chin.

We continue to collect numbers by region. In total, we're down ten thousand men, four hundred horses, and in desperate need of healers. Our crops and resources are dwindling.

It took two years for the war to commence after Jovie's betrayal. Just as she had insisted it would happen, the Alaha joined Roison's forces in the east. And because of her warning, we were able to muster our own army at the border in enough time to defend our land from their invasion.

It took another year before we were forced to concede ground to Roison. People are becoming less and less tolerant. There's not a family who hasn't sent at least one of their men off to fight. Many of those men haven't been home in years. Many won't return at all. But for all the tales of Wren's armies, I've yet to see anything unprecedented in their advance. Nothing extraordinary or commendable.

But in the last year we have become increasingly outnumbered, and we're in desperate need for more men after two years of constant battle.

My eyes flick to the miniature wooden ships on the map's surface, over the expanse of water separating Strou's land—our only ally—from us. The land bends into the shape of a crescent moon, with Maile's territory acting as an impenetrable barrier between Strou and Kenta. Evelyn's navy has intercepted any help the Strou has tried to send our way. While the queen of Maile has remained impartial to our plight against Roison, the reports of the battles over the northern sea between her navy and Strou have been abysmal and not in our favor.

"Bru," I say, glancing at the singular Strou warrior in attendance. He's fucking atrocious to look at and nearly twice the size of Hallis at his side. Why Irina's father, the king of Strou, would send *him* as regent is beyond my comprehension. "Any word of progress from the gulf?"

The mammoth warrior looks at the markers, then gives a single shake of his head. "One ship arrived at port about a week ago. It was the only one out of the last seven sent in the last few weeks."

I release a breath from my nose, making eye contact with Hallis. We've had endless discussions about what an ambush on Maile's northernmost border could mean for the war, but with supplies and troops dwindling, the reward of such drastic action is beginning to outweigh the risk. His expression holds, an unspoken question lingering between us. *Are you sure?*

And I nod.

He points to the hillside where the Strou and Maile borders meet in the north. "Let's divide their attention," he begins, and the very next breath in my chest feels tighter.

I swear to protect her with my dying breath.

The blood oath I made to protect Jovie consistently reminds me to stay within the parameters of my promise and I take the warning for what it is. While not directly against my Match or at my command, the order is a little too close to being so for my magic's liking. I signal to Hallis that I'm leaving.

In a foul mood, I return to my bedchamber to find it empty, much to my relief. A platter of half-eaten fruit and bread sits on the table beside the bed, two half-finished glasses of red wine accompanying it. Helping myself, I pour the leftover wine into one glass and carry it to my workstation. Books are splayed open across the surface, overflowing onto the floor where stacks of texts clutter half the room. Taking a swallow of wine, I skim a few of the spines in hopes that one catches my eye.

I've gone through bouts of obsessive searching for a way to break the oath, spending weeks, sometimes months, scouring pages of old texts in a bid to discover a remedy. Whenever I think I've stumbled across something even remotely promising, I've sent sentries to retrieve it. Herbs in the deepest of Roison's forests, rare stones found in the western springs, and leeches from the southern marshes. I've tried it all and all I've gotten in return is a weird rash and a stomachache.

Philosophers and scientists differ on their theories on blood oaths, but the one commonality they share is the belief that the same key that made the oath has to be what breaks it—blood. But aside from draining myself dry, there doesn't seem to be a viable option.

It's a worthless endeavor anyway.

I'll never be able overcome the blood oath unless I figure out how to eradicate the love I still have for Jovie. It's a strange conundrum, loving her while also wanting to hurt her the same way she did me. Sometimes I make myself sick, hating her as much as I miss the feel of her skin against mine.

Blood oath or not, Jovie will always be my greatest weakness.

Chapter 2

ACKER

The kitchen is the only place where I can eat lunch without being hounded by petitioners. They loiter in the halls in a bid to corner me. They're constantly angling to push their own agendas, to get my approval to send aid to their own lands. More soldiers, more wheat, more weapons. It pains me to lie to them, knowing their people need help. But dear gods, they're fucking vultures, willing to take from a neighbor if it means extra money in their coffers.

The cook has a plate ready for me. The turkey is dry, and I suffer down a few bites of even drier sourdough. It does little to satisfy my stomach, but I give Antony a nod of thanks anyway as I get up to leave. His culinary skills don't hold a candle to those of our last cook, but considering our previous cook, Henry, was a treacherous fuck, I remind myself to be grateful my meal is at least not poisoned.

I navigate through the maidservants' quarters behind the kitchen. The women are accustomed to me using their halls to leave the palace without being seen. Most of them are veteran staff and pay me little mind. But there are a few girls who see my brief appearance as an opportunity to vie for my attention with unbuttoned blouses and hiked skirts. Many of them would skin a cat for a chance to be my concubine, and I make sure to avoid their lingering gazes as I leave via the back entrance of the servants' wing.

The sky is overcast, hanging like an indictment over the capitol. After discovering the secret alcove under the library when Jovie was at court, I did some further digging and found a series of fail-safes around the grounds as well. The hidden passages behind the walls apparently aren't the only secrets the palace holds.

The smell of sweet vanilla permeates the air. The blanket of blooming vines overhanging the north side of the palace walls was planted to disguise the smell of rubbish from the kitchen. But underneath the foliage, set into an alcove, a gate is concealed. No one would think to go near the poisonous leaves for fear of the blistering welts the vine is known to cause on exposed skin.

Pulling my hood over my head, I assure all of my skin is covered before I duck underneath the vines. I place my palm against the iron lock, concentrating hard to slide the mechanism open despite the mangi stones around my neck. While they're a hinderance in my ability to use the full extent of my magic, I'm able unlock the gate and emerge into the back alley of merchants.

I'm mindful to keep my face hidden as I step onto the street. I could send a palace aide to do my bidding, but trust is no longer something I hand out so freely. My title alone doesn't afford me the luxury anymore. Besides, I want to speak with my friend face-to-face.

The city is quiet. Few people venture among the businesses and shuttered restaurants. The statue of Mother Nature stands barren in the city's central plaza. Water which once flowed between the figure's raised fingers has long gone dry. The children who often played in the fountain's basin are absent, and I can't remember the last time I heard a child's laughter.

There's a stillness I've only ever experienced right before battle. When the wind itself seems to be afraid of what's to come. Still as the breath the soldiers hold in their lungs as they await their fight.

It's not until I reach the blacksmith that the silence of the city is broken, the sound of iron striking iron and the grunts of men working.

Hearths are blazing on either side of the brickyard when I enter, the largest fire burning in the middle, turning the courtyard into an oven. Sweat instantly coats my neck and back as I look for my friend and fellow comrade through the haze of smoke. I find Wells barking at one of his men to remove a plate of iron from a fire, his skin blackened with soot. He returns to striking the weapon on the anvil before him and doesn't see me until I'm close, eyes darting to me between heaves of the hammer in his hand.

Sparks fly from the molten metal. Strike after strike after strike.

He inspects the blade before shoving it into the fire. "Yeah?" he says.

"Wanted to see if you had any update on the next shipment of armor."

Using the handkerchief from his back pocket, he rubs his neck, then his forehead. It's a losing battle as the moisture continues to sluice down his face. "I received word from Dusty in Auden and he said he'll be able to match my five hundred pieces by the end of the week."

Auden is four days east of us. "And Trey?"

He shakes his head. "His last batch of iron got intercepted by bandits a few weeks ago. He's still waiting for materials."

Fuck. The ever stirrings of a possible growing rebellion is another problem entirely.

"It'll take a further two weeks to get materials to the front lines," I say.

Someone yells for assistance and Wells looks over his shoulder to make sure it's being handled before his eyes snap back to me. "Anything else?"

I narrow my eyes at his clipped words. "Everything all right?"

He huffs and shakes his head, as if he can't believe I'd ask him such an asinine question, then leaves me standing in the middle of the yard.

I'm so caught off guard by his reaction, I'm frozen in place as I watch him return to the hearth to shovel coal into the fire's mouth. I debate the merits of letting it go, trying to convince myself it's just the stress of the war getting to him, but there's something about the way he looked at me that I can't shake.

My anger rises with my body temperature as I stalk toward him. "If you have something you need to get off your chest—say it."

He doesn't even spare me a glance. "I don't have the patience to appease you today, Acker. Go home."

"*Appease* me?"

"You heard me," he says, slamming the door on the kiln and latching it. "Every few weeks you come down here and demand more weapons and more armor and more bits, and when they're not ready *yesterday*, you act like it's unacceptable." He strips his gloves off and storms toward the door leading to his living quarters.

I follow close behind him.

The first alarming thing I notice upon entry is the dirty floor. Wells leaves boot tracks in the soot as I follow him into the dining area. Black daggers and swords in various stages of creation lie on the dining room table.

Wells throws an eyebrow up at whatever he sees on my face. "Oh, you didn't know?" He removes his apron and throws it over the mess. "Your father had a wagon full of hearthstone delivered weeks ago with orders to make as many weapons as I could with it."

The fuck . . .

Hearthstone weapons belong wholly to their makers. Whoever forges the weapon can recall the weapon to them anytime, anywhere, and they're lethal when used against an Heir, capable of killing someone's magic, making it impossible for them to heal—on land or otherwise. And it's impossibly rare. Too rare to mine this much without great effort. Yet, my father hasn't mentioned increasing mining efforts . . .

But what's the most concerning is the sheer number of weapons Wells is making. Upon becoming a blacksmith, he made a blood oath to never recall any hearthstone weapon he's asked to forge. And while it's typical for the king to occasionally demand a weapon here and there, this number is unprecedented.

I turn my gaze back toward Wells. "Why didn't you mention this the last time I was here?"

He shrugs halfheartedly. "I thought you knew," he says, continuing to the kitchen.

Following him, I ask, "Where's Olivia?"

"I sent her to stay with my parents."

That explains the attitude. Wells and Olivia haven't spent more than a day apart since they were sixteen. And it also explains the condition of their home. Olivia would be spitting mad if she saw the state that it's in.

Wells digs through the cabinets, knocking the contents onto the counters. There's a pinch between his shoulders, tension pulling his shirt taut. Once he finds a can of his liking, he removes a knife from the drawer and stabs it into the container, sawing it open. He folds back the top and tips the can straight to his mouth.

It's now that I notice how thin he's gotten. "When was the last time you had a real meal?" When he doesn't answer me, I pull a spoon from the drawer and shove it into the can of peas before he can raise it to his mouth again. "What's going on, Wells?"

He lifts the utensil, if a little begrudgingly. "She's pregnant," he says with his mouth full.

It takes me a moment for the words to register.

Olivia is pregnant. *Wow.*

"That's . . . incredible, Wells." I clear my throat in an effort to insert more enthusiasm into my voice. "Congratulations."

He nods, but it's without an ounce of excitement.

We're at war and there's no escaping it. As a royal blacksmith, he's well off enough to still afford food and necessities, but he's haggard. He's spent the last three years restocking the military's cache that we've run through in a fraction of the time it took to make it. It's not just a less than ideal time to bring a baby into this world.

It's the worst possible time.

"She and the baby will be safe on the northern shores," I say.

"For how long?" He drops his spoon into the now empty can, but he knows as well as I do that I can't answer that. "Olivia is under the impression Jovie originally offered you a truce," he says, meeting my gaze.

"She's spoken to *her*?" I ask, struggling to hide my outrage. He doesn't reply, knowing that even from him I won't stand for treason. "If Olivia is conspiring with our enemy—"

"*Your* enemy," he clarifies, cutting me off. Eyes of molten ore, he levels his glare at me—daring me to finish my sentence.

I lock my teeth together in a bid to hold back my temper.

Hurt and confusion muddy his features, eyes becoming glassy as he holds my stare. "None of this had to happen," he says, shaking his head. "So many lives have been sacrificed, for what?"

My reply is laced with disbelief. "She wanted my father's head in return."

In an instant, he's enraged, slamming the can onto the counter. "You spared the man who put this collar around my neck!"

I'm too stunned to react.

I never told Wells and Olivia the ultimatum my Match gave me. Anytime I broached the subject, I couldn't get the words to leave my mouth, the truth of what actually transpired that night almost four years ago. After a while, I figured it was best to let the story lie with the dead members of the council.

But, if I'm honest with myself, I always suspected that they wouldn't understand, having voiced their displeasure of my father's reign time and time again.

He spins about and slaps the cabinet beside him, taking his frustrations out on something—anything—to stop himself from doing something he can't take back. Like put his hands on me.

After a few moments of silence, he speaks with his back to me. "You know as well as I do that Maile could have used our vulnerability against us by now." When he turns around, he's a little calmer. "They know we moved all of our armies to fight at the Roison border. There's nothing stopping them from invading our land, razing our cities, hell—seizing the capital . . . but they haven't." His eyes are imploring. "You must have considered the reason."

I've considered it ad nauseam. Nothing about this entire war makes sense. Evelyn has had every opportunity to harry us from the west, but hasn't. Jovie had the makings of a rebellion within the walls of this very city, but never called upon it.

It leaves a singular, bitter notion that somehow makes me the sickest: that Jovie never had any intention of destroying my father's crown *or* Kenta. That she only went through with the plan to try and kill my father to appease her lover—Wren's son. *Kai.*

But I don't think right now is the right time to tell Wells of my suspicions, or that I've ordered the siege on Maile's northern border. I fought with the decision for months, and while Maile hasn't attacked us directly, they've hindered any ships trying to reach us from Strou. We're short on men, weapons, food, and even fucking *candle wax*, for godssake, and it's their fault we've stagnated for so long.

Of all the lives I've taken, none have haunted me like the ones I possibly sacrificed by saving my father. My people are dropping like flies. The longer this war wages, the harder it is to reconcile when a decision is right and when it's just *easier*, but like hell am I going to take the blame for the actions of one girl.

The memory of the moment I watched my Match hold a dagger to my father's throat—the very same dagger I carried around in her *fucking* honor—plagues me.

Wells's voice cuts through my thoughts. "It's the same collar he'll one day put around my child's neck, Acker."

"What are you saying?" I ask, meeting his gaze. "That you're against me?"

He shakes his head. "I'll never be against you, Ace," he says, placing a hand against his chest. "I'm asking—if you can end this war, by *any* means . . . *please* . . . do it."

Wells saved my life at thirteen by throwing himself in front of an arrow meant for me. A favor I returned by pushing him out of the way of the second arrow that followed, and it solidified our bond for a lifetime and beyond. It's something immeasurable.

It's why hearing his desperation hurts as much as it does.

He dips his head in the traditional Kenta gesture of allegiance. "A lot of blood has already been spilled, but . . ." He looks up and meets my gaze once again, a renewed vigor behind his eyes. "She's your Match. She'll listen."

My heart sinks. "She's not Olivia, Wells. Not all who are Bonded are a love Match."

He gives me the worst look of all—*disappointment*. "You can lie to yourself all you want, Ace, but you know as well as I do, she could have done worse. She chose war over killing your father because you asked her not to. If that's not love, then I don't know what is."

I'm too exhausted to argue with him about my Match's love for me or the lack thereof.

I turn to leave. "I'll see what I can do about getting you more iron," I say, walking away.

Unlike him, I have a wife to return to.

Chapter 3

JO

I keep my eyes peeled for any sign of purple amid the bodies, but the red of Strou's crest seems to be the predominant color. For that I'm thankful. A nearby soldier places a foot against one of the dead, using the leverage to yank the curved saber from the chest with a wet squelch. Curved blades have a tendency to get stuck once the blood thickens. He inspects the blade before throwing it in a nearby keep barrow.

At least the end of the battlefield is in sight. The last of the casualties littering the ground are being picked over for usable equipment while the dogwatch of soldiers piles the fallen bodies in a heap, ready to burn. It takes two of our men to carry a single Strou warrior. Meaty bastards, the lot of them.

In the northern reaches of the continent, where the winters rarely mellow and they eat oxen for breakfast, the most brutal of men are raised. If you can even call them that. *Men*. The scars marking their faces, arms, and chests give them a monstrous appearance. A slash of hearthstone across their skin for every life taken by their hands.

I've seen the count leave their mouths in the heat of battle.

Trophies, General Samasu called them.

This fight in particular was short. Nothing more than a squabble before bedtime. They've been toying with us for months since they've arrived. They send a few hundred men down at a time, sometimes a thousand. The numbers of men they ambush us with is always different, so we never know what the day will bring.

We're not naive to their tactics: dividing our military's focus, harrying us at random intervals to distract from their true intentions—getting aid and men across the gulf to Kenta. We knew what they were doing the moment we received word that Strou warriors were spotted in the hillside just beyond our border. It was expected, but not ideal as we hurried to spread battalions across the expanse of land neighboring ours, dividing our resources. Food and supply have to be diverted in two opposite directions. Things like food and water, as well as cots, clothing, and oil.

My breath escapes in a puff of fog as I release a sigh. Night sits on the horizon, the stars already visible as the sky fades to gray. Winter is closing in quickly this year and I'm not eager to embrace it. My mother told me I'd get used to the bite from the wind and the smell of ice in the air, but I've yet to do so.

"You shouldn't be out here." I look over my shoulder and find the source of the exasperated voice. General Samasu points a wordless order to a soldier before giving me his full attention. "You need rest."

I bend to pick up a stray dagger. "Speak for yourself, old man."

Fredrich, the soldier beside him, shucks the commandeered weapons into the uncovered wagon. I've heard the shielder speak all of five words in the months since we've been stationed here, so when he notices my stand-off with Sam, his slightly upturned lips catch me off guard. Especially considering there's no love lost between him and myself.

I first noticed Fredrich observing me back in Maile. Lingering on rooftops or inside alleyways. Always around, but never too close. When I mentioned a soldier had been following me to my mother, she admitted to speaking to Sam about getting me protection. Not wanting to upset her, I accepted the tail, thinking my mother's paranoia would wane over time. But when I realized he had followed me to the border, I'd had enough, and I, in no uncertain terms, made sure he knew to stay away from me. And in the face of my ire, all he did was stare at me with indifference.

I continue my search of the battlefield, swatting away the flies swarming around me with a wave, only for them to return a moment later. They're a constant nuisance. Their buzz has followed us since the first battle, as if they know dinner will come if they hover around long enough.

The eyes of the dead are their favorite.

My gaze catches on the purple emblem peeking out from under an overturned Strou; a portion of the golden butterfly of the Maile's crest is visible. I work my foot under the body, pushing the heavy warrior off of the man underneath.

My breath stutters in my chest.

The young boy's face is familiar. I've seen him around camp. Son of a farmer, I believe. He would often turn his gaze away in my presence. At first I thought it was due to shyness, but over time I realized he was trying to hide his disdain for me. I suppose that was a kindness.

It's odd. He looks almost peaceful, as if he were sleeping—if it weren't for the scarlet blood splashed across his bone-white face. Most soldiers die with stricken faces, eyes wide as if their fight continued beyond the veil of life.

The ache in my chest somehow feels comforting and I welcome the sensation.

I raise my arm and wave, signaling a need for help with the retrieval of one of our fallen brethren. "Maile," I yell.

A soldier nearby drops his weapons, another already stepping over the body at his feet as he moves toward me. I look back down at the Maile soldier and practically stop breathing altogether. His eyes are open, glossy as they stare up at me.

Alive.

He's alive.

I drop to my knees. "Raina!" Gently holding the face of the soldier, I inspect his pupils, then the slow rise of his chest—the very shallow breath that takes entirely too long to draw in. "Raina!" I yell. "Someone get Raina!"

I hear footsteps pounding closer. "She's coming," someone informs me.

It feels like an eternity before the healer is sinking to her knees on the other side of the soldier. "I'm here," she says, eyes already roving over the body, inspecting. "Remove his armor."

My fingers fumble for the buckles at the side of his breastplate and Raina helps me remove the metal, heaving it aside. Any breath left in my lungs evaporates at the sight of the blade sticking from his abdomen. The dark, oblong blade of an ax. Black. *Hearthstone.*

Raina's eyes meet mine and the dim resignation in her gaze is more fuel for the steady flame of anger that refuses to expire inside me.

"Try," I order her. "Roll him over."

I don't wait for her to help, gripping the soldier by his leathers and heaving him onto his side. A low groan escapes him but Raina and I share a look in stony silence when we see his back. The ax is cleaved straight through his spine.

Raina's voice is placating. "Jo—"

I ignore her as I wrench the blade out. The lack of blood that follows makes my heart sink again, and by the time I'm able to roll the soldier onto his back once again so I can see his face, his eyes have already glazed over—lifeless. The hand I place over his chest doesn't move.

Dead.

In the span of mere seconds, he's dead.

Sitting back on my haunches, I take in the soldier. No longer sleeping peacefully, his eyes—open and scared.

I wasted his last moments trying to save him, when I should have tried to offer him comfort instead.

Who am I kidding? He's probably cursing my name all the way to the afterlife at this very moment.

I blink as I look up and realize we're surrounded by fellow soldiers. Their faces are a barrage of pity and anger like mine, but some are indifferent, having seen enough death to be numb to the experience.

There's a flash of golden hair as Sam shoulders through them, motioning for them to disperse with a flick of his wrist.

I force my legs underneath me. "Come on," I tell him, standing by the dead soldier's feet. "Let's get him to the wagon."

Sam doesn't speak as he helps me lift the body. We carry him to the enclosed cart, laying him next to the other fallen. Sam removes the emblem from the soldier's shoulder and I take it from him, tacking it to the side of the wagon and smoothing it down with a closed fist. It'll inform the families of the soldiers' identities when they're transported into the city for claim and burial.

Today's count currently stands at seventeen. Not a bad number in comparison to others.

Sam stops me from returning to the battlefield with a hand banded around my upper arm. "You're done for tonight."

I move to shrug off his grasp, but he doesn't budge.

"Jovinnia," he says, using my full name. "You've done enough."

My hard stare meets his eyes, the color of wheat, and I consider putting him in his place, that ever-present anger in my chest eager for a fight.

As if sensing the fire ready to spew from my mouth, he lets me go. "The field is nearly cleared."

I look toward the clearing and, sure enough, the flickers of growing flames begin to envelope the dead of the Strou, a plume of gray smoke reaching into the sky. My gaze shifts to the dots of smoke in the distance. Up in the hills, our enemy settles in for the night. They can undoubtedly see the evidence of their comrades' cremation.

Relenting, I nod and Sam tries and fails to hide his relief.

The exhaustion in the camp is palpable when I reach its boundary. I can feel the eyes of my men on me as I trudge through. The same men I fight alongside, eat with, mourn with. It was important to prove my worth to each of them, those men sent to fight a war I initiated. I just didn't realize the scale of the guilt that would come in the wake of my choices, or how heavy it would make their regard. They bow their heads in a show of respect as I pass by, and I deny myself the reprieve of looking away.

The hours immediately after battle are always quiet, but there's something especially burdensome about the silence around the campfires tonight. Like the shortness of the skirmish makes the death of our men feel all the more senseless. The camp feels barren in contrast to the bustling tents from when we first set up camp. When there was only just enough space to walk due to the overcrowding.

At least everyone has a bed now.

Chapter 4

JO

Inside my billet, I unbuckle the armor from my torso, shoulders sagging with relief. I drop it by the door for the stewards to pick up for cleaning in the morning, then I strip off the mud-and-blood-soaked leathers, throwing them on top of the metal. Goosebumps immediately erupt across my naked flesh.

A long string of mangi stones wraps my body, a single chain connected to the loop about my neck, hanging between my breasts before it splits into two strings again under my sternum. It sits right over the scar I have from being shot with an arrow, over the place my magic resides, before meeting at my spine. The gyve took some trial and error to perfect, but it has enough give that I can fight in it, while still buffering my magic and the tether connected to it.

Usually hidden beneath my clothes, the complex swirl of stones weighs little more than an apple would in my palm but is somehow heavier than the iron plate I strap to my chest every day. The shame over wearing it never abates, knowing my people view such collars as a symbol of repression. How am I supposed to lead with strength and dignity when the Bond hangs over my head? I need the stones to prevent the

Bond from forcing me into Acker's presence, or he into mine. To protect my mind. And my heart.

I'm grateful for the small amount of clean water in my wash basin and I do my best to clean up before getting re-dressed in fatigues. The cot in the corner calls to me like the fabled sirens of the gulf. I want sleep desperately, but I know the horrors that await if I give in.

I've been running from my nightmares for a long time. Since Kenta. Dreams where Kai slits Acker's throat and I have to watch the life drain from his dark and loathing eyes. Dreams where Acker's trying to kill me, and I wake gasping for breath, clawing at the imaginary hands around my throat.

The worst, however, are the *good* dreams.

Like the unearthed memories of my stolen childhood, or of my time in Alaha with Kai and Messer. When I'm forced to relive the time I spent with Acker. In the boat, on land . . . in a soft bed and clean sheets.

Good or bad—I don't want any of them.

A chill seems to seep into my bones and I wrap myself in a coat before sinking into my desk chair. I finger a match free from the box lying on top of the table, strike it on the wooden surface, and use it to light the oil lamp, bathing the war map spread out before me in an orange glow.

I switch my attention to the stack of parchment and the letter I've left half-written, but the thought of formulating whole sentences feels too daunting at the moment. Instead, I slide the book from the top of the pile of texts I have stacked, and flip to the page I left off on—*Queen Asa.*

The last known light wielder is not a subject I wish to delve into tonight. I thought if I learned as much as I could from the previous queen of Maile that I could, I don't know, learn from her mistakes, but every time I read the tales of her impetuous reign, I only find parts of myself in bits and pieces of her story. As much as I tell myself I'm not vindictive or cruel, I'm not so sure that's how my actions will be perceived in history.

Given the chance, I'd go back and make different choices.

After leaving Alaha with Acker, I should have said fuck Kai and the rebellion when we arrived on land. Instead of going to the palace in Kenta, I should have begged Acker to come to Maile with me. Then he could have seen how different things can be without hindering magic underneath his father's tyrannical rule. Maybe things would be different.

I try to give myself grace, remind myself that I was young and naive and distrustful of . . . nearly everyone, Acker included. And it's not as if he's ever come for me, or sent a single message with a bird. I vacillate between being angry at him as much as at myself. If he truly loved me the way I thought he did, then he would have never married Irina.

I slam the book shut, leaning forward onto the table and propping my chin on my fist in sheer determination to keep my head up. The map stares back at me—taunting almost. I run my eyes along the marked embankments tucked between the hillsides. The Strou warriors have crammed themselves onto many of the rocky ledges, square pegs marking their known locations. I've been told in some areas those spaces are no more than a foot or two wide. They're cocky to hide in plain sight. Always having a view of us while knowing we can't meet them on their ground.

Too high. Too exposed.

Sam told me stories of yearlong battles, wars that went on for decades, and I pray to the gods I'll never have to see the like in my lifetime. I'm desperate for this war to end, and it's yet to get started. Not really, anyway. Frustration has me swiping my arm out, knocking the pieces down, and scattering them across the ground.

Steps sound outside my billet. Soldiers filing in from the battlefield. I expected war to be loud, and it is in the heat of battle, but after? The hushed quiet is painful.

My head feels so heavy.

I lay it down on the crook of my arm and close my eyes, listening to the steady march of the dogwatch as they come in for the night. It's comforting, somehow. Like the waves of the ocean. And after a while, I can almost smell the saltwater. Taste it in the air.

It's one of the worst dreams of all. The kind that brings to the surface the emotions I work to shove deep inside of me every waking moment.

Where my unconscious refuses to let me escape the true desires of my heart.

One of the best ones.

You're going to miss this, Acker says.

It takes all of my effort to look up at him. *Like hell.*

He smiles up at the sky, eyes still closed, and I watch a droplet of water make its way down the column of his throat. We've just taken an afternoon swim and he somehow convinced me to lay down on the deck with him. He's obsessed with my sleeping habits for some reason. With my cheek pressed to the inside of his bicep, I close my eyes and accept my fate.

You will, he insists. His thumb runs lazy circles on the back of my upper arm.

It feels so good.

A day will come when you won't kill a man at all.

Confusion penetrates my drowsiness. *What did you just say?*

All of a sudden the gentle rocking of the boat comes to a stop. *You'll wonder what's wrong with you*, he continues, voice a balm to my soul. *Because how could you miss the feeling of sliding your blade into another man's flesh?*

Something's not right.

I open my eyes and find him staring at me. Dark eyes, soft and sleepy in the daylight. *We're both terrible people, Jovie*, he says, fingers dancing in my hair. *It's okay to admit it.*

After a moment of confused consideration, I think . . . *maybe he's right.* As I relax further into his side, I allow myself to succumb to the warmth of his body and the sleep pulling at my eyelids.

Then something snaps me awake.

"The *fuck*, B!"

I blink up at Messer as I regain a sense of my surroundings. I'm in my billet, sitting at my desk, dagger in hand stabbed just a hair width from Messer's fingers that are flat on the table.

Not on a boat in the middle of the ocean.

Removing the dagger from the desk's surface, I set it aside as I sit up, wiping the drool from my cheek. "Why are you sneaking up on me?"

"You nearly took my finger off," he says, inspecting his hand with an offended expression.

I wave away his worry. "I'm sure it would have grown back the next time you shifted or something."

He looks at me in abject horror. "That's not how it works."

How would I know? I don't transform into a winged creature in my downtime.

I inspect his half-dressed state. "I'm glad you found pants this time."

"Swiped them from a poor fellow a couple of spots over. He'll be a sad chap once he wakes up though."

I definitely don't want to know if the chap was wearing them at the time Messer stole them or not. "Why are you here? You're not due to report in for another week." His expression turns more serious, causing the hair on the back of my neck to stand on end. "What is it?"

It takes him a moment to speak, but the beat is just long enough for me to already know what he's going to say. "Kai sent word this morning. I flew straight here."

My stomach flips and I swallow around the nausea. "Roison is ready to invade Kenta?"

He nods, solemn. "Yes."

It was only a matter of time, but it doesn't make the news any easier to digest.

Messer senses my dismay, moving closer. "B—"

I stand to evade his grasp, bending down to pick up the wooden pieces I knocked off the desk earlier. "Need a place to crash?" I ask him as I try to gather them all up in one swipe and fail.

He sighs before kneeling down to help. "I could use a night to rest before flying back."

After all the markers are collected, I scatter them across the map and slip back into my chair. "Take the bed. I have some letters to respond to."

He leans against the table. "You need to sleep, too. You look like shit."

I glare at him. "*You* look like shit."

He looks down at his bare torso, which—*objectively*—is nice, before narrowing his gaze at me. "We're friends, B. We don't lie to each other."

My eyes snag on the V carved below his collarbone, the scar stark against the rest of his unblemished skin before I slap him in the stomach to get him to move. "If I don't write to my mother at least once a day, she will send the cavalry to find me."

It works to loosen the tension around his mouth. "I don't doubt it."

"Stay for the night," I urge him. "Rest."

He takes a breath, inspecting my billet. "Sure you couldn't find better use for me here?"

Messer hates being landlocked, but his guilt over not following me into battle bothers him more. Despite my continual insistence that I'm fine without him, he mentions it every time he reports back to me.

"Drake would give me hell if I took you from his crew."

"He always puts me on head duty."

"For good reason, I'm sure," I say with a genuine smile. "Please return the pants before you leave in the morning."

He rolls his eyes, grinning. "As you wish, your—"

I throw one of the wooden pegs at his face "Don't you dare."

His laughter fills the billet and he flops belly first onto my cot, burying his face in my bedding with a groan of satisfaction.

Chapter 5

ACKER

The messenger slips the curled parchment paper into my hand and I nod, dismissing him as quickly as he appeared. I chance a look across the dining hall in my father's direction. He's deep in discussion with Paul in the crowded room. It seems the noble-born lord has somehow swindled my father into having a drink tonight despite his paranoia of possibly being poisoned once again. By the ruddy hue of their cheeks, it's safe to assume they're both feeling the effects of the wine.

"Poor bastard," Hallis comments behind his own goblet before taking a sip.

I follow his gaze, landing on my father's royal taster swaying in the corner. The lowly boy is no match for the potency of the palace wine. At least, not the amount Paul likes to consume.

I turn my back to the room, bracing a hand against the mantle above the hearth so no one can spot the disgust I'm struggling to mask. Less than an hour ago we walked out of the war room after hearing a staggering report of casualties at the border. Another ten thousand men are gone, and a key mining town is being occupied by enemy forces. We're running low on coal and a third of our grain reserves are spoiled from not being stored properly in the cellar.

Yet here the council is, eating and drinking their fill, unconcerned with the day's news. They were oddly chill in the meeting as well. As if merely being in my father's presence eases their coddled minds. He's been uncharacteristically available the last few weeks and it's worked to dull the tempers of the council.

Well, all but Tyreek, Johannes, and Daz. They sit by themselves at the far end of a table, not a crumb of food or drop of drink in front of them. By the looks on their faces, they're as off-put by the cheerful atmosphere and drunkenness of their fellow council members as I am. They aren't noble born. One could live inside these walls and remain entirely ignorant of the tragedies happening to our own people. But those three? They know the price.

Hallis angles his body closer, creating a barrier from prying eyes as I straighten from the mantle and peel the red wax seal from the scroll. My eyes shift over the words before I crumble the parchment in my fist.

Hallis is silent as he waits for me to reveal the message.

It takes me a moment to gather myself. "The Maile have sunk a third of Strou's fleet in the gulf in an ambush."

Shifting in place, Hallis checks our nearby surroundings for potential eavesdroppers before asking, "How?"

I fight to not look away from his gaze as I recite the message word for word, the last spat out like a curse. "*Eyun.*"

The mystical creature has been extinct for millennia, but there's one shifter who I know is capable of transforming into the deadly, man-eating bird. Jovie's *pet*—Messer.

Slowly, understanding settles into Hallis's features and I nod, my blood running cold despite the roaring fire feet away.

"*Fuck*," he spits, hands braced on his hips. "Your father is going to be insufferable when he finds out."

While my father's initial ire following Jovie's betrayal has abated, the insults he threw at me still burn. *Love-sick idiot. Dimwitted boy. Foolish.*

Over time, he's given his apologies for being so harsh in the weeks following that day. Even going so far as to express his understanding.

He had clasped me on the shoulder one night after having a nightcap in his sitting room and said, "Why do you think I keep Greta in the library? My Match has tried me a time or two as well."

But with his current state of inebriation, the last thing I want to experience tonight is to test my father's patience.

I toss the parchment into the fireplace.

Hallis and I exchange glances before departing in separate directions. I move past the helmeted guards, keeping to the wall of stained glass windows to avoid unwanted attention. I'm within steps of the hall's exit when I hear the disapproving timbre of my father's voice behind me.

"Son." The single word is spoken like a term of endearment, but there's no denying the underlying authority.

I stop, pivoting in place to face him. "Father."

"Where are you hurrying off to?" He steps away from his company, eyes suddenly astute in his buzzed state.

"I'm feeling a little unsettled." I place a hand against my abdomen. "Going to turn in early tonight."

His jaw works as he considers my words. He orchestrates these dinners as a show of confidence for the wider noble court as well as the council. Nothing is more important than maintaining the appearance of control in front of our people.

The people look to us to gauge the state of our territory. Never let on to the truth of your concerns.

He places his hand on my shoulder. "A prince should never leave his wife unattended with dignitaries at court."

The crack of my teeth echoes in my ears. "Of course."

Turning toward the dais, my eyes lock on Irina. She hasn't left her place since I pulled her seat out for her at the start of dinner hours ago. Poised and polished to perfection, I've often wondered if her appearance is due to dedicated time and consideration, or whether it is an illusion. Without her collar, either is possible.

Resentment makes the collar around my own throat feel all the more suffocating.

I make my way toward her. She fiddles with a square of cheese between her fingers before popping it in her mouth. Her eyes land on mine as I ascend the dais, and as she realizes I'm here for her, she straightens in her seat, ever the vision of attentive subservience.

We both know better.

"Husband," she greets me.

I take note of the dignitaries lingering nearby. Gossipers eager for a morsel to spread to the hungry masses. They've never fully taken to her and I'm partially to blame for her isolation.

"Wife," I drawl, pasting on a partial smile for their viewing pleasure. "I hope you don't mind if we turn in early for the night."

"Oh?"

"Yes," I say, imploring her not to be difficult. I place a hand on the back of her chair, leaning over her shoulder when I speak, my other hand upturned in front of her. "Right now."

It takes a beat too long for her to yield, but then she finally slides her hand into my awaiting palm. "As you wish, *your highness*."

I know my father wants me to parade my wife out the hall's grand entrance in order to maintain the illusion of a strong alliance with the Strou, but I lead Irina toward the back stairwell instead. She doesn't protest as we descend the narrow stairs that lead to the kitchen. The sound of pots clanging and chatter comes to a stop as we emerge from the darkened recess. I nod my apologies and urge Irina forward with a hand on her back.

She jerks from my touch as soon as we're alone. "You don't have to push me."

I'm glad her mask didn't slip in front of witnesses, but she knows as well as I do that servants make a habit of snooping around corners. She's grown increasingly hostile in the last year or so, and the last thing I need tonight is for word to spread of another spat between the prince and his wife.

As if coming to her senses, she softens a smidge. "Being in court all day has put me on edge," she mutters, even grinning a little.

Her swift change in demeanor is alarming, almost as if she wants to commiserate with me. I can't recall the last time I've witnessed her genuinely smile, let alone been on the receiving end of it. But the longer I stare at her, the more she reminds me of the girl I courted in Strou. It feels like it was another lifetime ago. When I wanted this marriage to work—not just for our two territories, but between the two of us. For *her*.

Irina has always been soft. Too soft for nobility. Her parents did her a disservice by sheltering her. I visited her territory as often as I could in a bid to court her, to nurture a rapport between us. And at the time, I looked forward to those visits. It afforded me reprieve from the army without having to return to the capital. Weeks where I didn't have anyone looking to me for the answers, without the watchful eyes of my father.

But the girl I went on long walks with, who I shared lingering sidelong glances with in her parents' presence, is gone. The same girl who lit up at the simplest of gestures, like receiving wrapped chocolates or a kiss to the softest part of her hand, *broke* the day I declared my intention to marry Jovie in her place. I did it before all of the congregation at the dinner meant to celebrate Jovie's return, and Irina was never quite the same after. Whatever affections Irina held for me were demolished, as was the kindness in her heart.

A flicker of guilt ignites in the back of my mind. But as quick as the feeling occurs, it leaves, and I turn to continue toward my bedroom.

Her huff of annoyance echoes against the walls. "Oh, we're reverting back to the silent treatment?"

I don't take the bait.

"You're a right bastard, you know that?"

Like my father, she, too, needs to find new material.

". . . sleep in *her* room once again and pretend I don't exist . . ."

Here we go.

". . . good for nothing, arrogant prick . . ."

Debatable.

". . . father you've been following him."

The door to the bedchamber is within sight when her last words catch up to me. Stopping, I slowly turn in place. "Say again?"

Her chest expands with each breath. "I said," she spits out as she stomps toward me. "I'll tell your father you've been having him followed every time he leaves the palace."

I have my hand around her throat, back pinned to the wall before she can blink. Pupils dilated, nails uselessly scraping at my wrist, her haughty bravado evaporates. The real Irina is frightened. And desperate, I realize, as she fights tears.

"What are you doing, Irina?"

"I want out," she hurls forth. "Out of this marriage and this palace with all of its godsdamn self-righteous fools under your father's thumb—"

I slap a hand over her mouth. "Are you trying to get yourself killed?" I hiss.

But she continues to shout muffled words behind my hand and I'm forced to pick her up, arm around her waist, and carry her the last few feet to our bedroom. She fights me the entire way and after I kick the door closed, I let her go with a growl of frustration. "You should be more careful about using the gods' names in vain, because they may have just spared you from execution."

Her face contorts, anger giving way to despair. "Please," she begs. "Let me go home."

"Where's Wesley?"

At the mention of her consort, the moisture building in her eyes finally spills over. "I don't want him." She grabs my shirt in both hands, my mangi stones tangling in her fists as she speaks in a rush. "I'll tell my parents to nullify the marriage if you don't let me go."

"Under what pretense?"

"That my husband refuses to make an Heir."

I can't stop the laugh from escaping. "You think I care what those pious bastards think?" I grab her by the wrists, squeezing until she's forced to release her hold on me. "They're about as worthless as your dowry."

My words only serve to further fuel her manic desperation. "I—I don't fault you for being Matched, Acker. All I want is to go home. Please let me go *home*."

Her voice breaks on the last word and I close my eyes. This whole arrangement is a sham and the last thing I feel like doing is consoling the woman who's made my life all the more difficult these past few years.

But I pull her into my arms anyway.

Her tears soak through my shirt and I cringe.

"Let's go to bed," I tell her, stroking her hair. "You'll feel better after a night's rest."

It takes her a moment, but she finally relents, nodding into my chest. I direct her to the neatly made bed. The room that was once solely my own before my father forced me to share with my bride.

Some battles are won by surrender.

And it seems Irina has grasped that concept, at least for tonight, as she silently discards her finery and slides under the covers in her undergarments. Tears continue to flow down her face and as black lacquer coats her wet cheeks, I realize it may not be her power of influence affecting her beauty after all. She's cautious, eyes half-lidded as she looks up at me, sobs quieting.

"The only way I could undermine my father's order to marry you was if I publicly denounced your hand in exchange for Jovinnia's," I tell her.

It's an apology . . . of sorts.

It was a choice made in desperation, like most of my decisions were when it came to Jovie, as shameful it is for me to admit.

Leaning over her, I wipe the streaks of make-up away with my thumbs. "But don't ever threaten me again."

Tears continue to drip down her temples as she rolls away from me. "You can be so cruel," she whispers.

I know.

I just can't find it in me to care.

Chapter 6

ACKER

The spare bedchamber is as I left it the last time I was here.

I unbuckle the strap of daggers at my chest, laying it across the back of the reading chair. I've ordered the servants to steer clear of this room, but I'm forever cautious about how I leave it. A thin layer of dust has accumulated on every surface, including the desk where Jovie's sketchbook remains after all this time.

I finger open the cover carefully to disturb it as little as possible. The image of a prized horse stares back at me. A stallion with a sash and crown befitting a queen. It's good. Cute, even. An inside joke I once found adorable. Now, all I feel is bitterness every time I look at it.

But it's the robe hanging from the corner of the armoire's door that I'm here for. I'm drawn to it like a dog in heat, saliva pools in my mouth in anticipation of indulgence. Each time I cave, I swear it will be the last, but it's beyond time I quit telling myself that lie as I lift the material from its resting place. I run my thumb over the softness before bringing the collar to my nose. My inhale is deep. The scent is faint. So very faint that I often wonder if I'm imagining the wildflowers and salt filling my lungs.

Desperation is a lethal drug.

This incessant need to see her will not abate.

Left unchecked, it becomes so strong it damn near cripples me. Consuming every waking moment, every thought, every second of every godsdamned day . . . until I *fucking* give in.

I used to blame the Bond, but I quit lying to myself a long time ago.

Hanging the robe back on the door, I sit on the edge of the bed, hating myself for what I'm about to do. It took me a long time to figure out that it's best if I just satisfy the craving. To give in instead of fighting it. It's the only way I'm able to get a reprieve from the constant longing.

I pull the string of stones from my neck and let them hang between my fingers before placing them on the bedside table. Like stretching after a long slumber, my magic warms in that spot in my chest. Metal sings to me from every direction, and my gift is swift to seek out every inch of it. From the copper of the bathtub in the other room to the specks in the crevices of the walls. I allow myself to savor the freedom for a moment, but it's short-lived as anticipation surges through my veins.

It's impossible to force myself into Jovie's presence while she's awake, especially with the chain of stones she's crafted to fit her body, smothering the connection of the Bond from her end. But she's been sleeping less and less as of late. Messages of her involvement in the battles at the Strou border continue to come in, and rest is vital when you constantly need to be battle-ready. She must be exhausted.

I can't tell if it's my oath or just plain irritation causing the pinch inside my chest.

I lie back, hands threaded behind my head, and let my eyes fall closed as I concentrate. I discovered the ability to overcome the mangi stones by accident when I was studying a text about an alchemist who believed ingesting mangi stones could possibly nullify a blood oath. He was wrong, of course. But after weeks of mixing in small amounts of finely-milled mangi stone powder to my tea every morning, I developed a sort of tolerance to the stones' ability to smother my magic, and, consequently, the Bond.

As burdensome as the stones feel for me, someone who has a fairly high tolerance, I can only imagine how heavy the stones Jovie wears must feel, given she never takes them off.

It usually takes all my energy to bridge the gap and I'm on borrowed time. Ever since my fight with Irina a few weeks ago, she's been around more. Her visits with Wesley have waned and that means we've been sharing a bed most nights. Just to avoid another fight, I had to wait for her to fall asleep before I could leave to feel for the tether to determine if Jovie was awake.

Jovie.

It's difficult to reconcile the girl I brought back with me from Alaha with the girl strong enough to take down Strou warriors. I don't know why, considering how easily she destroyed the Dark Forest, or how comfortable she was in allowing the blood of my father's entire council to spill across the palace floors. But the memory of her blushing cheeks and naivete still haunts me enough to make me doubt she could be as efficient on the battlefield as the reports say, regardless of how consistent they are.

The tether stretches as far as my mind will go and then some, to a strange place where nothing exists beyond *this*. Nothing more than a single thread woven between us. I'm blind as I feel my way along the Bond. There's no sound or smell or sense of up or down. Just emptiness.

The first couple of times I tried to chase it to the very end I nearly turned around out of fear of getting lost to the void. I begin to worry I'm getting lost this time, too, because it's taking so long.

But then it pulses.

A faint, lone vibration to signal that I'm getting closer. Each beat of her heart thrums in pace with mine, growing in intensity with each breath. Louder and stronger, it echoes in my body, my mind, flooding the emptiness between us.

Until it comes to an abrupt halt.

With my feet on solid ground, I take in the inside of the small billet for a moment before my gaze lands on my Match. She's very much asleep, head draped across her arm at her desk, chest rising and falling with the even measure of her breaths. Her hair fans over her shoulders in a tangle of waves, spilling over her face and onto the desk. The first set of buttons of her shirt are undone at her collar, the stained fabric askew enough to expose the chain of mangi stones around her neck. Blood and filth are splattered across the material, with most of the staining at the cuffs. Her bare legs peek out from underneath the desk, clean feet crossed at the ankles next to a bowl of muddied water. She must have fallen asleep in the act of washing up after battle.

I maneuver closer, taking in her haphazard sleeping position. It appears she washed up to her knees before the exhaustion claimed her. Sinking to my haunches, the crouched position affords me a better view through the curtain of her copper tendrils. I look over her features and a sharp stabbing sensation spears straight through me.

Even after all this time, it still hurts to look at her.

Beautiful, stubborn Jovie.

Gods know I've spent enough countless nights staring at her to grow accustomed to her beauty, but I've yet to become immune. I could stare at her forever and I truly don't believe I'd ever not crave the next moment, the next second, my next breath when I could lay eyes on her again.

Carefully, I lift my hand to move the delicate pieces of her hair away from her face. Her brows are pinched, lips pulled into a frown by whatever is plaguing her dreams. It makes me wonder if she's dreaming of me or of the atrocities she's just witnessed. I'm not ashamed to admit which I would prefer.

I know it's a futile effort, but as I've done every time in the past, I lean in close and inhale. The stench of war clings to her. Fear being the most dominant; an especially abhorrent scent. Undertones of mud and sweat and leather follow. But what I really desire doesn't reach my nose—that fragrance distinct to her. The perfect combination of wildflowers and saltwater and the iron that runs through her blood.

I've never been able to smell her through the Bond. It's how she must have been able to eavesdrop on the conversation I had with my father the night of her celebration dinner. It's become the only part of her I desire the most, simply because I'm unable to sense it. I'm not sure why the Bond allows for me to smell everything except her, but it's absolutely *maddening*.

The thump of her heartbeat is visible on the side of her neck. A steady pulse, proof of her vitality.

My mouth waters at the sight.

I don't know what comes over me, but I'm suddenly desperate to feel her pulse underneath my tongue. Bracing a hand against the edge of the desk, I lean forward. There's not a hint of her scent as I suck in one final breath and hold it.

I'm venturing into dangerous territory as I place my mouth against the tender skin there.

Heat blooms across my lips and it sends a heavy wave of lust through me.

I fight the impulse to sink my teeth into her soft flesh.

I could do it.

Right here, right now.

To tear through the flesh, let her blood spill and put us both out of our misery.

As my thoughts churn, my heart squeezes in protest and bitterness burns up my throat. As if her fucking fist is wrapped around the organ itself, an ever-present reminder of the power she wields over me because of the oath.

I *loathe* it.

I bet she tastes *so* good. Just the smallest touch of my tongue—

A low groan escapes from Jovie's mouth and I jerk back, snapping out of my bloodlust. I inspect her expression. Still very much asleep, just as before except for the slight part at the seam of her lips.

I slowly let out the breath I've been holding as I sink back to my haunches. A flood of desire muddled with fear inundates my senses as I take in her expression. Her emotions have always felt compounded through the Bond. The divide between fear and excitement has always been a fine line with Jovie. One emotion would often trigger the other.

Like when riding at full gallop or during a heated sword fight. Or when I kissed her with a little too much bite.

It's been four years since I've seen the color of her eyes, but I refuse to wait another four before I'm able to see for myself which emotion supersedes the other when she looks at me—fear or excitement.

A smile tugs at the corners of my mouth.

I'm looking forward to it.

Chapter 7

ACKER

Ace. Wake up," Hallis says, tapping my cheek with an open palm. "Get up."

I stir but the alarm in his eyes snaps me out of the fog of sleep. Sitting up, I note the shade of light filtering in through the balcony glass doors informing me of the early morning hour. "What is it?"

"Roison has invaded the valley in Tyreek's territory. They've taken the town and are setting up camps along the fjord."

"My father?" I ask.

"His bedchamber is empty. Zion sent a messenger from the battlefront. He's waiting downstairs." He picks up the string of mangi stones from the bedside table and tosses them at me. I catch them against my chest. "Get dressed," he orders.

He stalks out and I shut the door behind him with a flick of my magic. Cradling my head in my hands, shame clings to me as it always does when I wake in this bed, magnified tenfold since Hallis has witnessed just how weak I am.

I dress in yesterday's clothes and slip the stones over my neck as I make my way to my father's sitting room. Tyreek and Hallis are waiting, along with Draken and a couple of other lords. The soldier sitting in a tufted chair is staring at the war board with stark, unblinking eyes.

The eternal stare. An empty look soldiers get after staring death in the face for hours, days, sometimes weeks on end.

An oversized blanket hangs over his shoulders. Dried blood and mud and probably guts cover his body, hair plastered flat against his brow. The smell of weeks' old sweat permeates the air around him. Exhaustion lines his body, undoubtedly made worse by riding here through the night.

No one speaks as I squat in front of him, taking the glass of dark liquor Hallis hands me and offering it to the young boy. Like a doll being pulled by strings, he accepts the drink, taking a tiny sip without any indication of the burn as he swallows. He finally makes eye contact with me and there's just enough recognition in his gaze to make him sit a little straighter in his seat.

I thread my fingers together in a fist between my knees. "What's your name?"

His voice is a shallow whisper. "Darcy."

"Tell me what's happened, Darcy."

He seems to have trouble swallowing for a second and takes another small sip of liquor before speaking. "We were keeping rotations, so I was asleep when the first explosions occurred."

"A witch's brew?" I asked.

He shakes his head. "That's what we thought at first, but then we saw—"

The audible noise of another thick swallow is loud in the quiet room and I reach for the glass in his hand, encouraging him to drink some more.

After taking a larger gulp, he continues. "He was already swinging the flail for his second strike by the time we realized the troll had knocked out a portion of the mountainside underneath our base."

We listen to Darcy detail the horrors of the lost battle against the giants. Two of them devastating the mountainside in order to cleave a path so Roison could overrun the town, killing all but one hundred and forty-six of our battalion. Zion, wounded but alive, hidden in the mountainside, sent Darcy to warn us.

It takes three hours to debrief Darcy, but we're able to get a rough understanding of where the Roison had begun setting up camp when he left, including the building where they're keeping a handful of prisoners.

I have the young soldier escorted to a private room to be looked over by a healer as news of the battle spreads. The whole council convenes after breakfast in the war room and I lay out in no uncertain terms the tenuous situation we've found ourselves in. But they know. They blame me. Their hatred is evident as I send out orders for the rest of the front-line soldiers to fall back. All hands will be needed as a last line of defense between Roison and our farmlands—and the city.

War will be at our walls by winter's end.

"This wouldn't have ever come to pass if you would have listened to us when Tyreek first brought the problem to your attention months ago."

"That is neither here nor there, Paul," Hallis says, eyes surveying the map before us. "Let's save our breath for the most important thing at the moment. We need to make sure each province is alerted to the imminent invasion."

"No one could have prepared us for the trolls to join the war," Draken agrees. "In all known history, *millennia*, they've *never* intervened in human affairs."

As I pour the remaining dregs of liquor from a carafe into a glass, my back to the room, I say, "The city gates *will* fall. In the meantime, have the nearby farms render their winter wheat early."

"It'll just spoil," Hallis says. "There's not enough time for the wheat to dry."

I swallow the liquor in one go and place the empty glass on the edge of the map table. "We'll need hay for the horses and cattle."

The council members filter out, each tasked with disseminating updated decrees to their own territories. All but one remains. Tyreek has been silent throughout the morning, but I knew he was only biding his time.

"What is it your plan to retrieve my son?" he demands.

Hallis's eyes shift from Tyreek's sullen expression to mine.

Taking a deep breath, I give Hallis a dip of my chin. Unspoken, but understood nonetheless, and it settles Tyreek enough for him to leave without complaint.

I wait until we're alone before giving Hallis my final order. "You will come back *alive*, do you understand me? Go in, get our brother, and that's it." *Don't try to be a hero.*

Even though he doesn't like it, he nods. "I understand."

Chapter 8

JO

I'm annoyed but not surprised to find the general waiting outside my billet when I return from dinner. It's been days since our last skirmish against the Strou and he's dressed in his cleanest uniform, which tells me he visited my mother. I give him a look that conveys my lack of enthusiasm for whatever it is he's here to relay, before dipping inside the opening of my tent. He follows behind me uninvited.

I strike a match and light the oil lamp on the desk. "Just be out with it," I tell him.

He adjusts the hand braced on the hilt of his sword at his waist. "You're returning home tomorrow."

I expected the order, but his words ring hollow in the small space.

Home.

I haven't felt I had such a place in the years since I left Alaha. They're not thoughts I voice as I take a seat at the desk.

I straighten a peg on the map. "I will not," I say, looking up at him. "And you damn well know you have no place to give me any orders."

He sighs. "Jo—"

"Unless you have any actual news to report, you can leave."

Judging by the stern expression on Sam's face, that was not the thing to say if I truly wanted him to obey. "You've done your due diligence," he says, voice leaving no room for argument. "The men respect you. The people of Maile honor you. What else are you striving for?"

Absolution.

The thought occurs before I can stop it, and I hurry to shove it to the back of my mind. I remove one boot, then the other before looking up at the general. Concern shines back at me, and I reel in the anger that has lived on the tip of my tongue lately.

I lean back in my chair. It takes me a moment to choose my words. And when I do, I hate the waver in my voice. "You know, I never believed Kai when he would talk about the possibility of me being this . . . *lost princess.*" I struggle to swallow past the knot in my throat. "And now I have an entire army behind me just because of a title."

Sam leans further into the lamplight. "They follow you because you're worthy of being followed."

I wonder if he knows he's lying.

There's an entire faction of this battalion who resents me. I'm the very reason their brothers, fathers, and sons have died. All because I didn't kill Edmond. So few have got close enough for even a chance to try before, and I squandered my opportunity.

Sensing my mood, Sam changes tactics. "Your mother wants to see you." It's his last card to pull and he knows it's a good one. "She's worried."

"I wonder why," I say, dryly.

He at least has the audacity to appear sheepish. "I haven't told her anything she isn't already familiar with. She knows what war looks like."

My leaving for the border so soon after my return to Maile only served to rub salt in all of the unhealed wounds from my childhood disappearance. I hated to do it, but I had little choice. She knew it too, as much as it pained her to admit it.

"It wouldn't hurt to check in with Drake and the status of the armada," I concede.

He tries and fails to quash his enthusiasm. "I can have a wagon ready first thing in the morning—"

"No," I cut him off. "I'll leave in a fortnight."

He must see the finality of my decision. "I'll let Evelyn know."

Muttering under his breath about rabbits, he disappears altogether. There one second, gone the next, like he never existed here in the first place.

Magic will never cease to amaze me.

I prop my chin on the heel of my hand as my eyes fall on the map. The part of the border we're currently guarding sits in an area between Mount Zallis and the rocky hillside of Strou. I run my fingertips over the expanse of low-lying planes that have become our routine battleground before moving them up into Strou's hills. Today was one of the rare respites from their aggression, and despite spending the day closely monitoring for movement, there's been none from what we can tell.

Their numerous campsites sit nestled within the many caverns dotting the hillside, protected from the elements while maintaining a perfect view of us. They're impossible to ambush and we're basically sitting ducks, waiting day and night for them to move in for the attack. It's beyond frustrating.

My finger stalls on one of the largest caverns. It sits the highest on the east side of a rocky outcropping. We've frequently watched the Strou soldiers tote in their wild game kills. They hunt in the heavily forested terrain over the hills and hang the animals at the cave entrance for gutting and skinning, letting the blood mark their location in bright red spatters. It's undoubtedly an arrogant display, knowing we are unable to scale the terrain without them having the upper hand.

My eyes catch on the thin ledge to the left of the cave's opening for what feels like the hundredth time and—

Wait.

A thought forms, and I can't believe it hadn't occurred to me before. I jolt from my chair, quickly blowing out the lamp and yanking the map off the desk, sending the pegs scattering all over the ground once again. Rolling it up, I shove it under my arm as I rush out of my billet.

The camp is unusually lively tonight. Rejuvenated by the last few days of ease, the men and women congregate around fires as they drink ale and play cards and dice. They greet me with cheers. A few even try to recruit me to join in their hijinks, which I politely decline as I hurry to get to the far side of the camp. The billets become more dispersed as I reach the edge. The atmosphere is more subdued, less boisterous. Instead of smiles and waves, I'm greeted with polite nods and cautious eyes. Most of these soldiers come from smaller communities outside of Maile's capital. Even here, in camp, they choose to post their tents away from the fray.

My mother never held favor with the rural farmlands and villages. They're still angry with the mess from the last war and have been the least accepting of my return. They were fearful of what my reappearance would bring. Rightfully so, considering war followed within a couple of years. While I've done everything I can to keep the fighting off their farmlands, it's done little to appease the naysayers.

I can't say I blame them either.

I know which tent I need from the last and only time I've hunted Fredrich down. Soldiers linger around a fire roaring. Voices dim to a whisper before stopping altogether at my approach. I fight the urge to avoid their stares. These soldiers left their families, their homes, to fight in a war that has nothing to do with them. The *least* I can do is look them in the eyes. The slight head dips are purely out of courtesy, but it's a courtesy I return in kind before ducking inside Fredrich's tent.

Whatever the two occupants are discussing comes to an abrupt halt when I enter. The younger soldier leaps from where he was lounging on his cot, discarding the book in his hands and reaching for the shirt tossed at the end of his bed to pull it on. Fredrich is thankfully dressed. Judging by his stance and the belt swaying from a hook on the support beam, I arrived just in time to avoid seeing more than I needed to.

There's a long moment where I'm staring at him, and he's staring at me, eyes falling to the rolled parchment under my arm, and the soldier is staring at the both of us, frozen in place, dumbfounded.

Finally, Fredrich looks over at the other man, dismissing him with a jerk of his head toward the billet's opening. The young man grabs his boots from under his cot and dips his head in a tight nod before scurrying out, and Fredrich reaches around me to ensure the entrance closes.

I waste no time in shoving the bedding from the opposite cot, assuming it's Fredrich's, and kneel as I smooth the map out flat.

Fredrich looms behind me. "This is very uncouth of you—"

I stop him with a singular question. "How many men do you think the Strou have in the hills?"

It takes a moment, but he eventually unfreezes from his position, moving closer to look at the map. "Five thousand," he states. "Maybe six."

"How many do you think are stationed per cave?"

He shrugs. "A couple hundred, maybe a thousand at most in the bigger ones. Why?"

I point to the ledge I've been fixated on. "This is their weakest point." When I'm only met with silence, I look up to find his expression carefully blank and continue: "A man or two could easily ascend the southern face without detection. Smoke them out."

A twitch—*there*—in the corner of his eye is his only tell. "It would need to be someone skilled."

"Of course. And when they least expect it." I reach over and turn the flame down on the lantern sitting on the small table nestled beside the bed, deepening the shadows in the tent. "And no one would see us at night."

"Your mother would kill me if I aided you in such a reckless endeavor."

We both know he'd have to tell her first. "I'm going to do it with or without you," I warn. "And you know my mother would want you to protect me. That's why you were sent here, is it not?"

His gaze drops to the base of my neck. "Your stones—"

"I wear the gyve for assurance," I tell him. "I have a necklace. It's smaller." Not as effective, but the likelihood of my Match removing his own is . . . *unlikely*.

I await his answer, knowing he could easily turn around and tell

General Samasu of my plans, which would undoubtedly get back to my mother. Something tells me he won't, however.

"I'll need to acclimatize my magic around them," he says, eyes flicking up from my throat.

I nod, trying to reel in my excitement. "Is that a *yes*?" Anticipation already has the blood roaring in my veins.

There's a flash of teeth when the shielder smiles. "Yes."

Chapter 9

JO

Fredrich spots him first, his low cuss grabbing my attention. My eyes following his line of sight to the figure off in the distance. Sam's back is to us as he inspects the Strou hillside and I grumble my annoyance. We've barely made it to the other side of the valley toward the Strou's position and the light from the full moon reflects off his golden mane like a damn beacon to any Strou patrolling the higher terrain.

"Whistle to signal him," Fredrich whispers. "He's going to give away our location."

I do so and Sam's head whips in our direction a moment before he disappears, reappearing immediately in front of us. The speech I'd prepared in case of this exact scenario dies on my tongue at the look on his face. Anger like I've never seen before, or at least never directed at me. He's in plain clothes, having been woken by the soldiers tasked with keeping watch over me at night. I'm not supposed to know about the guarded rotation, like most things put in place to appease my mother's desire to protect me without making me feel smothered. It never works, but that's neither here nor there.

“Turn around right now,” he orders. His voice is level, at complete odds with the fury lining his features.

It takes me a moment to gather my words. “I don’t take orders from you.”

“You know the agreement, Jovinnia. You swore to Evelyn that you wouldn’t put yourself in unnecessary danger when you came to the border.”

“And I’m not,” I say, frustrated that my voice comes out higher than I intended it, almost a whine. I clear my throat before continuing. “I have Fredrich, who is more than capable of protecting me. You know that.”

His tone deepens with unleashed emotions. “I am the leader of this battalion. The first under your command. You should have come to *me* with your plans.”

“You would have tried to send someone else in my place—”

“As someone should be!” He points at Fredrich. “Take her back to camp.”

I all but bare my teeth at the idea that Fredrich should force my return. “No,” I say, making sure he sees the resolution in my eyes. “The longer you stand here, the more danger you’re putting us in.”

His expression cracks, revealing the raw emotion underneath—fear. “What am I supposed to tell your mother?”

“That I’m doing what she would do in my place.” The truth doesn’t comfort him in the least, but we’re already on borrowed time and he knows it. “We gave the orders to your second,” I continue. “The battalion will move into the valley tomorrow night. They are to rest in the meantime. They’ll need to be ready.”

A muscle ticks in his jaw as he glares at me. “I’ll wait for the smoke, then I’ll come.” Worry wars with the pride he’s trying to hide at my decision and I know it’s the best compromise I could ask for. He looks at Fredrich. “Do your job,” he says, resolute.

Then he disappears once again.

It is a few more hours before the sun breaches the horizon and we’re forced to find cover. There’s not much more we can do to hide ourselves than lay within a tall batch of grass and hope the Strou warriors don’t happen upon us. They do patrol, but seemingly at random. I originally suspected the unpredictability was meant to dissuade any attacks, but now I actually think it's due to lazy arrogance. They believe they're untouchable up in the security of the hills.

Fredrich unsheathes one of his many swords and lays it across his chest for easy access. "Try to sleep. We have a long night ahead of us."

A cover of clouds has moved in, blanketing the sun a little, but the shade does little to help me fall asleep. I fold my arms across my chest to help conserve heat, but I can't stop the involuntary shiver that racks my body. Winter is officially upon us.

"You're safe with me," Fredrich says, unused voice rough around the edges.

I peel my eyes open and turn my head to look at him. "What?"

He doesn't look at me when he speaks again. "You're fidgeting," he says. "If you're worrying, don't. I've got us covered."

Eyes closed, one arm folded behind his head, he's a picture of calm and relaxation as he lies within arm's reach beside me. Almost as if we were on holiday instead of hiding in enemy territory. The grass is tall enough to disguise our whereabouts, and coupled with the spotty Strou patrols, being seen isn't what concerns me. It's being *heard* in the case I fall asleep and my dreams are less than . . . *pleasant.* It's not uncommon for me to wake with a scream in my throat.

He sighs. "Nothing is going to get past my shield."

"I'm not doubting your capabilities," I say with a huff of annoyance as I watch the high reeds sway around us. "I'm just chilly."

"It's not that cold."

Maybe to you, I think, but don't voice it out loud. The ground is rock hard and icy against my back. The occasional gust of wind has me worried about the chance of rain and my breath comes out in tiny smokestacks with every exhale. I'm not about to let a man who's spoken a handful of words to me since we left camp last night manipulate me into believing it's *not that cold.*

It's freezing and I will die on this hill. Pun intended.

"Is it the guilt that makes you do that?"

My head snaps in his direction, unsure I heard his question correctly. "Excuse me?"

"You know," he says, motioning with the hand resting on his chest, as unbothered as ever. "This thing you do where you pretend you're fine when you're obviously not."

It takes me a few breaths to formulate a response that isn't snarky. "I have no idea what you're talking about, considering I just informed you that I'm uncomfortable."

"Yes. The cold. Your nemesis."

Leaning up on an elbow, I stab my next words directly at him. "You do realize who you're speaking to, don't you?"

He isn't outright smiling, but I can hear the smallest hint of teasing in his voice. "I'm aware of your title."

"Yet you speak to me as if I'm beneath you."

Out of all the things I've said, this is what makes him finally open his eyes. "No," he says, gaze relaxed as he looks at me. "I'm speaking to you as an equal." There's a surprising touch of kindness in his eyes. "Is that not what you've been working toward? With hope that your soldiers will respect you in spite of your title, and not because of it?"

"That doesn't mean I owe you my thoughts."

"No. It doesn't," he agrees, closing his eyes once again.

I lie back down, thankful the conversation has been put to rest and we can go back to pretending we're sleeping.

"But it has to be lonely," he says, voice cutting through my momentary relief. "Soldiers fight together. Live together. Hell, even *shit* together. They share everything, from their misery to their laughter. Whereas you . . . *you* go back to your billet all by yourself and presumably ruminate on all the things you've done that led you to this hellscape."

My chest aches at his scarily accurate assessment. I can't tell if I'm such an easy read or if he's simply been paying closer attention to me than I realized. It's General Samasu's assignment to keep tabs on me and report back to my mother, but I wouldn't put it past her to have more than one recruit. Maybe protecting me isn't Fredrich's only task.

"It's the people I dragged here with me," I whisper, my voice barely audible over the wind. "That's what bothers me the most about the results of my actions."

Fredrich's gaze is already on me when I finally gain the courage to look over at him again. "You believe you're the reason we're at war?"

"Isn't that what they say? We're fighting because of a *lover's quarrel*?"

The mention of the rumor whispered around the campfires at night has him shaking his head. "Don't listen to the rantings of soldiers who are hungry and mud-logged. They don't realize it takes more than two people to start a war."

"And you do?"

"Yes," he says with enough finality for me to not question him on the matter.

I can't believe I've just confessed my darkest thoughts to a man who has shown barely more than contempt for me. His odd bout of chattiness caught me off-guard and regret is already setting in.

"But let's say it is true," he continues after a beat. "That you and your Match ignited this war when you two broke each other's hearts. Is that so terrible?"

Isn't the answer obvious? "Yes."

He shrugs. "There are worse things to die for."

"Such as?"

"A greedy man who wants all the power for himself."

Any rebuttal I have gets smothered by the realization that he might actually have a point. A shaky one, at best, but life is all about different perspectives.

He settles back in place with a smile on his face. "If I had my choice, I'd prefer to go to war for a lover's revenge."

Chapter 10

JO

Every time I think I've grown accustomed to the temperature, a smattering of rain dampens us and makes the wind bite harder. The chattering of my teeth is involuntary as I keep my back pressed to the rock face, protecting the flint, oil, and weedgrass we foraged to throw on the fires to create white smoke to flush out the warriors from their encampment. We see the Strou's fires from the valley, so we know they keep them burning throughout the night.

We're balanced on a strip of cliffside that's little more than a few handspans wide. The sky is overcast. There's no light from the moon or stars to see by. I'm forced to rely on my other senses as I listen to Fredrich's steady breathing beside me, feeling the dirt and gravel under my palms and the uneven stone at my back, braced against the biting cold seeping through my leathers. The climb was too arduous to carry the added weight of a protective chest plate or other armor in addition to our weapons.

A violent tremble racks my body.

"Not long now," Fredrich whispers.

They're the first words either of us have spoken since we began scaling the rockiest and steepest section of the hillside before nightfall. They don't work to settle my quivering, but I find solace in those three words, knowing we'll at least be free of this ledge. Such an odd feeling considering my end could very well be just around the bend of the cliffside. Instead of fear, I feel only anticipation as I focus on the heavy beats of my heart, each pulse sounding like the ticking of a clock in my ears, counting down the seconds before chaos.

I feel the slow shift in Fredrich's stance. I hear the scrape of metal as he unsheathes his sword at his side. Following suit, I ready my own weapon, rotating my wrists to loosen the joints after being stock-still for hours. My neck and shoulders all ache as I begin to stretch them out. We've used a lot of our strength climbing and remaining alert as we waited for the time of night when most of the Strou warriors would be the least cautious and it has been draining. Being low on energy is one of our biggest disadvantages—other than being severely outnumbered once we're inside the caverns, of course.

His hand closes around my wrist and I freeze in place.

"Stay close," Fredrich orders.

"I know—"

"If we get overpowered, we make a run for it."

I nod. "Understood."

A gust of wind howls from above us, sending rocks crashing down the hillside. I duck and cover my head with a forearm, but the debris scatters around us, missing us entirely. I've seen Fredrich's shield work in battle, men and weapons rebounding off the invisible and unbreakable barrier that always surrounds him, but it's different to experience from the inside. To feel the pressure shift as the rocks hit, magic vibrating around us.

Again, magic never ceases to amaze me.

He pulls a second sword from the sheath across his back. I call my dagger, the weapon materializing in my hand in the next moment, and hold it with my thumb over the head of the hilt, blade flat to my forearm.

"Ready?"

I nod again.

"Let's begin," Fredrich says.

The sooner we begin, the sooner it can be over.

We shuffle along the slick precipice and toward the cavern's opening. Once we're clear of the bend, we'll be visible to any warriors camped out on this ledge. Our hope is that the few who are awake to keep watch will be easy to sneak past or to take down before we're able to smother their fires. I pray to the gods, the rest of the warriors should be sleeping.

When we emerge on the other side of the bend, the brutal wind stops altogether. The ledge expands in width, the rock face curving back into a natural shelter. The cavern is larger than I expected. The sudden drop in air pressure creates a ringing sensation in my ears. An orange glow burns from a fire at the edge of the cliffside at the opposite end of the cave entrance just as we suspected there'd be. A handful of figures huddle around it.

It takes a moment for my senses to adjust, for anything to pierce through the muffled atmosphere. But soon, as my eyesight adjusts and shapes start to emerge from the dark, a new, collective sound becomes audible.

Snoring.

I swing my sword out to my side, signaling Fredrich to stop in place.

Rows and rows of men sleeping on the ground. I count them as far as I can see, then again to make sure I'm not mistaken. The Strou rarely sent more than a thousand men at a time when they ambushed our battalion, but we suspected they had five times that scattered throughout the cave systems in these hills.

But we were wrong. *Very* wrong.

Judging from the cursory view, I guess there's at least five hundred in this cavern *alone*. If even half the caves contain the same number of men, I'd surmise their headcount is nearly triple of what we originally thought.

We have two options: turn around and scale down the escarpment and call the night a wash or proceed with the original plan and pray to the gods for success. Both are as unappealing as each other. I look at Fredrich over my shoulder, and seeing the question in his eyes, it's obvious he's leaving the decision in my hands. Proceed with our plan or flee back to camp?

I've observed him fight often enough to know he's skilled, but his true strength lies in his gift. Never have I seen his shield falter. Not even after hours of battle. If I choose to fight, it's not *his* life I'm gambling with—it's mine.

And like hell am I returning to camp just to repeat the cycle all over again tomorrow. Where we wait for the Strou to ambush just for us to lose men in the counterattack. No. I'm not returning to camp and confessing to my men that I failed.

Instead, I give Fredrich a nod, letting him know I'm okay to proceed.

The warrior closest to us grumbles in his sleep and we both still. We don't want to start the fight with our backs to the ledge. We wait long breaths for the man to settle again before we move. Crouching low, we take assured but quick steps. It's impossible to move without commotion, but as long as it doesn't sound suspicious, no one will be roused by regular footsteps passing by.

Even though we don't have an idea of direction, the cave system houses a series of interconnected tunnels and inlets. As we move alongside the cave's wall, we come upon a few of these passages. It's too dark to see into, but any could be a passage to a connected cave. But first, we need to create smoke, and that's going to begin at the fire burning ahead. We just need to take the warriors down as quickly as possible.

The five men at the fire have their backs to us; unbeknownst to them, death is creeping up behind them. The closer we get, the hotter the air becomes. And the faster my heart beats, the calmer I feel.

It's a strange high I've become accustomed to when walking into battle. My mind is empty except for a visceral need to kill and not be killed. A place and time where my thoughts cease and I'm nothing more than a girl using her body for what it's been trained for. Whatever the end may be—the eternal reprieve of death or the sweet pleasure of victory—I'm ready for the outcome.

Shifting my sword in my hand, I dare a look at Fredrich. He's positioning himself to take the right flank as I move left. Our eyes lock and . . .

. . . and he smiles. An impish grin I've never seen on him before. Something more fitting for the likes of Messer.

"Intruder!" The man to the far right of the small congregation points in my direction, drawing the attention of the others.

His protest dies on his lips as Fredrich swings his sword in a short arc, slicing through the side of the man's neck. He hasn't even hit the ground before Fredrich jabs his other blade through the throat of the man next to him—in one side and out the other—before yanking it free.

The men are wholly unprepared for the ambush and scramble for their discarded weapons. Using their surprise to my advantage, I slice across the larger one's back. Nonfatal, but painful as fuck, and it makes him arch in discomfort. It takes a flick of my wrist to sever the artery in his neck. Blood spews across the ground. His scream turns into gurgles as he drowns.

The shouts from hundreds of Strou warriors jolting from their sleep echoes in the cavern, but I keep my focus on the last man standing. He swings his sword toward my middle, and I leap back, waiting for his next move before advancing. Being smaller than most of my opponents, I'm often on the defensive until there's an opening, and I've learned that even patience has a place in a fight to the death.

His next move is predictable. A backswing aimed at my neck. I lift my blade to block it, but before the steel of his blade meets mine, it hits an invisible resistance. The warrior's rage morphs into undiluted fear at the realization. I can't stop the grin pulling at my lips and the memory of Fredrich's smile resonates within me. I get it now.

The warrior is shaken from the revelation that he's on the losing end of my sword; he begins to fall back, feet shuffling as he retreats.

The shield protects me from harm, but it doesn't prevent my opponent from defending himself. I continue my assault. Front swing, back jab. Again, again, and again. I fake a jab to my left—his right—turning my body at the last second and am successful in disarming him. His sword skids across the cavern floor.

In a last-ditch effort, he lunges for my throat with clawed hands, only for his fingers to snap from the force of meeting Fredrich's shield. He screams when I plunge my dagger into his gut. I hold his stare as I twist the blade, and his shrieks turn into choked protests as he fumbles for my wrist with gnarled fingers. I acquiesce, pulling the weapon out, blood gushing from the wound. It's too late for him to save himself though. His eyes roll back, body tilting in the same direction before he finally loses consciousness, falling onto the fire with a loud crack.

Darkness descends on the cavern, like a candle has been snuffed out. The commotion is extinguished at the same time as the light.

After a beat of silence, the Strou warriors voices begin to amplify.

"*. . . fucking kill you . . . Maile scum . . . another tally . . .*"

A vibration hums in the air, and it takes me a moment before realizing it's the force of the shield holding the warriors back. Something touches the side of my neck and I jolt.

"It's me," Fredrich says, voice somehow clear above the reignited chaos.

I let out a breath of relief, latching onto the sleeve of his shirt, afraid to lose him.

His grip is firm but gentle as he pulls me closer. "Not scared of the dark, are you, light wielder?"

At the mention of my gift, I still. I'd all but forgotten the part of me that I've constantly been trying to dampen in the years since I left Kenta. That place inside me where my magic and Bond reside together as one.

I finger the mangi stones at my neck. I never take them off. In a situation where I need to switch them out for my gyve, I overlap them before removing the necklace.

The noise becomes nearly unbearable. Deafening. *Violent.*

Fredrich makes the decision for me. "Show them how you burned down the Dark Forest."

Taking a deep breath, I unclasp the necklace, slowly sliding it from under my collar. I remind myself that Acker has never tried to breach the Bond through the tether. Not once since I left Kenta. And if he wasn't also wearing mangi stones himself, I'd likely already be forced into his presence.

I let the string of stones slip through my fingers and fall to the ground.

The men rage beyond the invisible barrier and I focus on the beating of my heart, drowning them out. Pressing my palm against the spot under my sternum, I concentrate as I beckon my magic forward.

Nothing happens.

It takes so long that I question whether I've smothered my magic to death.

Then I feel it.

As if unfurling from a winter slumber, my gift stretches. Slowly at first, but I feel it, nonetheless. Like taking a shot of good whiskey, it burns, growing warm as it spreads through my veins.

I gasp as a dusting of light shines from the exposed skin of my hands. I'd forgotten what this feels like. Painful, but delicious. Intoxicating. *Powerful.*

Then, in the blink of an eye, everything ceases to exist. The air stills. Silence descends so loud that my ears ring. And I'm staring at a textbook, laid open on a wooden desk, lit by a single candlestick. I struggle to make sense of what is happening, when I see them. Male hands I've stared at for hours on end. Hands capable of amazing and terrifying things, with a silver scar that mars the skin between the thumb and pointer finger.

The right hand slides underneath the tissue-thin paper and lazily flips the page.

In a panic, I attempt to squeeze my eyes shut, and just like in my nightmares the scene persists whether I want it to or not.

He reaches for something out of sight. His hand returns with a grape pinched between two fingers. The scar glints in the flickering light as he rolls the fruit between his fingers while he reads. More like skims, as I can barely make out the words on the page before he's moving on to the next.

Oh my gods.

The grape comes closer before disappearing. Sweat sugar coats my tongue, the crunch of the skin echoing in my ears as he chews.

This is not like the times after I accepted the Bond, when my mind could be in two places at once.

No. The Bond doesn't want to let me go. Beau's words ring in my head.

Magic doesn't like being denied.

I need the stones.

Fredrich's voice sounds hollow when he yells.

"Jo!"

Acker's gaze snaps up.

Pain lances across my face, and the last thing I see is the view of Acker's bedroom and the figure of a woman asleep in his bed.

Then I'm staring at Fredrich's heated gaze as he tries to shake me out of my skin. By the throbbing pain on the right side of my face, I surmise he hit me.

"Oh, thank the fucking gods," he says once he realizes that I'm aware once again.

Turning my gaze to the warriors surrounding us, I notice the entire cavern is lit. By me, I realize. *I'm* the source of the light.

Dropping my pack at my feet, I flick my sword in my hand. Somehow, I'm less afraid here than the place I was just in. At least here, I am the master of my own fate. Bringing my sword pommel to rest against the place my magic resides, the glow of my skin flows into the iron filigree in the handle, winding down the hilt like a river of pure light, spilling onto the sword's blade, a stark brightness in the night.

A torch to light the way out.

And my strongest weapon.

Chapter 11

ACKER

I can't *fucking* believe what I'm seeing.

The little I'm able to make out in the darkness, anyway. The only detailed glimpses I'm afforded are when Jovie swings the glowing blade in her hand, her illuminated strikes highlighting the severe expression on her face in quick flashes, her teeth bared, eyes deadly.

I'd be amazed if she wasn't outnumbered by hundreds.

What the hell was she thinking, storming the Strou in their caves by herself?

Oh, *excuse me.*

Not by herself.

The fucking bastard with her obviously helped facilitate this half-cocked plan to . . . I don't even know. Get themselves killed? There doesn't seem to be an outcome that doesn't end with both of them dead.

A warrior bumps into me, which knocks him off balance and he flails in the dark to find the cause for his stumble. When he comes up empty, unable to see my Bond-projection form, he blindly swings his sword in my general direction. Annoyed, I jerk the sword from his flailing hand and grab him by the front of his armor to keep him steady when I slice his neck open.

The other men around me hear their comrade dying, can hear the loud gurgling as he drowns in his own blood, but with the only source of light coming from the middle of the melee almost fifty feet away, they can't determine the cause. All they know is there's another threat somewhere and it diverts their attention away from Jovie, sending many of the warriors scrambling to find it.

And, *of fucking course*, Irina chooses right now to call to me, her worried voice pulling my consciousness back to my body, back to my bedroom where I'm standing at my desk. Her hair is mussed from sleep, robe dipping from her shoulder as she stands before me, hand outstretched as if she were on the verge of touching me.

Her dazed eyes take me in, from my heaving chest to my unadorned neck, before dropping to where the string of mangi stones lay strewn on my desk after I hastily ripped them off. "Everything okay?" she asks.

I don't have time for this.

Heart thundering, I reach for the shirt I discarded on the floor, and pull it over my head. A stabbing sensation sends fire through my chest, and I choke out my next breath. The oath reminding me of my promise. Irina calls out to me again, pleading for me to tell her what's wrong, but I ignore her as I march out of the door. I don't go far, choosing to escape into the nearby hidden passage before allowing the tether to yank me back to Jovie.

This time I'm closer to the fray. Bodies of warriors pound into me from all sides, but none of them are concerned by the invisible force they're knocking into. They can't be, with the threat of the burning sword in Jovie's hand so close, her companion cutting down any she may miss—and she doesn't miss often.

Jovie is a sight to behold. Small, but so precise in her movements. She doesn't hold back; no hesitation in her eyes as she wields the shining weapon. The warriors' screams don't faze her as the burning iron sizzles across flesh and bone, its heat hot enough to singe hair and skin from a distance.

But as marvelous she is to observe, my stomach revolts at the same time.

I've fought alongside and against a handful of soldiers who had the very same look on their face that Jovie wears now, and none of them are alive today. They fought without fear, that vital piece it takes to survive battles much like this one. I don't see an ounce of it in her intense gaze.

That is, until she senses my presence, head whipping in my direction. She can't see me, however, lost as I am amidst the mass of warriors and darkness beyond her sword's range. But she knows. Must know considering the Bond's insistence in taking any chance it's given to reunite us, the tether a burden even now when our lives are at risk.

I force myself back into my body, leaving her presence. Distracting her is the absolute last thing I need. Not for her well-being and the blood oath I swore, but also for my sanity. I let my back hit the stone wall inside the hidden passage, gulping down deep breaths of the stagnant air. My anger has subsided, replaced by an overwhelming sense of helplessness. The pounding of the blood in my veins drowns out my thoughts as I concentrate on the tether, knowing it will reveal whether she needs me.

The fuck is wrong with me?

I always thought her demise would bring me happiness, knowing it would have to come by happenstance or at the hands of someone other than myself. Yet, here I am, worried sick over what I just witnessed. I tell myself it's due to fear of the oath's retribution. There's no telling if the Mother would consider me at fault if Jovie were to die at the hands of men I've placed in her path. But even if I somehow outmaneuvered the oath's hold on me, I'm not so sure I'd survive her death.

Or worse, if I'd even want to.

Another piercing pain propels me back down the tether. Not my pain, but Jovie's, a gash visible across her cheek when she swings her sword in her attacker's direction. Whatever pain he caused her is short-lived, the wound already healing as she continues her fight through the throng of warriors. If she feels my presence this time, she doesn't let on.

For hours, I continue volleying back and forth along the tether. I do it for so long that I'm no longer able to tell what time of day it is, knowing only that I left my bedchambers well after midnight. Fatigue has me slumping to the floor, but I don't let it overtake me. And I realize . . . that even after everything she's done . . .

I'll never abandon her.

I *can't.*

Chapter 12

JO

I swing my sword over my head before bringing it down onto the neck of the warrior in front of me. As he crumbles, I'm already moving on to my next target. The sword in my hand is dim, the light of my magic fading. I'm burnt out, too, as I flip it into my opposite hand, raising it with just enough time to block the curved blade of a saber coming at me. My arm nearly buckles from the effort it takes stop the warrior from bringing the weapon down on my head. A feral sound escapes my clenched teeth as I spin out from under the pressure, calling my black dagger into my free hand and jabbing it into the warrior's side, through the space of his ribs and into his heart.

Someone jerks me from behind by my leathers and I flip my sword to stab blindly behind me. But when I'm spun around by the assailant, I discover it's not an enemy warrior. *Fredrich.* We became separated during our flight from the cave system. It was strictly dumb luck we escaped, that the plan didn't completely unravel.

I'm just noticing the fight has begun to wane. There're few Strou left, most of their men we let retreat once we knew we had the winning hand in the fight. But there's still a great deal of our men lying amongst the fallen. The valley has turned into a mud pit, the ground soft and slick with blood. In the distance, the sky is beginning to fade to gray, morning just beyond the horizon.

I try to think of something to say, but my mind is blank. I can't formulate a single word, let alone string multiple together. Judging by Fredrich's appearance, he's nearly as worn out as I am. It actually makes me feel a little better as I struggle to make my feet lift from the ground with each step.

"That's enough," he states.

Looking down, I realize he has a tight fist in the material of my sleeve. I can't find the energy to try and remove it. Instead, I let him drag me toward the battalion's temporary camp on the other side of the valley. My feet are as unhurried as the other soldiers who are headed in the same direction, at complete odds with the soldiers who are better rested returning to the dwindling fight. They pat us on the backs, issuing words of encouragement on our return.

General Samasu appears in our path just as we reach the outskirts of the gathered tents. "Jovinnia," he says, grabbing me by the shoulders, eyes wide as he inspects me.

The fear in his eyes works to knock me out of my stupor. "I'm fine," I say, voice hoarse.

He doesn't believe me, patting my shoulders and down my arms until he reaches my hands, where I still have my weapons locked tight in my grip. He takes them gently from me one at a time and hands them off to Fredrich.

"What happened?" he asks, but there's a sharpness in his eyes as his gaze swings to Fredrich.

Fredrich's eyes dip, and I'm surprised by the contrition clouding his features. "It's my fault. I should have been more tactful in my effort to down the men guarding the cave."

"That's not fair," I say in his defense. "We were spotted before we could cover the fires. After that, there wasn't a chance of getting out unnoticed."

For every one warrior we downed, there were ten more to take his place. We were able to break free of the horde by dashing into one of the winding tunnels of the cave system. Then it became a torture chamber of sorts. Running from the warriors chasing us as their footsteps and shouts echoed off the walls in seemingly every direction, only to think we were in the clear before coming upon the next cavern when even more warriors waited.

It took hours to finally find an opening where the hillside beyond gave way to a sloping terrain safe enough to navigate in the dark. The warriors kept funneling from the caves like ants. But once we were in the valley, our battalion folded in on them from all sides, preventing them from retreating back into the security of their cavernous hideout.

It's obvious Sam isn't finished voicing his anger at how things went, but he must see the fraying thread we're only just hanging by, because his mouth thins as he bites back his frustration.

"Come on," he says, tone softening as he places a hand on my shoulder. "Let's get you cleaned up."

My eyes meet Fredrich's and I hope he sees my silent apology as we depart. He stayed by my side for as long as he could until the weight of men pulled us in opposite directions in the valley. His muffled yells for me were desperate. And in the moment, they were the only thing I focused on as I fought.

Sam leads me inside a tent where two women are waiting for me, both healers, that he tasks with helping clean me up.

"No," I protest, holding up a hand to halt the women as they come toward me. "There are many others who are more urgently in need of care. Tend to the wounded. I can clean myself."

"Jo, you, too, have injuries—"

"I said *no.*" It takes nearly all of my remaining energy to spit the words out, but my tone leaves no room for argument. "My wounds are artificial and will heal on their own. There's plenty of those without gifts who need help more than I do."

And, once again he's forced to swallow his tongue. "Fine," he says, dismissing the women with a wave. "But the two soldiers outside stay. I won't hear anything about it."

He takes my lack of response as a concession, then he pointedly looks away from me before turning away and leaving.

This tent is meant to be a temporary shelter, so it's missing a lot of the amenities I have at the main camp. There's a cot positioned to the right, a stool with a bowl of clean water perched on top, and a lamp hanging from the apex of the covering overhead. The sounds of soldiers clearing the battlefield in the distance filters through the flimsy material.

I look down at my soiled clothes. Blood and mud and sweat have the material sticking to my clammy skin. Untying my leathers from each side of my abdomen, I peel my top over my head and realize I'm shivering, just beginning to register how much the cold has sapped my energy. But the rest of my gear needs to come off, so I remove my boots and pants, dropping everything in a pile by the entrance.

Aside from my undergarments, my skin is exposed to the frigid air, and my muscles spasm erratically as I remove the rag from the lip of the wash bowl and dip it in the water. It's colder than the night air, making my body quake in rebellion at the mere thought of pressing the damp cloth to my body, and I have to sit on the edge of the cot to stop myself from keeling over. I urge my hands to cooperate as I start at my feet and slowly work my way up. By the time I make it past both knees, the water is a murky brown, but I continue until I've scrubbed every inch of my body as thoroughly as I can.

A wave of exhaustion makes the world tilt suddenly and I realize after a long blink that it's because I toppled over sideways on the bed. I don't have the energy to even to pull the blanket over myself despite still shivering, instead just letting the abyss of sleep pull me under. It's my favorite kind of sleep, where I don't dream and my mind can't turn my best memories into my worst nightmares.

The kind of sleep that feels like bliss.

It doesn't last as long as I'd like, a dream tugging me into a series of memories. It's the kind where I know I'm dreaming of a time I try not to think about. Like the time Acker gave me saigon root to help me through the awakening. When the grass and trees seemed so vivid upon my arrival to land. Then to him sitting in the chair beside my bed in Fia's cottage. When he looked at me with such tenderness that it hurts to witness in hindsight.

That is . . . until something wakes me.

My eyes peel open, not to the murky light of morning like I was expecting, but to the dead of night. It's dark, the flickering of light from the oil lamp having burned out, but there's just a sliver of moonlight filtering through the gap in the tent entrance. Nocturnal insects chirp in unison, creating a hum of noise. There's an eeriness in the quiet.

My eyes scan the shadows for movement.

Then I see it: a shift in the darkness mere feet away. The form of a Strou warrior as he steps forward.

Huh.

Not exactly a coherent thought, that. A niggling voice inside my mind tells me I should recall my blade as he comes closer, but all my sleep-addled brain seems to ponder is how he got into camp, let alone past the soldiers outside my tent.

He takes another step and I'm able to see the unmasked rage splashed across his face, the subtle glint of the long knife in his hand. It's only then that I find it in me to summon my dagger. A moment too late, as the warrior is already lifting the hand holding the weapon above his head. But just before he's able to bring the blade down, someone's hand reaches out and grabs the warrior by the wrist, stopping him.

It's a hand I'd recognize anywhere, and I internally sag with relief.

It's just another dream.

A new, terrifying one, but I find some semblance of comfort that it's simply my mind playing tricks on me. It makes sense, given I felt Acker's presence at least once when Fredrich and I were inside the caves. For a moment I thought he had come to save me.

My eyes track up the attached arm, to where Acker's face is partially masked in shadow. He kicks the warrior's legs out from under him, sending the man to his knees. Twisting the weapon from the warrior's hand, Acker spins it in his palm before he shoves it right through the warrior's ear and into his brain, killing him instantly.

It doesn't matter how much I try to convince myself that my love for him has dimmed, I know it is the furthest thing from the truth. My mind knows it, too, hence why it concocted this stupid nightmare so I can never forget what I actually long for—*him*.

Acker's eyes flick up to meet mine as the warrior slowly falls forward onto the ground. "Were you just going to let it happen?" he asks, incensed.

I'm not sure.

Maybe.

What happens when you die within a dream? I bet it's peaceful.

Taking a measured step over the felled warrior, he bends down, crouching down to my eye level. He reaches a hand toward me, brushing the stray hairs that have slipped from my braid away from my face, the back of his knuckles dragging over my cheek.

His brows come down in a slant over his eyes as he touches my neck, then my shoulder. "Fuck, you're freezing," he says.

Actually . . . now that he mentions it, I am *really* cold.

He reaches for the blanket at the foot of the cot and covers me with it. It does little to warm me up.

When he pulls away, I reach out a hand to stop him. "Stay," I beg him, desperate to ease the ache in my heart. "Please."

He looks at the grip I have on his fingers, as weak as it is, before looking up at me through his lashes. There's a hint of hostility in his expression that would scare me if this was real, but this is nothing but my exhausted mind playing tricks on me.

And because it's one of the rare occasions my mind takes pity on me, Acker's face softens. He doesn't speak as he stands from his bent position before climbing onto the cot next to me. Heat radiates from his body and I savor it as he wraps an arm around me, pulling me in close as he weaves his legs through mine. He slides his forearm under my head as a pillow before slowly reaching for my hand with the other, threading his fingers through mine and tucking me into his body.

I can feel his heart beating against my back, the expansion of his chest as air fills his lungs, and the caress of his exhale against my neck. My dreams have always been particularly detailed, but out of all of them, this one is the most surreal. I suppose if I'm forced to endure my truest desire then I might as well enjoy it.

I sink into his embrace and a sound rumbles from deep in his chest, something so similar to the way he would hum when he'd finally convince me to nap with him in the boat, the vibration palpable against my back. A burning sensation creeps up the back of my throat, and it takes me a moment to realize it's the urge to cry. Such an odd thing to do in a dream, but there's no stopping a single tear from escaping, the trail of wet heat hot across my nose before dripping onto his forearm.

His arms tighten around me as he says, "Sleep, Jovie."

Then my dream transports me to our boat, where there's no war or death or cold. Just the stars in the sky and the gentle lap of the ocean.

Chapter 13

ACKER

I twirl the blade in my hand, sitting directly across from my father as I wait for him to reveal why he called this meeting. We're currently at a stalemate, sitting in complete silence.

Stay. Please.

I can't seem to quit thinking about Jovie's broken plea, the desperation on her face. It should be the least of my concerns, especially after watching her narrowly escape death against the Strou, both in battle *and* when the lone straggler managed to sneak into her tent. But the way she folded into me was both agonizing and ecstasy. It was the first time in the years since our parting that the ever-present thrum of the Bond didn't feel wrong.

I'm bone-tired after staying up all night to ensure she didn't find herself on the wrong end of a sword. Even my body is sore, as if I were physically there instead of manifesting through the Bond. It did, however, take all of my concentration to remove the Strou warrior from Jovie's tent. I didn't want her to wake to a dead body beside her, so after I was sure she was in deep sleep and her body temperature had risen considerably, I somehow found the strength to get rid of the bastard.

Worry has firmly taken root inside me at her apparent lack of care for her own well-being. I tell myself it's because of the oath, but a shameful part of me can't deny how good it felt to have her in my arms again, that it took me longer than I'd like to admit to peel myself from her. I try to convince myself *that* is just due to how long it's been since I've lain with anyone and has nothing to do with it being Jovie, but I can only lie to myself so much before it slips into the realm of delusion.

It was her tears that did me in.

"Would you like a drink?" my father asks, finally.

"No, thank you."

He waves away Stassia, the maidservant, and gives me his full attention. "You've been frustrated with me," he says, voice a low timbre in the empty room.

I've been expecting this conversation for quite some time now. My father likes to be in control of difficult conversations, disarming his verbal sparring partners by pretending the severity of the situation isn't as dire as they were led to believe.

I, on the other hand, have been dealing with this man for twenty-four years, and I'm well acquainted with his tactics.

"Yes," I answer evenly, holding his gaze.

He nods, a small grin tugging at the side of his mouth. "Navigating politics in the heat of a conflict isn't easy for any lone man. Yet, you've handled the pressure well. I'm proud of you."

I'm proud of you.

Never has my father uttered those words to me.

I've changed my mind. I do want a drink.

Leaving my dagger on the arm of my seat, I walk over to the liquor cart. Stassia moves to get me a glass and I hold a hand up to stop her, pouring a healthy dose of whiskey for myself and taking a swallow.

"I put a lot of responsibility on your shoulders with my absences," my father says, voice heavy. "Probably more than I should."

I turn to face him. "Then why did you?"

He looks at me for a long time, almost *thoughtfully*, before his gaze lands on the string of stones around my neck. "We both know the mangi stones are not infallible, son."

"You've entrusted me to man the ship for the past year by myself, and now I'm suddenly the liability?" I scoff, shaking my head. "You don't even wear the stones to shield against your own Match."

"Greta isn't the enemy, now, is she?"

"You're telling me you don't believe Greta had knowledge of her daughter's plans to help Jovinnia overthrow you?" I ask, incredulous. "She's a godsdamned fortuneteller."

"Greta couldn't have known. There are no secrets between the two of us."

"And yet she wears the mangi collar, unlike you," I challenge.

He's unfazed by my accusation as he stands and makes his way toward me. "I was informed you've been sneaking into the bedroom the princess of Maile had previously stayed in."

I force myself to not react. If I appear even the slightest bit guilty, he'll latch onto it. "You're the one who insisted I share my bedchambers with Irina. It's the only room in the entire palace where I know I won't be bothered."

"So you're telling me you haven't visited your Match through the Bond?"

There's something in the way he's eyeing me that makes my hair stand on end and it feels like a warning to not lie. "Now, I didn't say that," I drawl.

There's a tense moment where he inspects my unrepentant expression before he breaks, a knowing grin spreading across his own face. "I understand how luring a Match can be, son, but the difference between my Match and yours," he says, lifting a brow, "is that yours has proven to be a menace."

I can't stop my responding grin at his choice of description. "That's fair."

He places a hand on the top of my shoulder. "I have a plan," he says, tightening his grip in the same way he's done all my life. "But if we have any chance of winning this war, it's important it remains confidential. Do you understand?"

I nod.

The band of pressure that has stayed wrapped around my chest, suffocating the air from my lungs, finally loosens a degree. "We've lost nearly eighty thousand, the trolls have joined our enemy's cause, and we're low on iron—"

He cuts me off. "There's someone I want to introduce you to." And as if he planned it, the sound of the door's hinges creaks open behind me. He let's go of my shoulder, and in the blink of an eye, his expression flattens into neutrality. "Please, come in," he encourages with a wave of his hand. "Stassia, fix our guest a drink."

I down the rest of mine, eyeing the empty glass in my hand as I work to rein in the flood of hot frustration beginning to pump through my veins. Judging by my father's sudden shift in demeanor, I already know I'm not going to like the person behind me. The stranger's voice is unfamiliar as they thank the maidservant and a seed of dread takes root in my gut.

My father holds out an arm to direct my attention to our guest, playing the gracious host. "Ace. Son. Let me introduce you to an old friend of mine."

The scent hits me first. That strange aroma that anyone who has lived in Alaha carries with them. Like the metal in their veins is rusting, poisoning them slowly, blood turning toxic from being denied land for too long.

My father's voice drones on, but I barely hear him over the ringing in my ears. ". . . Wren and I go back centuries."

I finally turn in place, eyes landing on the Captain of the Alaha.

The man my mother told me scary bedtime stories about when I begged her. The man who massacred countless in his personal quest for power. Who incited my father's own men against him. At least, that's what the records say. The history written down for future generations as a warning about this one man's deranged mind.

He holds his hand out toward me now. An Alaha greeting, to clasp hands when meeting. I stare at it and imagine all the ways I could remove the appendage without so much as lifting a finger. Neither of us move for a long time before he finally concedes, closing his hand in a fist and dropping it.

"You'll have to excuse my son," my father interjects. "You don't exactly have the best reputation here in Kenta."

What my father's statement is failing to encompass is the depth of my disdain for the man who stole my Match's memories from her as a child and kept her in deplorable conditions. Regardless of my anger at Jovie, no one should be robbed of their mind. Any man capable of doing so, to a *child*, shouldn't be allowed to breathe, let alone stand in my presence.

Whoever helped Wren take Jovie to live in Alaha deserves the same fate. My father has always maintained his innocence. He claims it was solely Osiris's doing, stealing the princess of Maile and shipping her to live with the Alaha. It's the very reason Evelyn killed the previous leader of Roison, but I've grown increasingly suspicious my father didn't play a role in the entire scheme; I've just yet to figure out how. Or better yet: *why*.

Stassia reappears to hand Wren a drink. He accepts it with the countenance of a gentleman and gives her his thanks. My eyes drop to the glass in his hand. It's never concerned me before, but the thought of the glass I possibly used to pleasure my Match being in *his* hands has me seeing red.

"I'm sure that's none of your doing," Wren says, continuing their casual exchange, eyes cutting to my father in a shared conspiratorial glance.

I jerk myself away from them out of fear of doing something I can't undo, like removing both of Wren's hands.

Ignoring their mutual ribbing, I move to the drinks cart. The decanter clinks against the lip of my glass as I pour a generous measure and I take a calming breath before returning it to its place next to the other bottles. Instead of throwing it at Wren's head.

After taking a healthy swallow of liquor, I finally give the two men my full attention, hiding the violent shake in my free hand by sliding it into my pocket. "Let's skip the nonsense," I say, cutting through their bantering, leveling my father with a look. "Explain to me why the man exiled to live over the sea along with his entire people is allowed to move freely in our home."

My attitude sobers my father and he wordlessly leads Wren to the seating area. I follow cautiously, sliding into the seat I vacated moments ago. It just happens to be directly opposite the one occupied by Alaha's captain. He inspects me in a way that reminds me of his son. Kai's arrogance clearly comes from his father.

"Ace," my father says, crossing a leg over the other. "I understand the concept of an alliance with Wren may seem inconceivable to you, but there are a lot of dynamics at play you haven't been privy to."

I look at him with a calmness I don't feel. "I know he sent his son's puppet to overthrow you, then immediately upon returning to land himself, he joined Roison in their attack against our people *and* your throne."

Wren leans forward, and it's the first time I notice the collar around his neck. "We have been adversaries in times past, yes, but before that we were friends, and this time we've come to a mutual agreement that we believe will benefit us both."

"Hm," I grunt around a swallow of liquor.

My father tips his chin in my direction. "I'm sure you have many questions."

I suck on my teeth before saying, "Not really." I set down my glass and casually pick up my dagger. "The king of Roison made a deal with Evelyn that cut the Alaha out of territory. It's the only reason a self-serving leader like Wren would ever force his men to join the losing side of a war."

My father's voice is tinged with warning. "You speak about things you know nothing of."

I cock my head to the side. "Enlighten me then."

Wren observes our exchange with careful consideration. He tries to disguise his interest by taking a drink and I'm quick to divert my gaze from him to the dagger in my hand. I know I don't need full access to my gift to kill Kai's father. I could kill Wren in the span of a single breath. It would be so easy. I pinch the tip of the iron blade between my fingers. He wouldn't be the first life nor the last taken with this blade.

Wren's voice interrupts my murderous thoughts. "You see, my people have lost their magic. We've been away from land for too long."

"*You* haven't though." When I look up at him, his hands are empty, his glass discarded on the table alongside mine. "You and your kin haven't gone without."

His eyes linger a moment on the weapon in my hands before replying. "When we were exiled, I made the decision to smuggle soil to Alaha for my son's benefit, if that's what you're referencing."

"Does he know you're here? Pledging allegiance to his sworn enemy? Last I heard he was calling for my head."

His carefully curated mask slips, revealing the animosity he's been hiding underneath. My smile only seems to make it worse. He had to know I'd have had spies in his ranks. A divided house will always have plenty of gaps for vermin to sneak in. I've hung more men than I have fingers on my hands these last four years—men who, under his son's command, were sent to assassinate me.

"Kai will fall in line."

There's not a chance in hell I believe that.

"Wren's ideals align with our own," my father continues, ignoring our tense exchange. "We could live in harmony with our neighbor. Not as we are now, in a constant state of defense, subject to Chryse's every move to needle us from Roison, but with an actual ally on the other side of the border."

I nod slowly. Their goals would mirror one another's. They're both rulers who prefer to hold power over their people by wielding a heavy hand. But I don't for one moment believe either of them could coexist. Not on this land, in this realm, or while they're both still alive.

Power craves dominion.

"This puts your armies in a precarious situation," I tell Wren.

He looks rueful for a moment. "My men are too imbedded within Roison's army to change their orders at the moment. If Chryse were to find out about the Alaha switching allegiance, it'd be a bloodbath."

"To prevent such an event," my father adds, "we will keep the existence of this alliance between the three of us."

"Until the time is right," I conclude.

My father nods. "Exactly."

I manipulate my blade between my fingers. "We'll continue to lose men at an unsustainable rate if we wait too much longer."

"A sacrifice not made lightly," my father says with faux gravity.

Wren leans forward, drawing my attention toward him. "Once Roison's troops close in on the capital, we'll have the element of surprise on our side and can finally end this war."

The statement leaves his mouth with too much ease.

Chapter 14

ACKER

It's well after midnight when my father waltzes into my bedchamber. I knew when my father ordered his favorite wine from the cellar and called for his royal taster that it was going to be a long night listening to him and Wren swapping old war stories if I didn't recuse myself. But I also knew he was unhappy with my less than welcoming attitude to Wren and that I'd likely hear about it later. Likely at a time of inconvenience. Another one of his tactics to gain the upper hand.

I close the book I'm reading and rise from my place at the desk, sliding my hands into my pockets as I wait for his temper to make itself known.

He takes in the empty bed with an unimpressed raise of his brow, then turns his gaze to the barren walls and pockmarked surfaces as he leans against the mantle. "You've been following me."

I'm taken off guard by the accusation, but don't retreat from it. "I hired a shifter to track your scent."

At first I thought the rumors to be true, that he was just being cautious about his extra-marital exploits. After being lectured for years and years about maintaining appearances within the palace walls, his being elusive about such things wouldn't have been a surprise. Nothing is more important than keeping the status quo with the courtiers. But on his recent excursions it was his habit to visit the mines first, checking on the efforts to excavate more hearthstone, before moving south. And that's where the shifter would lose track of him every time.

"Who told you?" I ask.

"I have my sources," he says, noncommittally. "I suppose I should have expected as much. You are my son, after all."

With a flick of his wrist, the hearth erupts in a blaze of fire before dimming to a more normal smolder. It's a gratuitous display of the magic he's been hiding, and I stagger back a step.

"How?" I ask, trying to mask my fear, but I'm sure it's evident in my astonishment.

He looks at me with an amused glint in his eyes, enjoying my shocked reaction. "You shouldn't let the cold seep in like this," he admonishes, ignoring my question. "Then maybe your wife might prefer your bed over her consort's."

I don't tell him that I actually sent her away, having anticipated this confrontation. "Don't patronize me," I say instead. "Tell me how you've regained your gift."

"I believe it's best we sit for this conversation," he says.

The reading chair slides across the floor toward us and I take another step back, alarmed by its independent movement. That is, until my father sits down, and I realize with abject horror that he's also somehow developed the gift of a kinesis. A gift that allows for the moving of things with the mind. There's only one person I know of with that gift, and they were confined to the palace dungeons at the end of the last war, when the Alaha were first exiled.

He's unbearably smug as he leans back and crosses one leg over the other. "I've discovered a method that enables the transference of one Heir's gifts to another host."

"And what method is that?" I ask.

His eyes dip to the stones around my neck. "If the information was to leak . . ." he says as he moves closer, ". . . it could be catastrophic."

"You're killing people and stealing their magic," I deduce, warily.

He doesn't deny it, and there's no chance I'm able to disguise my true feelings, my upper lip curling in disgust.

He isn't the least bit offended by my reaction. "Only the ones who have used their gifts to harm others."

"And what of us?" I motion between us with a wave of my hand. "Should we be stripped of the Mother's blessing for those we've harmed?"

"We are kings." He speaks slowly, as if the concept is new to me. "We are granted . . . privileges."

I shake my head. "Not to take that which rightfully belongs to another."

"You and I don't use our gifts *against* our people." He levels me with an admonishing look. "We use them to fight *for* our people."

A number of responses run through my mind, but the truth is I *haven't* done much fighting. Not as of late. Not unless I count the other night when I fought to keep Jovie safe, but that wasn't even in defense of my *own* men.

Instead, I've been navigating court politics and plotting war strategies while being kept in the dark about the things that really matter. I might as well have gone to the front lines without any weapons, blindfolded. That's how useless I've been—just a very convenient placeholder in my father's absence while he was doing the unimaginable.

I've been waiting for this.

The moment I would know there's nothing redeemable about my father.

A dagger sits on the edge of my desk. The temptation to use it screams inside my mind. To remove the stones and send the weapon straight through my father's throat, ending his tyrannical rein right here, right now. His eyes flick down to where my hand hangs by my side, clenched into a fist, and I hurry to check that my mental shields are fortified. There's no telling how many gifts he's hiding.

He returns my stare. "Whatever you're thinking, just know any move you make against me will fail."

I need to calm down.

Pointing to the other tufted chair, I ask, "Will you?"

Without moving a muscle, my father makes the chair skid across the floor. I sit, then glance at the glass of wine I left at my desk. My father catches on quickly, and the glass floats into the air and over to my awaiting hand. I take a long sip of the contents.

"Cheeky," he states, a smile slowly coming back to his face. "But do you see? The possibilities are endless."

"I can agree that it has its benefits." I twirl the stem of the glass between my fingers, pasting on what I hope to be a believable enough expression. "My concern is making sure that we take from Heirs who have abused their magic in ways that go against Mother Nature's intentions."

"Of course. I've already sent word to the lords of the court that they're to turn over any prisoners they've detained and charged with magic-related infractions."

"It wasn't Roison's territory you agreed to give Wren, but magic for his people in exchange for this alliance," I say, putting the pieces together.

He nods.

I absorb his answer. "Do you have an idea of the numbers of prisoners?" I ask.

His mood shifts, smile dipping in response to my question. "If we're to appease Wren, then not nearly enough. This is where having an oracle would have been of great benefit, to help us find the truly bad eggs. I haven't been able to source one, however. At least, not one trustworthy enough. Or, say, if we had someone like Beau . . ."

I tense in my seat, my magic responding to the insinuation, burning through my veins like a wildfire. But I don't move. "She'd never agree to it," I say.

He gives me a look straight out of my childhood, like he gave me back when I used to advocate for my sister to train in the courtyard right alongside me.

Like he's humoring me.

"Her gift is one of a kind," he says. "It's truly unfortunate how everything went down with her. She was my best hand. Yours, too, I know."

I finish my wine and give a shrug. "Mm hmm," I murmur, noncommittal as I inspect my empty glass.

We discuss his plans to send soldiers to neighboring townships to begin rounding up imprisoned Heirs. I interject when appropriate, the wine in my stomach turning sourer with every minute that passes by. But I must do a decent enough job at appearing untroubled and invested, because it isn't much longer before he decides to turn in for the night.

I wait for a long time after he leaves to ensure the coast is clear before grabbing the oil lamp from my desk and slipping out. The alcove outside the door to my bedchambers hosts the bust of a princess long forgotten. I always found her sad expression comforting, as if she's always been sympathetic to my place as prince, having been in the same position once in time.

Behind her, the wall gives way to the hallway hidden beyond. The secret passages here run the length of both wings of the palace, but I've never explored them in their entirety. Just one of the reasons neither my father nor I knew of Beau's duplicity, only later realizing she'd utilized the passageways to sneak in the Maile soldiers.

The acrid smell of rat piss burns in my nose. Their scurrying feet echo down the corridor as I encroach on their space. Once I reach the end of the narrow passage, I feel along the wall until a portion of it gives, swinging open and allowing me to emerge into the hall before the closed doors to the library. It's impossible not to feel small before their enormous height. I can only imagine how Greta feels from the inside, having not been permitted to leave the library's confines ever since her daughter played a key role in Jovie's betrayal.

As my father's concubine during my childhood, Greta maintained the library as the record keeper for the king. He gave her the responsibility in a bid to disguise who she was to him, but it didn't take long for rumors to spread of their Bond. It was an unspoken understanding to never discuss the dynamic in court. Anyone caught gossiping was charged with treason. By my mother's doing, or so I've been told.

The library no longer serves that function. No one dares to step inside the library's walls. Ever since Beau's treason, people have shunned her mother, believing she *must* have known beforehand and therefore *must* be just as traitorous. Even though my father refuses to believe so.

I don't knock, opening one of the large doors just far enough to slip inside before pulling it shut behind me. Lamplight bathes the ground floor, providing enough light to see by, so I deposit my own lamp on the circular desk in the center of the room.

"Greta," I call, my voice traveling up the curved book lined walls, bouncing off the darkness-cloaked ceiling high above. "Greta!"

The sound of a bolt sliding out of place comes from below. On the floor beneath the open center of the desk, the intricate circular pattern carved into the stone on the floor slides away, revealing a haggard-looking Greta. Despite her frizzy hair and unbalanced spectacles, she still spares me a smile.

"Acker," she says, stepping out from the alcove in the floor. "I've been expecting you."

Of course she has.

I glimpse the smaller, secret library hidden under the floor for a split second before she shuts the hatch of the door again. Every time I believe I've reached the bottom of the well holding reminders of Jovie's time here, I'm mistaken, and I'm forced to breathe slowly past the pinch in my chest.

"Then you know why I'm here," I say.

She dusts her palms on her pants. "Your father quit asking for my view of the future almost a decade ago." She drops into the desk's chair, pushing her hair out of her face as she leans on the desk with her forearms. "He never liked my answers."

My father has never hidden how little regard he holds for Greta's sight. *We create our futures, not experience them,* he'd say, dismissing his Match's gift.

"I'm not *asking*."

My tone gives her pause. "Your father will know," she says, warning clear in her voice.

"I know."

Admittedly, I'm ashamed it's taken me so long to gather the courage to come to her, and I think it's because I've spent the majority of my life desperately clinging to the idea that my father was right. That we are able to forge our own paths. But I've never felt more like an onlooker in my own life since Jovie's betrayal.

"What makes you think you can handle the reality of what is yet to come?"

"I don't," I tell her, honestly.

She must see the thin string I'm hanging by because she sits a little taller. Removing her spectacles from her nose, she places them atop the desk before standing. "Could you help me with my collar?"

Lifting the portion of the desk that allows for entrance to the center, I move to stand within the circle with her as she turns in place, giving me her back. The mangi stones Greta wears around her neck are the only reason my father didn't lump her in with Beau and Jovie in their betrayal. Like her daughter, Greta can get overwhelmed with her gift and has always worn the collar for her own sanity. But though her collar was never meant to be a shackle, it has become exactly that in my father's insistence she never tell anyone her visions.

Greta grabs the collar in both hands as I use my magic to turn the metal locking mechanism, releasing her, and as if a weight has been lifted, she stretches out her spine.

It's a feeling I know all too well.

Her back is still to me when she goes still, utterly motionless in place.

As children, Beau would recall tales of waking to the ghostly sight of her mother at the foot of her bed, eyes unseeing yet aware as she recited her visions aloud. While Hallis, Wells, and I had all assumed she was exaggerating, it scared us enough that we never dared cross Greta. We were all very diligent in returning our library books on time.

But as I slowly take a step around to look at her, I can honestly say Beau never embellished the truth. Not even slightly. If anything, she didn't emphasize the horrifying reality enough. Eyes glazed with a sheen of white, Greta's expression is haunting, face slack and devoid of any emotion.

And *nothing* could prepare me for the unwavering, monotone voice when she speaks. "Bodies lay in waste. More will switch their allegiance," she says flatly, as if reciting lines. "One will prevail."

Chills break out across my skin, and I take a step back as if the premonition will happen at any moment.

She blinks and the life returns to her face and body, her features becoming animated once again, but she still utters one final, terrible statement: "The king of Kenta will prevail."

My breath catches in my throat. "Do you know when any of this happens?"

She gives a small nod. "Likely this winter, judging by the snow on the ground."

I'm at a loss for words.

There's a shakiness in Greta's hands as she reaches for her spectacles.

I move closer to her. "Are you okay?"

She waves away my concern. "A little out of practice is all." Her eyes linger on the string of stones around my own throat. "If you're not careful, you'll be just as out of shape as I am one day."

"Not if I can find a way to break the blood oath."

She smirks, but there's no real humor in the gesture. "I've searched every text, boy. No such thing exists. Nothing aside from killing yourself along with your Match."

Her obvious certainty works to grate on my nerves. "You've had plenty of opportunities to kill my father, so why haven't *you*?"

"Like yourself, I didn't stop loving him until it was too late."

I got what I came here for, so I don't know why the next question leaves my mouth. "Is that why you didn't leave with Beau?" *When she and Jovie betrayed me . . .*

Her smile falls away altogether, leaving an unshakable look of despair in its wake. "If there was even a *chance* I could evade your father, that I could outrun him and go somewhere he'd never be able to find me, I'd take it in a heartbeat." She sighs, as if the truth exhausts her. "But we all have a part to play, and mine is as inevitable as your Match's."

She speaks as though Jovie's fate is set in stone and I don't like it.

I always thought my father kept Greta locked away in the library out of sheer possessiveness. He found her after already marrying my mother, and he couldn't bear to part with either of them. I've since learned that no one can deny the Bond, king or not.

Greta is correct, though. It wouldn't matter where she went. As long as my father is alive, she'll never be able to escape him, as they'll forever be drawn together by their Bond.

Maybe I can relate to my father more than I'd care to admit.

Chapter 15

JO

The capital of Maile sits at the base on Mount Zallis. The salt from the gulf mixes with the snowy draft sliding down from the top of the mountain, creating a rejuvenating sensation in the air, adding energy to my tired bones. The horses are all but dragging their feet, heads lulling with each step, but we don't push them. It's best to be quiet as we pass through the city in the dead of night, anyway.

Fredrich didn't protest when I suggested returning home in the earliest hours despite the lack of sleep we've gotten the last couple of weeks. This is exactly what I needed: to be able to return without the weight of my title on my head. Without eyes watching my every move and the shame over my decisions trailing behind me.

The lamps dotting the paved streets stay lit all night. Cottages sit along the winding roads, their stoops leading to brightly painted doors. Their shutters are closed, but they'll open at sunrise and the streets will flood with people. The scent of ocean and ice will be masked by cafes, warm breads and spiced teas, and horses as they move their cargoes and carriages.

That's my favorite time of day. To have breakfast on my veranda and watch the city wake up as the sun rises over the gulf in the distance.

While I found something striking in Alaha's resilience, in their survival in a nearly uninhabitable place at sea, and saw the appeal of Kenta's grandeur, the true beauty of Maile is in its people. Everyone plays their part, not because they have to in order to survive, but because they understand that if Maile prospers, the people prosper, too.

I cover my yawn in the crook of my arm. When I look up, I'm equally relieved to see the yellow door to the palace courtyard as I am filled with dread. But a warm bath and clean clothes call to me and the remaining distance feels nearly insurmountable as we trudge onward.

Tucked between the neighboring cottages, the single door looks unassuming. The white-washed stone walls framing the courtyard match the walls of the palace behind it. The third and tallest story is just visible above the trees surrounding the property's edge. My mother said she wanted to live near the people, but she still appreciates privacy.

Dismounting, I untie my bag from the saddle and turn to Fredrich, handing him the reins to my horse. I look up and meet his stare.

The need to acknowledge the journey we've been on together nearly suffocates me, but nothing I could say would ever suffice. Any words at all would be an injustice.

He nods. "Drink the tea," he says.

The tea?

Without elaborating, he clicks his tongue at his horse, continuing toward the stables near the training arena at the edge of the city.

Shouldering my pack, I move to the potted garden next to the yellow door and dig my fingers into the soil. It's early winter, so I'm not sure if I'll find anything of use but am relieved when my fingers find a hard root. I pull the carrot out. It's small, but enough to pacify my mother's guard animals.

I dust off my hands and grip the iron handle to pull the door open. The courtyard is beautiful, even at night. Lamps flicker off the trellised vine-covered walls, highlighting the winding pathway through the gardens and to the front door.

Within just a few steps, the hissing begins.

They call to each other as territorial instincts take over. The light of the moon reflects off their red eyes as they move in. Six—no, seven of them. Scattered throughout the decorative landscaping, they bare their teeth at me. I click my tongue placatingly, but it's no use. What they really want is the food in my hand . . . or the soft flesh of my ankles.

The first rabbit to hop within striking distance has its fangs fully extended and I know from personal experience that its warning hiss isn't just for show. I break off a bit of the carrot and toss it at its feet. The rabbit's nose twitches, fangs retracting as it leans down to inspect the morsel. Then it chomps down, the loud crack of root between its less threatening teeth signaling to the rest that I'm not an intruder. The chorus of their hissing ceases as they hop closer, standing on their hind legs to get my attention. I break off more and more carrot pieces and scatter them on the ground as I continue forward.

I fuss when they begin squabbling with each other, snapping my fingers to break them up. "Dang rabbits," I mutter.

My mother's choice of guard animals is unusual, but they're vicious and surprisingly efficient in taking down unwanted intruders regardless of size. They are also just an overall nuisance to anyone entering or leaving the courtyard *with* permission.

I knock on the inner door and the wicket slides open. Iona, the palace's nighttime doorkeeper, appears in the small opening. She doesn't react to my arrival. I'm fairly sure I've never seen the old woman blink, let alone smile. The peephole snaps shut again and a moment later the locks click and the door swings open to the entryway.

Iona looks me over, eyes stilling on my feet. The floors are polished to perfection and her unspoken reprimand for having dirty boots is loud. I murmur my apologies as I bend over to remove them. Only then does the old woman allow me to pass.

"Please don't alert my mother," I tell her. "There's no need to wake her at this hour, okay?"

Iona stares at me, still unblinking, and the best I can do is assume she's in agreement.

As always, a lamp hangs at the entryway, lit and available for any and all who enter. I lift it from its post and hold it high to help me navigate the wide hallway. The flame licks at the darkness, but it never fully recedes. Not that I need it to, really. I've walked these halls enough to know them like the back of my hand. They're the very halls I walked night after night when I nursed my broken heart. Where I learned of my past and who I really am when my mother kept me company in my grief, unable to sleep herself.

The main floor of the palace is mostly empty. There's a dining hall, sitting rooms, and guest bedchambers that sit empty, not having visitors in many, many years. Aside from the kitchens, not much of this area gets utilized. The entrance to a curving stairwell is tucked at the end of the hall and I take the stairs up to the landing that leads to my room.

Movement catches at the corner of my eye and my mother comes into view from the opposite side of the landing where the stairs continue up to the third floor. Appearing like an apparition, her fair skin and red hair shining in the lamplight as she moves closer. Her eyes are like glass as she tries and fails to hold in her emotions.

My voice breaks in the stillness of the night. "I'm fine—"

She has me in her arms as soon as the words are out of my mouth. The lamp swings in my hand, throwing shadows against the walls. I drop my boots to hug her back. It hurts, muscles aching from the journey, her embrace tight as she squeezes, but I don't pull away. I hear as well as feel the tremble in her breath as she holds me. I know I reek, but her familiar scent envelopes the both of us. Like lilacs and clean bedding; I soak it in.

Pulling back to cradle my face in her hands, she gets a good look at me. The intense gaze feels like it lasts forever, but I let her take as long as she deems necessary, knowing she needs this. The reassurance that I'm alive and well and before her, not lost once again.

"My girl," she whispers in a shaky breath.

I risk a smile.

She doesn't return the gesture as moisture continues to collect in her lashes. Guilt fights to overwhelm me, but I shove it down as I hold my own metaphorical ground. I won't let her see my regrets. She can't suspect I'm anything less than sure of my actions.

"Go," she says, releasing me. "I'll have Karla send you some tea."

"There's no need to wake her—"

"I already did. She's making it now." She bends and retrieves my boots. I reach for them, but she pulls back, pinched between her fingers with disdain. "And I'm throwing *these* away."

She leaves as quietly as she had come. On a mission.

In a daze, I walk the remaining distance to my room. Right next to my door is Beau's own, and there she stands in the threshold. All of my plans to sneak inside without anyone noticing have failed *spectacularly*.

Arms folded, Beau eyes me suspiciously as I come closer. "Your colors are muted."

The words hurt, but only because I know they're true. "I *feel* muted."

Sadness lines her features as she lunges in to hug me. It's a short, tight embrace and then she's pushing me away again. "Go wash up," she says, shoving me in the direction of my room. "The stench of war clinging to you is making me nauseous."

The door creaks as I push into my bedroom. It puts the tent I've been sleeping in at the border to shame. Fur rugs line the stone floor, panels of sheer linens drape across my bed's canopy, cocooning the made bed against the far wall and a clawfoot bathtub on the other. In the center of the room sits my desk, angled to face the terrace doors so I can look out over the city when they're open. That's where I set down the lamp, on the edge of the surface, which is just as messy and chaotic as I left it. Books and parchments scattered across it.

It's the same bedroom I apparently used as a child, although I still have no recollection of it from before I returned to Maile four years ago. When I escaped from Kenta, I was hopeful that being back in my childhood home would jog the forgotten memories free, but I was only left disappointed by the lack of familiarity I felt when I walked through the door. The very same feeling I have right now. This doesn't feel like home any more than anywhere else ever has.

But that shiel back in Alaha calls to me still.

I note the soaps and towels left beside the tub and surmise General Samasu must have given my mother ample warning of my imminent return. I strip off everything but my necklace of mangi stones, dropping my clothes on the floor, also in desperate need of being discarded.

Kneeling in the barren tub, I undo the knot from the base of my braid and begin to untangle the matted strands. I did my best to care for it during my time at the border, tying it up and rinsing it as soon as I could after battle, but it was little use. Its length stopping just below my breasts. I turn on the spigot, waiting for the water to turn warm before I dip my head under. Brown sluices from my hair as I work my fingers through it and it takes a long while before the water runs clear. I then scrub my skin raw with a cloth and a liberal amount of soap and rinse myself clean before filling the basin fully. I pour in a generous amount of oils and soap before settling back into a more comfortable position so that I can finally—*finally*—allow myself to relax.

It doesn't last long.

A knock at the door rouses me. "Come in," I call, voice cracking from underuse and exhaustion. I look over my shoulder to see Karla stick her head into the room.

She must deem me decent enough, because she scurries in with a tray. "I've brought some tea." The older woman keeps her eyes averted as she deposits the cup and saucer on the bedside table before carefully placing the steaming teapot down as well. "It's to help you sleep," she explains.

There's an awkward moment where her gaze locks with mine. As my mother's longest-serving maid, Karla's the only person my mother would trust to deliver anything to my personal room. For good reason. She doesn't linger unnecessarily or gossip among the staff. This is her duty, and she treats it with the appropriate gravity. It's why I'm taken aback by the worry in her eyes. Fretting with the material of her skirts, she averts her gaze again before swiping my dirty clothes from the floor and making her way out.

"Thank you," I tell her, but I'm only met with the sound of the door squeaking shut.

I drop my head against the basin's side, sinking further into the water. Exhaling slowly, I turn my focus to my next breath, then the one after, and continue this way until breathing feels natural again. I wanted to avoid all of this. My mother's concern sometimes feels heavier than my title does.

I poke at a few bubbles clinging to each other, and the black line of crust under each of my nails snags my attention.

Gross.

I call for my blade, the black dagger appearing in my hand in an instant. I twirl it in my fingers. Over my knuckles, under, over again, and back into my palm. The blade is dull and the hilt tweaks as I manipulate it. I'll need to repair it soon. For the moment, however, it still serves to pick the grime out from under my nails.

My mind clears as I perform the task, body going lax. To think I once was horrified by the thought of eating with a knife used for killing. Yet, here I am, picking at my nails with one. Each scrape and snick of the blade feels cathartic. Like carving out the last remnants of the weeks I spent at camp, the night scaling the rocky hillside, digging my hands and fingers into anything I could find purchase on, sometimes places slick with mud and clay and—

The earth is cold beneath my knees, but the blood coating my skin is warm. It doesn't stay that way for long as the freezing air whips around me. The man underneath me is ghostly white, eyes vacant as he stares up at the night sky. He never saw us coming.

My hands shake.

They're saturated with red, and I try to wipe them clean on my pants. It's futile. The more I wipe, the more it spreads. It drips from my fingers like water from a faucet, flooding the ground around my knees. Panic takes over as I try to stand, only for the ground to slide out from under me, melting into a rising tide and all of a sudden I'm drowning in a sea of blood. I open my mouth to scream, but the liquid chokes me.

I go under.

I break through the surface, sucking in a lungful of air before breaking into a coughing fit.

Not a red tide, but soapy bath water as it sloshes over the sides, slapping onto the hard floor. I clutch onto the rim of the basin, heart slamming in my chest as I attempt to ground myself.

I'm home.

I'm *safe.*

My magic is surging underneath my breastbone. A violent stirring that sets my skin alight. It's not the first time this has happened, although it is still rare, given the gyve of mangi stones I normally wear; the necklace I currently wear around my neck apparently isn't strong enough to stop my magic from bursting out.

I place my palm against the place it emanates from, reassuring it that I'm fine. I must have fallen asleep. It was just a bad dream.

Then I feel it.

Him.

The tether that twines through my magic. One doesn't exist without the other and the longer it takes for my magic to calm, the more likely it is the other side of the Bond will respond. A ghosting of what feels like breath on the back of my neck makes goosebumps spread across my skin. I spin toward the door to see what's behind me, only to find nothing.

An echo of a familiar chuckle sends fear flooding through my veins.

I leap from the bath, throwing even more water onto the floor as I hurry to my bedside table. Jerking open the drawer, I grab a handful of mangi stones and necklaces from the hoard I have stashed there and hold them to the place my magic resides. It's nauseating, stifling it this way, but I swallow down the bile until it eases and the glow of my skin no longer leaches through my closed eyelids. When I find the courage to open them again, I'm met with humiliatingly loud silence.

There's no one here.

But I affix an extra layer of stones around my neck, and another. Just to be sure.

I look down at the porcelain cup Karla left and pour the tea from the teapot with shaking hands, splashing some of the liquid onto the saucer in my haste. It's black and opaque and I bring the cup closer to my nose before recoiling from the bitter scent. It smells worse than the bootleg mead I had in Alaha.

Fredrich's words float through my mind. *Drink the tea.*

I sit on my bed, heedless of my damp state, and down the terrible liquid in two gulps, holding the back of my hand to my mouth to stop it from coming back up. *Anything* is better than feeling like I'm slowly losing my mind but still being aware of it, because there's no other explanation for the sensation at the base of my neck. Like I'm being watched.

Then the world goes dark around me . . .

I don't remember anything else after that.

Chapter 16

ACKER

Wells stands in the center of his courtyard. "Don't try to stop me."

The threat of violence is unspoken, but heard nonetheless.

"I'm not," I assure him.

The fires that constantly burn in the hearths have been smothered within the last hour, evidenced by the smoke billowing from their mouths and the faint heat lingering in the kilns. He's cleaned up, skin clear of soot for the first time in seemingly years. The lack of a collar around his throat is the most telling.

His escape has obviously been planned for a while.

"Good," he says, shouldering past me. "Then if you'll excuse me, I have a boat to catch."

There isn't time to dwell on the familiar sting of betrayal, so I speak up before he can leave. "I'm going to Maile and I want you and Olivia to come with me," I say.

He stops in place, head turning to the side so he can look at me out of the corner of his eye. "Why?"

"I'm going to ask Evelyn to help me overthrow my father."

This gets his full attention.

Pivoting sharply, he faces me head on. "What's happened?"

"My father and Wren are working together."

He shakes his head in disbelief. "There's no way his council would just accept that."

I take a deep breath, then step closer and say, "They would if he promised to give them magic in return."

Shock renders him speechless, jaw hanging open as he tries to make sense of what I just told him. "I—how . . . *what*?"

"I'll tell you everything I know in the carriage. It's waiting in the street, but we need to hurry to pick up Olivia if we want to get to our boat before my father realizes I'm gone."

His clear suspicion drives the proverbial knife in deeper, but he knows me well enough to know I'd never abandon my post or my people for my own safety. I especially wouldn't risk Olivia's either. After a long, tense moment, his shoulders drop.

"Okay," he concedes, eyes losing some of their heat. "Let's go."

Harold holds the door open as we step out of the courtyard. It's after midnight and the streets are barren. I slide inside the carriage first and I realize my mistake a moment too late. Wells stills at the sight of my wife, Irina, sitting beside me in the small space. Any progress we made in the past few minutes is immediately undone, and Wells face hardens.

Irina lifts a challenging brow in his direction.

I slap a hand against the door to stop it from swinging shut when he takes a step back. "We need her. We won't stand a chance of getting to Maile alive on a Kenta ship without an illusionist."

His expression is accusatory. "You didn't send word to Maile first?"

"And risk the chance of my father finding out?" I shake my head. "Listen, we can send a bird when we reach your family." This seems to appease him some but not by much, and I'm starting to lose my patience. "Wells . . ."

With a shake of his head, he gives in, sliding onto the bench opposite us. Harold shuts the door, and we're instantly encased in darkness. We ride through the city streets in stunted silence.

It doesn't take long for the sound of the carriage's wheels turning over stone to change to pavement before becoming muffled by the softer ground of dirt as we leave the city. Only then do I reach for the lamp by my feet and pass it to Wells. With a snap of his fingers, the wick erupts with light and he hangs it on its designated hook by the door.

"I suppose we were bound to meet at some point," Wells directs this toward Irina. "I'm Wells."

"I know who you are." Her answering smile is polite, but there's no mistaking the calculated look in her eyes. "I'm glad to finally be able to thank you in person for our incredible wedding gift."

Tension radiates between the two of them at the mention of the pointed present Wells and Olivia gifted us. A dagger Wells made himself. I could tell by its craftsmanship. That alone would have been a nice gift, but it was the images inscribed inside the lid of the wooden box it was delivered in that was the real insult. Butterflies painted in varying shades of purple—Maile's colors.

Irina's expression had soured in front of the congregation when it was opened, face turning a blistering red. It was an obvious mockery of our nuptials considering that Wells and Olivia refused to attend our wedding. My father was equally as livid as my new wife, but even he knew it would be stupid to hang our best blacksmith ahead of an impending war.

Wells doesn't look the least bit repentant. He doesn't apologize either, instead turning his attention away from her entirely. Silence envelopes the compartment, and, after a while, Irina get comfortable enough to fall asleep.

Thank the gods.

Wells observes the way she's curled into my side, head resting on my shoulder. "She's going to kill you, you know."

I don't need any clarification as to who he means, and I don't dispute the possibility. The thought has crossed my mind plenty since I made the decision to travel to Maile. Jovie's wrath might very well be my demise.

But I guess we're about to find out.

Chapter 17

JO

"Where are you two going?"

Beau and I freeze in place, turning to find my mother in the door leading to the kitchen. Dressed in a nightgown, hair falling in waves around her shoulders, one would believe she just rolled out of bed if it were not for the flour dusting her fingers. Her favorite time to bake is late in the day, sometimes well into the night, but it appears she's calling it quits early tonight.

"To the tavern," I answer. "We're meeting with Drake."

"Oh," she sounds. "How's the new commander doing?"

"Sam is impressed," I say.

Drake used to be second to General Samasu, but my mother convinced Sam to hand the reins to his successor so he could follow me to the border. While young, Drake has proven himself to be a skilled leader.

"Good," my mother says. "Anything interesting on the docket?"

Beau offers a casual shrug. "The usual."

There's a long pause where all three of us trade glances, and I already know what's coming before my mother asks: "Are you sure you're ready?"

"Yes," I say, nodding. "Word is already spreading of my return."

"It's only been a week's time," she reassures me, stepping closer. "You're allowed a period to settle."

I'm steadfast in my response. "The people need to see me."

The conflict in her expression is evident. The pride of a ruler who agrees with my decision, having had to put her title before her own well-being many times, battles for precedence with the worry of a mother for her daughter who has only just come back from battle.

My reliance on the sleep aid tea hasn't helped to alleviate her worry either.

A small grin pulls at her mouth, regardless. "Let me at least pack some of my toffee cakes. Messer loves them."

This time my smile is genuine as we watch her scurry to the pantry. She *adores* Messer, always saying he's like a puppy you don't have to train, which is *mostly* true. He still could use a bit more edifying.

She returns with a basket and a bottle of champagne. "To celebrate your victory at the border," she explains, handing the bottle to me and the basket to Beau. "The people will be excited to see their champion." Then she pinches my side, and I yelp, rubbing the sore area. "Quit sneaking out. You're too grown for that nonsense."

Beau's eyes slide to me, the smugness radiating from her. When I knocked on her door and told her to schedule the meeting, she advised me to inform my mother of my intentions to venture into the city. I didn't, obviously, but only because I knew she'd worry.

I confess as much as I embrace my mother. "And don't wait up," I tell her, finally.

She pulls back, cupping my face in her hands as she stares at me. "Much like yourself, I am also grown and will do as I please." Smiling, she swats me away. "Go have fun. Tell everyone I said hello."

And by *everyone*, she means *Messer*.

I grab a fistful of sugar snap peas from the bowl by the door on our way out. The rabbits hiss as soon as we step into the courtyard, and we sprinkle the peas like confetti, which subdues them with relative ease and allows us to weave along the winding paths toward the door at the front of the courtyard.

We wait for a carriage to pass before crossing to the other side of the street. I pull my woolen coat closed to ward off the chill in the air, knowing that any effort to remain anonymous is futile. No one in Maile wears overcoats this early into winter unless they're new to the city.

Tonight is particularly busy. People are out to enjoy the weather before the first snowfall. And while I was used to living in a bustling community in Alaha, it's vastly different in Maile.

Here, magic intensifies everything.

A family spills from a nearby eatery onto the street. Two parents and three kids; there's nothing particular about them except for the youngest of the children, a girl who can't be any older than six. She skips alongside her sister and when she glances both ways to check for buggies before crossing the street, her eyes reflect off the lanterns, flashing a ghostly white before returning to a more normal color. An early indicator that she has the gift of foresight—the same as Greta's.

There's a pastry vendor on the corner and he delivers the desserts to the customer's hand on an invisible gust of wind. Across the way, one of the city's fire starters stands on a ladder, refilling a burned-out lamp with oil before reigniting the flame with a strike of his finger. And a little further down, a resident is tending to her rose bushes by her front stoop, the petals unfurling just the slightest at the touch of her fingers.

The term Heir isn't used here much, if at all. There are simply people who have magic, and others who do not. Having magic is still considered a blessing from the Mother, but the religious association has waned with time. At least, that's how my mother explains it. It's undeniable that the land still holds secrets because even those who are giftless suffer from their eyes leeching of color when traveling at sea.

It doesn't take long for people to *really* take notice of me and my bulky coat, and I try not to appear too hurried as Beau and I maintain our steady gait toward the tavern a few streets away. I wave and give thanks to compliments and congratulations for the battle won at the border. Kids are the boldest, running up to me to bow, sometimes wrapping their little arms around my middle before their parents wrest them away with apologies.

My mother loves being in the heart of the city, to be accessible to her people. She's the type of queen I aspire to be. The smile she gives me is the same she gives to her people: honest and open. She radiates joy and kindness, making anyone that comes across her feel seen just by being in her presence. It's a skill I've yet to master.

Sensing my discomfiting thoughts, Beau takes my hand and squeezes it.

"I'm fine," I reassure her.

"You know better than to lie to me of all people, Jo."

I suppress a sigh. "Can't you let me get away with it every now and then?"

My question brings a begrudgingly small smile to her mouth. "*Never.*"

She looks beautiful in a pleated skirt that reaches her ankles. Hair twisted into a braid, with gold strands woven in and out and a tiny golden butterfly ornament at the end. Maile's symbol and my family's crest. Many of the refugees fleeing the spreading war also wear the butterfly as a symbol of appreciation for the safe harbor, but Beau wears it simply because she loves Maile. And my mother.

"I received word from my mother late last night," she says.

I lift a curious brow. Beau has kept regular communication with Greta since we left Kenta, but she rarely mentions it to me unless there's news worth sharing.

"She said there's tension in the palace. A rift between the king and my brother."

She's long since quit referring to Edmond as her father, but she hardly ever mentions her brother unless there's something particularly noteworthy, and my heart stutters in my chest. "Any idea why?"

"One can only speculate. The reasons could be endless, considering . . . well, everything."

Even though it's little more than nothing, it's *something*. A morsel of hope.

"It wasn't supposed to take this long," I mutter under my breath.

Beau tilts her head, looking at me from under her lashes. "Four years doesn't undo a lifetime of manipulation, Jo."

"I thought the king would have shown his true colors by now." That Acker would see through his father's manipulation tactics.

"Edmond doesn't need magic to be persuasive," she says.

I hear the unspoken words she refrains from tacking on. I need to give Acker the same grace I would ask in return. Not that I have or ever will ask him for forgiveness for my betrayal, but that's irrelevant.

"It takes people years to come to terms with who their parents are, even without being the subject of heavy magical influence," she says.

Our spies have informed us of Acker's reluctant participation in leading the council during his father's frequent absences. It was due to his orders alone that forced me to the northern border to defend against the Strou. Meanwhile, Edmond's been biding his time while he rebuilds his power, and there's nothing I regret more than not ending his existence when I had the chance.

My dagger was there, poised to sever his lifeline with a single slash, something none have been close enough to even *try* before, and . . .

I failed.

I thought that ignoring Acker's plea for his father's life would make me as evil as the man I was trying to kill, but being merciful was just as selfish as any self-serving action the king himself has taken. I knew if I killed his father that Acker would never look at me the same way again. That adoring gaze I'd grown accustomed to would be forever twisted into disgust. The mere idea of that gutted me. And with one hasty decision fueled by the hope that Acker could one day forgive me, I damned the lives of countless innocent people.

A day, I realize, that will never come.

It took me entirely too long to admit to myself that Acker never loved me, not truly. He only wanted me because of the connection we share, the Bond that Mother Nature forced upon us. What he thought he felt between us as children before I went missing. But what he really wanted was someone like Irina. A placid placeholder in his life. A trophy. *A prized horse.*

And I hate that I proved just how useless I am by not fulfilling my promise to Kai. To the rebellion. To myself, in the process.

Since I betrayed Acker and left Kenta, I've regretted not killing the king every single day. It's because of my cowardice that the continent has been thrust into chaos.

"Maybe it's best Acker never realizes who his father really is," I say, admiring the gulf in the distance, the moonlight sparkling off the glassy water. The boats dotting the horizon are a reminder of the life I left behind in Alaha. "Sometimes ignorance is better than facing the guilt."

She doesn't disagree.

Considering all the time that has passed and everything that has transpired, maybe I need to come to terms with the idea that Acker may see his father for who he is and agree with him. That maybe Beau's and my betrayal pushed him so far that he no longer cares, and corrupting Acker's pure heart might be my worst crime of all.

The tavern is tucked into an alleyway not far from the wharf. Patrons linger around the entrance, smoking tobacco before heading inside, and I spot Fredrich leaning against a nearby lamppost as he waits.

"You invited *him*?" Beau asks.

"I did."

Her gaze swings from the soldier, then to me, then back again. "You trust him?"

When we left Kenta, I told Beau I'd never use her gift as a tool, but there's something in her expression that gives me pause. "Is there a reason I shouldn't?" Something she's able to see that I can't, perhaps . . .

"I don't know." She shrugs. "He doesn't have an aura."

What?

"How is that possible?"

"I think it's another level of protection his shielder gift offers him, but I don't *think* it's anything to be worried about. Your mother wouldn't put anyone in charge of your guard that she wasn't sure of."

He straightens when he sees us approaching and it's strange to see him outside of a war camp after months of being at the border. He wordlessly offers to take the basket from Beau's hands, and she pulls it from his reach.

"Nice try, but as the new guy, you don't get first dibs."

He lifts his hands in mock surrender. "Fair enough."

He grins, and I'm slightly taken aback by the gesture, but it's not unpleasant to look at. Matter of fact, he should do it more often and I tell him as much.

"Duly noted," he says with a slight uptick at the corner of his mouth.

The tavern looks like just a dingy hole in the wall, but as soon as we step through the entrance, the room beyond opens into something warm and inviting. A lone fiddler plays on stage against the far wall and bustling tables fill the space to one side of the room, with a dance floor taking up the other half. Servers weave between the patrons with giant pitchers of ale and platters of food. For the first time in what feels like ages, my stomach rumbles with hunger at the scent.

Beau takes the lead, Fredrich at my back, and I can't help but wonder if they consciously realize they're buffering me from the public's eyes. It doesn't work, of course. It takes one drunk soldier recognizing me to make my presence known to all. Acknowledgments ring out from all sides of the room, and I'm momentarily taken aback by the cheers. Fredrich urges me to keep moving as a chorus of chanting begins. I recognize the song instantly; it's one of the few I remember from my childhood in Alaha, about a siren who enchants an entire fleet of ships.

I motion for the crowd to calm with a wave of my hand, and the volume in the room lowers just enough for me to tell the server who approaches us to put the next round of drinks on my tab. The cheers become deafening and when another young man escorts us to the room tucked at the far end of the bar, we duck inside the moment the door slides open.

Messer rises from his seat at the round table to greet us, pulling me into a hug first. "I figured it was you causing all the ruckus."

As if on cue, the sound of celebration erupts again through the wood paneled door. Maybe buying another round wasn't the brightest idea . . .

"And Beau, this is a nice surprise," he continues. "Looking as delectable as always." By the glassiness of his eyes and the level of mischief in his smile, I can tell he's already tipsy as he leans in to kiss Beau on the cheek.

"Save your efforts for someone else, you pigeon," Beau snarks.

Not one to be deterred, Messer sets down his cup of ale to take the basket from her hands. "But you brought me gifts." He eyes the contents before beaming at her. "Are these toffee cakes?"

"From my mother," I say, forcing him to take the bottle of champagne from me as well. "She says 'hello.'"

"She knows me so well," he says, his grin becoming more salacious, and I know I'm going to despise whatever comes out of his mouth next. "I'll have to stop by one day soon so I can return the favor."

I shake my head at his teasing. "I hate you."

His laughter dies in his throat when he sees Fredrich. "You brought your stalker with you?"

"Messer," I warn.

"What?" he asks, face the picture of innocence. "I'm just surprised to see him indoors, is all. Usually, he does his stalking from a rooftop nearby."

Fredrich doesn't take offense. If anything, he finds the assessment amusing. "Best vantage point," he says, dryly.

"Everyone, sit."

The order comes from Drake, the youngest man to ever captain the Maile navy, but he's also a damn good archer and military strategist. He has served us well since General Samasu decided to step down. Or, rather, he was forced to step down at my mother's insistence that he accompany me to the border.

"It's good to see you," I tell him.

He tilts his head forward in a pseudo-bow and I narrow my eyes as I slide into the chair beside him. I've harped on at him enough that he knows I hate bowing, especially outside of formal situations. My mother insists that it's a sign of respect I should graciously endure, but Drake isn't in uniform, and I consider him my friend before my liegeman. And because he's my friend, he takes after Messer and loves to goad me.

Messer begins to twist the cork in the champagne bottle. "Who else are we waiting on?"

"The general," Drake answers. And, as if summoned, Sam appears beside Drake, making the young captain nearly leap out of skin. "Good *gods*," he shouts. "I wish you came with a warning."

The cork Messer's been working on finally pops and everyone opposite ducks to avoid being hit by the flying object. "My question is, how are *you* the one who's always late?" he asks right before he drinks directly from the bottle.

"I've been busy," Sam replies. "Lots to be sorted. Soldiers to disperse. Camp to relocate." He settles in next to Drake and palpable exhaustion lines his face as he watches Messer take another swig. "Unlike some of us."

"Hey, I've been doing my share," Messer protests, pointing at himself.

Drake makes a face. "All you do is eat people until you look like a stuffed turkey."

"You failed to mention how I puke up belt buckles and shoelaces afterward. Very useful bits of equipment, those."

Beau wiggles her fingers for Messer to pass the champagne her way. When I lean around Fredrich to eye her, she says, "You can't expect me to be sober in the company of so many insufferable men."

Chapter 18

JO

"So, Wren decided to join Edmond in exchange for knowledge on how to gain another's magic?"

Messer chomps on a toffee cake, crumbs falling everywhere when he speaks. "More or less."

Even though we've gone over the information Kai sent to Messer, it still doesn't seem real. The ability to transfer someone else's magic is . . . inconceivable. But the more I think about it, the more it feels like the only possibility. Edmond held the power of influence, used it on me to kneel before him upon our meeting when his true gift was elemental. The only explanation for him gaining more magic is if he was able to take it from someone else.

"Edmond would never give away his methods to anyone, let alone Wren," Beau says.

Messer swallows his food. *Finally.* "Kai doesn't believe so either. I suspect that's why he's continuing the advance toward Kenta's capital from the front lines instead of joining his father at court."

Kai.

Such a frustrating-shaped piece of the puzzle, never quite fitting with anyone else's plans. Somehow more unpredictable than any of our adversaries. He does what he wants, when he wants.

Sam throws up his hand. "Are we sure we're worried about the right Alaha leader here?"

Messer and I trade looks. Kai's communication with me is minimal. Cut and dry and to the point. He sends most of his updates through Messer, and they offer little of his state of mind.

He's likely still angry with me.

I was supposed to overthrow Edmond and take the crown, holding the throne until Kai could usurp his own father, Wren, and make his way to land with the rest of the Alaha. The perfect solution to all our problems—if all went to plan. But my decision to not kill the king of Kenta ruined everything.

Once Kai sent word he had made it to Roison years ago, Messer flew out to tell him of my failed mission. He was livid. Not just with my failure, but the fact that I spared Acker as well. And Messer defying his orders by following me to Maile just added insult to injury.

Kai felt like I chose Acker, and that Messer chose me in turn. Which is true, but we didn't do it to spite him.

I'm not sure Kai will ever not see it that way, though.

Messer dusts his fingers on his shirt before speaking. "No one wants this war to end with Wren's head on a spike more than Kai. He'll do whatever he feels he needs to do to ensure that."

Drake interjects. "And when Kai usurps his father, what are his plans then? Will he still have a horde of trolls to do this bidding?"

"Let's focus on one problem at a time," Fredrich adds.

Beau begins rubbing her temples. "I'm starting to get a headache." I bite back the *I told you so* threatening to escape my mouth, but she sees it in my expression, regardless. "At this point, we're talking in circles. Nothing is going to be solved tonight."

Drake leans back in his seat. "The Strou have seemed to slow their attempts to move across the gulf for now. They're either rallying their ships or have taken their loss at the border as a signal to regroup."

Nodding, I remind everyone, "The objective remains the same. Protect Maile. Keep up our end of the deal we made with Roison to stop the Strou from crossing the gulf. When Kenta fails—"

"*If* Kenta fails," Beau interjects.

Her repeated warnings to not underestimate her father have not gone unnoticed, but I continue as if she hadn't spoken. "Chryse promises to maintain the accord between our two territories once he assumes Edmond's throne."

Sam nods. "The Strou situation is being handled for the time being. All we can do is wait to see what Edmond has hiding up his sleeve."

I tip my chin in his direction, acknowledging his words. We've only spoken once since I left the front lines, and even then it was curt. He nods back before he blinks from existence, and everyone takes his departure as the signal to head out.

"I'm going to walk to Catuxa's if anyone would like to join," Drake offers.

"Count me in," Messer says, turning toward me. "B?"

I roll my eyes. "I'd rather gouge my eyes out."

While the Catuxa is leagues above the brothel I experienced on the outskirts of Kenta where Hallis had accidentally booked our group rooms on our journey to the capital, I do not consider watching the women and men there fawn over Drake and Messer as a favorable night out.

"Same," Beau agrees.

"I can escort you two home," Fredrich offers.

As if it's the first time he's noticed him, Messer's eyes narrow at the man who has sat beside me all night. "Since when do you *ask* before following her home?"

I'm poised to reprimand him, but Fredrich speaks first. "Since when are *you* concerned?"

Messer freezes. The easygoing persona he perpetually wears slip and seriousness pinches the edge of his mouth. "Are you trying to court her?"

I thought I outgrew my tendency to blush, but I can feel the sensation of blood creeping up my neck and into my cheeks at the suggestion. Those were the very last words I expected to come out of Messer's mouth. And that says a lot, because I'm usually prepared for just about anything possible when it comes to him. I'm contemplating how to clip his wings the next time he tries to flit by my terrace for a visit when I realize Fredrich still hasn't spoken.

Dread sinks like a stone in my stomach as I slowly turn to look at him.

He's grinning, but in a pitying way that doesn't quite reach his eyes. "As much as I would be honored to court you, I have no interest in contending with a Matching Bond."

It wasn't like I was actually interested anyway.

But I manage to keep the retort to myself. It's not his fault Messer is a meddling asshole.

My nosy friend then makes the awkward move to slap Fredrich on the shoulder, shaking him playfully. "No one said it had to end in marriage, right?"

"Messer!" I hit him in the arm with the back of my hand.

"I'm kidding!" He smiles around the last dregs of his drink, then shrugs. "Mostly."

"I mean," Drake interrupts, drawing our attention across the room, his smirk more than telling. "*I* don't care if you're Matched."

The statement doesn't even have time to register before Fredrich intervenes. "*Absolutely not*," he snaps.

Everyone goes silent at Fredrich's declaration. Messer is struck dumb, and the disgust on Beau's face would be comical if my own wasn't practically glowing with mortification. I can feel the heat radiating off me as I close my eyes and beg for the gods to end my misery.

My voice comes out in a whisper. "Fredrich, please wait outside." I can feel him heed my request, the door opening and then then closing softly behind him.

When I open my eyes, Messer has the decency to at least appear contrite. "B—"

I shut him up with a pointed glare, not in the mood to hear the nickname he's called me since we were adolescents. "I will kill you where you stand if you say another word. *Stay*."

For once in his life, he's smart enough to keep his mouth closed. I don't see as much as feel the death glare Beau levels at Messer on our way out the door. The tavern has mostly emptied, aside from just a handful of dutiful card players still sitting at a table in the corner. They are graciously more subdued than the patrons from earlier in the night and let me pass by with just tips of their chins and a raised pitcher of ale.

Fredrich has returned to the position we first found him in, leaning against the lamppost outside.

"Want me to wait?" Beau asks.

I shake my head. "Go ahead. I won't be far behind."

She hesitates.

While Maile is safe, there's no such thing as *too* safe when it comes to me, given my position. "I'll have Messer or Drake escort me."

"Okay." She squeezes my hand gently before letting it fall as she pulls away. Her gaze lingers on Fredrich as she walks past.

Sighing, I meet his stare. "I'm sorry—"

"Don't apologize," he cuts me off, hand to his chest. "I'm sorry if I overstepped."

I nod. "You will never speak for me again, is that understood?"

It takes him a moment, seemingly fighting with what he wants to say, but he eventually nods. "Understood."

"Good." I nod. "Now go so I can read Messer his last rites."

Fredrich laughs. Loud enough for it to bounce off the alley walls. It's the first time I've ever seen him express genuine happiness so openly and I can't stop myself from smiling at the sight.

"May the Mother have mercy on his soul," he says.

I watch him saunter down the street in the direction of the harbor. He lives in a modest residence above a tailor shop. When I realized he was keeping eyes on me all that time ago, I followed him home and then spoke to the tailor to get more information about his tenant.

Keeps to himself. Tidy. Pays on time.

When I turn around, I'm not surprised to find Messer standing outside the tavern door. His attempt to appear nonchalant is laughable considering it's very obvious he was eavesdropping. This is a good instance where he could use more training.

My voice comes out biting. "Where's Drake?"

"I told him to save himself."

Smart, honestly. "And what about you? Are you not scared?"

He grins, eyes crinkling at the corners. "*Terrified.*"

Rolling my eyes, I move past him, and he falls in step beside me. Mount Zallis looms up ahead. It's dizzying, staring up at its magnitude. I like how small it makes me feel, like the weight on my shoulders is less significant in comparison.

"I'm sorry," he says.

I look at him from the corner of my eye before sighing. "You're forgiven."

I have too much to worry about to be petty about some teasing. Plus, it's actually impossible for anyone to stay mad at Messer, myself included. It's much like staying angry at a puppy who piddled on the floor.

"It's just . . . if you did like Fredrich—"

"I don't."

"But if you *did*," he stresses. "There's no reason you shouldn't act on those feelings."

"I don't have feelings for Fredrich." Seeing that he's not going to let this go, I shake my head. "You wouldn't understand."

"Try me."

"You don't . . . *view* things the same way I do."

"Try me."

"Messer, you've never . . ." I trail off, not wanting to hurt his feelings. Been in love. Felt the insistent pull of a Matching Bond. Experienced a broken heart.

"B," he says, grabbing my elbow. Not in a punishing way, but hard enough to hold my attention. "*Try me.*"

The streets are mostly empty, but I cut through an alleyway for some added privacy. "I saw something through the Bond one time," I say. "Acker. Irina . . ." I'm not even sure I'm making sense. The words are so hard for me to find and spit out.

"But the stones . . ." he says.

I've explained the Bond to Messer before, how the tether forces me into my Match's presence without my permission if I don't wear the mangi stones. I didn't always need them. In the time after I accepted the Matching Bond, it was as if the Bond was satisfied to let us be. But once we were apart for too long, it surprised me by being less forgiving.

"I had to remove them during battle." I finger the exposed stones at my neck, the full extent of the gyve hidden under my clothes. "But that wasn't the first time," I say, eyes flicking up to meet his.

I don't need to delve into the specifics for the realization and subsequent horror to settle over his features.

The memory of Acker's eyes flashing to mine is vivid in my mind. Irina was straddling his lap, her back to me as she kissed up his neck, dress pristine white. He had *smirked* at me when I appeared in his room. The tilt of it was such a foreign sight. The expression of a man I realized could never have possibly loved me. His gaze had held mine as he opened his mouth in invitation to Irina, letting me see the way her tongue dipped in to taste him. The delight in his eyes was cruel as he glided a hand over the curve of her spine, under the hem of her dress to what awaited underneath.

I watched, not just because I couldn't look away, but because back in my room in Maile Beau was desperately searching for more stones. It was the first notion I had that a single strand of mangi wasn't strong enough to withstand the tether's pull if Acker wasn't wearing any to block his end of the Bond. I was forced to witness the man I loved allow his new wife to shift sensually on his lap.

It was their wedding night.

"Sometimes I make myself sick," Messer says, breaking me out of my depressing thoughts. "Over the thought of Aurora and Kai." He laughs without humor. "My fucking childhood best friend."

Aurora had been Messer's intended, but when he met with Kai upon his return to land, he discovered the two of them had married. At their parents' directive, I'm sure, but Messer has refused to speak about it since.

"I don't know what I would do if I had to watch it," he says. "Gods, I'm sorry, B."

"I had no idea you cared for Aurora so deeply."

He tucks his hands into his pockets and shakes his head. "No one did. Not even Kai. If my father knew, he would have leveraged her against me. I knew the only way to ensure our arranged marriage went ahead was to pretend like it was the worst thing he could do to me."

And it worked.

But then Messer followed me when I left Alaha . . .

"Messer."

"This is why I never mentioned it," he says, pulling me to a halt at the end of the alley. "I don't want you to feel any more guilt than you already do. I didn't tell you to make you feel bad, but so you know that I *get* it." His eyes look hollow in the shadows. "Even if I wish I didn't."

I step closer and wrap my arms around his middle, burying my face in his chest so he can't see the sympathy in my eyes, knowing he'd hate it. "For what it's worth, I'm sorry, too," I say.

He squeezes me once before releasing me. "It helps," he says, looking up at the sky. "Being with someone else. At least for a little while."

I give him a dubious look before shoving him away.

But maybe Messer has a point. Given the lack of information I can find on breaking a Matching Bond, I need to consider the possibility I may never get rid of the tether. I might have to accept the fact that the stones around my neck and body are permanent accessories. Even if I were to ever be intimate with another.

I can't think of anything worse than Acker witnessing me with someone else. To know he was there would overshadow anything pleasurable about the experience.

"It's not like I have suitors lining up at my door," I joke.

He pulls me in with an arm around my neck, jostling me as we continue toward the palace. "I don't know, B. Drake seemed pretty open about his interest back at the tavern."

Even if Drake was being earnest, which I don't believe for a single second, I wouldn't muddy waters by getting involved with the commander of Maile's entire naval armada.

The rest of the walk home is quiet, and Messer drops me off at the front door of the palace with a mischievous grin. I shake my head at him, knowing he's eager to meet Drake at Catuxa's. I tell him if he wakes up to anything strange going on with his nether regions after tonight that he can find a healer all by himself, regardless of how much he's suffering.

He winks as he walks backward in the brothel's direction. "I appreciate you looking out for me, B."

Iona informs me that my mother left honey biscuits in the kitchen, and I swing by to snag a couple before heading up toward my room. Beau's door is shut, and she's likely already down for the night. I expected as much, given her level of frustration and subsequent alcohol consumption at the tavern. She had insisted on coming even though I had told her that she wasn't needed. When she stumbles from her room in the morning hungover, my sympathies will be minimal.

Sometimes I wonder if it's hard for her to turn off the sense of duty she has toward the people she loves, or if it's her guilt of betraying her brother. While our attempted coup didn't go the way we wanted, I'd do it all again even if it only meant finally getting her out from under her father's heel, so that she's no longer forced to do things she despises.

Putting people in cages. Collaring the gifted.

I light a lamp and draw a bath, adding a selection of calming oils as it fills. One of the hardest parts of being stationed at the border was being without this, I think, as I sink into the water. I soak until I'm pruned, then wrap myself in a robe and sit at my desk to try to decide which text I'm going to tackle next. I'm nibbling on a piece of biscuit when there's a knock at my door.

I check the timepiece I keep nearby and it's nearing three in the morning. While Messer will occasionally use the palace as a place to crash, what with it being closer to Catuxa's than his flat by the gulf, it's not typically until sunrise when I see his face at my door.

When I open the door, I am instantly taken aback by the sight of

Drake standing on the landing. I hurry to make sure I'm fully covered, pulling the collar of my robe more tightly closed.

"Drake," I choke out. "Hi. Is everything okay?"

"Everything is great," he replies, face unreadable.

I let out a breath, relieved, before asking. "How'd you get up here?" Iona would never allow him in without approval first.

"Messer told me you requested me," he explains, shifting on his feet. "To service you."

Unease begins to trickle into my nervous system. "Service me?"

He doesn't look away as he dips his chin in a nod. "Messer told me you requested me . . . *specifically*," he says, eyes holding a touch of heat in them, and I gasp at the realization.

And, for the second time today, I blush. "I'm going to kill him."

Drake's eyes narrow. "I—did you not?"

"No!" I all but yell, absolutely mortified. "And you can tell Messer that I'm issuing a warrant for his arrest, so he better flee the city before dawn if he wants to keep his head."

Then I slam the door in his face.

Chapter 19

ACKER

Olivia is driving me fucking crazy.

I suppose I didn't think to ask, but Wells failed to mention just how pregnant his wife really is. She's *pregnant.* The kind that can still be hidden behind a loose top, which is how they kept it from me when she was still in Kenta, but without layering clothes her swollen belly is very evident. And she wields her condition like a weapon, knowing I can't defend myself against her anger, which follows me wherever I damn well go on this boat.

We boarded the ship at the port not far from where Wells's parents reside and allowed the current to take us down river to the sea. It's quicker than traveling to the coast by carriage, but nothing is quick enough when trapped with a childhood friend who currently curses the day I was born with every breath.

When Olivia isn't openly yelling at me, she gives me the silent treatment. Which would be fine, preferable actually, except Wells's only reason for living right now is to cater to his wife's every whim. Meaning when she goes silent, he goes silent. He can't risk being seen fraternizing with the enemy, and that's a fucking problem.

We've resorted to sneaking around like teenagers in the middle of the night. I've been waiting for him on the bow for two hours when he finally makes an appearance. Hair unkempt and clearly sleep deprived, he's a nervous fucking wreck.

"She's sleeping," he whispers, as if she can hear him from below deck.

"Good." I mean for it to come out positively, but the chastising look he shoots me tells me I didn't succeed. "She's less spiteful when she's rested," I amend.

He braces an elbow on the railing, cradling his head. "She would be giving you hell even if she wasn't pregnant."

Accurate, honestly.

Olivia has never been one to skirt around a topic for the sake of anyone's feelings. Her own or anyone else's for that matter. It's why she and Beau gravitated toward each other as children. That, and because there were few other girls their age at court, certainly none who wanted to be caught befriending the king's bastard child. But Olivia didn't care about any of that, much to her parents' chagrin.

Between the two of them, I've never gotten away with anything reckless without getting an earful.

"At least I would be able to give her hell in return."

"She's disappointed in you," he says.

"Obviously."

"And she thinks you're up to something."

"She does?" My brows hit my hairline. "Or you do?"

He grins. "Oh, I *know* you are."

Leaning on my forearms, I stare at the inky black of the night beyond. The sky and water merge together, impossible to tell where one ends and the other begins. It reminds me of that space between me and Jovie. The nothing that exists when I follow the tether to her. Of our time on the boat.

I take a deep breath, gathering the courage to speak the truth. "My father has been manipulating me my entire life, Wells."

He moves closer, posture mirroring mine. "What made you realize? This alliance with Wren?"

"I think in some ways I always knew. Even as a boy, he demanded things of me regardless of my feelings about it just because it served his interests. I just didn't realize the extent of it until . . ." I huff out a breath at the incredulous notion. "Until Jovie took his magic."

The days following her betrayal are a blur. The council was dead and their families were demanding retribution. When my father refused to attack Maile, they became incensed and withheld necessary resources from their lands. Sent their men to join the uprisings in the capital city. The protests became violent, riots broke out, and the only answer my father provided was to have the remaining relatives of his murdered council members slain.

"I want you to handle this," he had ordered me one night in his sitting room.

And I refused. "I will not have deaths of innocents on my hands."

He wanted to kill entire lineages, right down to the youngest children. He wanted to rebuild a council out of untitled landowners. Men who worked under the previous lords but never held real positions of power. I suspect he believed that if he gave them titles and money that he'd gain their blind loyalty.

I never outright defied my father. My insubordination was usually underhanded, never blatant enough to require harsh punishment. At least, not until I chose Jovie over Irina and the Strou alliance. He blamed me for the problems my darling sister and my Match created when they killed his entire council.

And when I swore to him in that moment I would not kill on his behalf, he looked at me as if I was the enemy. As if me not being a blade for him to wield, meant that I might as well be nothing.

I left his sitting room feeling sick to my stomach and it was the first time I felt like I was seeing a glimpse of who my father was for the first time.

"You're going to have to kill him," Wells says.

"I know." I figured as much the moment Wren walked into my father's sitting room but it was confirmed when he revealed his newly acquired magic in my bedchambers. "I had a chance, and I . . ." Swallowing around my shame, I dare a look at my friend and am grateful to find there's no judgment in his gaze. "I didn't take it."

"It wouldn't do any good right now. Without Wren's army, Kenta would fall, and Wren and Chryse would be there to scavenge your crown off your dead body."

"Nevertheless," I say, straightening my back and hardening my resolve. "I'll handle my father after I have an army to back me."

A wry smile pulls at Wells's mouth. "And what's the plan, exactly? You've yet to reveal anything aside from just wanting to make it to Maile's wharf without being identified, but *then* what are you going to do? Stride up the palace doors and knock, bold as brass?"

"With Olivia, yes."

"My wife?"

"Jovie has been begging Olivia to seek asylum in Maile until the war is over." His eyes jump between mine, searching for a clue as to how I was able to find this out. I grimace at the truth I'm about to reveal. "I intercepted one of their birds."

At first he appears perplexed by the idea of a secret his wife has been keeping from him, but then anger replaces any confusion, his jaw hardening. "You have to control everything, don't you?"

I shake my head, because he's got it all wrong. "I was jealous," I admit. "Olivia had been in contact with her when I couldn't and I was sick with the need to know her thoughts, to read her words. To have a single scrap of her, even if it wasn't intended for me." The smell of wildflowers barely clung to the parchment.

That's one thing Wells can wholly understand. Pity shines in his eyes, and I'm not even bothered by it. Not when I feel it so deeply for myself.

He cusses, shaking his head as he turns back toward the main deck. The second crew shift maintains our course while the rest sleep. Although at least half of them are playing a card game on deck, drinking ale.

"Olivia didn't tell me because she knew I'd want her to go."

"She would never leave without you." My voice comes out sharper than I intended.

"All this talk of my wife, but you haven't once mentioned what you're going to do about your Match once we're there."

"You're going to tell me your opinion on the matter, anyway, aren't you?"

"The smartest and most obvious tactic would be to seduce her. Again."

While the thought is appealing . . . "I don't see how that would be possible with my wife in tow."

A grin tugs at his mouth. "It's not like it stopped either of you before."

"That was different," I insist, leveling him with a hard stare.

He rolls his eyes. "Groveling it is, then."

The mere thought alone has my lip curling in disgust. "I'm not sure that would look advantageous while I'm negotiating a possible alliance for military support."

He bumps his shoulder into mine, leaning in and forcing me to look him in the eyes. "I just want my best friend to be happy."

"You should temper your expectations."

"Fine, but making up with Jovie accomplishes two things at once: ending your current state of celibacy, *and* gaining possible sway with her mother."

It's not like I hadn't thought about that—*wait.* "How the fuck do you know anything about my sex life?" *Or lack thereof.*

He looks at me like I'm stupid. "I'm Matched, remember? I know how the Bond works."

The memory of my wedding night with Irina comes to mind.

Jovie appeared like a phantom across the room. Thin and ghostly white, frozen stock-still as she took in the sight of Irina straddling my lap. I had been dreading the wedding night, but one look at Jovie's stricken face had ignited the need to hurt her just as much as she had me. For her to feel the same pain in return.

So I dug my hands into Irina's flesh, urging her on, keeping my eyes locked on Jovie's as Irina's mouth descended onto mine. At the time, I loved it. *Reveled* in the pain splashed across her face. She broke the connection before it went any further with Irina, disappearing from my presence, but I was determined to finish what I had started, fueled by spite.

I stripped Irina bare and threw myself into the final act. It could have been anyone underneath me and I wouldn't have cared. All I wanted was a release. An escape. Anything to fill the open wound of my heart. I couldn't even register which part of her my mouth was on. There was no taste or feeling or sound.

Then, like a growing inferno, a sensation unlike any other filled my chest. I tried to disregard it at first, but it became unbearable, to the point where I had to tear away from Irina's flesh, feeling dazed. It took me a moment to realize: I was going to *cry*. The urge was so violent that I leapt from the bed and ordered Irina from the room. She undoubtedly thought I was crazy, barking at her like a madman when a moment before I had been all over her. Nothing could stop the tears.

"I thought I was just experiencing Jovie's feelings," I say.

"You likely were," he explains, expression contemplative. "And I think that's the point."

For reasons unbeknownst to me, the Bond made it to where Jovie could see into my mind, where I could only sense her emotions. And while I could always sense Jovie's emotions through the tether, I never experienced it quite like that. Potent. Brutal. Unrelenting even when I put on the mangi stones.

I never touched Irina after that night.

Chapter 20

ACKER

"Do you think the message to Jovie made it through?" Wells muses.

Hard to say with the winter storm that brought snowfall to Mount Zallis's peak in the distance, but I keep my eyes set on a Maile ship as we sail by. A purple flag with an emblem of a golden butterfly on it waves above a white flag inscribed with black lines. The markings are distinct, and it is easy for me to surmise their significance. The similarities between them and the scars the Strou warriors are known to wear are immediately apparent.

"If I'd had more than an hour's notice before we left Kenta, I could have sent a bird well ahead of time," Olivia smarts.

Wells attempts to sooth with her ire. "Liv, you know why. We couldn't risk the message getting intercepted."

"According to Acker," she retorts, shooting me what feels like the hundredth glare today already.

"Will you all shut up?" We turn and look at Irina. She's standing with her eyes closed and her back to the main mast, bare feet on a patch of soil in a shallow crate we brought specifically to enhance her ability use her magic over water. "I'm trying to concentrate."

She was unsure of her full capabilities, as was I, considering she's never used her magic on a scale of this size before. As the princess of Strou, she's never wanted for much, and she had no call to use her magic more than superficially. But the Maile ship is the first we've come across since moving closer to their waters and they don't seem to be making any move in our passing direction. I'm not sure what they're seeing from their perspective, but whatever Irina came up with has them barely sparing a glance.

Olivia glares at her, sourly. "She can't be the only option we had for an illusionist."

Gritting my teeth, I share a look with Wells before walking away.

I give orders to the crew to get the pinnace ready. We'll be at Maile's breakwater before nightfall, and I don't want to waste time getting the small boat into the water. I instruct them to remove and stow away any personal weapons below deck on the off chance we get intercepted, not wanting to appear hostile by any means. But my nerves are getting the best of me, voice coming out clipped when I give the orders.

I've been fending off the familiar craving to see her for days now. Ever since I left the palace two weeks ago, the need has intensified. Every inch, every breath, every heartbeat is filled with anticipation. I'm less than a day away from being able to look her in the eyes. I spend my time watching the shoreline, and *fuck me*, I wasn't even this anxious to see land after being stranded at sea for weeks.

My hands feel empty without a blade as I pace the deck.

We pass fourteen more Maile ships without any issues before the wharf comes into view. I've heard stories of the stone dock, but none of them did it justice. Giant masonic arches stretch over the water in both directions, curving from the land like a shield. Evelyn built the wharf to divide what she considers to be her water from everyone else's beyond. The only ways to reach Maile from Kenta are either a precarious trek over the mountain range branching from Mount Zallis along our shared border, or by sailing directly into their waters through this defensive wharf.

We set anchor a distance from the breakwater. A contingent of

Maile's armada sits inside the protective barrier of rocks set before the wharf, ready to defend the city from direct sea attack. Each one with the same flags as the one before it: the butterfly emblem with the death count flying below it.

Wells meets me at the bow. "This is going to be tricky," he says.

It's easiest to cast an illusion that's believable from far away, which is why we're safe for the meantime, Irina's gift still shielding our ship. Up close, however, things become much more difficult.

"We're going to have to take the pinnacle the rest of the way," I tell him.

"And what of this ship?"

I look at Irina. She hasn't moved for hours. Sweat cascades from her hair and down her temples. She's never stretched her ability to this level before and is likely to pass out as soon as she's relieved of her duties. Hopefully she can hold on long enough to continue hiding the pinnacle once the ship is underway.

I return my attention to Wells. "Do you know if there's a water or air elemental on board?"

He tilts his head in contemplation. "If there is, I doubt anyone would be likely to admit to it."

I suppose not, considering my father's history of collaring Heirs, so I nod, accepting his statement for truth. "We need to turn, and as soon as we drop the pinnacle in the water, the crew will open the sails and make a run for it."

The crew is quiet as we tack, shifting the boat to face the opposite direction, back toward Kenta. Wells helps Olivia into the small boat, kissing her on the cheek when she's settled and running his hands reverently over the swell of her belly. Wells speaks softly into her ear and whatever he says makes her smile shine, sweet as pure sugar, her eyes softening for the first time I've seen in the time we've been together on the boat. As strange as it is to me for my childhood friends to be on the verge of becoming parents, it's impossible not to admit that it suits them.

One of the crewmen on board tests the line to the smaller boat, then gives me the *go* signal with a dip of his chin. "Ready, sir."

When I turn to tell Irina she's next, I find her swaying on her feet, moments from losing the battle to stay upright. I wrap an arm around her waist and assist her into the boat, and she falls heavily onto the bench next to Olivia. One of the crewmen hands me a couple of waterskins and I pass them to Wells.

"Don't waste time," I instruct the commander standing nearby. "Sail as fast as you can. We're far enough away right now that they might not notice you in time to catch up."

He acknowledges the order, wishing us godspeed and waving to us in farewell as our pinnacle is lowered.

Once we hit the water, Wells and I release the lines, using our oars to push away from the vessel. Irina looks as if she's going to lose her lunch and I urge her to hold the mirage on the ship for as long as she can stand it. Taking pity on her, Olivia takes one of the waterskins and helps her to drink a few sips, but it's no use. Irina's abilities can't hold up with the increasing distance from her current target, especially considering we're over open water.

Slouching, her breath comes out in a rush. "I'm sorry," she says. "I can't anymore."

I dig the end of my oar through the water in sync with Wells, pulling the handle in toward my chest forcefully and pushing out again. "Do you have us?"

She nods. "Yes, yes. We're concealed."

This boat is almost the same size as the one Jovie and I sailed in from Alaha. We're crammed together, knees knocking into one another, but it doesn't take long for color to return to Irina's face, the strain of her magic easing now she's working to illusion a smaller target.

"I think they've spotted the ship," Olivia says, focused on the Maile ships still between us and shore.

Sparing a look behind me, I can see the nearest ship pulling anchor, the crew readying for departure. Wells and I pick up our pace. Irina's already at her breaking point, so we have to hope that the fleeing Kenta ship is enticing enough to keep the navy's attention.

The water calms once we're inside the line of rocks that makes up the breakwaters, although the wake of the warship that glides past us on their way out sets us to bobbing again. It's the closest we've come to one of their ships, but though Irina seems nervous, she's wholly focused on maintaining her shielding illusion.

The first ship is just the beginning. One after another unfurls their sails and heads toward the open water. The shouts of men echo over the water and we're able to make out that they have, in fact, spotted our retreating ship in the distance.

The wharf is lined with soldiers. They stand about every fifteen feet, inspecting the water below. With our backs to it, Wells and I are helpless, relying solely on Olivia to monitor for any particular attention aimed in our direction as we row. By the grace of the gods and Irina's hard work, we manage to row underneath the wharf without being spotted.

It's the first time we're able to get a good view of the capital. The city ascends up toward the base of Mount Zallis. Cottages are nestled close together, streets cutting a winding pattern up the hillside. Trees sprinkled throughout. It's daunting to see it from below. The beach itself is rocky and manned in the same manner as the wharf with soldiers dotting the shoreline. Boats are anchored along the wharf, closer to the shoreline.

Wells cusses.

"They're either really prepared or really paranoid," Olivia muses.

"Both," I say.

"If we can make it to shore and past the initial line of guards," Wells says, "I can take Olivia to the palace while you two find somewhere to lay low." I begin to protest when he cuts me off with a look that leaves no room for negotiation. "I'm already letting you use my pregnant wife as leverage to prevent yourself getting killed on sight by your own Match. At least let me be the one to deliver her there safely."

I concede with a tip of my chin.

"Besides," Olivia says. "The princess consort here is going to need a nap."

We all look at Irina's disheveled hair and sweat-soaked clothes with concern. She normally takes a lot of pride in her appearance, but she doesn't even have the energy to snipe at Olivia's observation. If anything, a nap probably sounds incredible to her.

We resume rowing, leaving the shade that the wharf temporarily provided. Squinting against the onslaught of sudden sunlight, it takes a second for my sight to adjust. In the next moment, I'm finally able to set eyes on the wharf from the Maile side. A soldier stands on the edge of the stone bridge, bow at the ready.

"Can he see us, Irina?" I ask.

She shakes her head, gritting her teeth. "I don't know."

"Just a little longer," Wells assures, urging her to fight her exhaustion.

But it's too late.

I hear the whiz of the arrow right before it pierces the hull of the boat with a loud thunk of splitting wood. Water immediately begins to seep in. Attached to the arrow is a rope. A line, I realize, that they're using to reel us in.

Olivia moves to yank the arrow free, but Wells and I both move in to stop her. "We'll sink," he says.

"It's best if we just surrender," I agree.

She lifts her hands as if to show she's not a threat. "It's your funeral."

Irina groans, shoulders dropping as she releases the illusion she couldn't fully maintain. "I tried. I promise."

It was a lot for me to ask. Too much, apparently. There's no one to blame but myself.

We're ankle deep in saltwater by the time we're towed back toward the wharf. Underneath one of the arches, there's a loading dock of sorts. A host of soldiers wait on the small platform. There are steps leading to the top of the wharf behind them and there's a slew of soldiers overhead with arrows knocked to their bows, ready to be drawn and fired in an instant. The message is clear: don't do anything to provoke them. But the soldier who released the first arrow stands at the top of the stairs with his bow drawn, wooden arrow pointed at me . . . *specifically*.

It's apparent he knows who I am, or that arrow would be tipped with metal.

Our little boat has lost some of its buoyancy, and it rocks jarringly when I climb onto the wharf. I turn to help Irina, but a soldier whips his sword up in front of my chest to stop me. Gritting my teeth, I eye the steel, gaze flicking to the archer atop the stairs before finally taking a step back. Irina stumbles a bit but is successful in pulling herself up onto the dock. Then Olivia, and Wells last.

Olivia is slow to move clear of the boat, obviously struggling with the transition from rocking boat to firm ground in her condition, and when a nearby soldier attempts to prod her forward with the tip of a sword, Wells barks at him: "She's pregnant!"

I say his name in warning, but it's of no use. He knows how important it is to not cause a disturbance, but he doesn't back down. Instead, he hops quickly out of the boat, immediately reaching for Olivia to help her regain her equilibrium. As soon as Olivia is steady, the soldiers move in to separate them, which Wells does not take kindly to.

I lose sight of them in the commotion, but there's no mistaking Olivia's yelp of pain.

It happens so fast. Wells grabs who I assume to be the offending soldier by the back of the neck. I don't know where the dagger in Wells's fist came from, but he has the blade to the man's throat in the span of two heartbeats.

"Don't kill him!" I yell.

I allow myself to be knocked to my knees, keeping my eyes locked on my friend and his hostage.

The archer shouts down from above. "Tell him to release our man and we won't."

I don't waste breath clarifying that it wasn't him I was speaking to.

But Wells knows.

"Don't," I repeat, holding my hands out in a placating gesture.

It feels like the moment stretches out forever before he finally relents, his teeth clenched as he shoves the soldier away. Wells keeps his gaze on the man to make sure there's not any intention to retaliate, only dropping the blade when satisfied. I risk a look at Olivia to make sure she's okay. Another soldier has her arm in a viselike grip, which he promptly releases when Wells levels him with a murderous glare, fearful of the clear threat.

I'm grateful for the man's instincts, because I know I could do little to stop Wells from torching every soldier on the wharf if he wanted to.

Chapter 21

JO

My arms shake. Each strike of my blade against Messer's sends pain shooting through my hand. The sound of metal against metal rings in my ears so loudly that I miss his protests.

"—B, easy, easy, *easy*. *Shit!*"

If he thinks I'm going to let up now that I have him where I want him, he's sorely mistaken. The heels of his feet are clipping the line of chalk drawn on the ground. I'm three good strikes away from pushing him out of the circle.

Spin, strike. Dodge, strike. Backhanded swing, and—*fuck me*. He's expecting it, and instead of me bullying him out like I'd intended, he pivots at the perfect moment and my blade cuts through nothing but air. I pushed too hard, too fast, and momentum causes me to lose my balance. I stagger forward . . . and out of the circle.

Panting with each breath, I walk off my frustration to the edge of the arena, heart thundering in my ears as I tug on the gyve around my neck. It's been bothering me. Maybe I got too used to wearing the smaller necklace, because I've been fighting the suffocating sensation caused by the gyve all day.

I try to focus on the scenery around me instead. Soldiers spar at different stations on the temple floor. Built high above the city, the temple was converted into an arena, carved from the stone mined from deep within Mount Zallis. It's open on all sides, the arched columns affording the most gorgeous view of the sloping grasslands outside the city and toward the farmlands beyond.

The irony of leaving behind Alaha's limited space and dual-purpose training arena, only to condition with farm animals is not lost on me. Horses graze in the pastures, the stable hands readying their afternoon feed, moving in and out of the stables located at the edge of the city. A guard stands at the break in the low-lying, stacked stone wall, chatting with one of the farmers venturing in with a cart filled with goods.

Messer appears, holding a waterskin out toward me. "Do you feel better?"

I accept it, but don't reply as I gulp down what's left of the contents. My eyes catch on Fredrich, who's currently weight training, two bags of horse feed thrown over his shoulders as he lunges across the arena floor.

Messer waves a hand in front of my face to pull my attention back to him. "How long are you going to punish me for, huh?" He looks down at his ruined shirt, slashes littering his torso, and another on the outside of his thigh. When I continue to ignore him, taking another sip, he jerks the waterskin from my mouth. "That's enough of the silent treatment. You're being a brat."

I wipe my mouth with the back of my hand. "Would you prefer I bar you from Catuxa's?"

His expression shifts from excitement about the fact I've spoken to him to abject horror. "You *wouldn't*."

I'd thought about it but couldn't bring myself to do so. Not after he revealed his feelings about Aurora and Kai to me. If Catuxa's does truly offer him some semblance of reprieve, then I'd hate to take that away from him.

I turn back to the hillside and sit on the edge of the arena, letting my feet dangle over the side. Because the arena floor cuts into the hillside, there's a sizable drop to the ground below. Not enough to seriously injure if I were to push Messer off, but enough to stun at the very least.

He must sense my thoughts because he sits with his back to the column, facing me. His hair is blonder than it's ever been, even compared to the years he spent in Alaha. The sun gleams off the strands, creating a halo effect around his head.

Leaning back on my hands, I tell him, "I haven't been angry with you."

He makes a face. "Well, of course not. That would be ridiculous, because I've done nothing wrong."

Try as I might to stop it, a smile pulls at my mouth.

I've been lost deep in my own head these past few days. I'm so used to Messer understanding my moods better than most that I didn't foresee him mistaking my silence for anger toward him.

Messer and I share a level of understanding that neither Kai nor Aurora have ever reached with either of us. Along with Beau, he knows everything I know. What *true* loneliness feels like. What it's like to lay your head down at night with a sadness so deep that it threatens to swallow you whole, unsure if it'll ever get better.

But something we talked about the other night at the tavern has been pestering me.

"I think we need to prepare for the possibility of Kai turning on us."

His smile slowly wanes as my words sink in, until it no longer exists. "We don't have any reason to doubt him. He's continued to feed us solid information," he says, defending our childhood friend. "He's told us both that he's no longer angry with us."

I eye him. "Since when has Kai been a beacon of honesty?"

He bites his lower lip between his teeth for a moment. "Maybe we should consider—" Stopping mid-sentence, he sits forward, eyes narrowing at something in the distance.

I follow the direction of his gaze, alarmed to see the three stallions racing up the path from the city and headed our way. Rushing to my feet, I race down the length of the arena to the steps that lead to the end of the path below.

Messer follows right beside me. "They're from the wharf," he says, noting their uniforms.

My heart pounds in my throat, and I unconsciously tug on the mangi stones at my throat.

Then, my heart stops altogether, because . . . *no.*

It's impossible.

But the pulling sensation below my sternum says otherwise, the tether humming with a resounding *yes.*

Fredrich appears from the arena floor above, joining us as we wait for the three horsemen to come to a sharp stop nearby. The commanding officer dismounts, dipping into a bow and I cut the formalities short with a sharp question that I'm positive I already know the answer to.

"What is it?"

The officer stands abruptly. "We stopped four individuals attempting to cross the bay. Two males and two females. One is with child. They're currently being detained—"

I don't let him finish before I step around him, seizing the reins of his horse. "Have word sent to Beau," I tell Fredrich. "Inform her that her brother has arrived." *Just in case she wants to see him.*

He nods, already jogging toward the entrance to the city.

Messer grabs the pommel of my horse and pulls himself up behind me. I tug the reins, steering the horse around and squeezing my legs to urge it forward. The wind whips at our face as we traverse the curving path of the hillside, the two other soldiers following right behind us. It's a steady decline toward the water's rocky edge and I slow from a canter to a trot when we're within sight of the wharf. The afternoon sun reflects brightly off the water, making it impossible to distinguish individual figures in the mass of people. Half the city's current rotation of soldiers must be present.

I urge my heart to calm as I direct the stallion onto the stone dock. The tether gives a strong jerk and I struggle to catch my breath. My magic is all but writhing in anticipation as I get closer. His presence lures me in like the heat from a roaring fire on a frigid winter night.

Messer, still pressed close behind me, places a hand on my shoulder and asks, "You good, B?"

Nodding, I ignore the chill in my bones, and pull the stallion to a stop, handing the reins to a waiting soldier. Messer dismounts first, the picture of ease, but I know him well enough to notice the tension lining his shoulders.

I look him squarely in the eye, my focus only on him. "*Don't* antagonize him."

He places a hand to his chest, affecting a wounded expression. "You would think so low of me?"

I just give him a deadpan look, words not needed.

Turning toward the waiting soldiers, I make myself take a step forward. The men separate, gazes affixed to me as I move through, their bowing forms creating a rippling wave in the line as I pass by. It's not the time to try and dissuade them from performing this formality, and if I stop to speak to them, I don't think I'll get going again because I'm not sure I can feel my legs.

Acker has come to Maile.

So, I put one foot in front of the other, taking it one step at a time.

One breath at a time.

Our last interaction flashes through my mind. When he kissed me with the heat of a thousand suns, only to strike me across the face immediately after. He threatened to kill us both if I didn't leave, and, even after all this time, the ache of the memory hasn't abated. The sting of my flesh still feels real.

The soldiers continue to move out of the way, bowing in succession as I move farther and farther down the wharf. Their heads and shoulders fall from view out of the corner of my vision, but I keep my gaze straight ahead, locked on Drake who stands at the far end of the congregation, bow and wooden arrow in hand.

The four of them stand in a line, their backs to me. Olivia is on the far right, and she looks at me over her shoulder, lips pulled into a small, soft smile as we make eye contact. Then there's Wells immediately next to her, as to be expected. It's the person next to him, however, that makes my heart stop. Irina shifts in place but doesn't trouble herself with looking back at my arrival at all. And its her presence that makes me realize . . .

He didn't come for me.

A tidal wave of dejection washes over me, and I struggle to continue forcing one foot in front of the other. Each breath feels like a waste of effort, as though the oxygen never reaches my lungs. My vision blurs and I bite my tongue hard enough to draw blood to force back the burning in the back of my throat, a knot wanting to form there.

Whatever remnants of hope I held for us withers away and dies in that very moment. I never voiced them. Barely let my mind wander to the deeply hidden desire that Acker would one day realize—*what exactly*? That he loved me more than his pride? His title? The woman at his side?

I've spent years guilt-ridden and ashamed of my decisions, hating myself for breaking his heart, and it's obvious he is nothing of the sort.

I refuse to let on how much it hurts.

Last in line, but certainly not least, Acker stands tall, with his shoulders back and head tilted as he listens for the sound of my approach. There's a glint from his gold nose ring as he pivots, turning his body just enough to lay eyes on me.

Dark eyes that are exactly as I remember them.

I thought my imagination might have colored my impression of them, enhanced my memories beyond reality, but no. They're as potent as they've always been. Enticing. Powerful. Intoxicating. As ensnaring as ever.

Maybe even more so.

I let my gaze slide smoothly away as I pass, moving around him to stand with Drake, and I think . . .

I think I'm in as much trouble as I was when he arrived in Alaha all those years ago.

Chapter 22

ACKER

Her eyes dismiss me without a backward glance.

Completely unfeeling, she stalks toward the archer, stepping purposefully as the soldiers continue to bow in succession.

They fucking *adore* her.

Gone is the girl I stole from Alaha.

At first glance, everything about her appearance is the same as when I've watched her sleep, but now awake, its *more*: facial features sharper, body honed to perfection. I always found her beautiful, but now she's something *else*. Something I can't quite identify. Alluring, maybe? *Divine.* The word feels like liquid as I roll it on my tongue, so damn close yet not enough. She swipes her braid of hair over her shoulder imperiously and I swallow the excess moisture pooling in my mouth.

I'm compelled to keep watching as she stops in front of the archer standing before us. They're speaking too low to make any sense of what they're saying, heads dipped close as they whisper, but the archer looks over at Wells before pointing to the gulf, to where our ship has been taken over by Maile soldiers. Jovie follows his stare before turning back to continue the conversation. Whatever he says makes her smile and he grins back at her.

Up to this point he's demonstrated as much personality as a dead fish, but now he's acting like he's made of sunshine and happiness. *Get the fuck—*

Standing off to the side, just beyond the archer's shoulder, I catch sight of Messer.

I'd forgotten about her *pet.*

He smirks. He's been watching me this entire time.

I'd been too enthralled by my Match to notice him. His eyes slink to Irina at my side, before flicking back on me. Back to Irina. Back to me.

He lifts a brow. "That's . . . *a choice,*" he smarts.

A dumb one, he means.

And yeah, *I know.*

Jovie's heads snaps toward him and she barks, "What did I say?"

His shrug isn't the least bit repentant.

Sighing, Jovie turns her attention back to us, as if just remembering why she's here. She briefly looks at Irina, before taking in Wells and Olivia, avoiding me completely.

I never fully let on to Jovie what I'm able to sense through the Bond. She was always good at hiding her emotions, but it didn't stop me from being able to *feel* them. Like right now, as she walks toward Olivia, there's not a glimpse of the unease she's disguising so well. The sense I get of her inner turmoil isn't strong, with the mangi stones smothering the connection of our Bond, but an echo of the tightness in her chest still filters through to me.

There's a note of affection in her voice when she says, "Liv." Her eyes fall to the round belly Olivia is cradling, paying no mind to the way Wells leans closer to his Match defensively. "I was worried you weren't coming, after weeks without any word from you."

"I'm sorry," Olivia says. "I wasn't given time to send a message before we left."

Jovie nods in understanding. "How was your journey?" she asks. "The baby?"

Olivia runs a hand across her stomach. "He was very active while we were on the ship."

"He?"

"Well, Wells thinks it's a girl, but I'm not convinced."

Jovie glances up at Wells's towering figure, a hint of a smile playing on her lips, before she looks back to Olivia. "Men think they know everything."

Olivia laughs.

"Listen," Jovie continues. "I'm sure you're in need of rest, so let's cut to it: why are you trying to *sneak* into Maile after you've turned down all of my invitations?"

Olivia looks at Wells and he nods, encouraging her to answer. "I'm here to seek refuge for my husband and child. That is all."

There's a beat of silence as they hold each other's stare, and I'm just realizing how familiar they've become. Olivia won't speak against me, but she's not going to lie to her friend, either.

A swift assessment of the soldiers visible nearby tells me everyone is balanced on a delicate edge. All of their eyes are on their princess, their leader, as they await her instructions. Jovie wears leadership well. There's an air of confidence about her that wasn't there before. An authority in the way she holds her head, her stance sure but at ease.

She's . . . *magnificent.*

Wells's suggestion that I should make amends with my Match comes to mind as I take her in. He believes I should get on my knees for the woman who betrayed me and beg like a dog for her help. *Seduce her if you have to,* is what he'd said. I'm not above it. It's basically what she did to me, letting me fall more and more in love with her all the while having every intention of stabbing me in the back.

If I believed it would work, that seducing her would save my people, then I'd more than enjoy getting on my knees at her bedside. I'd make sure she'd beg me in return, to make her come with my mouth between her legs, for release. I can practically feel the heels of her feet digging into my shoulder blades, her hands fisted into her bedding as she caves to her base urges. I'd turn her into a fucking mess.

I can't imagine a sweeter revenge.

Her head snaps toward me, eyes flashing with anger before she's able to mask it. The blaze emanating through my chest from her side of the Bond makes me grin. She can't hide the connection anchoring us together, regardless of the mangi stones she's wearing. The pull of the tether is too strong, too demanding to ignore. A single thread of magic stretching the mere feet between us that's been vibrating since the moment we saw one another.

It's stronger than it ever was before. Even then, I could never discern when she slipped into my thoughts versus when I was just thinking about her of my own volition. My years of training as a child, learning how to shield my mind, are worthless against her, as are the mangi stones when we're this close.

She stalks toward me, and the smell of wildflowers wafts over me on the sea breeze, nearly crippling me. "Get on your knees," she orders. To punctuate her point, she makes the demand again, voice eerily calm as she says, "*Kneel.*"

I have no reason not to acquiesce.

One knee hits the hard stone, then the other, and I tilt my head back to maintain eye contact with her. A pin could drop, and it'd be as loud as the sound of a witch's brew exploding in the silence. This is a show of power, to demonstrate how tightly she holds the reins here, and exactly how little I control in comparison.

And *fuck me* if I'm not struggling to stave off an erection.

There's a flicker of satisfaction in her eyes before she looks to the woman beside me. "And you, Irina," she says. "Why have *you* come here?"

"We came—" I begin, but Jovie cuts me off.

"I wasn't talking to you."

She doesn't even bother to look at me in her reprimand.

It's a casual rebuff meant to put me in my place. I grit my teeth, clench my fists. Partially in a bid to keep my mouth shut and partially to stop myself from acting on the impulse to punch Messer right in his smug face. I can see him grinning at me again from behind the archer.

"Acker told me we were coming here to speak with the queen," Irina says with a haughtiness that surprises me, given her weakened state. "As for the reason, you'd have to ask him."

"Did your husband not coach you on what to say?"

The term she uses for me does not go unnoticed.

Irina sways slightly in place. "My husband does not give me orders."

Risking Jovie's ire, I dare to interrupt: "She knows nothing of my intentions."

Jovie cocks her head to look at me, hazel eyes bright in the sunlight. "Then what is it you seek?"

"An alliance." I have to give her credit for not balking at my answer. "I am sure you've heard by now that the joint forces of Roison and Alaha are nearing our capital. I have come to petition Maile for aid."

"Aid? As in . . . from *my* men?"

I hold her stare. "Yes."

A grin begins to grow on her face as she lets out a small laugh of incredulousness. She looks over her shoulder at the archer and Messer, smile blooming to fullness, and I'm beyond envious that they're the recipients of it.

By the time she faces me again, her smile is gone. "And what in all the gods' names gave you the idea that I'd ever send my men to fight in a war I want nothing to do with? Idiocy or arrogance?"

"Neither," I tell her. The stone wharf is beginning to bite into my knees, but I don't dare move, knowing to do so will reveal my discomfort. "It's a war you're already embroiled in—"

"By your command," she clarifies. "You ordered the Strou to attack my territory along the northern border, did you not?"

This is going to be a tough sell. "You've refused to let our allies cross the gulf." Maybe seduction won't suffice in persuading her, but maybe my misery can. I'd offer to stay on my knees for eternity if it would save my people. "Choosing sides is the same as choosing conflict."

"Your father can't possibly approve of you being here."

I give a slow and measured shake of my head. The soldiers flanking us visibly react, discomfort evident in the shift of their feet and shoulders as the news travels down the line in hushed whispers.

"The Alaha have switched sides," I tell her. "Wren and my father have struck an accord."

She lifts a single brow. "You've received first-hand knowledge of this alliance?"

"Yes."

This, above all else, begins to thaw the ice in her eyes. "Why would Wren switch to the losing side of this war?"

I hesitate and I can practically see her shield going back up. "I'd feel more comfortable sharing what I know in private."

The archer steps toward her and touches her arm to get her attention and she pivots to speak with him. Messer leans in to listen, his eyes shifting between the two of them. Their whispers are once again too hushed for me to overhear

When Jovie looks at me again, her expression is shuttered once more. "Stand."

I unfold to my full height as she saunters closer. Her hazel eyes look up at me, calculating, so different from the wide-eyed gaze of the girl I fell in love with. Tension pinches her brows and I follow the lines down the straight of her nose to her pursed mouth. So severe in the bright daylight. But I know what she looks like when she thinks no one is looking, in the dead of night when all of her ice melts.

"I'm sorry," she says, sounding anything but. "I can't help you."

"Are you prepared for when Chryse or Wren come for you? Because they will. They're as power hungry as my father."

She isn't swayed. "If the situation should arise, I'll handle it."

I take a step toward her but am immediately halted by the creaking sound of a bow being stretched to its limit. In the span of a breath, the archer has readied an arrow and has it pointed directly at my face.

"I wouldn't," she warns.

I lift a brow. "Perhaps your queen will have a differing opinion to yours."

There's a low chuckle from the archer. By the matching set of smiles he and her pet are both wearing, I have a feeling I'm not going to like whatever she says next.

"Haven't you heard?" Jovie asks, her tone taking on a condescending lilt. The archer's gaze lingers on the side of her face with reverence as she continues. "I *am* the queen."

My mouth parts in surprise. I share a look with Wells and he seems as baffled as I am.

Olivia is the first to break the silence. "*You're* the queen?"

Jovie nods.

"And *that* is your royal attire?" Irina asks.

Messer chimes in, a mocking glint in his eyes. "Her crown is being fitted."

It takes me a moment to find my voice, but when I do it comes out like gravel. "Since when?"

There's not a drop of uncertainty or hesitation in her features or stance, and it mirrors the lack of emotion emanating through the Bond. "My mother relinquished her title to me a year ago."

"Why?" Irina challenges.

The way Jovie's gaze brushes over my wife is the same way a tiger would glance at a gnat before dismissing it.

She directs her next words to Olivia. "I'll have a selection of healers ready once you've settled, so you can choose a midwife. They'll be able to check on the baby."

"You speak as if you know our decision already," Wells says.

For the first time since I've laid eyes on her, Jovie offers him an honest smile. "You'd be a fool to do anything else but stay."

Wells can't hide his surprise. "You're just going to let us into your city without an oath in place?"

"Are you telling me you have ill intentions toward me or my people?"

"Ah, no," he says, blinking owlishly. "I am not."

He doesn't so much as look at me as he falls silent. Everyone awaits their queen's final judgment. Wells may not be here with ulterior motives, but he still poses a potential risk to Jovie if Olivia's safety was at stake.

"We're in need of another lamplighter," she says. "Fire elementals aren't as common here, but there are also a couple of blacksmiths if you would prefer to continue your forging." Then her gaze finds me, and her words turn as sharp as knives. "I'll have your boat moored and stocked by midday the day after tomorrow. I'll give you a couple of nights to rest before you return to your fight. Against Roison, Alaha, or your father. I don't care."

Her gaze encompasses Irina, too, indicating that this directive is for the both of us. Irina is unhappy and she's determined to make it known. Her nails dig into the flesh of my forearm. Clenching my teeth, I grab her by the wrist and move her hand back to her own side. My grip isn't hard enough to leave a mark, but there's enough pressure to warn her to keep her hands to herself.

Jovie doesn't miss the silent battle of wills between us, but she flicks her gaze toward Wells and Olivia. "Put them in one of the empty cottages on sailors' row," she tells her lackey, the archer, who motions to a handful of his soldiers.

Determined to leave in the same way as she came, without a backward glance, Jovie stalks past, the smell of wildflowers once again washing over me.

I'm not willing to let her get away with it this time.

I release Irina, stepping out of line to call out toward my Match's retreating back. "And my sister?"

Stopping in place, Jovie turns to look at me, gaze assessing. "She wasn't sure you'd care to see her."

I'm taken aback by her answer. I assumed Beau's position here would be as a resource. A tool for Jovie to use. It never occurred to me that she might be wary of facing me. The oath I swore only protected Jovie from my rage, and did not include my sister. I could have sent sentries after her, put a bounty on her head. After all, she conspired behind my back and chained me to a chair. But as angry as I've been with her for her treason, she's still my little sister.

"Please tell her I'd like to."

Maybe I had hoped for validation or support from Jovie of some kind, but I'm sorely disappointed when she doesn't reply. She simply turns and leaves, Messer following close behind. A puppy trailing after its master.

A voice comes from close behind me. *Too* close. "Step out of line again, and I'll kill you quicker than you can blink. Do you understand?" the archer challenges.

I understand completely, but the sound of hooves on paved brick holds my attention. At the end of the wharf, Jovie's figure on horseback cuts up the city street, strong and confident as she picks up speed, her hair snapping in the wind. A black eyun flits overhead, tracking her movements. It's wingspan ten times wider than the last time I laid eyes on it.

The tether in my chest aches the further away she gets.

Wells's voice is effective in breaking my concentration. "That'll be seven pence, my dear."

"She made him kneel!" Olivia protests.

"The bet was whether or not Jovie would *wound* him," Wells says, folding his arms and nodding, satisfied. "And she did not. Therefore, you owe me seven pence."

"But she did." We all look at Irina, and her voice comes out hollow when she continues. "She hurt his pride."

Olivia is damn near giddy as she looks up at her husband. "Pay up," she insists.

Wells opens his mouth to further argue, but the archer, Jovie's lackey, puts the matter to rest by saying, "Just pay the woman what is owed."

I can't help but grin.

Who needs pride anyway?

Chapter 23

JO

I *think I hate him.*

My mother throws the ball of dough onto her workbench in the center of the staff's kitchen. She's stress baking loaves of bread. "You need to eat," she insists as she begins to work the dough.

Beau eyes my mother, then me, but keeps whatever she's thinking to herself. Probably a good decision considering I feel like I want to rip off my skin. Or someone else's. That seems like a better option.

He brought his wife.

"Who are we waiting on?" Messer asks, sitting at the end of the kitchen table, feet propped on the edge of the surface, chair tilted back on its hind legs.

"Sam," I state.

"Of fucking course," Drake mutters.

My mother eyes me as she kneads furiously. "Will you *please* eat something?"

I take a deep breath to temper my reaction. "I'm not hungry."

She dares to look to Beau for confirmation, who shakes her head in caution. "She's not hungry."

I slap my palm down on the table "I just said that!"

Everyone shares looks of trepidation, the room falling into uncomfortable silence. I squeeze my eyes shut, massaging the pressure building in my temples with my fingertips. The sound of Messer's chair slamming back to the ground has me opening my eyes, and I watch him leave the open doorway of the kitchen, heading into the pantry. He's gone for less than a minute before he returns again with an apple, placing it on the table before me.

I give him an exasperated glare, but I bring the apple to my mouth anyway. The bite is loud and obnoxious. Each successive audible crunch emphasizes the stretching silence. It's not as terrible as I thought it'd be, putting food in my belly. I suppose I didn't realize exactly how hungry I was after skipping dinner. The clock on the wall tells me we're nearing midnight.

Sam snaps into existence on the other side of the table, right in front of the last vacant seat. His uniform is clean, indicating there hasn't been any further fighting with the Strou since I last saw him.

"Fill me in," he says, pulling the seat out and sitting.

No one answers, all of their gazes flitting between the other occupants of the room, wondering who was going to be the first to broach the topic at hand.

I all but roll my eyes, rotating the apple in my palm with my fingertips. "The metal slinger has arrived."

Sam's eyes widen a fraction, head tilting back at the revelation before he adjusts to the news. "Let me guess," he says. "He wants to reconcile."

My mother spits Sam's name in admonishment at the same time Beau does something underneath the table's surface that has him flinching with a bark of pain.

"A little sensitivity, please?" Evelyn hisses through clenched teeth.

I feel foolish for having fantasized about a different kind of reunion with Acker. He didn't come for me. He came for my men.

I think I hate him.

Messer rocks his chair back on its rear legs as soon as he sits down again. "Believe it or not, he came to seek an alliance."

Sam's eyes lock on mine and I hurry to reassure him. "I declined, obviously."

"Bringing his wife didn't exactly help his case," Drake murmurs, scratching at his chin.

There's not an ounce of tact in this room.

"For all that, he did reveal that Wren has decided to jump sides in the war," I say, inspecting my apple, debating if I want to take another bite. "And he hinted at having knowledge of his father's iniquities."

This gets Beau's attention. "And you believe him?"

I shrug. *Who the hell knows*. And it doesn't matter; I won't agree to join his cause either way. "Drake put them in one of the abandoned cottages. I have a small contingent of soldiers keeping watch over them."

"Wait, you didn't send them on their way immediately?" Sam asks.

"They'll be on a ship back to Kenta the day after tomorrow, but I believe Wells and Olivia will choose to stay," I say.

His expression turns incredulous. "You can't be serious."

"Olivia is pregnant. She's currently being seen to by some midwives."

The confirmation that I'm letting them remain in the city by offering them resources seems to upset him even further. "That's the equivalent of handing the enemy a knife and inviting them to stab us in the back. You know that better than anyone," he accuses.

"Watch it," Beau warns.

He stands from his seat and appeals to my mother. "Evelyn, you can't possibly allow this."

My mother places a portion of dough into a bowl before covering it with a cloth. "It is her decision to make."

Sam balks at her calmness, looking over the rest of the room's occupants for support, outraged. Messer continues to rock in his chair with a grin on his face, but Drake doesn't look up, unwilling to speak against his queen *or* his previous commander.

"I'll meet with them," Beau says. Her nervous swallow is audible but she seems firm in her decision. "I'll be able to get a sense of their intentions."

I tilt my head as I look at her. "Beau—"

But she's quick to stop me. "I need to speak with my brother anyway," she says. "For my own sake."

She's never said it aloud, but I know she still wrestles with her own feelings of guilt about betraying her brother.

I had assured her and her mother, Greta, that I'd never use Beau as a tool for my own gain. It was a condition I made in exchange for Beau helping me in taking down the king of Kenta. And I meant it, too. No matter how tempting the idea of utilizing her gift to see Acker's aura is, I never want her to feel pressured into doing so by me.

It was at my insistence that we had offered Acker the choice to take his father's throne, but Beau felt Acker's allegiance to his father was too strong to be included in our plans ahead of time. That if given too much time to dwell on it, he might reveal our plans to his father. Then, after the conversation I overheard where his father insisted that Acker marry Irina, I was doubtful enough about him to follow her guidance. We agreed that the best way was to spring the option on him at the very last minute, but he never saw the chance to usurp his father as the mercy I meant for it to be, just as another layer to my betrayal.

In hindsight, it was probably for the best, despite the pain Beau suffered at having to be the one to strap her brother to the chair. She was the only person capable of subduing Acker, even if only for a few minutes, as he would never have seen it coming. Those last moments she shared with him in their home were so difficult, the guilt biting as painfully as the spikes on her metal rope that cut into her brother's skin.

After she gives me a look of assurance, I nod. "I'll send Fredrich with you."

General Samasu is flabbergasted, shaking his head. "And the prince? Do you at least have him restrained with mangi stones?"

I take a bite of my apple, ignoring his question.

The slight shake of his head turns into nods. "All right. *Fine.* Since you're not interested in my council, why have you requested me?"

"I need you to travel to Roison and update Chryse on the situation." I made the deal with Chryse when it appeared Kenta was on the losing side of the war, I still don't want to ruin the alliance on the chance things go south with Edmond and Wren. Which is likely.

"A bird is not sufficient?" he asks.

I shake my head. "I'm not risking it getting intercepted. And with winter closing in, your arrival is both quicker *and* guaranteed."

His mouth thins. "If Chryse finds out secondhand that the prince of Kenta is here, he's going to come to the wrong conclusion. The sooner we inform him of the truth, the better," he says.

"I'm glad we agree."

Neither of us point out the potential ramifications of the Strou finding out that their own heiress may be conspiring against them, especially after her marriage was intended to secure their alliance with Kenta. Or worse, if they believed we were holding her hostage here in Maile.

I ask Drake to retrieve a map from the library and we slide some of my mother's bowls to the side when he returns, making room as he lays the map flat on the surface. We all huddle around it as we go over the last known whereabouts of the Roison leader and what his potential movements might have been since then. It's likely Sam will have to do a bit of jumping about in order to find him.

"It shouldn't take me longer than a day. Two at most," he says.

Drake soon has to leave, needing to return to the wharf and pass along the instructions to keep the Kenta ship anchored offshore. The crew will be fed and well kept, but confined to the ship; we don't need them spreading news of the prince's arrival. Whether Acker coming here is an act of treason against his own father or an act of aggression against me, it's imperative we keep as tight a lid on the situation as we can for the time being.

My mother gives an assortment of baked goods to Messer before she departs for bed, and he makes an off-color joke about my mother that has me chucking my half-eaten apple at his retreating head as he ducks out of the kitchen. Sam disappears not long after. Then, it's just me and Beau left to make our trek out of the kitchen, into the main hall toward the stairs to our bedrooms.

When we first came to Maile, Beau lived in a flat next to Messer near the gulf, but it didn't take long to figure out that living in the city wasn't a viable option for her. She would go days, sometimes more than a week at a time, not stepping a foot outside. There were too many people. While she's gotten a lot better at not getting overwhelmed in large crowds, she said their auras had started seeping through the walls, the population too dense for her to get any reprieve. She needed a more isolated place to reset. It took some convincing, but eventually Beau moved into the palace.

The oil lamp swings in her hand, throwing our shadows dancing on the walls with every step. "How are you feeling?" she asks, voice barely above a whisper.

I release a long-suffering sigh. "I hate it when you do this."

"Do what?"

"Ask me how I'm feeling when you already know."

"I'm trying to be polite."

"*No*, you want to know if what I say aligns with whatever it is you see in my aura. Then you'll do your emotional sorcery where you sneakily lead me to the truth of my own feelings, because you don't want me to suppress things. And, frankly, I don't have the energy for it tonight."

She blinks at me. "I see you're frustrated."

"*Beau*," I all but growl at her, as we reach the landing that leads to our rooms.

"Fine." She swings open her bedroom door. "But as much as you believe you hate him, you really don't." Then she slams the door shut, taking the lamp with her.

Alone in the darkened hall, I let out a breath that finally doesn't feel forced—an exhale that I don't have to concentrate on holding steady in order to appear put together, when everything inside of me wants to scream.

He didn't come for me.

In my bedroom, I don't bother lighting a lamp as I undress down to my undergarments. The cup of tea sitting on my bedside table is ice-cold when I take a sip. Then I take another, but only a little one. I'm too nervous to drink all the sleep aid, given the circumstances. Not with the tether refusing to settle below my ribs, riled up by Acker's proximity. It pulls even now in his direction. Insistent and frustrating, and I need something to dull the ache.

Before I climb into bed, I retrieve another necklace of stones from the bedside drawer, draping it on top of the gyve around my throat. I inhale shakily at the weight of them, the pressure increasing as they smother my magic even more. The tether is still heavier.

I'm chilled to the bone as I slide under the blankets. The tea is already lulling me into a dreamlike state. I usually down the entire concoction, which knocks me out within moments, but the smaller dose is dragging out my thoughts and memories of the day into long strings of vivid images. My only solace is that I won't remember any of this when I wake.

Even though I know he's not here for me, I can't seem to stop flashes of the fantasy I saw inside Acker's mind when we were on the wharf from coming in quick succession. Me in the dress I wore the night I betrayed him, an unkempt bed, skirts hiked to my thighs as I teeter on the edge of the mattress. I could sense the stone under his knees when he knelt at my command today, as if he was anticipating the slight edge of pain. I could tell he enjoyed it, even though his face betrayed nothing.

I fight the druglike pull of the tea, trying to control my own thoughts, but the dream plays on. My hands pulling at his hair, legs draped over his shoulders, heels digging into his back. The vision is sweet torture and I can feel my heart racing as I claw for a way out. I don't want to see the strength of his hand as his fingers dig into my thigh, or the shift of his forearm when he splays a hand over my stomach, or the—

Something about the sheets . . .

The perspective skews to a view of my hands as they grip the material between my fingers. Then to a wisp of gauzy material hanging from the bed's canopy filters through the vision and I gasp, eyes opening at the realization.

On the wharf, I dismissed Acker's fantasy as nothing more than an attempt to goad me into reacting. Which I did, like an imbecile, forcing him to kneel. But I hadn't considered anything of it beyond that. I'd been so incensed by his audacity that I missed the obvious.

The bed. The sheets. The canopy.

My bedchamber.

How would he know what the inside of my bedchamber looks like?

Unless . . . unless he's come through the Bond. Without my knowledge. Like when I'm . . . *asleep*.

Horrified, I reach for the lamp I know is on my bedside table, but the motion is lethargic. The tea is too strong to fight. I consider yelling for Beau, but what could she do? Keep watch over me in case an Acker that she can't see appears in my mind?

Touching the stones around my neck, I'm at least assured by the extra set I added, and in the knowledge that Acker can't hurt me. Not unless he figured out how to break the blood oath. But, just in case, I call my blade, keeping the dagger's hilt tight in my fist as I finally allow sleep to claim me.

When I wake up the next morning, the weapon rests on my bedside table.

Its blade?

Sharpened.

Chapter 24

ACKER

The figure on the roof across the street sits with his back to the smokestack, leg swinging lazily where it hangs over the edge as he sharpens the sword in his lap. Long, steady sweeps of stone against metal. He's been out there since we were deposited at the cottage yesterday.

"Isn't it a little early to be drinking?"

Letting the curtain fall back over the window, I turn to see Irina in the doorway of the bedroom, looking a tad rumpled, but surprisingly lively considering what she went through yesterday. She was lucky the bedroom was in such close proximity to the front door, as it took her less than a minute to fall asleep after face-planting into the bedding.

I inspect the tumbler of liquid I've been nursing since I awoke hours ago and shrug. "What else is there to do when you're imprisoned?"

As if it finally occurs to her where we are, she takes in the living quarters of the cottage. It's clean, but there're little trinkets that feel personal to someone who lived here once before. A half-used bottle of men's fragrance was left in the bathroom, along with a beard comb. And the pots and pans in the kitchen are well worn. Worn boots sit beside the door. If I had to guess, this was a soldier's personal residence. Someone who will no longer be coming back to it.

The walls are a soft white, the furniture crafted in varying shades of wood, and rugs covering the floors. Not very prison-like, no, but the soldiers making regular sweeps of the perimeter have made it abundantly clear we are not merely guests. At least, *I'm* not. Wells and Olivia, on the other hand, are apparently guests of honor.

"It's a bit disappointing, isn't it?" Irina asks, gaze moving back to me as she sits in one of the armchairs in front of the fireplace.

She has a tone she sometimes uses that never fails to grate on my nerves. It's meant to come across as light and conversational when it is, in fact, incredibly patronizing.

I waver on whether to ignore her or not, but the drink has me sliding into the opposite chair. Maybe. "What is?"

"Having your Match do the same to you as you did to her."

"I think you're mistaking my father's actions for mine." I swirl the liquid in my glass. "I did talk him out of the collar he wanted her to wear, though."

I realize my mistake a moment too late.

Irina's gaze falls to my neck . . . to the *absence* of stones. Now that she sees me without them, there's no hiding the obvious implication. I did visit Jovie last night, but it's not as scandalous as she probably believes it to be. I thought that giving Irina a lover would lessen the hurt of living without my affection, but I'm not sure it has. Ever.

Irina's emotions play across her face like the flicking pages of a book, telling me everything without saying a word. I am the cause of her perpetual heartbreak.

Olivia shuffles into the room. "You're drinking already?"

Fucking maddening, these women. I down the remainder and hold the empty glass up for them to see.

"Nope."

Rolling her eyes, Olivia lays out on the settee, head lolling on the armrest as she looks over at me. "I heard you pacing around in here for hours. Did you even sleep?"

I'm surprised by her concern, having gotten so used to her ire as of late, but I am not one to turn down grace when it's given. "I did," I tell her. It wasn't more than a couple of hours, but sleep is sleep. "But it sounds as though you didn't."

She groans as she rubs her distended stomach. "I think the boat made him unsettled. Like you, he has yet to quit moving."

The midwives had come within an hour of us arriving at the cottage. The four women disappeared into the second bedroom with Wells and Olivia and were dismissed one by one. They finally chose an older woman dressed in layers of practical linen, her years of experience and positive demeanor highlighted by the laughter wrinkles bracketing her eyes and mouth.

It seems that arriving in Maile has calmed Olivia in some sort. Even clearly exhausted, she rubs her belly gently, a peaceful grin on her face. I know it's because she believes her unborn child will be better protected here. And as glad as I am that Jovie has offered my friends sanctuary, I can't shake the feeling that it's a false sense of safety, not now that I know my father can steal magic from Heirs. That type of power feels inescapable, no matter how far one runs from it.

My magic suddenly shifts. It's been a while since I've given free rein to my gift, but the sensation of metals moving closer sends my blood buzzing and I look in the direction of the front door a moment before a knock sounds. Irina shoots to her feet, instantly on guard, and I urge her to calm with a raised hand. Olivia sits up, albeit a bit wobbly.

Wells appears in the open door of the bedroom, doing up the last few buttons on his shirt. "Who is it?" he asks, smoothing down his mussed hair.

Only one way to find out.

I'm somehow unsurprised by the sight of my sister at the cottage's door. What is shocking, however, is how . . . *mature* she appears. There's a touch of make-up enhancing her strong features; her lips are painted a soft pink, lashes curled. A lavender dress hangs from her shoulders with a gold butterfly pinned to the neckline.

She stares at me in the same manner I do her, as if struggling to merge the memory of the sibling we grew up alongside with the version of them standing here now. Foreign, yet familiar. Familiar, yet foreign. Her inspection goes deeper than just the physical, her eyes flitting over the air around me, seeing colors and shapes I've never been privy to. I don't move, nor so much as blink, knowing this moment is pivotal if I'm to be trusted.

But I can only withstand the silent judgment for so long. "Well," I say with a tilt of my head. "What's the final verdict?"

Her dark eyes, near identically to my own, fix on my face. "Let's go for a walk."

They are the first words she's spoken to me since her betrayal. I suppose a simple *hello* would be too gauche. "Sure."

Beau steps back, waving at Olivia and Wells as she turns. "Hey, you two," she says, and then pauses, eyes lingering on my wife. "And you, Irina."

While her tone is dry, it's not unkind either, and Irina offers a brief tight-lipped smile in return.

I keep an eye on the man on the roof as I step outside. The cottage we've been housed in sits on a bend in the road near the gulf, the water within walking distance and the wharf within sight. Aside from the rooftops of the cottages situated on the street up hill, I have no sense of where we are in relation to the palace.

"Where are we going?" I ask.

Beau simply stares at me standing on the stoop. Her eyes are lethal as they scour my skin. Like I'm being gutted, sliced right to my core, like she's trying to dismantle me from the inside and there's not a godsdamned thing I can do about it. Finally, she takes mercy on me, eyes cutting to the direction where the road slopes down toward the coastline.

"This way."

I fall into step beside her. Both of us are quiet and I use the time to take in the city once more. When we were marched up the hillside yesterday, it was dusk, and the lamps dotting the roadside were a beautiful sight to behold. The warmth radiating from the lamps made it seem like a blanket had been draped over the city, their glow making the white stone cottages all the more ethereal looking and I'm eager to see the city in the daylight.

"Does he go everywhere you go?" I ask, tilting my head to the figure leaping across to another nearby roof as he follows us.

"He goes where the queen tells him to go."

If Jovie believes I am capable of harming my sister, it's another stone stacked against me. Beau is more than capable of defending herself. Even if she weren't, I never felt the same anger toward her as I did for Jovie. Her betrayal felt like it was born out of desperation. Beau suffered at the hands of our father. Trapping her mother, making her vie for a place at court by doing his bidding, constantly pitting us against each other just as he did with his wives.

Jovie's betrayal just felt cruel. Like a punishment for something I wasn't even aware I'd done.

People begin to trickle out into the streets as they start the day. They wave to Beau, well acquainted with her presence, it seems. A horse-drawn buggy heads toward us and we step to the side of the road to let it pass, a sweet smell following in its wake. "Bread delivery," Beau explains. "Evelyn makes bread as gifts for people in the capital."

"As in . . . for everyone?" I ask.

She smiles as if I'm a toddler asking if the sky is going to fall one day. "Yes. Every family gets a parcel at least once a year. Evelyn says it keeps her busy. She enjoys it."

The path curves around a cottage with pink shutters, and as we round the bend it's as if we've stepped foot into an entirely different part of the city. The path splits to the left and right of a theater sunk into the ground ahead, steps leading to a stage at the bottom.

Despite the cold temperatures, the trees bordering the round seating area are green and full. Flowers bloom on them in bright shades of purple. And, as gorgeous as they are, it's the flutter of gold between the swooping branches that holds my attention. The way the sun glimmers off the butterflies' wings looks like tiny fissures of lightning, a tiny spark of reflected light here and there before it's gone, hidden by the beat of a wing.

Wow.

"I know," Beau says. "It's beautiful."

I don't know if I accidentally spoke the sentiment out loud or if she was able to surmise it from my aura. It's been like this since we were children; she's always been able to sense my thoughts without me having to say them.

As we approach, the sound of chittering diverts my attention to the seating area where children are congregated on the tiered stone steps. On the stage, a chalkboard stands next to a desk. A teacher's desk, I realize.

I'm struggling to take it all in—the outdoor theater filled with children ranging from roughly nine-years-old to twelve, but also the butterflies flying overhead, and the sweet, perfumed smell of nectar from the flowers. I stand under the shade of the trees taking it all in, when I notice my sister walking down the stone steps and toward the stage, the children's voices quieting as she passes.

"Good morning!" Her voice is lilting and a smile overtakes her features.

The class sings back: "Good morning!"

I promptly take a seat on the highest row as I come to the realization my sister is the teacher. My *sister*, who has arguably taken the lives of as many men as I have, picks up a piece of chalk and plays with it between her fingers as she looks over the students.

"Who did their reading assignment?" she asks, and every hand shoots up. "Good. Then everyone should be able to answer a question if I call on you."

She opens a text on her desk and runs a finger down the page before asking the first question. Her eyes scour over the array of students until she chooses one, calling him out by name. Alec is swift to answer, and he beams when Beau gives him a pleased smile. She continues her interrogation—because that's what it is—as she paces in front of the kids, figuring out if anyone has skimped on their assignment.

I've seen her in action enough to know when she's sizing someone up, and most of the class sits at attention as they wait to be called upon. One boy, Mason, cowers in his seat when her eyes land on him, and I pity him as he stutters over an answer. He's wrong, of course, and Beau's disappointed expression is punishment enough for his lacking effort.

I spend the morning observing her as she lectures. The noise of the city bustling around the amphitheater mixes with the sound of wind in the trees and the buzzing of bees. As the sun rises in the sky, the canopy of trees keeps the theater shaded. It's idyllic and makes me melancholy for the people back in Kenta. There's a peace here I haven't felt in years back at the capital.

Beau has always said children have the best auras. I never thought much of it but watching her interact with them reminds me so much of how her mother was with us when we were young. Still as intimidating as hell, but also forthcoming with her joy.

In Kenta, Beau existed.

Here, she's *thriving*.

Jovie has given her so much more in a few years than my father ever did in her whole life.

At the end of her lectures, she gives the kids the day off from assignments and they're boisterous when they scramble to leave, running to the parents waiting for them around the circumference of the theater.

I wait for Beau to clean her chalkboard and tidy the supplies on her desk before she comes to meet me at the top of the stairs. We fall into step as we take a different path back to the cottage.

Maile is a city unlike anything I could have ever imagined, as if it was pulled from the pages of a fairytale. Magic is as common as breathing. People exercise their gifts out in the open, free to use them however they please. I can practically feel the magic in my lungs, on the breeze as it dances across my skin. It's intoxicating.

"Is this how it always is?"

Beau's smile is earnest when she answers. "Always." She swings the excess material of her skirt as she leads me higher into the city. "Your aura has calmed since this morning," she says, eyes flitting over me. "Although, you're still angry with me."

The soldier from this morning has been replaced by another, and I keep my eyes on him as he scales the roofs a street over from us. I don't remove my hands from my pockets, making it clear that I pose no threat. To my sister or otherwise.

"Tell me," I say, returning my attention to the sloping street ahead. "When exactly did you decide to overthrow our father? Was it an impulsive decision influenced by Jovie, or was it something you had planned since we were children?"

Beau's never been one to be dismayed by my attitude. "I saw the deception in Jo's aura as soon as I laid eyes on her." Smirking, she reaches out and plucks a stray flower petal from my shirt. "Much like I see it in yours."

"That's news to me."

"You've always had a little bit of deceit hiding in there," she says, twirling her fingers in the air. "Whether you mean to do anything or not."

"Doesn't everybody?"

"It was always my wish to overthrow our father," she says without a hint of remorse. "It wasn't until meeting Jo that I ever hoped it was a real possibility."

"And what was I? Collateral damage?"

"Yes." She looks away, at nothing and everything all at once. "It wasn't an easy decision. Jo wanted to bring the offer to you sooner, but I warned her against it."

My heartbeat seems to still as I absorb her words. "Why?"

"You love too hard. Always have." She shrugs. "But there's one thing you value over love . . . and that's loyalty."

I exhale a burst of air through my nose in a huff as I shake my head. "You have no idea how wrong you are."

"I know." She looks back to me, the corner of her lip quirked up in a small, humorless smile. "I can see that now."

Something in her face sends a frisson of unease down the nape of my neck. "Oh, yeah?"

"I believe our father had been planting falsehoods in your mind for a long time. Probably starting before you even left to join the army. But your aura is vastly different from when I left home," she says, swinging her skirt as she walks. "Loyalty is still there, but it's divided."

I look up at a flicker of butterflies floating on the breeze. "I hadn't been home more than a handful of times since I joined the army, so when I did return, my perspective of our father was still that of a boy. I was just too stubborn to see him for he was—*is*."

"Jo told me there was something you refused to speak of, on the wharf. Something about the reason Wren switched sides."

A humorless breath escapes me. "She's not willing to have this conversation with me herself?"

Beau looks at me as she has done for the majority of our lives—admonishing, with a knowing tilt to her brow. She doesn't need to voice the obvious, and that's the fact Jovie doesn't want to speak to me at all.

"Our father has found a way to regain his magic."

By the way her expression doesn't falter, it's apparent she already suspected what was going to come out of my mouth.

"How do you know that already?" I ask.

She gives me a look that says everything without having to say it; she's not dumb enough to reveal her sources.

Sighing, I nod my understanding.

"Listen, I think you're being honest about wanting to take the throne from our father, so please believe that what I'm about to tell you is in your best interest." Her mouth thins as she inspects me before she looks away, as if she can't stand to look at me as she speaks. "You're wasting your time here. Jo will never help you."

There's something in the bluntness of her statement that tells me she's being truthful. Whatever Jovie's reasoning, it's nonnegotiable, which makes me believe she's holding on to an alliance with Roison. For what, I'm unsure. What could Chryse have offered her to not even *consider* hearing me out? Besides my marriage being an obvious point of contention.

"Does she draw anymore?" I ask, solemnly.

If Beau is taken aback by the sharp deviation in the topic of my question, she doesn't show it.

"No," she answers, softly.

And that's the worst news Beau's given me today.

Chapter 25

JO

I had hoped I was wrong, that he hadn't been spying on me without my knowledge. But here he is. Appearing at the foot of my bed well after midnight. Collar of his shirt pulled open, hair messed, feet bare. It's nearly the exact image of him from our time together on the boat that I've reminisced about. Without inhibitions or influence from the outside world.

His expression is tempered, but his voice holds the weight of every emotion coursing through my own body. "*Jovie.*"

It's been years since I've heard the moniker outside my dreams, and it sends chills down my spine.

Nobody calls me by that name. Ever.

But it was never *only* a name with him. It felt like more. Like a claim.

I don't so much as blink, refusing to let on that the heat threatening to bloom across my face is due to anything other than the anger I've been harboring all day.

The light from the oil lamp beside my bed flickers. I drop the spare string of mangi stones next to it before lifting the teacup and taking a sip with forced casualness. It's the perfect temperature. I take a moment to relish the steeped spices as I swallow. It's a far cry from the bitter taste of the sleep tonic I've become accustomed to.

I set the cup back down before giving him my full attention. "How long have you been watching me?"

He tilts his head thoughtfully, gaze heavy as he holds my stare. "I think you already have an idea."

The oath protects me from physical harm, but it seems emotional torture is fair game. All the dreams I've been desperate to escape, the ones I wake from with my heart pounding in my throat. Sometimes from fear, sometimes in pleasure, and all too real. Both equally as painful.

There's no telling which dreams were possibly influenced by his presence or the workings of my own mind, but they started not long after I arrived in Maile. One in particular, however, stands out more than the others. The most recent one from my time at the border. When I thought I awoke to a Strou warrior, only to be convinced otherwise in my drowsy state of mind when Acker appeared. And, with a stunning realization that I . . . I *begged* for him to stay.

Humiliation burns through me, scorching my cheeks. While I expected the anger, I was not expecting the tears that sting at the corners of my eyes. I jerk my gaze away from him as I move from the bed, trying to hide the emotion on my face as I tighten the cinch of my robe, willing the gathering moisture to dry as I face the doors leading to the terrace.

All of this time, I've accepted his hurtful actions as if they were fair payment in return for my own. Marrying Irina, relishing my misery on their wedding night, ordering the Strou to attack our border. Transgressions I believed that would finally equal my own and we could call it even. But this feels like the tipping point. The remorse I've been carrying for my actions in Kenta dissolves into nothing, and all it leaves behind is burning resentment.

I'm done longing for someone who only despises me.

I turn and find him leaning against the foot of my bed, hands in his pockets as he watches me. "I'll have Drake escort you and Irina back to your ship in the morning, but you're no longer welcome *here.*" I finger the gyve around my throat, realizing it'll need more revisions. Something stronger to withstand Acker's ability to somehow overcome them to bridge the gap in the Bond. "Invited or otherwise," I clarify.

His gaze hesitates on where I toy with the string of mangi that disappears beneath the cut of my robe before returning to my eyes. "You became queen, so that makes your word law, does it?"

I cock a brow. "Last time I checked."

He makes a noise in the back of his throat and it's as if the vibration cuts straight through me. Pushing off the foot of the bed, he moves closer, steps measured and precise. I hold my ground, refusing to give him the satisfaction of making me retreat, my head tipping to maintain direct eye contact.

"Then why'd you let me into your city?" he asks, voice low in the still night air. "You could have killed me on the wharf, sent me back to my ship. You knew I would never ask for personal sanctuary. Unless you thought I came here for *you*." His gaze dips to my mouth before flicking back up to my eyes. "Is that it? You were hoping I'd finally come for you?"

"I thought—" I swallow to soothe the rasp in my voice, letting my eyes convey my distaste. "You must truly be desperate."

He's unmoved by my change in demeanor. If anything, he seems to become more motivated to prove me wrong. "I can feel you, you know?" He wets his lips, eyes lazy as they drip down the front of my body, as if he can see straight through the material of my robe. It's a blatant and salacious look meant to knock me off-kilter. "I know when you're lying."

"Oh, *now* you can tell?"

"When it comes to your desire, Jovie . . ." He smirks, something dark and devious that makes me nervous. "There's no denying the truth."

Godsdamn him.

Inside I'm quaking. Being this near to him is borderline euphoric. His eyes feel like the weight of a thousand suns as they hold steady on mine. The tether steadily urging us to get closer. I could touch him if I wanted to, reach out and skim my fingers over his jaw, his mouth. Kiss him if I wanted to.

Which I don't . . .

His grin grows, snapping me from my torrid thoughts.

I close the little distance between us, nothing more than a finger's width separating the two of us. "Or," I say, "You feel what I want you to feel."

"Really?" He reaches a hand up; the movement is slow as he tucks a stray hair behind my ear. "Like all those times you sucked my tongue into your mouth," he purrs. "Or when you clung to me as I entered you." There's no teasing glint in his eyes, just need reflected back at me as his lips hover over mine. "Or those times you came on my cock—"

"You think I fucked you because I wanted to?" I shake my head, forcing a small smile playing on my lips. "I needed to accept the Matching Bond, or risk myself by denying it. I don't want you. I *never* wanted you."

He stills, dark eyes unwavering as he looks down at me. "And how well did that work out for you?" he asks, eyes on the stones around my neck.

I sneer at him. Mostly because I hate that he's right. I thought accepting the Bond would mean I'd have control over my own mind and my body, but I'm still having to fight the pull of the tether every waking moment of every day. And apparently when I'm sleeping as well.

Seemingly satisfied by seeing his blow land, his expression shifts, and he looks entirely unbothered again in the blink of an eye. His shoulders lose their tension as he takes a step back. "Whatever you bargained for in exchange for providing aid to Roison's side in this war, I'll pay tenfold."

I'm taken aback by the sudden shift in conversation but manage to paste on a placid expression of my own. "You can't afford what I want."

"Try me," he says.

The challenge in his voice touches something inside of me. Something dangerous and indulgent, and by the way he's fighting a smile, it was likely his intention.

A knock on my door cuts through the tension.

Acker's expression shutters. "Expecting someone?"

Unease settles in my stomach as I slowly move around him toward the door. Acker spits my name as I pass, but I ignore him. Picking up the extra necklace I left on my bedside table, I slide the stones on top of the gyve. Acker's voice gets swallowed by their weight, and when I turn around, he's gone.

I let out a breath, but there's no relief to be found.

The knock comes again. I add one more extra layer of mangi before I walk over to open my bedroom door, but I'm surprised by who is standing on the other side.

"I sent for Drake," I say, confused.

Fredrich nods, face solemn. "I know."

I lean around him to check the hallway, ensuring it's empty, that Beau's door is closed, before motioning him in. "Is everything okay? Drake? The armada?"

"Yes, everything is fine," Fredrich says, eyes roaming around the room once, efficient as ever, before coming back to me. "I just couldn't let a man walk blindly to his death."

Death? "You think I summoned Drake to my bedchambers to kill him?" I ask, dumbfounded.

"What you were seeking from him would unequivocally sign his death warrant."

Realization dawns, my cheeks burning as I hold Fredrick's gaze. "Who told you?"

"Sailors talk, Jovinnia."

Crossing my arms over my chest, I'm immediately on the defensive. "It's not as if my Match would have ever known I'd taken another to bed, if that's your concern."

Fredrich's mouth thins, his expression conveying exactly how dense he thinks I'm being. Frustration drives me to cuss as I stalk away from him, back toward my bed. The tears are back with a vengeance. I just want these . . . these . . . *overwhelming* emotions to end. I keep waiting to reach the bottom of the well, for my heartache and anger and frustration to run dry, but my conversation with Acker has solidified the truth—it won't end until I make it end.

I'm done hating myself for something I can't change, for a man who doesn't love me.

Pushing past my embarrassment, I untie my robe, letting the material slip down my shoulders and to the ground as I turn to face Fredrich. His eyes dip to my body only briefly, but the glance is intense enough to heat straight through the sheer slip I'm wearing.

He reaches for the sword strapped to his waist. "Are you sure?" he asks in responds to my unvoiced words.

Not in the least.

"Yes."

His eyes don't shift from mine as he sets his weapon on my desk. "As a service?" he clarifies, undoing the top button of his shirt.

I take a second to gather my thoughts. "As my friend, but nothing more."

His expression doesn't change as he begins rolling one shirt sleeve up his forearm, and then the other. "Okay."

The single word makes my heart skip a beat. "The bed?" I'm surprised by how steady my voice sounds.

He looks at my empty desk chair and shrugs. "Here's fine."

I'm wholly unprepared for his decision, and even less so when he grabs me by my hips and spins me, pushing me onto the cushioned seat. He sinks to his knees before me, and when he places his hands on my legs, my skin heats instantly.

"Tell me to stop and I will," he says, rough palms trailing up the length of my thighs, pushing the hem of my slip upwards.

When his fingertips reach the crease where my legs part, I stop him with a hand over his. "You're under no obligation to do this because I'm your queen."

A grin I've become familiar with eases some of my doubts. "Trust me," he says, right before he grabs me by the back of my knees and pulls me to the edge of the seat. "This is by no means a hardship on my part."

He tugs at my panties and I lift my hips to help him remove them. The sudden escalation of events has my head spinning and I cling to the reminder this is what I want.

No. This is what I *need.*

He looks up at me as he spreads my legs, exposing me to him. I feel the heat of his breath against the inside of my thigh as he dips his face to place a gentle kiss to the skin. Finally, his gaze falls to the task before him and even still I struggle to dispel my doubts. The urge to retreat plagues me, to tell him I changed my mind, but I don't. I *won't.*

I realize now how pathetic I've been, and the only thing I haven't tried to make the hurt stop is doing what Messer said—to move on with someone else.

I need the hurt to end.

My breaths come in short bursts, anticipation making my body tremble. It works in my favor, making me appear eager about the way Fredrich's tongue and teeth scrape along my skin. It's meant to be enticing, teasing, but I'm somehow already impatient to get this over with. For his mouth to be on me properly, so I can move on with my life.

Widening my legs even further, he reaches the apex of my thighs and wastes zero time before licking his tongue over my center in a long, sweeping motion that makes all of my thoughts stutter to a complete stop. The teasing is over. His mouth moves over me in a devouring kiss. This is exactly what I needed, because suddenly there are no thoughts or emotions or desire making me want to escape my own skin. There's simply . . . *nothing.*

He makes his way higher and I have to grip the edge of the chair's arm cushions when he sucks firmly on my bundle of nerves. A shocked burst of sound escapes my parted lips at the jolt of intense pleasure. He's clearly pleased by my reaction, but he eases off a little, his mouth curving into a smile—right before his tongue plunges inside me, and I'm stunned by how much I think I like it.

Then the worst thing imaginable happens.

Acker appears.

I pitch forward with a shocked gasp, which Fredrich takes it as positive feedback, delving in deeper, and I grab him by the hair in a bid to halt his movements. Instead, all it does is draw a low groan from his throat, which I feel vibrate against the most sensitive part of me.

For a heartbeat, Acker is frozen in place.

I say Fredrich's name in warning, but it comes out breathier than I intend, and it does nothing to stop him. Acker's expression falters a moment before a wave of outrage floods his features. His figure flickers as he surges forward, the stones still around my neck doing their best to keep him out, but they're not enough in the face of his wrath.

This time, my warning is sharp. "Fredrich!"

But I'm too late. Acker slams into Fredrich's ever-present shield, his outrage palpable as he yells out his anger. There are no coherent words, only searing hatred as he slams a fist against the invisible barrier again, teeth bared. I'm momentarily stunned by the raw emotion shining in his eyes.

Looking up from between my legs, Fredrich's pupils narrow as he angles his head in the direction of the unseen impact. I scream in alarm as the sword Fredrich had discarded on the desk flies through the air toward us. Fredrich doesn't flinch as the sword snaps, the sound of ringing metal reverberating against the air around us.

A cocky smirk stretches across his glistening mouth as he returns his eyes to me. "You didn't say stop."

Before I'm able to comprehend the meaning of his words, he's thrown my legs over the crook of elbows and dives back in. I cry out, fingertips scraping against the material of the chair. My eyes are locked on Acker's as the feel of Fredrich's mouth and tongue make me squirm and *oh my gods . . .*

I arch as one of Fredrich's fingers slips deep inside me.

Acker's chest is heaving with the force of his breaths, eyes wild as he watches me suppress a silent cry. Fredrich introduces a second finger and it's too much. All of this is too much. I don't know how I got here or how Acker's able to push past the power of the mangi stones, but when Fredrich returns to suck exactly where I need it at the same time, he curls his fingers . . . I *whimper*.

"Is this repayment for my wedding night?" Acker's upper lip is curled in disdain, but it isn't very convincing, not with the way his eyes are glued to the scene before him. "An attempt to hurt me like I hurt you?"

I shake my head from side to side.

He's not even supposed to be here.

Closing my eyes, I bite my lip in an effort to hold back the sounds threatening to spill from me due to the buildup of pleasure, but it's becoming more and more difficult to ignore the way Fredrich is determined to end me.

"Look at me."

Acker's voice comes from closer than I expect, and my eyes shoot open, landing on a gaze as dark as night. He's leaning over the back of the chair, and unless I'm mistaken in my lust-fueled haze, his expression looks almost wounded as he takes me in more closely. Everything about the way he's looking at me makes my heart squeeze painfully in my chest. Not a look of disdain or resentment, but how he looked at me when we were on the boat, just the two of us: with restraint and . . . and maybe even a little admiration. Like he can't help but appreciate the sight of me in the throes of pleasure regardless of where it's coming from.

His voice is rough when he says, "Tell him to make you come." My eyes widen at his words, but also from the way he wraps his hand around the column of my throat and angles my head back toward him. "Tell him," he growls, looming over me.

My words tumble out between breaths. "Make me come."

Fredrich hums as he continues to suck at the bundle of nerves and pump his fingers in and out. A moan slips from my mouth.

"A footman obeying his queen," Acker drawls. Wetting his lips, he leans closer, eyes hazy as he fights against the mangi stones. "You *like* knowing you have him at your bidding." His breathing nearly matches mine as his eyes fall to my open mouth. "At your *service*," he says, before swiping his tongue over my parted lips.

My eyes fall closed as I savor the taste of him.

Acker jerks back from my mouth, tightening the hold he has on my neck. "Look at me," he orders again.

I obey, my gaze landing on his dilated pupils, his eyes nearly black with need. He opens his mouth, telling me without words what he wants, and I open my own so he can lavish his tongue over mine. The memory I've held of what it's like to kiss him has done the reality of it little justice. It's all power and struggle and dominating in every way possible. I cave to it, letting Acker devour me as my hips buck, chasing pleasure against Fredrich. There's nothing I can do but submit to the moment.

Releasing Fredrich's hair, I cup the back of Acker's neck, pulling his face lower. He understands, mouth descending to my exposed neck and shoulder. It hurts, his teeth, as they scrape along my skin. Biting, tasting, punishing. The blood oath won't allow him to truly hurt me without dire consequences, but I need him to know my surrender is *my* choice and not *his*, and I dig my nails into the meat of his neck in warning.

I'm desperate as I race up the last stretch of pleasure to the peak, squeezing my eyes shut. There's a chorus of rattling and I have the vague sense that every mote of metal in my bedchamber is in danger from Acker's failing composure.

"Look at me."

The words are a demand. The powerful echo of an order, bordering on intrusive. But still, I obey. I'd do just about anything right now as long as it brought me to this moment. Blurry in my vision, Acker's dark eyes watch me as I come apart, my breath leaving me in a punch of ecstasy. I pull his mouth back to mine, wanting to disappear within him in this singular, perfect moment.

I never want it to end, but the high does eventually ebb into a simmering afterglow I'm not yet ready to face. And just as I think I'm fully spent, emotionally and physically, Acker removes his mouth from mine . . . and there isn't even a hint of that soft haze of adoration in his gaze.

He brushes his thumb over the apple of my cheek, eyes hardening further with each swipe. "So, you do still blush after all." Satisfied, he lets me go. "That was your one and only concession, Jovie. Don't let another man touch you again."

Chapter 26

JO

The clock on my desk ticks the night away until the sky begins to lighten, the rising sun casting a haze of gray across the sky. I tap the end of my charcoal pencil against the parchment on my desk.

My mind has been spinning all night, sleep a futile endeavor.

After Acker left, Fredrich gave me a wolfish grin, and after making a teasing remark about hoping my Match had as much fun as he did, he left before any awkwardness set it.

I still can't believe Acker was able to withstand the three layers of mangi I was wearing. On the rare occasion I've removed the stones from my body, it felt as though the far end of the tether was unmoored. Like a fishing line that snapped in the ocean. I've never tried to follow it, assuming any attempt would be in vain, knowing how smothering the mangi can be.

But Acker's found a way. He's conditioned himself to withstand the power of the stones.

It'd be impressive if it wasn't horrifying.

My mind is in chaos as I try to untangle the memories. There were so many nights I'd awoken from a dream that felt too real. Or mornings where I'd find something wasn't where I'd left it the night before. Letters shuffled around on my desk, texts open to a different page, the blanket pulled over me when I had no recollection of covering myself. Mind tricks meant to torment me, to figure out my agendas.

But the haunted look on his face when he saw me with Fredrich has polluted my mind, filling me with doubt. That moment when he realized there was nothing he could do to stop Fredrich. Despite that, I don't regret my decision. Not with the way Acker's gaze had heated and he decided to give rather than take away, as if it were *his* taste and *his* voice and *his* touch driving me to the peak, eclipsing everything else.

I look at the ticking clock once again. I'm supposed to meet Messer for conditioning soon, but there are only a couple of hours left before Drake is due to escort Acker and Irina to their awaiting ship. I've spent all night wavering over whether or not Acker deserves to know the full depravity of his father's doings, or if he'll just use the knowledge to further hurt me.

I suppose I'll find out.

By the time I get dressed and make my way to the stables, the sun has made its full appearance. The stable boy is unprepared to see me at this hour of the day, but he's quick to get a gelding tacked and ready for me. I slip him a couple of coins as an apology for disrupting his morning chores.

The horse handles well as I push him into a full gallop once we're outside the city. The wind is frigid, the sun not yet having had the chance to burn off the early morning chill. I head east toward the farmlands, where the river flows from Mount Zallis and curves far inland before swooping back toward the gulf. Farming families flourish near the fresh water. Cottages dot the landscape, but there's one in particular I'm interested in.

Once I see it from a distance, I stop the gelding, allowing him a moment of rest and a drink from a shallower stretch of the river. I refill my waterskin and take the opportunity to wash away the fine layer of sweat that chills my skin. I wipe my forehead dry with the back of my riding glove before I remove them both and stuff them in my pocket.

As I reach for the layers of stones around my neck . . . I hesitate. I chose not to take them off the entire way here just in case I changed my mind, but now is the moment of truth. I decide to quit letting doubt dictate my decisions. I take off the necklace and then the gyve, having to lift my shirt to pull it from around my abdomen.

My magic immediately responds, coming alive below my sternum, warming me from the inside out. A slight glow radiates from my hands as I prepare my mind to split, for the Bond to take me to Acker of its own volition. But when long moments pass and nothing happens, I feel for the tether. Unlike how it's felt for years, lax and unattached, it's now clearly anchored to the other side. Keeping a hand on my horse's reins, I follow it.

His voice reaches my ears before I see him, inflamed temper evident in the way he clips his words.

"—told you I would, didn't I?"

When I open my eyes, I'm standing in the bedroom of the cottage. Acker's pinched gaze swings to me instantly.

I'm relieved they're at least dressed.

Irina doesn't notice the shift in his demeanor. "If I get on that ship, I'm never going back home, Acker, and you know it."

His eyes never leave me, as if we're the only ones in the room. "Let me talk to Jovie. I believe after last night she owes me a favor."

Arrogant of him to assume . . .

"She wants to return to Strou?" I ask Acker.

"Yes," he says with a small nod.

Catching on, Irina's eyes widen as her gaze flits about the room, but of course she's unable to detect my presence. "*Please*," she pleads, knuckles white as she grips the footrail of the bed tightly.

I consider the odds that they're hiding motives unknown to me, but I can't think of any reason Irina returning home would benefit either of them.

"I have something to show you," I tell Acker.

He looks at Irina. "Give us a moment."

She's not happy with the lack of engagement from either one of us regarding her situation, but at least she knows better than to push. Acker shuts the door behind her. A new tension settles over the space between us. When he left last night, it was with a look of mixed anger and desire, and it seems he's still battling with himself, unclear on which emotion supersedes the other.

"There's someone I need you to see," I say, before he's able to decide.

"It wouldn't be the executioner, would it?"

I'm surprised by his levity, and I shake my head with a small smile. "No, but you may witness my own life end, depending on what kind of mood she's in."

"She?" he asks, stepping closer.

"It'll make more sense if I show you, instead of trying to just explain."

He eyes the open pack on his bed. "I'm supposed to be getting on a boat in an hour. By your order," he reminds me.

"Yes, but I can't let you go back without knowing everything. We should have plenty of time if you follow me through the Bond."

For the first time since I appeared to him, his defenses lower the tiniest amount, and he nods in acquiescence. He sits on the bed with his back to the headboard, feet crossed at the ankles and hands folded over his stomach. There's something so inherently primal about seeing him laid out on a bed that I take a fraction of a moment too long to look away.

He smirks. "After you," he directs.

Back in the field, I refocus on the reins in my hands and the wind in my hair. Acker appears moments later, blinking against the sun. He takes in our surroundings and the cottage in the distance, before setting his dark eyes on me.

"That's where we're going," I say, nodding toward the cottage.

I lead the horse by reins, and the gelding moves smoothly beside us as we traverse the field of tall grass. I'd expected things to be awkward between the two of us after last night, but we fall into a comfortable silence. Even during those first days when he was hiding in my shiel in Alaha, after I broke him out of the brig, it was easy to be in each other's presence.

It doesn't, however, make it easy to look at him. That's more painful than ever.

My curiosity gets the best of me. "Why does Irina want to return to Strou?"

"Her life at the capital hasn't been easy for her," he says, walking with his hands in his pockets. "She's homesick."

Interesting. "And you convinced her to flee the palace with you?"

"I promised I'd do my best to get her home in exchange for her help protecting us from your armada as we crossed the gulf."

I'm perplexed by his answer. I inspect him for any sign of dishonesty, but can't find any in his seemingly open expression. Then I recount Irina's pleading when she realized I was present in the room with them and it felt like raw emotion.

"I can't help facilitate her over the Strou border," I tell him, "But if you want to sail across the gulf to their shores, I won't stop you. I'll tell my armada to stand down to let you through."

He tilts his head to look at me, and it makes me feel out of depth for a moment. "That's very kind of you," he says, almost as of he is shocked I'm capable of kindness at all.

Once we reach the cottage, I speak as if I'm whispering to the horse as I tie him to a post anchored in front of the short path leading to the front door. "I can't let on that you're here, so don't do anything stupid." I check the windows to the cottage before risking one last look at Acker. "No matter what you learn, okay?"

He must sense my nervousness because he takes my warning seriously, eyes searching my features for an explanation. "All right."

His steps sound behind me as we walk up the stone pathway. While none of the plants and bushes lining the path are in full bloom this time of year, there's no mistaking the care and love that went into maintaining them. The garden curves around the steps, along the front of cottage before disappearing around the small home.

Taking a deep breath, I knock, nerves sending my heart into a frenzy. When the door finally opens, Grenadine's appearance is exactly as I remember it from our time in Alaha, when she lived in the shiel below mine on Urchin Row. Gray hair, withered features, and a hunched posture. Her expression is as derisive as ever, a smile revealing yellowed teeth.

"Brynn," she says. "Or do you go by Jovinnia, now?"

I lift a brow. "Either is fine. Although, 'your royal highness' has a nice ring to it, don't you think?"

Her smile grows. "And to what do I owe the pleasure of your presence, *my queen*?" she drawls.

"I'm sure that by now word of your son's arrival in the capital has spread this far."

Only I can hear Acker's intake of breath behind me.

I hold my features still as I inspect Grenadine—I'm sorry, *Cadence*—for a reaction, but come up empty-handed. Acker's presence at my back looms nearer. I can feel the heat of his body between my shoulder blades, the hint of his breath across my neck. He's standing *that* close to me.

"You know my stance on the matter," she says sharply.

I nod, because I do know. But . . . "I think you should reconsider."

She thinks about it for a long moment, her gaze shifting over my shoulder before she relents, standing to the side as she opens the door wider to allow me to enter. "I just happened to put a pot of tea on."

My heart races in my chest as I step over the threshold. I'm careful to close the door slowly enough to allow Acker time to follow behind me. I hold my breath as I feel his fingertips press into the center of my spine, a signal that he's with me the entire way.

Cadence's cottage is quaint but filled with luxury. The furniture is made with the best craftsmanship, textiles woven from the finest silks, and gold-embossed paintings hang from the walls. After she and a handful of other fugitives from Alaha arrived in Maile by commandeering one of the ships, my mother gave her a hefty amount of wealth to live on. *She may be your mother-in-law one day,* my mother had explained.

The old woman walks to the small kitchenette and takes down a second cup and saucer from the cupboard. "Sugar?" she asks with her back to me.

"Yes, please."

"Did you always know?" Acker asks, voice low even though Cadence can't hear him.

I take the moment to steal a glance at him. It's nothing more than a flick of my gaze, where I offer him a wordless shake of my head before I avert my eyes, but by the stonewashed color of his face, I can see he's in shock.

"One or two cubes?"

"Two, thank you."

"Sit," she instructs, carrying a serving in each hand.

I slide into one of the two chairs at the small table and accept the tea she slides toward me. She motions to the plate of uneaten toast and jam, already plated. I shake my head and she huffs in annoyance at my turning down her hospitality.

She adjusts her robe into a more comfortable position about her ankles as she sits, eyes full of mirth as she watches me tentatively sniff the scalding liquid before blowing on it. "It's not poisoned," she assures me, "but we can switch if you'd like."

I watch her over the lip of the cup but follow Acker's movements out of the corner of my eye as he ventures closer, steps imperceptible as he navigates more clearly into line of sight beside us, in front of the windows overlooking the small garden.

"You love my mother too much to harm me," I remind her, unnecessarily.

One eyebrow shoots up as she risks burning her tongue with a sip, licking her lips after. "That is true."

She places her cup down and settles her gaze on me.

My mother always says the first to speak in a stand-off is the first to lose. Cadence isn't my opponent, any more than I am hers, yet the tension in the room suggests otherwise.

I need to tread carefully. "Acker leaves within the hour."

"Hmm."

Fiddling with my cup, I make idle circles around the rim with a finger as I inhale the steam. "I think he should know the full scope of what his father is capable of before he returns to Kenta."

"Was he able to sway you that easily?" she asks, eyes dancing over the table. "A couple of days is all it took to weaken your resolve?"

"Beau believes he's being honest about his determination to take his father's throne." When she doesn't comment any further, I lean forward. "Don't you want to warn him?"

In the blink of any eye, anger shines from her eyes. "*You* tell him."

"Given our history, I'm not exactly considered a trustworthy source. Plus, I don't know everything. Not really."

She sneers before turning her head toward Acker. My heart skips a beat before I realize she's staring out of the window, and not at her son. A little color has seeped back into his face, but there's a carefulness to his features, something wary and guarded as his eyes remain fixed upon his mother's now aged face.

"How do I tell him that I ran to save myself?" Her voice is reedy, like she's squeezing the words from a closed throat. "That I abandoned him to be raised by a monster for my own sake?"

My mother had told me Cadence had apprehensions when it came to facing her son, to not push her on the subject if it were to arise, but I never expected this level of emotion from her. Her eyes are misty as she continues to look through her son and at the morning sky beyond.

"Maybe explain why you needed to run in the first place," I suggest.

Her face sours with disgust. "Edmond had been siphoning my magic from me for *years*."

I ask, "How?"

"With a slatstone," she says, like it's obvious.

But I am as thoroughly confused as I am disgusted by the concept. "What's a slatstone?" I repeat, dubiously.

She rolls her eyes, as if my skepticism is bothersome before leveling me with a look. "It's a stone that's been lost to history. Thought to be a myth by most scholars, but capable of pulling the magic from someone."

I'm almost scared to ask, but . . . "How does it work?"

And I'm only subjected to another withering look. "It acts much like a magnet. If someone knows where to find where the magic resides within a person, it's essence can be extracted through a wound."

"Is it only Edmond who has the stone?"

"He did," she says with a smug grin, brow raised. "That is, until I stole it and dropped it into the deepest parts of the ocean. If he's stealing magic, he must have found another."

Acker's voice is gravely in the small space. "The mines," he says, knowing only I can hear him. "That's why my father has been disappearing to them for years."

Mangi stone is found in the ocean, and hearthstone from deep within the earth. And now there's slatstone?

I resist the urge to look at Acker, but I can see him shift from the corner of my eye. "He used this stone on you."

"He needed to test the method. I didn't want to give him my magic, but I volunteered to let him try in the hope it would pacify him enough to leave Acker alone." She rolls her eyes. "As if Edmond could ever be capable of restraint, even when it came to his own son."

A new, unfettered fear weighs heavy in my gut. It takes everything in me not to look at him standing mere feet away when I ask: "He *took* from Acker?"

Blinking, she shifts in her chair before turning her gaze to her tea. "No. Acker hadn't shown any signs of awakening, but Edmond began to get restless around Acker's tenth birthday. I could see the idea taking root in his mind, to force magic upon our son before he was ready. Before his awakening."

I shake my head, horrified. "Most don't awaken until fully through puberty."

"Most, yes. But other powerful families in the territory have had children awaken early. I thought, if I could withstand the slatstones' pull that I could impede his efforts. Delay him, somehow. At least, until I could figure a way to get us out."

"My mother never explained how Edmond managed to do it," I say, dancing around the truth.

She swallows, the sound loud in the tiny apartment. "He started not caring how deep he cut, desperate to get to my magic, using hearthstone to stop me from healing."

From the corner of my eye, Acker wipes a shaking hand across his mouth, and I can only imagine how difficult this is for him to hear.

"I'm not sure if it was his desire for power or the euphoria that propelled him to become so adamant, but by the time he was finally able to source my gift, I'd nearly bled out."

"How did you manage to get free?"

"Greta." A small, almost imperceptible smile tugs at the corner of her mouth. "She told Edmond my death was inevitable, that she had seen it in her dreams, and to cart me off with the bodies already rotting from a flu that had swept through the city. She paid a merchant to get me on a ship to Alaha."

"Where you couldn't heal."

She shakes her head. "I think Edmond took every drop of magic I had that day, making it impossible for me to truly return to the way I was before, not even if I'd remained on land."

My voice comes out shallow. "May I ask what your gift was?"

A small, almost imperceptible smile tugs at her lips. "I was an elemental. *Metal.*"

The same as Acker's.

Something like a choked cough comes from Acker, having come to the realization of who his mother is: the old woman I lived above through my teenage years. The very same woman we bribed to be quiet during our escape. Not dead, as he's been led to believe.

"If I am to tell all of this to my son," Cadence says, leaning forward, and there's a glint in her eyes I don't like. "Are you going to tell him the real reason your mother handed you the crown?"

I do my best to appear indifferent, fingers tightening around my teacup to keep my hands steady. "It won't change anything."

"No?" she says, her smile turning more serpent-like by the second. "You don't think my son would care to know the agreement you made with Roison was in exchange for sparing his life?"

My blood freezes in my veins. She knows. *She knows Acker is here.*

She looks around the space as if she might actually see her son. "You think I was married to a man who was Bonded to another without learning their tricks?"

I rise from my seat. "You don't know what you're talking about."

She does the same, planting her hands firmly on the table as she leans toward me. "I don't?"

With a quickness I didn't expect her to possess, she yanks the knife from the open jar of jam and has it poised for my jugular in the blink of an eye. I reach for her wrist, but the dull blade is pulled from her grip before I ever make contact. Both of our heads whip toward Acker. My heart breaks as I take in his expression. Stony, with red-rimmed eyes. He looks between me and his mother, fist tight around the knife.

Cadence tracks the movement of the knife in his hand, the only thing she can see as her eyes flood with tears, as if she didn't truly believe he was here until now. "Son," she says, voice cracking. "Please, forgive me."

He shakes his head slowly, either in response to her plea or simply because there are too many emotions happening for him to voice anything. His hands are still trembling.

Cadence's tears fall steadily, eyes darting around as if she could see him if she just looked in the right place. "You have to understand, I never wanted you to see me like this."

Acker swallows hard before looking at me. "Leave," he orders.

"Acker—"

"*Now.*"

Rightfully chastened, I take one last look at Cadence before I turn for the door. The sound of her heartbroken sobs follow me outside.

Chapter 27

JO

I'm immediately concerned when I see Beau waiting for me when I return to the palace. "Why aren't you teaching?"

"I have a parent covering class for me." Beau's eyes narrow as I approach. "Where have you been?" she asks, borderline accusatory.

I pause in the kitchen's doorway and realize Sam has returned. Given the look on his and my mother's faces, it's not with good news. I've had enough revelations in the last three days to last a lifetime, and I suspect I already know Chryse's response to finding out my Match is in Maile.

"He's nervous you'll quit upholding your end of the bargain if you suspect the war is no longer in his favor," Sam says.

Sagging against the door frame, I push my windblown hair away from my face. "He knows Wren has made a deal with Edmond?" I ask.

"He didn't say, but he certainly suspects something is amiss. He went as far as mentioning a blood oath to ensure you're not going to turn on him."

My mother doesn't need to voice her opinion. I can see the displeasure in her face at the concept of me swearing a blood oath. When I came to her with the request to take over the crown, she promised to allow me the space to make my own decisions—and mistakes. But if I ever want any advice, all I need to do is ask.

"Thank you, Sam. I think it may be best to just let the pieces lie where they are at the moment."

He nods. "I agree."

Exhaustion lines his features, clothes rumpled from repeated leaps across the land, and it's unsettling. I've seen the man walk away from a day's battle and appear as if he had simply gone out for a gentle stroll.

"Did you see the front lines?" I ask.

His mouth thins, eyes sorrowful as he answers. "The Roison have pushed the fight well into Kenta's territory, leaving the land and Kenta people scarred in their wake."

My mother *tsks*. "Mother Nature isn't going to be happy."

"No, she isn't," he agrees. "We're going to be in for one hell of a winter."

I groan. "Does anyone have any good news?"

"Actually," Beau says, grimacing. "I received word from my mother this morning. She's found something . . . *interesting*."

By the way she jerks her head toward the stairs, it's clear this is a conversation she wants to have in private, so we leave Sam and my mother in the kitchen. He'll do the best he can to ease her worries, but he knows there's little he can say to reassure her. My decisions will, at the end of the day, be my own.

Beau and I don't speak until we're alone in her bedchamber. "Your aura is all over the place," she says, shutting the door behind me.

Beau's room is decorated in soft shades of neutrals. Everything from the curtains to the bedding to the rug on the floor is void of any patterned designs or starkly contrasting hues. It's at complete odds with her home in the ornate gaudiness of the Kenta palace. The only pop of color comes from the stack of mystery novels she has piled on her bedside table.

And as I sit on the edge of her made bed, I can maybe understand the calm such a minimalist style brings to her. "What did Greta find?" I ask, avoiding responding to her assessment.

She opens her mouth, as if to push me further on my current emotional state but then seems to think better of it. Standing at her desk, she picks up a stack of papers and hands them to me. They appear to be pages that have been ripped from an aged text. I skim the first few lines before I realize what I'm reading. It appears to be an old handwritten note, specifying exactly when and how an oath can be utilized.

"Where is this from?"

Beau pulls the last page from the pile and passes it to me, tapping on the emblem stamped underneath the philosopher's signature. The Strou's emblem. Red with the depiction of antlers. "My mother found it hidden in a text in Acker's bedchamber."

I return to where I left off, but most of it seems to relay things I am already aware of. A blood oath must be sworn using the blood of the person performing the oath mixed with soil from the land. The cost of breaking the oath, regardless of the oath's content, is the person's magic. But creating a blood oath with another while telling a lie, the price is higher: death. And due to this high price, it's a tool that can be used to reveal truths.

The next line has a hand drawn asterisk next to it.

If a sworn oath is given with an accompanying declaration of truth, the sworn promise is tied to that truth itself. As long as the declaration remains true, then the oath's binding will remain intact. In the event the truth no longer holds any value, then the oath will be null and void.

It feels like a stone drops to the pit of my stomach as I look up at Beau.

She nods. "My mother said it's from before she met my father, likely before Edmond held the thrown, even." She comes to sit on the bed next to me. "She found it in a text not contained in any of Kenta's archives, and after examining the simpler binding technique used on the pages, she surmises that Acker likely brought it back with him during one of his many visits to Strou."

Holy shit. *He knew.*

He knew when he made the oath with our combined blood that his promise to protect me would only hold as long as his declaration of love remained true.

And, I love her.

"But who's to say this is accurate?"

Beau shrugs. "We can't. Blood oaths are notoriously difficult to navigate. People have always looked for loopholes."

"Were you able to tell from Acker's aura if he still loves me?" I hate that I asked as soon as the words are out of my mouth, knowing it's not fair to her, but I need to know if he came to Maile to test the bounds of the oath after all this time.

Beau shakes her head, forlorn. "I would need to see how his aura interacts with yours to know. How did he react to Fredrich coming to your bedroom last night?" she asks, slyly.

My mouth parts in surprise. "How do you know about that?"

"I was worried when all of my hair pins went flying," she says, pointing to the wall behind me. Gold and silver metals dot the stone wall; the pins are embedded in the stone. "I was concerned, obviously, but just as I was about to rush into your room to save the day, I heard . . . *things*."

A blush creeps up my neck. "Great."

"I thought it was just my brother, so I waited outside, not wanting to intrude, but still wanting to make sure you were safe." She makes a face at the recollection that I don't think I've ever seen on her before; something like a mix of horror, embarrassment, and nausea. "Imagine my surprise when Fredrich was the one to walk out of your room."

"It was a terrible decision, I know," I groan.

Beau shrugs, expression contemplative. "Did it achieve what you wanted it to?"

I ponder her question as I remember the night before. How desperately I wanted a reprieve from the pain, so much so that I was willing to take the second option that walked through the door, only for the entire plan to be foiled by Acker's presence. How he became enraged. Then, in his own desperation to take me from Fredrich, it was almost as if he was . . . helpless to not participate. Like he couldn't *not* be involved in something—*anything*—that brings me pleasure.

"I don't know," I answer, honestly.

"Well, just a warning, Iona absolutely told your mother."

The doorkeeper is very much a tattle tale, but, somehow, my mother finding out about my nighttime debauchery is the least of my worries. "What time is it?"

"Wouldn't know," Beau says, flicking a hand toward the scattering of metal shards. "My timepiece is crushed into the wall."

I roll up the papers and hand them back to Beau. "Messer and Drake should be escorting Acker and Irina to their boat imminently. If he did come to test the oath, he's out of time."

"You took him to see Cadence this morning, didn't you?"

I nod. "Possibly another bad decision."

"Sometimes decisions aren't good or bad. Sometimes they're just decisions."

As I let her words soak in, everything feels heavy all of a sudden. There's still so much to be said, especially considering everything Cadence revealed to me. I look at Beau and she gives me a sad smile, knowing without words the weight I'm carrying. She sees it as much as I feel it.

I stand to leave, stopping at the threshold of her door. "Can you organize a meeting tonight?" I ask her.

"Sure," she says. "Want me to reserve the room at the tavern?"

I shake my head. "No. I want it here at the palace."

I don't want to risk the chance of anyone overhearing, not with this kind of world-altering information.

The evidence of last night's liaison is gone from my bedchamber. My robe, my lingerie: removed from where I left them on the floor when I bathed afterward. The made bed calls to me, but as I consider climbing in for a mid-morning nap, I realize I've made a grave mistake. My fingers reach for the gyve at my neck, but it's not there; I must have left it around the pommel of the gelding's saddle. I open my bedside drawer and find the last necklace of mangi stones I have. It won't be enough to stop Acker from breaching my side of the Bond if he wants to, that much is clear, but it's better than nothing. At least while I'm awake.

I'm hesitant to put it on.

Even though he needs to leave Maile for multiple reasons, the Bond is already protesting. It's been four years since I left Kenta, and the three days he's been in Maile have felt like the first time I've been allowed to drink my fill of water after being deprived of even a single drop. As if being apart from him is equivalent to being in those mysterious lands of rumor where there's only desert and sand and no drop of water in sight. My magic hates being deprived of my Match's presence.

Stepping out onto the terrace, I lean against the balustrade as I stare at the white sails in the distance. From here, the wharf is but a tiny curved line jutting into the gulf. I can't differentiate which ship is Acker's from the rest of them tied to the wharf. Yet, my eyes linger on one in particular. The tether below my breast wants to lead me straight to him.

I'm toying with the necklace between my fingers when I feel him behind me. I don't move as he takes a deliberately loud step forward to signal his approach, his hands appearing on either side of me on the railing, caging me in between his arms. I call my dagger, holding it in one hand, and the necklace in the other. The latter won't do much good if he's no longer bound by the oath, but its familiar weight makes me feel better.

His chest presses into my back and warmth blooms through every inch of my body.

"I've always craved your scent," he says, nose trailing up the side of my neck as he inhales deeply. "The iron in the blood running through your veins mixed with the scent of wildflowers." My heart picks up its pace and I know he can feel it. "I thought it was just because I wished to see it spill . . ."

Steeling myself, I turn in the circle of his arms to meet his gaze. Dark and guarded and so godsdamned beautiful that it feels unfair. "Did you come all this way just to kill me?"

"Kill you?" A confused smile pulls at his mouth, and I find myself enamored by it. "Why would I kill you?"

"I know about the oath," I say, despising the breathlessness of my voice. "How it's tied to the truth declaration."

His smile only grows, teeth flashing when he speaks. "I thought it was clever."

I tighten my grip on my blade, but he is unbothered by the weapon as he settles more of his weight along the length of my body. Tucking my stray hairs behind my ear, he has unfettered access to the exposed, vulnerable part of my neck where my life source flows. He leans in, and I'm surprised when his lips land on the edge of my jaw instead. I hold my breath as his lips trail toward my mouth. I try to turn my head away, but he stops me with the grip of his fingers on my chin, keeping me in place.

He tilts his head back to look me in the eyes, searching. "You negotiated for my life."

The denial sits on the tip of my tongue, but there's a hint of softness in his gaze that stops me.

His gaze descends to my open mouth again, lingering there for a moment before dropping lower. I try to temper my breaths, but they come in large gulps. He releases hold of my chin, fingers coasting over my jaw to my exposed throat. Goosebumps spread across my neck and chest at the feeling of his featherlight touch.

Licking his lips, his eyes flick up to meet mine once again. "You would never do that for someone you don't love."

I swallow in a bid to clear my throat. "On the contrary, I'd do it for just about anyone."

He laughs, low and delicious. "You're still so beautiful when you lie."

I neither confirm nor deny his accusation as his lips return to my pulse, tongue dipping out to taste me, and I clamp my teeth shut in an effort not to reveal how much it affects me. I can feel his smile as he places open mouth kisses up the side of my neck until he reaches the shell of my ear.

His voice sends chills down my spine as he says, "I was *always* going to come for you."

My heart stops, the stone necklace falling from my hand as I reach for him. In defense or otherwise, I'm unsure, but I'm left aimless when he disappears. It's not Acker's sudden departure that has me nearly leaping out of my skin, though, but the man standing in the open doorway of my bedchamber.

"Fredrich," I whisper, shoulders sagging with relief. "What are you doing here? Everything okay?"

He doesn't immediately respond, and there's something in his eyes that puts me back on edge.

I take a cautious step back.

Then he blinks, as if snapping out of a trance, and a small smile pulls at his mouth. "Of course. Are *you* okay?"

His confusion is noticeable enough to make me question my sanity. Acker has well and truly fucked with my mind. "Yeah," I say, with a relieved huff of breath.

I look down over the railing, at the last of my mangi stones lying in the courtyard below. A rabbit is nibbling on it. When I call out for it to stop, it decides to pick it up and hops off with it. *Dang rabbits.* I'm going to have to risk life and limb to get it back.

Fredrich's voice comes from directly behind me. "I want you to know, I think you're the best leader I've ever had the honor of serving. Strictly speaking as a soldier of the crown."

The statement makes my hair stand on end, and when I turn back around, he's within arm's length. My discomfort returns in full force as I retreat a step, back hitting the railing.

"Although, the perks of serving under you in particular were definitely nice," he adds, a playful glint in his eye.

I'm beyond confused as I watch my friend undo the top button of his shirt, pulling out a handkerchief. He takes one last step forward, putting us toe to toe. There is neither hostility nor heat in his eyes as he looks at me. If anything, he appears . . . apologetic? Then my eyes snag on the exposed portion of his chest, the mottled skin and the single letter carved into it. My blood runs cold in my veins. The V-shaped scar stands out in stark contrast against his pale skin.

I open my mouth to scream for Beau, but he shoves the cloth over my mouth and nose, pinning me to the railing with his body, his other hand grips the back of my scalp to hold me still. The bittersweet scent of the fungi we had used to ease the passing of the mortally wounded after battle fills my lungs.

The sky above fades to black.

Chapter 28

ACKER

The sound of something heavy hitting the wharf has me pivoting in place and I find Wells standing with his bag at his feet.

I level an unimpressed look at him. "What the hell are you doing here?"

He lifts his chin in determined defiance. "When it comes down to it, if you're set on killing your father I don't want you to have to live with being the one to do that."

He knew something was wrong the moment I walked out of the cottage bedroom after Jovie pulled me with her this morning. I told him the horrifying truth about my mother, about how my father has managed to regain magic and what it costs. It took everything I had to keep my voice from trembling as I told him what I saw. My mother, withered beyond the point of recognition.

I recall the days leading up to my mother's death. No one explicitly told me she had fallen ill with the same sickness that was sweeping through the territory, but I was able to put the pieces together myself. After, when my father called me into his sitting room to break the news, it felt unreal. I was numb. I remember feeling as though she couldn't be dead, because . . . wouldn't I be stricken with sadness, if she were?

But the sadness never came. The tears never fell. Aside from the slight pinch in my chest, all I remember feeling was lost. Confused, as my father poured me a glass of wine. My first ever. He spoke to me like an equal, something I hadn't experienced from him before, and I was perplexed by it. His change in demeanor was not enough to satisfy my cravings for his attention, but I was also oddly relieved. As if I'd finally accomplished what I had always wanted, which was to make my father proud.

Now, I realize, none of my feelings were a natural reaction to being told my mother had died, regardless of how minimally she participated in my upbringing. I never felt unloved by my mother, but moments when I received her affection were few and far between. Once Greta came into our lives, my mother became a shell of her former self. Whether it was my father's doing or her own, I may never know.

Bearing witness to my mother's remorse muddles the image I've held of her for most of my life, and I'm not exactly sure what to do with it.

Taking a breath, I shake myself from my thoughts and try to take the emotions welling up inside me and meet my friend's gaze. "Olivia," I say, letting his wife's name hang between us as an unspoken question.

"She knows I'm here."

"And she's fine with it?"

He shakes his head with one quick motion. "Not in the least. She's afraid, and she hasn't had the utmost faith in you as of late. But she also doesn't want our child to grow up without our families." Shrugging, he lifts his brows. "If given the chance, we'd like to return to our lives in Kenta. I want to try to help make that happen."

Wells and Olivia have long been hinting that I should be the one on the Kenta throne. They've been critical of my father's leadership and laws since we were young. I can't help but feel undeserving of their friendship and it makes the weight of my mother's revelations somehow heavier and lighter at the same time.

"I'm not sure I'm going to do any better as king."

I inspect the crew loading our ship with goods—the exact amount for the time needed to sail home. No more, and no less—under the supervision of the Maile soldiers that congregate on the wharf, and then the flags flying on the masts of the Maile ships moored nearby, displaying the tallies of the men they've killed—men from Kenta.

"Kenta's territory has already been ravaged by my hands," I tell him.

"Hands your father has tied behind your back." His presses his hand to my shoulder, drawing my gaze toward him. "You were his puppet."

Wells had wanted to flee Kenta, was willing to cross swords with me to ensure Olivia's safety. And now he's offering me something worth more than a king's ransom—to be the one who ends my father's life so I won't have to do it myself.

"I can only live with your choice if it doesn't come at the cost of your life."

He grins, cockiness peeking through. "It won't."

"Wells, you have a baby on the way."

"And she'll be here waiting to meet me when I get back."

I give him a skeptical look, and he sobers, tension lines bracketing his mouth right before he pulls me into an embrace. It catches me off guard. Wells doesn't hug. *Ever.* The only person I've ever seen him be affectionate with is Olivia. I take a deep breath, prolonging the embrace for as long as I can until I'm forced to let him go.

"Adorable," the archer chirps as he approaches, motioning for us to embark from the end of the gangway. "Let's go."

We grab our bags and board the ship and I turn toward Irina, already waiting on deck. She's sullen and I know there's nothing I can say or do that will lift her mood. I didn't tell her about the offer Jovie gave to allow us to cross the gulf to Strou. It wouldn't do any good. I have to order the ship to return in the direction of Kenta, and if she were to find out the reason why I didn't bring her home, it would crush her.

The Maile ships escort us outside the breakwaters, watched nervously by the crew of our ship, who are as concerned as they are relieved to see our return.

"At least I'm not going to be worked half to death this go-around," Irina mutters. "I'm taking the first officer's cabin." She doesn't wait for anyone to dispute her claim and takes the stairs leading below.

We waste no time setting the sails and moving while the wind is on our side, and by dusk we've put enough distance between us and Maile's shoreline that the wharf and city beyond are no longer visible. Once I'm sure we're out of sight, I issue the command for the crew to drop anchor. I ask the helmsman about our position in relation to the nearest shoreline. We're orientated toward Kenta, and no more than a mile offshore. I order the crew to keep a close eye on the water as we wait.

I'm anxious.

The sun is dipping toward the horizon fast and it'll be hard to find anything in the water after dark. The Bond has been smothered most of the day, but I can't tell if it's Jovie's doing or if it's due to the sedative Fredrich planned on using to subdue her. There's no way to know if he succeeded, having most recently spoken to him last night, but the lack of tension from the tether is pissing me off.

One of the deckhands yells and I follow his pointed finger to the starboard side. The dingy rocks alarmingly in the swell and the crew is quick to get ropes cast in order to hoist it up to safety.

That's when Wells chooses the worst possible time to appear from below. Not that I intended on hiding my plans from him, but it would be so much easier to explain myself after the fact, instead of him being here to witness this happening firsthand.

I twirl the blade in my palm, needing something to alleviate the restless anticipation of her arrival.

The sound of the mangi chains clanking as she thrashes against her bindings makes my chest tighten. My back is to them as they're hauled aboard. I stand between Wells and the proceedings, but I hear Fredrich grunt during the commotion. I keep my eyes on Wells's face as he comes to understand exactly what's happening, his expression contorting in anger.

"You stole the fucking *queen* of Maile."

"No," I correct him. "I stole my *Match*."

Her screams are muffled, her mouth gagged, if I had to guess. Wells's eyes watch them avidly over my shoulder and I begin to turn around just as Fredrich finally hauls Jovie out of the dingy and onto the deck.

There's a heavy thunk, followed by a cuss from Fredrich that brings a smile to my face. Then a sharp, stinging sensation echoes across the Bond, and I still the twirling blade in my hand.

"Watch it," I snarl, head turned just enough to see my friend out of my peripheral vision.

He bends down and hefts the writhing queen over his shoulder. "I'm not hurting her," he assures me. "Whatever pain she's feeling, she's inflicted on herself."

He somehow manages to keep hold of her flailing body as he marches toward the main cabin. I risk a direct glance in the last moment before they disappear behind the cabin's door. Jovie's hair is a wild mane around her head as she thrashes, hands threaded together in a prayer position with rope to block her ability to call her blade, feet cinched together tightly to stop her kicking. I once threatened to hog-tie her, when she thought I would ever leave Alaha without her, and a deranged part of me is bothered by the fact that Fredrich is the one to actually do it. Her head twists in my direction but I divert my gaze before she's able to make eye contact.

The door swings shut behind them, and as if snapping out of a trance, the crew returns to their normal tasks.

"The oath," Wells says, eyes wide as his gaze swings to me. "How?"

I return my dagger to the strap across my chest and begin rolling up the sleeve of my shirt. "She's safest with me," I explain. "By taking her, I am protecting her."

"Bull. *Shit.*" He points to the cabin's closed door and the muffled noises emanating from beyond it. "*He* wasn't in Maile by *chance.*"

The door to the cabin swings back open and Fredrich steps out, looking a little worse for wear. He jerks the door closed behind him and scrubs a hand over his mussed hair, before straightening the collar of his shirt and turning to lock eyes with me.

He already knows what's coming, because he holds up a placating hand. "Before you start, you should know I was saving a comrade's life. If it wasn't me, it would have just been someone else and you would have undoubtedly killed him."

Wells is rightfully confused, his head swiveling between the two of us as we close in on each other.

I finish rolling up my other sleeve. "Does it look as though I give a fuck?"

"You should be thanking me." Fredrich's smug grin ratchets my anger up another degree. "I could have fucked her."

My fist connects with his jaw before he can take his next step, sending him stumbling backward. Wells cusses as all work ceases around us, the crew once again distracted.

"Shut your fucking mouth," I snarl at him.

Rubbing the sore spot on his jaw, he has the nerve to hold a finger up to me. "That was your one free pass. Try to hit me again and you'll regret it."

It's doubly infuriating to know he's only speaking the truth. He *let* me hit him. If he hadn't dropped his shield, it's likely I would have broken every bone in my hand and wrist. Over water, it would have taken forever to heal, maybe even incorrectly.

"You could have told her 'no.'"

He gives a half-hearted shrug, as if the effort to give a whole one is not worth the effort. "Where would the fun have been in that?"

Retrieving a dagger from my harness, the metal like an extension of myself, I sling it directly at his throat. It hits the wall of invisible resistance surrounding him but doesn't shatter or rebound, not as I continue to drive it forward, my hand outstretched as I take a menacing step toward my friend. The blade vibrates as it creeps closer to its mark.

His eyes don't even stray to the weapon, gaze unwavering as he looks at me. "I watched the sacrifices she made for her own men. Saw her go days on end without sleeping. Stare down death without an ounce of fear."

A crack sounds and my hand shakes as I struggle to keep up the pressure on the dagger. The distaste in his expression makes my stomach twist.

"And I wish you could have seen her face when she was informed of your arrival. It was so fucking filled with *hope*. It was the first time I'd ever seen that level of emotion in her in all the years since you asked me to keep watch over her. Only for you to fucking crush it by showing up with your *wife*, wanting her *men* instead of *her*."

My tone is warning enough as I say, "You know better than anyone exactly why I came, and it has nothing to do with her men."

He huffs. "You may want to kill me right now, Ace, but I think we both know it's not me you're really upset with."

His words are clearly chosen with the intention to piss me off and it fucking works. There's no way I'm mistaken about exactly who I'm angry with, and it's definitely the friend I entrusted with my Match's safety. Not that Fredrich would ever be able to understand. The few times in the past we were able to drag him to a tavern for a drink or two, he turned down every person who ever made an advance on him. He's never spoken of a fling, never even hinted at a love interest. I mean, we all thought the man was fucking celibate, for godssake.

Fredrich slaps Wells on the shoulder. "It's good to see you, my friend," he says, sending one last glare in my direction before heading below to find a bunk.

Wells's gaze slides to me and there's a look on his face that I can't identify. "You're a rightful mess," he says, then leaves me alone on the deck with my thoughts.

Chapter 29

ACKER

By the time we arrive at the port town deep into Kenta, I'm itching to step foot on land. I thought being stranded on a boat with Olivia's ire was bad, but it doesn't hold a candle to the misery of the trip back.

My days have been spent listening to the sound of chains rattling through the thin walls of Jovie's cabin. She's livid. The kind of angry that can be felt in the bones. I know the feeling well, having felt it for long after her betrayal.

But in the night, when her exhaustion wins over and she's too tired to fan the flames of her ire, the desire to go to her is all-consuming. And she's so close. Too close, honestly. It's become a true testament to my self-control, when all I want is to hear her say the words to me. That she loved me then, even when she betrayed me, and may love me still after all this time.

I try to hold on to the reminders of why I'm angry with her, but they all seem weak in comparison to what we're facing. The plans that my father has concocted and the darkness of this war on the horizon. But Jovie could see it. She lived it in Alaha, and she always knew change was coming.

While I've been contending with my fragile restraint, Irina has been sullen and only comes out of her room for meals. Fredrich and I have barely spoken, mostly due to my own lingering frustrations with him. And Wells has been quiet. I can practically feel the judgment rolling off him every time he sees me.

Snow flurries over the port, the flakes melting as soon as they hit the ground. We had to sail far upriver. Farther than I would have liked, but the larger ports near the mouth of the Yanka River were swamped with soldiers from the palace. This port, for instance, is small and not usually manned by more than a handful of men, but there's a handful of soldiers present on the dock with a jail cart full of prisoners waiting to be loaded onto a boat, their clothing filthy and hair matted from their time kept in the town's prison. Collars adorn their necks.

Heirs to be transported to the palace.

To my father.

We're not close enough to the palace that I worry about being recognized, but I pull up my hood and keep my head down as I walk through the streets, just to be safe.

No one seems perturbed by the heavy presence of soldiers. People meander from storefront to storefront, congregating on the walkways to chat, as if everything is normal. The farmers' market I'm looking for is tucked into a wide alley between two buildings not far from the dock. These are vendors who travel far and wide across the territory to sell and trade their goods, the very ones who would make the trip to the southern coast for the annual Market with the Alaha. If there's gossip to be heard, it'll come from their mouths. There's one vendor I'm looking for in particular, and I find her stall at the very end of the row. She doesn't notice me at first. Her back is to me as I approach her table to take a look at the pastries she has on display.

"I was hoping to find you here," I say, drawing her attention.

When she turns around, her pierced eyebrow lifts in surprise. "The metal slinger of Kenta," she says, smile growing wide. "To what do I owe this honor? It's been, what? Five years? Six?"

"The final Market," I answer, remembering the last time we connected.

I look at the bustling crowd around us and she gets the hint, waving me behind her counter for a little more privacy. She places a sign on the table before pulling a string, lowering a cloth over the front of the booth.

Once alone in the shadows, her smile turns flirtatious. "Rumor has it you've flown the coop," she says.

"Gossipers do love to spin tales," I say in turn.

Her fingers dance over the collar of my shirt. "Hmm," she sounds. "Is this unexpected visit one of pleasure then?"

I let her indulge in her fantasy for a moment while we talk. "What's the word on the street about why the palace has sent so many soldiers here?"

"We've been told they're here to relieve the town prison's overcrowding problem, but there have been rumors saying that only Heirs are being moved, that there's another crackdown on any Heirs who commit so much as a minor infraction."

"Such as?"

"Things like vandalism, getting caught saying anything remotely negative about the king, or just being too drunk or rowdy at a pub." She continues to fiddle with my shirt, slipping a button free, fingers digging to the exposed skin of my chest. "But I heard of a town nearby where *everyone* was taken. Even the *babes*."

My blood runs cold. "Where?"

"East," she says, hands slipping down to the waistline of my pants. "A town where no one wore collars."

"Have you ever seen or heard of a slatstone?"

Her fingers dip under my shirt, touch skimming the skin of my stomach. "Slatstone," she says, almost absently. "I think I remember my grandmother used to tell tales of a stone called something of the sort, but I've never seen one myself. Why?"

Having gotten what I need, I stop her ministrations with a gentle hand on her wrist. "Thank you, Phoebe." Leaning forward, I kiss her on the cheek, letting my lips linger. "Go home, okay?"

When I pull away, the flirtation in her eyes is gone, understanding in its place. She's as good at swindling information as I am. If she was needing confirmation that things are going sideways in this war, I'm more than happy to give it to her, no flirtation needed.

"Maybe next time, then?"

I smile at the teasing in her voice. "Be safe," I say in answer and farewell.

I make one final stop at the dovecote on the outskirts of the town. The elderly man behind the counter eyes me long enough that I'm positive he knows my identity, but I'm grateful when he doesn't pry. I write my message and seal it in a metal cylinder with wax. When he goes to take it from me, I shake my head and slide a few extra coins across the counter.

"I want to see the bird released." There's no room for argument in my tone.

He stares at the coins before sliding them into his palm. He disappears through the door behind him, returning with a pigeon in his hands. Without saying a word, he shows me the identifying band naming the town we're currently in on its left leg, and the destination it's trained to fly to on the right. I tie the message to its harness and when he walks out from behind the counter I follow him to the front door of the dovecote. Opening the door just wide enough to stand in the threshold, he throws the pigeon into the air, and we both watch as the bird gets its bearings before turning to the west.

"Happy?" he asks.

I nod, smiling at his evident annoyance. "Very."

I give him one more coin just to completely ensure that he'll keep his mouth shut about my identity, but something tells me he's read and seen enough in his life that he couldn't care less as to who I am or why I'm here. If anything, I've only insulted him for being distrustful of his discretion.

Returning to the ship, I hunt down Fredrich. He's not on the deck, or below in the cabins, so I venture down into the hold in a bid to find him. It's been emptied of provisions. Any of the few remaining supplies from Maile were dumped once we reached the mouth of the river. It's here that I find Fredrich sitting on an empty wine barrel.

Our conversations were minimal throughout the voyage. After I explained my father's alliance with the Alaha and the gifts he's acquired, Fredrich asserted that the best chance anyone has of killing my father would be with his help. As much as it pains me to admit that I agree, his shield is too valuable to not utilize.

He sits with a knee bent and his sword balanced across his lap as he runs a stone down the length of the blade. An empty glass is perched on a beam next to him.

"Well," he says, glancing up at me. "What's the plan?"

"There's apparently a nearby town that's been emptied in a raid by palace soldiers. Hopefully we can find some lodgings that have been abandoned in a usable condition."

There's a slight pause before he continues to sharpen his blade. "I thought you wanted to usurp your father," he says.

"I'm not going to take my Match anywhere near the man who's siphoning magic from Heirs like a leech."

Fredrich's expression is contemplative. "How are we going to get her through the port without being found out?"

"Irina."

"Even if she can cast an illusion over all of us, it won't matter if the queen doesn't cooperate. All it would take is a good scream and they'll see straight through Irina's glamor."

His insistence in referring to Jovie by her title irks me. "I'll handle Jovie," I tell him before turning to leave. "Be ready to disembark in thirty."

It's his huff of annoyance rather than his words that has me stopping in place. "I watched you and Hallis run through plenty of brothels in our youth, you know," he says, curtly. "I know it's different, because Jo is your Match, but I made the love of your life come, Ace. I didn't fucking kill her. When are you going to let it go?"

Grinding my teeth, I turn to eye him. "How many glasses of wine have you had?"

"A few," he admits.

"Still haven't gotten over your fear of water?"

"It's not a fear of the water," he protests. "It's being stuck on a boat that drives me mad. There's nothing to do but . . ."—he waves a hand in the air—"drink."

"It wouldn't have anything to do with being unable to fully access your shield, would it?"

My words give him pause, his eyes cutting to the strap of daggers across my chest. "Is that a threat?"

I shrug half-heartedly. "Just an observation."

After assessing me carefully, he returns to sharpening his blade. "I'm not scared of you, Ace. Shield or no shield."

I tell myself to walk away, to let the issue lie for the time being, but I simply *can't*. I clench my jaw before I'm able to force the words past my lips. "Thank you. For protecting her."

He could use this moment to mock me, to drive the proverbial knife a little deeper, but he doesn't, merely dipping his chin in customary Kenta fashion as he says, "Of course."

Truth is, I never doubted that he'd do it and do it well. I didn't have to lie awake at night and wonder if she was okay like I had done for so many years growing up, when I hadn't known if she was alive or dead. I knew she was safe *because* Fredrich was with her.

"But let's be honest," I say, narrowing my eyes at him. "It may have been your mouth that was on her, but it was *me* she was submitting to."

His smirk returns, but it's good natured. "Whatever you need to tell yourself, my friend."

I turn before he can see my grin. "You can't even whistle."

"Hey! You swore to keep that a secret."

Chapter 30

JO

I've been kidnapped. *Again.*

My body aches from being stuck in this unnatural position for so long. Shackles lock my wrists together, the same at my ankles. But it's my hands that hurt the most, the thin rope woven around each finger and across my palms, tying them together in a position of prayer. It has been sort of helpful while asking the gods to strike Acker down with a giant bolt of lightning since I've been in this bed. The bed I'm chained to, just in case I manage to undo all of my bindings, which truly would require an intervention from the gods.

There's a knock on the door followed by a silent pause, and I roll my eyes at the idea of anyone attempting to appear polite, given the circumstances. I'm chained to a bed, for gods sake. There's nothing hospitable about any of this.

The knock comes again.

For fucks' sake. "Come in!" I yell, begrudgingly.

When Acker's figure is the one to slip through the door, I sit up. There's no mistaking his height and stature in the dim cabin. Dark hair, strong shoulders, every inch of him lean muscle.

Neither of us speaks as he closes the door behind him. Leaning against it, the back of his head lolls against the wooden surface. Tiny streams of sunlight filter through the gaps between the planks of the ship's deck, the only bit of light in the otherwise dingy space. It offers little to see by, though, and shadows shield the expression on his face.

Venom pools at the tip of my tongue, ready to be spat at him, but something holds me back. Strange, after having nothing better to do for days but fantasize about all the things I would spew at him the moment he finally appeared in front of me. Now, here he stands, and I can't seem to muster the energy to say anything at all.

"We need to walk through the town to get to the stables and I need you to behave like an honest prisoner."

For a brief moment, I'm confused. Then amused, a giggle escaping from my mouth, followed by full-throated laughter. The sound bounces off the cabin walls. It can't be stopped as tears leak from my eyes, my stomach cramping as I struggle to get myself under control.

After many deep, shuddering breaths, I'm able to wheeze out a few words at last. "Honest prisoner? Compared . . . compared to *what*?" I hold up my wrists, and it sucks all the humor from my voice, my tone turning steely in the blink of an eye. "*This?*"

He strides forward, a beam of light scorching across his face for a split second as he moves toward me. "You've been in Maile for too long. Have you forgotten the ways in which my father likes to handle traitors?"

No, unfortunately not.

I've seen enough death on the battlefield to know the cages strung from the walls of the Kenta palace were worse. At least dying in combat is normally quick. The memory of running past the emaciated father crying for his family in one of the cages still haunts me.

"And you never once saw the dungeons," Acker says, knowing exactly what I'm thinking about. He's standing at the foot of the bed, close enough for me to make out the slight tilt of his head and downturned gaze.

"Well, I guess I'm going to find out, aren't I?"

"We're not going to the palace."

"Where are you taking me, then?"

"Somewhere safe."

His answer has me clenching my teeth. "I was safe in Maile," I snipe.

"No, you weren't. I had a man tailing you for years and you never suspected a thing."

I sneer at the reminder of Fredrich's treachery. "Then maybe I should say: I was safe in Maile from everyone but *you*." I can hear the grind of his teeth as his jaw flexes, but still, he keeps his face hidden in shadow. I lean forward as much as I'm able in the shackles. "Why aren't you looking at me?"

He swallows, the sound audible in the small space.

"You can't, can you?"

"No."

The single word washes over me, making my blood run cold for a single heartbeat before turning blistering hot in my veins. "Why not?" I ask, voice coming out flatter than I intended. "Are you ashamed? You've done the very same thing that was done to me as a child. Or is it that you're still disgusted by me after all this time, despite finally realizing that I was telling the truth about your father all along? As appalled as you were four years ago when I betrayed you, it's not like you were so fucking innocent—"

"*Enough*," he snaps, grip tight on the bed frame. "It's already difficult to *hear* your restraints, let alone *see* them." He pushes away from the bed, turning his back to me. "And I have no intention of testing the oath's limits."

I suck in a sharp breath.

A shameful kernel of hope threatens to take root inside of me. But without trust, it doesn't have any nourishment to help it grow. He could be lying. Distracting me from the fact I'm currently his prisoner.

"It's not the oath you should be scared of anyway," I say. "Because my mother is going to kill you."

"Your mother wouldn't kill your Match."

He speaks as if it's an undeniable truth and I scoff at his arrogance. "She killed her own Match for hiding me in Alaha. She definitely has no reservations about killing *mine*."

His head snaps up in my direction but manages to keep his eyes averted from my bound form. "What are you talking about?"

"My father became fearful of Edmond's relentless pursuit of other gifts, and when I showed early signs of awakening, he took me to live with the Alaha, knowing Edmond would never leave land to look for me. It wasn't until years later that my mother found out he was responsible . . . and then he refused to reveal my location."

"But Osiris confessed to taking you during the annual conclave, claimed your death was an accident, and she killed him on the spot. There were witnesses. Unless . . ." He turns his head to the side, never looking at me fully. "*Osiris* is your father."

"Yes."

"What of Leo, your mother's guard? The one she married and crowned king?"

"That's a story for another day. But if you believe being my Match affords you any protection, you couldn't be more wrong. There's likely an entire army already headed your way."

After a moment, he nods. "Good," he says. "We're going to need the men."

At first, I'm taken aback by his cavalier attitude. Then it hits me. "You plan on using Wren's power of influence on my men," I say, voice hollow to my own ears.

Acker's response is swift, cutting. "You know my stance regarding enforced loyalty, yet you believe me capable of controlling an army of men by robbing them of their free will?"

"I don't know if I ever really knew what you're truly capable of."

He smiles, the upturn of his lips visible from his profile, but there's no humor in it. "You don't like the taste of your own medicine?"

My words come out sharp. "*Fuck you.*"

His responding chuckle as he leaves the cabin has me seeing red, and

I have nothing better to do in the silence than think of all the ways I can rip out his tongue. *Hate* isn't a strong enough word for what I feel for him. Doesn't even skim the surface of the ocean of loathing I'm swimming in.

Every breath, every heartbeat, fuels the fire raging inside of me.

Chapter 31

JO

Acker pulls a hood up over his head, obstructing my view of his face as we—Fredrich and Irina on either side of me—follow him and Wells through the streets of the port town from a distance. My legs are stiff after being chained together for so long. The eyes of two passing soldiers land on me, and Fredrich picks up his pace, Irina's arm brushing against mine as we hurry to keep up.

Once we departed the ship, we split into two groups. The five of us together is sizable enough to draw attention and I was given strict instructions to be as unassuming as possible. Difficult, considering my hands are still shackled and tied beneath the cloak I'm wearing. It makes walking surprisingly awkward.

My gaze darts in every direction. The buildings are all two or three stories high, dwarfing us on either side. The town is small, but it's jam-packed with pedestrians. Each alleyway is filled with vendors selling different food and wares. These must be the very same vendors who sell at the annual Market, or . . . they did when it used to take place in the cliffs on the southern coast of Kenta.

"Whatever you're scheming," Frederich says under his breath. "Don't."

I suppress an eye roll. As if I want to trade one sort of captivity for another. No, if I'm going to escape, I'm going to do it when there's not an even worse adversary in the vicinity. As difficult as it is to admit, even to myself, Acker's warning isn't to be taken lightly. The very last hands I'd ever want to fall into belong to Edmond.

It's as if Fredrich has reverted back to that soldier I used to despise. Too serious and frustratingly ill-mannered. I'm all the angrier that I didn't see him for what he really was the first time I laid eyes on him, hiding in an alleyway, as I began to explore Maile on my own. I saw him again the next day, and again the day after that. He never approached me or appeared hostile, so I assumed he was sent by my mother to keep an eye on me, after the many arguments we'd had about me wandering around alone. Later, when I'd asked her about a soldier following me, she admitted to directing Sam to have his men keep an eye on me, making my conclusion an easy, if dumb, one.

"How were you able to infiltrate my mother's forces without raising suspicion?" I ask, keeping my voice low.

"It was a process," he says, and I can practically hear the weight of that statement in his voice. "Started at the tavern, found some of the lower ranked sailors who had enough ale in them to squeeze out information. I learned the military structure, where men were positioned across the territory, and who commanded each battalion. Once I figured out that soldiers from the neighboring farms would sometimes get put on duty within the city, it was easy to slip into the ranks as a reluctant soldier in a stolen uniform after dropping a few well-chosen names."

Well, that's embarrassing.

"I'm sure it's quite humbling, knowing it took so little," he says, eyes crinkling at the corners with self-satisfied amusement when I look over at him. "If it makes you feel any better, it was before Acker even knew you were alive. It took years to accomplish, and even longer to get in the general's good graces."

My smile is dripping with sarcasm. "We'll see how far that gets you when he catches up," I say.

He tilts his head in contemplation, but the flatness of his expression reveals that I've struck a nerve. "I suppose we will."

Snow hasn't gathered on the ground yet, but as the sun dips, so will the temperature. The livery stable is the last structure on the street and when we arrive, we find Wells loading the horses with supplies. He makes quick work, tying the packs to ensure they're secure.

"That should do ya'," a stable boy declares, handing the reins to the last horse to Acker.

I take a quick inventory of the total number of horses and deduce that we're going to be partnering up. The arrangement is made without discussion. A simple jerk of Acker's chin is all the direction Irina needs to mount the horse he's holding the reins of. Fredrich doesn't even wait for my consent, lifting me by my waist and hoisting me onto another horse. It's difficult to maneuver with my hands tied, but I manage to straddle the horse properly and get my feet into the stirrups, using the pommel as leverage. Fredrich heaves himself up behind me, and I'm grateful for the barrier the saddle creates between the two of us.

No one says a word as we turn onto the street that leads out of the town. The little bit of snow ceases, but the cold is relentless and I shiver as the wind whips at my cheeks. I'd be more self-conscious about my lack of bathing over the last week if it weren't for the fact that I'd wish the worst on the man at my back, even if my revenge is as pitiful as subjecting him to the stench of my unwashed body.

This far inland, Kenta is mostly flat. There's nothing remotely interesting to distract me from the predicament I've found myself in. Not a bird in the sky or a scurrying creature on the ground in the distance, just endless wind drifting across the grassy planes, and, swaying on the horse in front of me, the back of the man who makes me want to commit violence every time I look at him.

I hate that I've allowed myself to be put into this position. That I didn't see Acker for who he truly is, the very person Beau warned me about. She said her brother wasn't to be reasoned with, but I was adamant that she was wrong, that I knew better. Laughable, considering she could see his aura, and all I could see was the man I fell in love with.

Worst of all, I hate that he still hasn't looked at me. It feels like a punishment. And I loathe the way Irina is relaxed against Acker's chest.

How it makes my stomach clench in disgust. Four years after witnessing their wedding night, it still hurts to see them together, especially after I saw her in his bed just weeks ago. It's evident their marriage hasn't been without its benefits.

But his admittance that the oath still clings to him niggles at me. No longer a kernel of hope wishing it is true, but another reason for my anger to fester. Even if he does love me, is this the kind of love I want? We've been spiteful and petty and vengeful, fueled by our own pain. I mean, he's chosen to pair with Irina, his *wife* for gods sake, and I'm contemplating whether the man loves me or not. All the while, I'm being held captive.

Things are beyond twisted.

The temperature continues to drop as the sun's light dissipates. Acker makes the call to set up camp for the night and he and Wells begin to erect a tent. I stand idly as I watch them, useless in my shackles. Acker uses his gift to lodge stakes into the cold ground. Wells works behind him, trying the canvas to the stakes, and I recognize the sailors knots instantly. Now that I think about it, it's the same knots he used to tie the packs to the horses.

When he sees me watching him intently, he winks.

I suck in a sharp breath right as Fredrich leads me into the tent.

It's modest, meant to protect us from the elements more than anything. But as I enter, I'm confronted with the fact that I'm going to be sleeping in a confined space with my Match, his wife, and the man who went down on me. And *Wells*.

I don't care what Beau says; I've had to deal with the consequences of enough bad decisions in my life to just accept this predicament right now.

Choosing the spot at the far side of the tent, I lay down on the bedroll Fredrich lays out. The thin material does little to protect from the hard and ice-cold ground underneath, and I know tonight is going to be very, very long.

"I'll take the first watch." Acker's voice is pitched low.

"Nothing is getting past my shield," Fredrich says. "Let's just try to get some rest."

I roll onto my side, wedging my bound hands under my cheek as a pillow. I hear them shuffle about, then whispering too low for me to hear. Although, I get the sense it's a mildly heated discussion before I eventually feel someone press in close as they get situated beside me. I clench my teeth, but it does nothing to stop them from chattering.

"Wells," Acker says. "Can you burn a flame for a few minutes to take the chill out?"

I listen for his response with bated breath.

"Do we want to risk someone seeing it?" he asks.

There's a beat of silence before Acker replies. "No. I suppose you're right."

And I release my breath with a whooshing sigh.

Despite the cold, it doesn't take long for everyone's breathing to even out. I try my best to relax and let the wind lull me into some semblance of sleep. But after what feels like an eternity, I find myself shifting onto my other side, trying to get comfortable, and discover Fredrich is the one lying next to me. It's pitch black but his posture gives him away, flat on his back, hands folded across his chest. He has this insane ability to close his eyes and by his next breath have fallen asleep.

I think I resent him a little bit more, just for that alone.

Sleep has evaded me for days. At least, it's felt like days. I'm unsure of exactly how long I've gone without sleep. The time since my kidnap has blurred together, but despite the exhaustion and stress, my restraints were so wildly uncomfortable on the boat that they made it impossible to relax enough for proper rest. I'm also positive I've become too reliant on the aid of the herbal tea Karla would leave by my bedside every night.

I whisper Fredrich's name, afraid he's already too deep into his slumber to wake, but his responding *harrumph* lets me know I've caught him just in time.

"How did you know about the tea?"

He takes a deep breath as if he's finding the energy to answer. "It's an old Maile practice to give soldiers the tea when they return home from war." I hear more than see him tilt his head in my direction. "Cold?"

"No."

He huffs. "It's just in your nature to lie, isn't it?"

There's no sense in complaining about something I can't change. Unless . . . "Are you able to shield us from the cold?" I ask with a smidgen of hope.

I can hear the grin in his voice. "Unfortunately, I have a difficult time with shielding againt natural elements. The weather doesn't inherently pose an imminent threat."

Great.

I do my best to make peace with the long night ahead and my miserable existence and close my eyes. Only for them to shoot wide open when Fredrich wraps an arm around my waist and drags me toward him. I'm so taken aback that I freeze up. But then he rolls onto his other side, giving me his back, and while I want to refuse his offering, I'd be only hurting myself out of stubbornness. Shuffling toward his heat, I remind myself once again that this is all temporary.

All suffering ends, one way or another.

The wind picks up, and though it sends a draft of wind through the gaps in the tent's material, I'm grateful for the noise. It drowns out everything, including my thoughts. Soon enough, the cold doesn't feel as punishing. Almost invigorating, in fact. Kind of like jumping into the ocean during early spring, when the bite of the water offers a reprieve from the burning sun.

Come here.

I wipe the water from my eyes, spinning toward Kai's voice. He's over by the lone tree that stands on the outskirts of the grove, the one that we liked to climb as children. I recognize the memory; it's from less than a year before we visited the Market.

A smile stretches across his face before he disappears under the water. I swim the distance to the tree and duck underneath the surface to find the opening in the trunk, which was hollowed by a lightning strike. When I resurface inside, Kai's waiting for me, his hands braced on either side of the small space. We're close enough that I can feel his warmth despite the chilly water.

Can you imagine, he says, voice echoing up the tree's hollow shaft. *One more year and then we're out of here.*

No, I tell him honestly, but I so desperately hope for it to be true.

He reaches out, running a fingertip over my collarbone. *We'll find a way*, he says, eyes following in the wake of his touch. *Just promise me: that even if the prince is there waiting for you, you'll find a way to take me with you.*

I'm very skeptical about the idea of this "lost princess" he claims me to be. The title doesn't feel like it could belong to me. *Urchin*, however, feels much more fitting, but I don't bother arguing with him. Regardless of my possible title or lack thereof, there must be a way to get on land once we're at the Market.

We go together or not at all, I remind him. I can't imagine a scenario where I'd ever leave my best friend behind.

Messer yells from above. *Are you two coming up or what?*

I roll my eyes. *Both* of my best friends.

Just a second, Kai yells back right before he kisses me.

My heart thunders in my ears as heat spreads through my veins. I chase the feeling, wrapping my arms around his neck, using his shoulders as leverage to stay above water. He's always seeking reassurance, making me promise not to leave him behind, and I don't know how he could ever believe I'd be capable of doing such a thing.

When he pulls away, the sensation of the kiss still hot on my lips, it's no longer Kai I'm clinging to . . . but *Acker*.

His brows are slanted down in agitation. *He's influencing you, Jovie.*

I push away from him as much as I'm able to in the small space, alarmed by his sudden appearance.

He was always *using you*, he says.

I dip under the water and swim back through the opening in the tree, out into the open ocean. But when I come up for air, the water is no longer blue, but dark red. The grove is gone, and I'm standing in a current that's waist deep. Lifting my hands, I realize they're tied together with shackles, the rope threaded between is coated with droplets of blood that glisten like jewels.

When I look up from my bound hands, Acker is standing a ways away. I'm stunned by the intensity of his gaze. So much so, I instinctively take a step back, causing a red wake around me. But as Acker's eyes continue to hold my own, I realize it's not anger reflecting back at me . . . but fear. He begins to wade through the blood to get to me.

Bodies.

They're everywhere, floating up from the depths of the viscous liquid, all of them in military garb. Every insignia of every territory are present within the steadily emerging graveyard. Bubbles appear right in front of me, a body becoming visible slowly, emerging with a curved saber lodged through the spine. And as he bobs onto his back, the familiar bone-stricken face of a young man in a Maile uniform comes into view.

I stumble backward, falling, and the last thing I see is Acker's terrified gaze as he struggles to push through the bodies, yelling something I can't quite hear. I scream when I go under, but it's muffled by the dense blood. The taste of copper fills my mouth as I struggle, helpless as I sink deeper and I realize . . . *this is it.*

This is the end of my suffering.

For a moment, everything goes quiet aside from the beating of my heart. A steady rhythm inside me. That is, until muffled voices penetrate through the viscous liquid.

Wake her!

"Wake her up!" Acker's yells are muted. "Godsdamnit. Wake her!"

The scream trapped in my throat finally escapes the same moment I awake to Fredrich jerking me by the shoulders. I suck in a desperate lungful of air as I sit up shakily. Nausea burns in my throat. Everyone is awake and bleary-eyed as they look at me in the early morning light. The last thing I need is to add to my humiliation by dry heaving.

"It's okay," Fredrich says, hands hovering over my shoulders. "You're okay. It was just a dream."

That's putting it lightly.

I can't stop my eyes from straying to Acker. Sitting with his knees bent, chest heaving as he cradles his face in his hands.

And, even still, he can't bear to look at me.

Chapter 32

JO

We navigate the horses straight through the unmanned entrance into the small town. The dirt roads are empty and storefronts lining the main street are vacant, their doors left open on their hinges. There's no familiar smell of food cooking coming from the local tavern or sounds of life anywhere other than from a wandering goat munching on a piece of parchment the winds have scattered across town.

Fredrich is the one to break the silence. "Did the vendor at the port say if anyone was left behind?"

"She just said that soldiers from the capital descended on the town nearby," Acker answers.

"What were they looking for?" Irina asks.

"Not what," Fredrich says. "*Who.*"

Heirs, I realize with a startling spike of dread.

"But why take the whole town?" Irina asks.

Beau told me that there were defiant communities of Edmond's reign within Kenta. Unbeknownst to the crown, these towns protected Heirs who were charged with bogus crimes and developed a way to find others in need of hiding. She'd discovered them during travel in the army, seeing through the townspeople's auras as well as their illusions that a lot of them possessed magic. It was the beginning of her journey of unraveling everything she was led to believe while under her father's thumb and gain an idea of sorts of what he was up to.

We stop in front of the tavern.

Acker dismounts from his horse before helping Irina down. "There's likely to be rooms up top," he says. "Wells, do a sweep of the town. See what you can find in terms of food for the horses."

Fredrich lifts me from the horse's back, planting me on my feet, and I follow the three of them into the desolate tavern. It paints a bleak picture of what might have happened here. Chairs and tables are overturned. Flies buzz around the uneaten food and drink still left out. Acker disappears through an open doorway behind the bar, likely to survey the rear of the premises. I round the counter and am relieved to find multiple glass bottles of wine underneath the counter, and given the circumstance, a glass of wine sounds nice right about now but my bound hands prevent me from grabbing the drink for myself.

Sensing my predicament, Fredrich lifts a bottle from the shelf and uncorks it. He raises a brow, asking without words if it's okay for him to do the honors. I tip my head back and he rests the glass rim against my mouth, tilting the bottle carefully until he's sure I'm not going to let half the wine escape down my chin. The first swallow is small, but my sips quickly turn into a gulp, and I pull back to swallow. Fredrich wastes no time downing some himself.

"Excuse me," Irina says, drawing our attention.

Fredrich grins. "My apologies." He retrieves an overturned glass from where it had been left to dry next to the wash basin, sliding it onto the bar in front of her. Then he grabs another bottle and uncorks it, glass clinking against the tumbler as he pours her a helping. "On the house," he jokes.

Acker walks back through the doorway. He lowers his hood, and it gives me an unfettered view of his face, and it's as if I've finally take a sip of air after holding my breath since I woke up this morning. I've felt off-kilter all day, the nightmare haunting my waking thoughts. It's getting harder to differentiate where my memories stop in my dreams and where my own mind begins to play tricks on me. But seeing the easy and steady expression on Acker's face instead of undiluted fear comforts me somehow.

He accepts the bottle from Fredrich's outstretched hand and tips his head back to take a drink. I can't help but watch his throat working as he downs the wine.

Wells's voice draws our attention to the front door. "The stables are empty. I'm going to move the horses inside. Just in case anyone comes looking."

Acker nods his approval and wipes the excess liquid from his mouth with his hand. "They likely took the horses and feed to be used on the front lines."

"Supplies are that low?" Fredrich asks.

Acker's mouth thins. "It's not great."

He continues to keep his gaze averted from me as he explains the supply issues the Kenta have been struggling with in recent years and months. He looks at the open tavern doors, the dirty bar, and at any and everything that's not me before he says he's going to see if he can find any food in the kitchen. Fredrich finds a liquor bottle that's to his liking and takes it with him as he follows his friend through the door and into the back of the tavern.

Left to ourselves, I meet Irina's gaze across the bar. I can't tell if her passive facade is real or put on, but I make note to be careful not to turn my back on her. Sometimes a threat can appear weak when in reality it's actually quite the opposite.

I would know.

My gaze slides to the open tavern door behind her, waiting for Wells's figure to return. The silence seems to expand until the pressure of it causes a ringing sensation in my ears, only for me to realize it's just Irina gliding her finger around the rim of her glass.

"We have a lot in common, you know?" she says.

I'm caught off guard by her assumption. Curious, but not enough to inquire further, so I don't acknowledge her words. I don't want to think of Irina in any capacity. I've had enough of her to last a lifetime.

A placeholder wife to Acker, taken to keep his father happy. A warm body, I presume.

She's not dissuaded by my lack of response. "He was my first love. He was my first heartbreak, too."

If she expects me to feel sorry for her, she's sadly mistaken. Although she's not wrong about that being something we share. I just don't want to give her any validation. And I don't have the energy to feed into whatever rise she's trying to get out of me. She must realize as much, because she vacates her stool and stalks out of the room. I listen to her fading footsteps as they ascend the stairs to the floor above.

And then, I'm well and truly alone.

The open door of the tavern gives a temptingly framed view of the empty street beyond. Two windows on either side lend a partial view of the buildings across the street, and I inch out from behind the bar and toward the door. Looking back at the kitchen door, I listen carefully to Fredrich and Acker's movements in the room beyond.

"We need her skill set," Fredrich says.

Whatever Acker says in return is muffled, but I catch the tail end of it. "—are secure."

I keep my steps light as I move toward the tavern's entrance. The wind nips at my cheeks as I pause on the threshold. My heart picks up speed at the freedom just inches away from my fingertips. But then I look down at my hands and realize I'm fairly useless in shackles. I run my gaze over the vacant street, to the rooftops of the buildings on the other side, and the sky above. It seems snow is likely.

"What are you looking for?"

A surprised yelp leaves my mouth at the nearness of the voice behind me. I spin in place, finding Fredrich standing alarmingly close. His gaze is upturned, as if he's attempting to see something through the doorway that I can't. When his gaze drops back to me, he's grinning, but it doesn't quite reach his eyes.

"I may not be able to shield from the cold, but just about everything else is easy to block out. When Irina illusioned us at the port, it's likely your bird friend lost sight of us pretty quickly."

He doesn't say his name, but we both know who he's referring to.

He reaches around me to pull the tavern door closed. "Come on," he says with a jerk of his chin. "Let's get you settled."

Acker isn't around as Fredrich escorts me up the stairs. We move down the corridor to the last bedroom, its door already open. The floor creaks as I step inside. The room reminds me of the brothel we stayed at on the journey to Kenta, but thankfully the bed looks clean and unused.

Fredrich turns toward me. "Let me see your hands," he says.

I raise them, as instructed, then watch as he inserts a small skeleton key into the lock of the shackles. It doesn't release my hands from the bindings entirely, my fingers still woven together with rope, but a low groan leaves my mouth as my wrists are exposed to the fresh air for the first time since we left Maile. I begin to thank him, but before I can form the first syllable, he's dragging me toward the bed by my arm. I try to jerk from his hold, but he outmaneuvers me, forcing me down onto the mattress with little more than a sharp push. He threads the cuffs around a bar of the metal headboard and wiggles his fingers for me to give him my hands again.

"You can eat shit if you think I'm going to let you chain me to this bed."

He just stares at me expectantly, his hand outstretched . . . waiting.

I contemplate the merits of fighting, but the simple truth is I would lose ten times over against him and never land a single blow, and it would only serve to shame me further. Sighing in defeat and shifting my gaze to the space over his shoulder, I lift my arms to the headboard. I feel the cuffs close around my wrists, anchoring me to the bed, and the click of the lock engaging solidifies my entrapment.

"Wasn't my decision," he says, somewhat repentantly.

Oh, I know *exactly* who's decision it was. "Tell him to do his own dirty work for now on," I say, snarky.

I watch Fredrich leave out of the corner of my eye, quietly shutting the door behind him, and I return to fantasizing about what I'm going to do the moment I'm free of these bindings.

Then I make it my mission of the night to do just that.

I wait until I can no longer hear any footsteps in the hallway and the light from outside my window dissipates fully before I begin working on freeing myself from the bindings. Sawing my teeth across the rope visible between fingers, I slowly loosen the stranglehold on my hands, little by little. I have to take breaks to breathe, letting my arms go slack for moments while I rest. I do this for what feels like hours, my jaw and shoulders aching fiercely, but sheer fury propels me to keep going. I maneuver my bite back and forth. Again and again, feeling for the slackening in the rope with my tongue until finally—*finally*—the binding gives way.

A burst of relief escapes my throat, but I'm quick to snap my mouth shut and cut it off out of fear of getting caught. My hands shake, both from exertion and excitement, as I wiggle them free from the rope, my anger morphing into something predatory as sensation slowly trickles back into my fingers. I recall my dagger, the familiar hilt comforting as it appears in the palm of my hand.

One last hurdle.

It's too dark to see the shackles around my wrists properly, but they clink as I stretch out my hands. They're sore and slightly numb from being bound for so long, but I'm too anxious to have access to my magic, just in case the Bond forces me into Acker's presence. Shifting the dagger in my hand, I feel for a link in the chain that secures my wrists to the bed and position the tip of the blade through the open center of the metal. I grit my teeth as I wedge the tip of the blade through the loop, pushing with all the strength I can muster between the awkward angle and my weakened hands and wrists.

It doesn't budge. The blade nor the chain. Neither of them has any give.

I adjust the hold I have on the dagger and try again, holding my breath as I do my hardest to jam the blade through. Still, nothing.

Taking a moment to re-evaluate, I try to rotate the blade as I press it through the metal loop instead of shoving it with just brute force. And it works. The metal gives just enough for the blade tip to slip into the small gap where the ends of the link have—finally—been pushed apart. But as

I twist the blade further, I hear a terrible crack, the wood hilt splintering from the pressure.

I freeze. My heart hammers in my throat as I realize what I've done. This dagger is the only thing I have of my father. We made it during one of the summers we spent in Kenta. Not that I remember it. I don't remember much of that time at all; other than the few memories I've pieced together from my dreams. And those are warped and hazy, so I'm never sure of what's real and what my mind has conjured.

I feel for the crack with the tip of my fingers and the sadness that it elicits only serves to further fuel my anger. At this point, the damage is already done, so the least I can do is enact my retribution.

After I finally escape these shackles, that is.

Clenching my teeth, I tighten my grip and twist the blade with enough force to spear the chain apart. I catch the slackened links in my hands to stop them from making too much noise as I pull them back through the headboard, freeing my arms at last. The cuffs are still locked around my wrists, but I have free range of motion as I sit up and inspect my dagger. I run my thumb over the fissure that runs the length of the handle. The hilt is fully fractured, rendering it a hazard to wield. I'm just as likely to injure myself as I am anyone else if the tang slips free during an attack.

But it's still useful enough to carry out one last item of business.

Chapter 33

ACKER

I wake with a start and immediately tense when I feel the sharp point of a blade at my throat.

Jovie looms over me, expression murderous in the light of the flickering oil lamp I left on the table in front of me in the otherwise darkened tavern.

It's the first time I've looked directly at her since we stood together on her balcony in Maile. She's beautiful, undoubtedly, but there's a sliver of cold calculation behind her eyes that I overlooked in the past. Cunning and devious and sly like a fox. Her auburn hair, like a wild mane around her face, has never looked more fitting.

I attempt to lift a hand to disarm her but quickly realize I can't because my hands are bound. Another jerk of my wrists reveals the bite of rope into my skin, arms tied behind me, attached to the back legs of the wooden chair I'm sitting in. Even though I knew better than to underestimate her, I'm still impressed by her stealthiness, both in breaking free and by not waking me.

"How does it feel?" she asks, yanking my hair to further expose my neck to her. "Finding out you've been left exposed and vulnerable while you've been sleeping?"

She's furious. I can feel her anger burning down the tether. It pulses with the pace of her heartbeat. Steady and relentless, and it's exactly what I've been waiting for. After her nightmare a few nights ago, I . . . *fuck.*

Fredrich thinks I don't care about Jovie's feelings, but nothing could be further from the truth. When I first had to smother the Bond with the strings of mangi, it was like she was missing all over again. The severing of my tie to her emotions felt like I'd lost my own heart right along with losing hers.

The pulse of her anger begins to beat faster.

The sensation makes me want to smile, but I swallow down the urge, throat bobbing against the sharp tip of the blade in her hand. "If your intention is to kill me, then at least be merciful enough to make it quick."

She's not amused. "You think I won't?"

I definitely think she would draw it out just to spite me. "It feels good, doesn't it?" I ask on a low breath, relishing the way her eyes track my lips as I speak. "Having me at your mercy."

The blade pierces my skin, cutting into the place where my jaw hinges at the top of my throat, and the sight of my blood momentarily distracts her enough that I'm able to grab her shackled wrist.

She gasps.

"Did you think simple rope would be enough to hold me?" I ask, standing from the chair.

She steps back to accommodate for my size but doesn't remove the dagger from my throat. I hold up the severed rope, the dagger in the same hand I called into my palm while it was still tied before dropping them both at my feet, the metal blade clinking against the tavern's floor. I grab her wrist to hold her in place when she tries to retreat. The action causes the blade to slide even deeper and I suck in a hiss of air through my teeth.

I can feel the trickle of heat down my neck.

Her eyes widen. "Acker." She says my name in what I assume she intends as a warning, but the slight tremble in her hands gives her away.

"Kill me or don't," I tell her. "But understand: if you don't end my life right here, right now, then know that I am never going to let you go."

Her anger flashes through the Bond. "You're telling me my options are only to be with you or kill you?

"No. I'm saying there's no escaping the Bond, and if you want any chance of being free of me, you might as well kill me. My death is of little consequence."

"This is lunacy."

She tries to jerk her hand away, but I refuse to release her. "Aren't you sick of fighting it?" I ask.

Her expression stills. "You don't get to decide that."

I lean a little closer, enjoying the way her eyes falter on the blade she has at my throat. "It's no different than when you made me choose between you and my father."

She becomes eerily calm in the face of my anger. "Let go of me."

I take a moment to consider the possibility she might actually kill me before I finally relinquish my hold, undoing the mangi shackles on her wrists with a touch of my magic, and letting them, too, fall to the floor in a loud clank of metal. Her hands immediately begin to glow, her gift revealing itself as they shake.

Her eyes flick to the blade in her hand, to the blood dripping down the hearthstone edge. Then, ever so slowly, she takes a measured step back, lowering the dagger to her side. "I see we're at an impasse, so why don't we negotiate for my release?"

I bite back my huff of laughter. "Even if I was willing to negotiate, I would advise you against it."

"And why is that?" she asks, lifting a challenging brow.

"Your deal with Chryse," I explain, wiping the dribbles of blood from my neck and chest with a wipe of my palm. "It's a terrible agreement." Her glow intensifies and it's been so long since I laid eyes on the beauty of her gift that I can't help but admire it. "He had no incentive to uphold his end of the bargain after you already carried the heavy lifting on your end of the deal."

Her gaze stutters on me. "I considered it," she says. "But Chryse knew there'd be dire consequences if he didn't."

"So, what was your plan if he did kill me? Start a new war after this one ended?"

"No," she says like I'm the biggest moron to ever exist. "I was going to kill *him*." She wipes the dagger clean on her pantleg. "Obviously."

"*Obviously*," I repeat, sarcastically.

"You're welcome, by the way," she snarks dryly.

I can't believe this.

I take a step forward and dip my head, so my eyes are level with hers, which has her readying her dagger again defensively. "You're crazy if you think I'm going to *thank you* for anything," I growl.

There's a flicker of vulnerability in her gaze before it's gone again with a blink. A hint of her true emotions underneath. "You were on the losing side of a war—"

"That *you* started," I correct.

"That you *allowed*," she yells back, losing any semblance of calm. "If you would have taken your father's throne and made a new peace treaty with the Alaha, *like I proposed*, none of this would have had to happen."

I can feel the shift of the metal in Fredrich's blood as he rouses from sleep upstairs. "What did you expect me to do?" I shout back. "You had me pinned to a fucking chair and a blade to my father's neck."

This, out of everything, seems to suck the wind from her sails. "It was still your choice."

The solemn and cold tone she uses hurts more than they should. Like the sharp sting of a proverbial knife long buried in my chest being wrenched free.

I take a step back, needing distance. "How dare you put all of this on me."

She shakes her head. "Oh, I've blamed myself plenty."

Eyes full of regret, she looks up at me at the same time Fredrich's footsteps sound on the stairs and continues. His head peeks from around the banister before fully entering the tavern's main room.

"All good down here?" he asks.

I'm slow to turn away from Jovie after that revelation, but I eventually meet Fredrich's gaze. His eyebrows are raised with a mixture of concern and exasperation.

"Yeah," I tell him. "Give us a few."

He looks at Jovie for confirmation that she must answer with a nod. I grit my teeth, annoyed that my word wasn't enough alone, but keep it to myself as he says to holler if we need anything. It's a thinly veiled offer to the both of us. Whoever screams first, I guess.

Alone again, Jovie steps toward me as I turn back to face her.

I eye the dagger still in her hand.

"Why am I here, Acker?" she asks.

Aside from the fact that I was always planning on coming to get her, I say, "Greta had a vision."

As hard as I try to not let my worry seep through, I must do a terrible job because her eyes narrow. "What did she tell you?"

"She believes my father is going to win the war."

Confusion creases her brows. "She would have sent word to Beau if she thought it necessary," she argues.

"Would she?" I challenge. "Think of all the deaths she would have seen in that vision. Yours, mine. Her own daughter's. Your mother's, *my* mother's. Who do you think takes precedence?"

"Greta—"

"Believes the future is inevitable, laid out by the gods, so why would she try to alter it by warning anyone, regardless of how much she loves them?"

It's this piece of information that causes the tension to melt out of Jovie, her shoulders drooping as the truth slowly sets in. Her glow begins to dim as the fight leaves her. "Then there's nothing we can do," she says.

"How can you say that?"

She stares at the blood drying on my shirt before her eyes lose their focus. "You can't stop fate, Acker."

Grabbing her by the face, I force her eyes on me. "I refuse to accept that. I'll fight fate itself if it means I can right my wrongs."

"Acker—"

I slam my mouth onto hers in an effort to shut her up, and she surprises me by immediately accepting the kiss. Her easy submission drags a guttural groan from my throat. She swallows the sound with the same eagerness. I relish the warmth lingering on her skin from her diminishing light, her radiance dancing behind my eyelids. Each drag of my tongue against hers, each breath of hers I take in as my own, I let the tether reveal my darkest secrets to her.

The love I've been harboring. The obsession I've struggled to keep in check. The suffering I've endured at her hands.

I let her see and feel it all.

She gasps from the onslaught of emotions, tearing herself away from the kiss.

I don't let her get far, hand cradling the back of her head to keep her within the circle of my arms. "Help me end this," I insist. I'm not even sure what I'm asking. To end this war. My pain and suffering at her hands. "Put me out of my misery."

Feeling her trepidation through the Bond, it makes me want to shake her, but I know it would be counterproductive. It'd likely only instigate another row. So I kiss her again, instead. She's less receptive this time, mouth stilted against my movements, and when I pull away I'm disheartened to see the tears welling in her eyes. With her hands against my chest, she presses until I let her go.

"I can't," she says, voice barely a whisper.

I don't know if it's in reference to the kiss or my plea for her to fight for me, for her own life, but the way she tightens the grip on her dagger has me taking a step back. Then another, until I'm no longer forcing my legs to move, and I'm able to walk out the door of the tavern without doing something stupid.

Like actually let her kill me.

Chapter 34

JO

The water is freezing, but the shower is just what I needed. I stand under the spigot for longer than necessary, just letting the water pour down my face and soak into my hair. It feels like a ritual cleansing of some sort after last night.

I could have run once Acker had walked out of the tavern. Likely should have, at least that's what I keep telling myself.

But his kiss.

It was all-consuming. No longer me or him, just *us,* as we gave in to the desire. For a few sweet seconds, it was pure need. Only for me to be blindsided by the onslaught of his emotions.

I never knew the true extent of what the Bond allowed him to sense from me, but it's apparent my emotions have been more readily available to him than my thoughts ever were. He wanted to give me the same in return.

The hurt and love and desperation . . .

All of it was too much.

Overwhelming, even as I recall it now. And as cathartic as it is to know I was wrong in my assumption that Acker never loved me, it doesn't erase my anger. He's been against me for so long. I can't help but wonder what ulterior motives there are that I can't see. What he *didn't* share.

The marks around my hands and wrists are physical reminders of his transgressions. Marrying Irina, spying on me, sending the Strou to my lands to kill my people. All things he's proven to be plenty capable of while still loving me. Showing me his cards feels like a very convenient distraction.

I wring out my hair and braid it before putting my tunic back on. The rest of my clothes I wash under the spray as best I can, then hang them over the door to dry. I check to make sure no one is in the hallway before I hurry back to my room. There, I am surprised to find fresh clothes folded at the foot of my bed. I'm shivering, skin prickling with the cold, and I waste no time getting dressed. I'm pleased with how well the riding pants and linen shirt fit.

I shove my dagger into the waistband of my pants before heading downstairs, following the voices to the kitchen.

I recognize Wells's voice first. "Can we trust her?"

Fredrich's comes next. "Absolutely not."

"Then what—"

Acker hushes Irina before she can finish speaking and they all turn to look at me when I step through the doorway. The kitchen is long and narrow, without windows. Candles line the shelves above the prep station, where used bowls and utensils were left out by the missing cooks, pots still sitting on the wood stove against the far wall. The four of them are nestled around the butcher-block table in the center of the room and my eyes go straight to the meal they're sharing. My hollow stomach clenches and I can't remember the last decent meal I had.

Fredrich is the first to speak. "Good afternoon," he says.

Afternoon? "What time is it?"

"A smidge past one," he says, holding up his fingers in a pinch.

It was light by the time my mind finally turned off, but I don't usually sleep longer than a few hours at most. My eyes lock with Acker's and the tether hums at our close proximity. I'm concerned the kiss we shared may have encouraged the Bond somehow.

Slowly, Acker's dark gaze trails down the length of my body. Accessing my newly acquired outfit, I presume. There's nothing scandalous about the simple garments, but it doesn't stop a blush from trying to creep into my cheeks.

Put me out of my misery.

The desperate man from last night is nothing but a distant memory. *This* is the Acker I'm accustomed to, the one who's self-assured and daring enough to not care about the two other men in the room when he looks at me with heat in his gaze. Or his wife, for that matter. It somehow lessens the pressure in my chest.

I know how to handle *this* Acker.

Irina's eyes flick from her husband's profile to me, and back again. Acker left the tavern not long after trying to . . . recruit me? Or maybe he really was trying to end his own life. Who the hell knows? Whatever his end goal, he failed, and it was late into the night before he would have returned to her bed. I try to conjure a sense of guilt for kissing her husband, but it doesn't come. Out of all of my transgressions in this life, I'm afraid it doesn't hold a candle to the worst of them.

My eyes stick on the gash under the hinge of his jaw. It's no longer bleeding, but it isn't healing as it should, either.

"Come eat," he says, with a tilt of his chin.

The plethora of dried meats and cheeses on the table draws me in. Fredrich shifts his stool over to make room for me, and I give him my thanks as I reach for a piece of cheese.

A shocked grin pulls at Wells's mouth. "Take the girl out of restraints and she remembers her manners all of a sudden."

Layering a slice of meat on top of a square of cheese, I pop it into my mouth, then follow it with a bite of bread. It's stale and instantly dries out my mouth, making it difficult to swallow. Grinning, Fredrich slides over a waterskin. I thank him, but it comes out as a mumbled mess before I take a drink.

"Okay," Wells says, "maybe *manners* was a bit generous."

I make an obscene gesture with the hand I'm not using to pick out the best bits of cheese.

"Now that we're all here," Acker says, running a hand across his jaw, "we need to discuss our next course of action."

"I thought you were all in agreement that I'm not to be trusted," I say between bites.

No one refutes my statement.

"There's not a person at this table I trust," he says. When everyone turns their offended gazes on him, he leans back in his seat and raises his hands defensively. "Not even myself."

I stop mid-chew, stunned by his admission.

"I misled you into believing I went to Maile in a bid to seek an alliance, and while that is *partially* true, my father believes I went to retrieve my sister."

"Ace," Fredrich says, voice mixed with disbelief and anger.

Acker ignores him, continuing as if he hadn't been interrupted. "My father currently holds the magic of three gifts: fire, kinesis, and influence. At least, those are the ones I was made aware of when he was actively trying to manipulate me into pursuing Beau for her gift."

I swallow. "How were you able to resist it?"

"I'm not sure I did." Acker's eyes fall to the table for a beat before he looks back at me. "I wanted to kill him just moments before. He knew it, too, and yet . . . I *didn't*. It might have been the mangi stones I was wearing that shielded me from some of the influence, but I suspect he's either weaker than he wants me to believe, or he's being very careful not to overdo it and tip his hand."

"Fucking hell," Fredrich says, blowing out a large breath.

"That's where he believes you are now," I say. "Retrieving Beau?" His gaze slides to Irina, and I wiggle a finger around the table. "Circle of non-trust, remember?"

Acker's eyes darken with something I don't like. "Before I share any more of my secrets, why don't we share one of yours?" There's a poignant beat before his stare shifts to the man beside me.

The smile on Wells's face looks unnatural on him. Too reckless. "How'd you figure it out?"

"It was a number of things," Acker says, leaning an elbow on the table.

"The first was the fact that Wells would be hard-pressed to leave his Match in the first place, let alone now that she's pregnant. Then there's your scent. Wells smells like scorched iron and bergamot. You, *Messer*, smell like a wet dog."

Fredrich makes a face. "What?"

Pulling a dagger from the strap on his chest, Acker twirls it in his hand. "But the biggest giveaway was when you refused to light a flame to keep us warm. If you had known anything about Wells, it's that he hates the cold."

"If you knew this whole time, why didn't you say anything?" I ask Acker.

"Because he's had ample opportunity to rescue you, and didn't," he says, eyes holding mine. "I figured at worst he could provide another level of protection."

For me, he means.

Wells's eyes meet mine. Or, I suppose I should say, *Messer* looks at me, because it's clearly not Wells behind the brown irises.

"It was a long shot," he says, voice distorting, the inflection sounding more like himself than the man he's been mimicking.

Standing, he toes off his boots and stretches his arms out to his sides, shaking them. He shifts before our eyes. Taller by two, then three inches, hair curling out at the ends. Brown eyes swirl to blue as his facial features rearrange into something more familiar to me. The cracking of bones and cartilage makes the whole ordeal sound painful. At least he's able to remain dressed, given that Wells's stature isn't too different from his normal size.

"I think I'm going to be sick," Irina groans, covering her mouth.

Fredrich also stands from his seat and it's the first time I've ever seen him truly unsettled. "Good gods," he murmurs. "Since when can shifters replicate humans?"

"According to the old texts, only the most powerful ones are able to do so. Such as one capable of maintaining their shifted form over the open sea." Acker uses the dagger to point at my friend. "Cocky of you to think you could get away with it twice. The both of you," he says, eyes straying to me.

I wasn't aware the first time.

"How the fu—" Fredrich stops and shakes his head, thoroughly floored by this turn of events. "How'd you know I was planning on taking her?"

"When B didn't show for morning conditioning, I figured she was busy and flew to the wharf to check in with Drake. He made an offhand comment about Jovie likely being too tired from the night before," Messer says, returning to his stool. "He said a palace aide came to the tavern to retrieve you, Fredrich, personally, and I immediately knew something was up, because B would never send a request for a late-night rendezvous."

But when both Fredrick and Acker's gazes land on me with the same knowing expression, Messer notices instantly, eyes widening at the heat slowly coloring my cheeks. "It's not up for discussion," I tell him firmly.

"No shit?" he says, a sly grin quirking his mouth. "This makes this whole dynamic *much* more interesting." He looks from Fredrich to Acker. "That explains the skirmish on deck."

Acker's eyes darken. "She said it's not up for discussion."

The longer Messer stares, the more uncomfortable I get. Eyes darting between the three of us for a long, assessing a moment before he nearly jolts out of his seat at whatever he sees. "Both at the same time?" he asks, turning to me with eyes wide.

I cradle my face in my hand.

He slaps the table, a sharp bark of laughter escaping him. "I'm damn proud of you, B!"

I elbow him with enough oomph behind it that it shuts him up, his smile faltering as he grunts with pain.

Irina's eye roll is practically audible. "As if using your title to procure sexual favors is something to be proud of."

Acker's eyes flash with anger as he turns to snap, "And how do you classify your relationship with Wesley, then? Are only you allowed to have a consort?"

It's Irina's turn to be embarrassed, her face turning beet red. I don't allow my curiosity to get the best of me. I don't need to know who this

Wesley is or what he means in terms of their marriage. None of it is my business.

"Anyway," Messer says, alleviating the tension as he dives back into his explanation. "I flew to B's balcony but found her room empty. I almost didn't think anything of it. Except, right before I was about to take off, I saw one of the rabbits in the palace courtyard carrying something odd in its mouth." He leans forward with his hands braced on the table, the sleeves a smidge shorter on his arms than they were on Wells's. "Imagine my surprise when I realized it was a string of mangi stones."

I instinctively feel for the stones around my neck even though I logically know they're not there.

"The scent of both you and B were still fresh in her room, but it was the smell of the sleeping fungi that confirmed my suspicions," he says to Fredrich. "I followed it out the palace's front door before I lost the trail, but I figured that if I stuck with Acker, you'd come to me with B in tow."

"He could have been acting alone," Acker says, noncommittal.

Messer gives him a look that says something like *do I look stupid to you?* and Acker returns the look with one of his own that says Messer wouldn't like his answer.

"And Wells?" Fredrich inquires.

Messer shrugs as he begins to graze on the remaining food. "Evelyn has likely put the pieces together by now, and she's undoubtedly pissed. I'm not sure what that means for your friend, considering he arrived with her kidnapper, but I imagine there's a tiny bit of torture involved."

Acker's mouth thins as he considers the position Wells is in. The position *he* put him in.

"Beau won't let anything happen to him," I assure Acker and Fredrich both. "My mother will question him, yes, but not in the way Messer wants you to believe."

"You could have let him worry for a little longer, B," Messer says, his mouth full. "So, what's the plan, *Ace*?"

Acker only gives Messer an acrid look in reply.

"Please tell me I didn't subject myself to your wonderful company for days on end only to find you don't even have a plan of action," Messer says.

Sucking on his teeth, Acker cocks his head to the side, eyes sliding to Irina. An understanding passes between the two of them that has me averting my eyes, and I once again have to remind myself that my curiosity will be the death of me if I don't get it under control.

He returns his gaze to Messer, then myself, before he says, "I want to cut off the head off the snake."

"Oh, we knew your father had to go a long time ago," Messer says. "Don't take credit for our idea now."

An amused smile tugs at Acker's mouth that makes me sit forward. "Not just my father. *All* of them."

"You want to kill all the current monarchs?" I ask.

He tilts his head back and forth. "More or less."

"That won't solve anything, only allow more power-hungry fools to take their places," Messer says. "My father's been third in command of the Alaha for decades and has been itching for Wren's title the whole time, and I guarantee you we don't want that fucker sitting on *any* throne."

"*We* replace them," Fredrich interjects.

As I look around the table, the puzzle pieces begin falling into place. Irina, Acker, and I all have legitimate claims to a territory. That's three out of five already present and accounted for. One of us with a secured title already—*me*.

Acker nods, as if he can see me coming to the right conclusion, and says, "We will be the ones to choose who gets to wear a crown."

"And if the councils object?" Messer asks.

Acker shrugs as if the answer is as easy as it is simple.

"Then they die."

Chapter 35

JO

Messer sits on the ledge of the roof of the tavern, back to the edge, watching me pace as I work through my thoughts. "We need to talk to Kai," he says.

"I need to talk to my mother," I amend.

"I can't fly to two places at once. You're going to have to pick one over the other."

I turn my head to the west, putting my back to the freezing wind. "She's probably sick with worry."

Messer nods. "I know. And I know how much it's bothering you, but even if she is getting the army ready to invade Kenta, it'll take Drake a week to sail to the mouth of the Yanka River, another to set up a blockade and set up camp on land."

While I hoped to keep my people out of the war, I knew it was never guaranteed. They know it, too. The people of Maile aren't naive. Preventing Strou's warriors from crossing the gulf was just the preamble. But Kai was supposed to have crippled and taken Kenta by now.

Choosing sides is the same as choosing conflict.

"You're actually considering this," I say, voice flat.

He gawks at me. "You're not?"

"You mean, rule in accord with Acker and his wife? Why the hell would I agree to that? I can't trust either one of them!"

"They're not any worse than Chryse, and if we can get Kai to agree to the alliance, it's practically smooth sailing straight to the end of the war."

I close my eyes, dreading his reaction to what I'm about to reveal. "There's something I haven't told you."

"For the love of the Mother," he mutters. "What is it?"

"Chryse is my uncle."

His face screws up in confusion. "What?"

"It's complicated, but Chryse's brother, the previous king of Roison—Osiris—was my real father." Sighing, I take a seat next to him on the ledge. "My mother killed Osiris when he admitted to taking me as a child. That's the reason she relinquished her crown to me, because Chryse refused to negotiate an alliance with her."

Understanding dawns on his face. "But he would with you, his niece."

I nod.

His face slowly turns grave. "You don't want to screw over your own blood," he says, putting the pieces together.

"It's not that I have a particular connection to Chryse. We've never met. I don't even know if he still considers the alliance in good standing after Sam went to inform him of Acker's presence in Maile, but Messer . . ." He watches as I struggle to get the words together. ". . . the last time I betrayed someone; it ate at me." I shake my head. "This is not a decision I can make lightly."

Messer stares at me for a long beat before he rises to his feet. It's his turn to pace, hands on his hips as he stares at the tavern's roof, golden hair blowing in the wind. The only time he ever shuts up is whenever his emotions get too big. He once told me it's because he doesn't like saying things he can't take back. I had made a joke about all the other things he has no problem saying, but he'd only shaken his head and said, *when it's important, I want to be careful.*

"Let me go talk to Kai and get a feel for what he thinks before you're forced to make a decision."

I hesitate a moment before voicing the thing I'm most afraid of. "If we tell Kai the plan and he tells his father . . ."

Messer nods in understanding. "It's a risk, but I think it's one worth taking."

I can't believe I'm even considering this, especially when there's not even one of them that I remotely trust. Not Kai, Irina, *or* Acker. But I suppose I have just as little faith in Chryse.

I'm grateful to at least have Messer. I'd feel lost without his council.

"I should leave before nightfall," he says.

"You're going to lose a wing if you fly in this temperature, Messer. At least wait until morning."

"One night can be all it takes for word to spread that Acker stole you," he says. "Then we have a whole new set of problems on our hands. I need to speak to Kai myself and spin the story in our favor; tell him you left Maile of your own accord."

And I can't help but feel as though Acker timed this entire scheme with that exact problem in mind, knowing I'd be forced to decide in a hurry.

"I hate to give Acker the satisfaction by agreeing to do anything he suggests," I admit.

Messer smiles and it actually relieves me a little to see it. "Don't let your pride overrule your sensibilities."

"Since when did you become one of his supporters?"

His brows furrow. "B, I've always believed he was *it* for you."

My face goes slack at his words, disbelieving. "What?"

"Ever since we left Kenta you've been a shell of yourself and I get the sense he's been very much the same."

I'm too stunned to formulate a response.

"No one goes to the lengths he has unless they're a fool in love," he says, "and Acker is the most foolish man I've seen."

"Messer—"

"The kidnapping you thing was a tad excessive," he adds, cutting me off. Then he rolls his eyes. "But I kind of have to admit . . . I really do think the man loves you."

I shake my head. "Even if he did, it still wouldn't be enough. He married Irina—"

Grabbing me by the shoulders, he turns me so I'm forced to face him. "He's never touched her."

My daze gives way to skepticism. "I saw it with my own eyes, Messer."

He shakes his head. "I don't know what you think you've seen. I'm telling you what *I* see, and that man has never laid a single finger on little miss ice princess."

"Just because you're a self-proclaimed expert of sexual escapades doesn't mean you can tell if two people have slept together just by looking at them."

"I can when it's as obvious as the color of the sky. There might as well be a whole fucking ocean between them. He doesn't even like breathing the same air as her, I promise you."

The conviction with which he says it has me doubting myself. Or maybe I'm just desperate to believe it is true. I don't like either of those options.

He releases me. "Oh, and he stayed apart from her the entire time on the boat here. Then last night, he slept on the floor in Fredrich's room. That was after you two squabbled loud enough to wake the dead, of course, but that's neither here nor there," he says conspiratorially.

I narrow my eyes at him. I would accuse him of spying on me, but it's kind of his job, especially when I'm being held captive.

We take the fire escape back to my open window, then return to the tavern's kitchen to find that Fredrich has opened another bottle of wine and made himself comfortable on the counter. Acker straightens from where he was leaning against the washing basin, and Irina looks up from inspecting her nails at the table.

"Kai would need to be on the Alaha throne," I tell them. "We'd give him Roison's territory as compensation for past grievances."

Fredrich's eyebrows tip up. "He wasn't a part of the deal."

"Take it or leave it."

His gaze swings to Acker who simply stares at me, the reminder of his promise to end Kai's life hanging between us. "He's sent multiple paid men to kill me."

My eyes shoot to Messer who returns my stare with an equally baffled look of his own.

"And you're sure it was him?" Messer asks.

"When faced with death, men often like to bargain for their lives, and more than one of the mercenaries offered up Kai's name." The twirling of the dagger in his hand slows as he contemplates the question. "But that doesn't mean the attacks couldn't have come from closer to home. My father has the power of influence. And Wren. Either could be responsible."

"There's only one way to know," Messer says. "I'm going to leave tonight and fly straight to Kai."

"You know where he's based?" Fredrich asks.

"No, but I'm sure he does," Messer says, nodding at Acker.

Acker walks to the butcher block and pushes what little is left of the food to the side. Using the dagger he's been toying with, he carves into the tabletop, and it doesn't take long to recognize the rudimentary map he scores from end to end of the table. He marks the boundaries, then stabs the dagger into the place where the Kenta palace stands, almost center of the landmass that makes up Kenta.

"We're west of the capital, about here," he says, placing a piece of cheese at our location. "Before I left Kenta, this is where the front lines stood. That was a few weeks ago." He scatters dried meat near the Roison border, but inside Kenta territory. Then he stacks cheese on top of each other, north of the main battleground.

"What is that?" Irina asks.

He doesn't look at her when he responds. "Trolls."

"Nice diagram, but we're aware of all of this already," Messer says. "Where's Kai?"

Acker isn't bothered by Messer's attitude, pointing to an area not far from the trolls' location. "The giants have been finicky. We've gotten word that he spends much of his time keeping them compliant."

"That's about a two-day flight. Less if the wind is on my side," he says.

"One last thing," I say, drawing Acker's attention. "There's a dovecote on the eastern edge of town. I'm going to see if any birds have been left behind. If so, there might be one that can get a letter to my mother." I hold Acker's stare, letting him know I'm not asking his permission, merely informing him of my decision.

"Okay," he says without argument. "I'll go with you."

Fredrich polishes off his wine with a flourish, setting the bottle down on the counter with a heavy thunk. "I'm going to head east in the morning to try to find some feed. The horses aren't going to survive in this weather without proper food."

We're all in agreement as we disperse from the kitchen.

Messer and I convene in my temporary room. We're now too used to having to part from one another to make a big fuss about it, even knowing something harrowing could happen to the other while we're separated. He promises to shift into a leopard if the weather worsens on his way to Kai, and I promise to always keep my wits about me. The guilt and worry he usually struggles to his hide during our goodbyes isn't there, and it makes me believe that he feels I'm safe with Acker.

Which is comical, because the man literally had me chained to a bed last night.

I keep that fact in the forefront of my mind as I venture downstairs hours later. Acker's there, waiting with his feet propped on a table and a dagger in his hand. But I knew that already, the tether leading me right to him. His eyes follow me as I move toward the open entrance of the tavern. The scrape of the chair and his feet hitting the floor sounds behind me before his footsteps follow me out into the street.

"Where's your lap dog?" he asks.

The snap of wings draws my gaze to the bird leaping from the tavern's rooftop. Black wings stretch wide, the span now reaching the length of a small fishing vessel. It's truly a sight to behold. Feathers as black as night underneath the overcast sky, but I know how they shift to pearlescent and blue in the sunlight. Messer's squawk has transformed into a full bellow that would scare the most battle-hardened men into wetting themselves. It's a common occurrence, according to Drake.

When the eyun disappears behind the buildings and the beating of his wings dulls to a faint thump in the distance, I look at Acker. "You were saying?"

Even he cannot deny Messer's grandeur, a hint of a smile pulling at one side of his mouth. "After you," he says, tilting his head in the direction of the dovecote.

Chapter 36

JO

Messer says pigeons are nothing but flying rodents with brains the size of a pea, and that they're dumber than rocks. He swore that he was less intelligent when he shifted back to normal after that one time he forced himself to change into a pigeon. But I don't care what he says; I'll always have a soft spot for birds.

The sound of shuffling wings and feathers whispers from inside the wooden structure, indicating there are still live birds despite being left behind without care. Square windows spiral up the outside of the cylindrical structure, giving view of the birds within their cages. We step through an iron archway and into the small workroom. A counter divides the space, with an enclosed stairway tucked behind it. Shelves stuffed with rolled parchment and tiny metal message tubes line the walls. Quills and inkwells clutter the counter, and a half-written letter has slipped to the floor, abandoned. A wash basin sits in the far corner; the inside stained with splatters of black ink.

I round the counter and approach the stairwell, Acker right behind me. Signs hang from the wall at regular intervals, indicating the territory each section of birds has been trained to fly to. The birds alongside the first twenty steps are designated only for Kenta. Plaques on the front of each individual cage are engraved with the name of the town the occupant delivers to. It's not until step forty, nearly all the way to the top, that the hanging sign above reads *Maile.*

There are only a few cages, and all are empty.

"A town of this size wouldn't correspond with foreign territories much, if at all," Acker says, tone apologetic.

I consider my options. "Wells's parents live in one of the port towns north of the capital, correct? I can send *them* a letter in the hopes that they can pass it along to my mother."

When I look at Acker, I can see his worry in the pinch of his mouth. "It would take weeks for your message to make it to Maile, if Wells's parents can even send it on," he says.

Too long, he really means. "It's the only chance I have," I say.

As we begin our descent, a quiet flutter of wings stops us in our tracks. We move closer to the front of the cage and peer in. Tucked at the very back, hiding in the shadows, is a tiny bird. I check the plaque, and it reads *Maile: Capital City.*

Unlocking the cage, Acker reaches in and grabs the pigeon. It's so small, it nearly fits in the palm of his hand. Acker extends each wing before flipping it over and inspecting its feet; the bird coos in response to being manhandled. The band on its leg is marked with the emblem of the town we're currently in.

"He's small, but healthy. I'm going to find some food and water for him, so he doesn't stop mid-flight to hunt." He places the bird back and looks at me, and if I'm not mistaken, there's a hint of a smile behind his eyes. "Go write your letter."

Most of the materials are easy enough to procure; parchment and ink were clearly not considered important enough to take during the raid. I search the shelves for a new bottle of ink and fresh quill. I flatten a piece of parchment on the counter with a paperweight and unscrew the lid of the new ink. Dipping the quill in, I scrape the excess black liquid from the nib and carefully begin to write out my message. I keep it short and to the point, and blow on the parchment to ensure everything is dry before rolling it up.

At that same moment, Acker appears from the stairwell. "Ready?"

I stuff the parchment into one of the cylinder tubes and snip a piece of twine from the roll behind the counter.

Calling my dagger, I twist the fractured hilt of the hearthstone blade in my hand, gripping it by its spine to not further damage it. I angle the sharpened-tip against the tube and engrave a jagged letter into the side—*J*. A marker for whoever receives it in Maile to know the message is from me and meant for my mother.

We return to the top of the stairs, where Acker retrieves the pigeon once again, holding it on its back so I can tie the message to the leg without the town emblem band. Reaching through the cage to the latch on the other side, I push open the door that leads to the sky beyond. Once secured back inside the cage, it takes so long for the bird to waddle to the opening, its feathers all fluffed up, that I begin to worry it's too young to be of use. But one good gust of wind encourages it to take flight, and then it's gone.

I sigh, relieved.

Regardless of there being a chance the small bird doesn't make it to Maile, I can at least say I tried. Acker looks at me with a soft expression I almost forgot he was capable of and it flusters me.

"Don't look at me like that," I say, sharp voice echoing through the cages and disturbing the remaining birds.

He does a poor job of attempting to tame his grin. "Like what?"

"You're *married*, Acker," I say as I stalk past him, heading back down the stairs.

"It's not like me being promised to another stopped us before," he says flirtatiously as he follows me.

I don't have much in the way of a counterargument, but I stop and spin toward him, spitting out my next question as a challenge. "Why would Irina agree to overthrow her parents?"

"She wants to spare their lives."

"You'd kill them?" I ask, curious. "Your own wife's parents?"

"If they don't take a knee, then yes."

The way he says it with such nonchalance doesn't sit right. "How does that make you any better than the rest of the terrible men already in power?"

A closed-lip smile graces his features as he takes the next step down, bringing us closer. He reaches forward, movements slow and deliberate as he brushes a finger over my brow, into the dip of my temple. His gaze follows his hand before he meets my eyes again.

"Because I don't want them to bow to *me*," he says, voice low. "I want them to bow to *you*."

His words rattle me, so much so that I have to brace a hand against the stairway wall to prevent myself from losing my balance. "Wha . . . Why would you say that? I don't—" I shake my head. "I don't want *anyone* to bow to me."

"But they already do. Your people love you," he says, pride making his eyes shine. "You were able to sway my own people right out from under my father despite the fact that they could barely tolerate your presence when you initially arrival in the capital."

It takes me a moment, but then I figure it out, figure *him* out. "You know that if you win this war, the support of the people will be critical if you're to hold on to the throne afterward. You want to use me to bolster the public's opinion of you." Just as he wanted to the first time he brought me to Kenta.

"No," he says, sharply, eyebrows shadowing his dark eyes as he frowns. "I want to rule with the wife I originally wanted. The wife I should have fought for. Your favor with the people is to be expected, because it's fucking impossible not to love you. I should know. I've *fucking* tried."

I tilt my head away from his lingering touch. "I don't believe you."

He tilts his head and raises an eyebrow. "Rightfully so. I just kidnapped you." Then he brushes past me, leading the way down the stairs.

Dumfounded, I spin in place as I watch him descend, trying to get my mind to catch up with everything he just said. I hurry so as not to lose sight of him around the curve of the stairwell, but just as I catch up, he halts suddenly, and I have to pinwheel my arms to stop myself from toppling into him. He reaches out and unlatches the door to an occupied cage and leans in to open the external hatch. This bird doesn't waste any time before leaping from its perch and winging away.

"What are you doing?" I ask, still off-kilter.

"They're only going to die if we leave them," he says, moving to the next cage. "Might as well let them go."

He has a point. They'll arrive at their destination without a message attached, but at least . . .

I stop him with a hand on his shoulder before he's able to open the next cage. "Wait," I tell him. "I have an idea."

Once I explain, it doesn't take him long to give his assent and we spend what little daylight remains executing the plan. I write the messages and stuff them into the little tubes, and he ties each to a bird before releasing them. He sends the birds with the longest flights out first, and by the time we reach the last one, night has fallen.

I inspect the parchment bearing the last message to make sure none of the ink has a shine to it. *All hail Captain Wren, the new king of Kenta.*

Edmond will know the messages aren't Wren's doing, but the damage will already be done. The people will be confused. Some will flee. Tales of Wren's depravity are far-reaching and woven deep into the collective memory of Kenta. If Edmond defends his alliance with Wren, he'll appear weak, and most will believe he's been manipulated by the captain. And if Edmond forsakes him, he'll lose Wren's army.

"You really are the queen of deception," Acker says, with a wry smile, taking the message tube from me.

Of all the things he's said to me today, this is the one thing I know he actually means.

As he ascends the stairs to send the last note, I move to the wash basin to clean my hands. The bar of soap is specially made to remove ink, but it still takes a lot of scrubbing to make the black fade from my skin. The stain under my nails can't be helped at all.

I'm drying my hands with a towel when Acker returns. I move out of his way so he can wash up, too, and take stock of the mess I've made of the room. Even though the people of this town are long gone, it bothers me to think of leaving it in a worse state than I found it. I busy myself with capping the inkwells and returning unused parchment to its rightful place on the shelves. I hear the water cut off a moment before I sense Acker's presence looming behind me.

Bracing a hand on the edge of the counter beside me, he cages me in. He peers over my shoulder and inspects the parchment pieces I had discarded due to one error or another. "You never told me what you wrote to your mother."

I've been wondering when he would broach that subject. "Wouldn't you like to know?"

I hear the teasing in his voice when he replies, "Hopefully it read something along the lines of . . . 'Please don't kill my Match. He's been nothing but a perfect gentleman.'"

I can't help my smile. "You want me to lie? To my own *mother*?"

He leans in close to my neck and inhales. "Sometimes lying has its benefits."

My eyes flutter closed for a moment before I'm able to pull myself together. Pivoting in place, my body brushes against his front as I face him. I brace my hands on the table behind me and meet his dark gaze. "You mean, you want me to lie when it benefits *you*."

"When it's believable," he says, voice low.

"I think we both know I can be very convincing." *Ironically, a lie.*

He grins, but it doesn't quite reach his eyes. "Then convince me," he says.

I've craved him for so long, but my memory failed to capture just how intoxicating he is in person. His smell, the warmth of his body, the weight of his dark gaze. It's shameful how much he affects me. I shouldn't crave him the way I do.

His eyes drop to my mouth. "Tell me you don't want me to kiss you," he says.

"I don't want you to kiss me."

He isn't dismayed in the least. "Tell me you don't want me to touch you."

The words leaving his mouth shouldn't make me want the exact opposite. I try to respond, but find myself swallowing my own voice, the sound audible over our mingling breaths.

He leans closer, hand grabbing me by the waist. "Convince me, Jovie," he demands.

"I don't want you to touch me." I'm impressed that the words come out of my mouth at all, even if they're little more than a pathetic whisper.

"Tell me you don't want me to slide my hand between your legs and make you come on my fingers."

"I . . . I don't—"

There's absolutely no chance I'll be able to make myself say the words, a blush burning across my face. The grip he has on my waist tightens before being released completely, and the breath that leaves me is mixed with equal amounts of disappointment and relief. That feeling lingers only until he lifts the hem of my shirt, the back of his fingers skimming my lower stomach.

My voice is shaky when I say, "I don't want you to make me come."

A real smile graces his lips. "Good," he encourages. Fingers dipping under my waistband, he uses the material to yank me toward him, his mouth touching mine as he speaks. "But you can do better. Tell me again but *mean it* this time."

Then he *is* sliding his hand into my pants, and I *do* want him to make me come. But I know the only way I can ensure that it happens is if I continue to lie—and we both damn well know I'm not good at it. I was *never* good at it. It's just easier to get away with when no one looks for the truth.

I hate there's a part of me that wants to continue this game just so he doesn't stop. I've craved his touch, his comfort, for so long that I'm desperate to see this through. But I know I'd hate myself if it happens this way.

I meet his hooded gaze. "I *want* you to make me come," I say, steeling my voice.

His expression shifts entirely, eyes darkening into something more sensual, smile slipping as his gaze heats. "There she is," he croons.

There's no teasing or slow lead-up before he grasps the most intimate part of me. My eyes lose focus and my breath catches in my throat as his fingers dip to my center, the heel of his hand pressing firmly against my bundle of nerves.

He hums against my lips. "Like this?" he asks, mouth dragging over my cheek, up to my temple.

I nod eagerly. "Yes."

He squeezes and my knees nearly buckle, eyes falling closed with a moan. Wrapping his other arm around my waist, he keeps me upright, body pressing mine back against the counter. He inserts a single finger, and I hate that his mouth isn't on mine to muffle the gasp that escapes my throat, the sharp intake of breath punctuating the quiet of the small room.

His lips coast to the shell of my ear, his voice sending shivers down my spine. "Don't fight it."

As if I needed his permission, I let my mind go blank. His panting breath mirrors my own, as if he's the one on the verge of falling apart, not me. He doesn't relent, teeth nipping at the tender skin below my ear, tongue lapping in its wake to soothe the sting. I let go of the counter, grabbing his forearm for purchase, hips chasing the pleasure with every stroke of his fingers. I'm so, so close . . .

"Tell me, Jovie," he pants, arm flexing as he works me closer to the edge. "Do you love me?"

His words are the equivalent of being doused with freezing cold water. My eyes fly open, the gravity of the situation hitting me full force at the same time my body betrays me. Clenching my teeth, I close my eyes and refuse to make a sound, smothering any signs of physical pleasure.

Then, as soon as the waves abate, I open my eyes to find him staring at me with a smug fucking grin.

I shove him away from me.

He dares to slip the wetness on his fingers past his lips for a taste. I cannot be held responsible for what I do next, because I act purely out of blind rage.

I punch him in the face.

I don't even register I've done it until he touches the split in his lip, inspecting the red on his fingers, and I have to shake the throb from my hand.

His expression shutters as he licks the cut, but it doesn't bring me the satisfaction I really want.

"What was this, Acker?" I ask, furious. "Punishment for the thing with Fredrich?"

His answer is swift. "No." Then he rolls his eyes. "Although, if it was, I'd say it was a more than *lenient* punishment."

Unbelievable.

Defeated, tears threaten to emerge and I turn away from him before he can see them. I adjust the waistband of my panties, and it's only once I get my emotions under control that I dare face him again.

"I'm sorry," I say as I try and fail to stop my voice fraying around the edges. "Is that what you need to hear? That I regret what I did, and if I had a chance to choose differently, maybe I would?"

Hurt flashes across his face. Or maybe it's anger or surprise. I'm unsure and no longer trust my judgment when it comes to him. He's too much of everything and I'm obviously not capable of withstanding him in any capacity.

I continue, more firmly: "But what's done is done, Acker. I can't change what I did with Fredrich any more than I can my betrayal of you all those years ago. If you're searching for ways the oath will allow you to get retribution, then you're going to have to get more creative."

His head jerks back in confusion before he steps back toward me. "Let me make one thing known, Jovie," he says, cornering me against the counter once again. "Oath or no oath, and no matter what has already happened or what has yet to happen, nothing will *ever* negate the fundamental truth that you are, and have always been, *mine*."

I shake my head in astonishment. "You can't claim me," I protest.

His earnest expression combined with the indifference in his voice when he speaks is perplexing. "Even if Mother Nature hadn't already given me permission to do so when she made you my Match, it wouldn't make any difference." He steps closer and I hold my ground when he stops within reaching distance, dark eyes shifting between mine. "There's no other ending for us."

Chapter 37

ACKER

I sense Messer's arrival back at the tavern long before he appears, the blood in his veins is heavy with iron. He came in through the window Jovie left cracked open for him in the spare bedroom, and he must have seen the clothes I left out for him. As he's coming down to the main room, he's still shoving an arm through the sleeve of his shirt when he reaches the bottom of the stairs. He looks exhausted, with dark circles under his eyes, after flying across the territory to speak to Kai and back again in just three days. Faster than any bird on record.

Fredrich kicks out a chair for him, which he graciously accepts, falling into it with a heavy sigh.

"B's sleeping," he says.

I already knew that, but it's more difficult to explain sensing her through the Bond than it is to just nod my acceptance.

He holds my stare. "Kai wants to meet in person to discuss the possibility of an alliance before he'll agree to anything."

Figures. "I don't think that's a good idea."

Messer nods as if he, too, suspected that would be my answer, but it's Fredrich who speaks up. "Wait. Let's think this through before we write it off."

"There's something I need to explain to you before you decide," Messer adds.

I can feel Fredrich's stare slide to me, but I don't take my eyes off Messer. Stuffing my hands in my pockets, I place my back to the bar and lean backward, tilting my head toward him in acquiescence.

"You have the floor."

He smirks, sharply. "I may like you, Acker, but that doesn't mean a lot because I tend to like everyone."

"It's true," Fredrich remarks.

"But I do have my limits, and, let's face it, you've pushed them about as far as they can go."

For a moment, a part of me believes he's angry about what happened between me and Jovie in the dovecote before I'm able to rationalize he'd likely have already bitten my head off if that were the case. "By stealing your queen," I infer.

His smile turns bitter. "By stealing my best friend."

Anything I have to say wouldn't be productive *or* nice, so I bite my tongue instead.

"I understand that she's your Match—"

"I don't think you do."

He sucks his teeth in annoyance. "Were you born this arrogant or is it just a side effect of being a spoiled prince?"

Fredrich answers for me. "It's kind of a requirement for the position."

The bastard only shrugs when I look at him.

Messer sighs. "B—*Jovie*—is important to me. Probably the most important. If I had to create a list, her name would be at the very top." He stops to clear his throat before continuing. "She's my family, but, even so, I am careful about how I speak of her when talking to Kai."

I dislike where this is going already. "In what regard?"

"Kai has always held this belief that Jovie belongs to *him*."

Heat immediately scorches through my blood.

I have to remind myself that Kai is a long way from here and there's not any way for me to correct the very misguided beliefs of Jovie's childhood friend—the man to whom she was formerly betrothed—right now.

The tether begins to stir and the sensation of iron moving more swiftly overhead letting me know that Jovie is waking up.

"When we were growing up, he would get territorial if he felt like she and I were getting too close." He rocks back lightly in the chair, his expression blank as he recalls the past. "He monopolized her."

I remember the hovel she lived in out over the sea. Alone, high above and far from the busiest parts of the grove in Alaha. I knew then that it was intentional, her isolation, but couldn't figure out why Wren would have taken the Princess of Maile only to treat her like an inconvenience.

There's a hesitant look in Messer's gaze when he meets my stare. "He eventually told me his father gifted Jovie to him."

And now my veins are ice-cold. "Under what fucking authority?"

He doesn't react to my anger as he continues. "You see, Kai hates his father. His mother, Faline, spoiled him and he became rebellious as he got older. Any time the captain would try to discipline Kai, try to keep him in line, Kai would only retaliate harder. When Wren asked Kai what it would take for him to obey, Kai asked for Jovie's hand in marriage."

Fury has me reaching for the blade I left on the bar, spinning it in my hands, needing something to do with the energy buzzing through my veins.

"But then Wren began . . . *training* . . . Kai in the ways of the land. At first, we believed it was just an old wives' tale, Jovie and me. We thought Kai was making it up. Magical gifts imparted onto humans from Mother Nature. We wanted him to prove it by influencing one of us to hop on one foot, but his father made him perform a blood oath, to swear not to use it on anyone without his permission."

"The soil he used was old," I say, having experienced its lack of potency myself.

When I was held prisoner in Alaha, Wren had made me swear a blood oath not to reveal Jovie's true identity to her when I requested to speak with her, but I was able to overcome its bonds within a week's time.

He shrugs. "Days later, Kai snuck through my window with some soil he had stolen from his father and gave me instructions to handle it in my bare hands every day, but to hide it well. That after some time my gift would make itself known."

Fredrich seems particularly invested in Messer's spiel, eyes steady on the shifter. "How long did it take?" Fredrich asks.

"Nearly a year. I turned into a cuttlefish on the floor of my bedroom. Thought I was going to die without oxygen before I could switch back." He smiles to himself at the memory. "I pissed all over my floor."

We all chuckle.

"The first thing I did was look for the image of a bird I'd seen in a book from my father's study. It had always been my favorite, for as long as I can remember, and I flew straight to Jovie's room as soon as I shifted."

Impressed, I ask, "You flew on the first try?"

"First try," he confirms, grinning. "But I was terrible and hit just about every branch in the grove along the way, injuring my wing."

His story triggers the memory of Jovie explaining how she had garnered a bird as a pet.

"I was too weak to shift back when Jovie found me in her shiel. She didn't know it was me, obviously, but she kept me in her sink and fed me sardines as she tried to nurse me back to health. Even though it was against the law to keep pets."

Soft footsteps sound on the stairs, and we all pause, waiting for Jovie's arrival. Hair escapes her unkempt braid, still mussed from sleep, her freckles are on full display in the last golden rays of daylight. She's been fighting her nightmares at night, choosing to pace her bedroom floor instead of sleeping, and it finally caught up to her today. I found her crashed out right after around noon, but it seems our voices may have woken her from her slumber.

She's radiant, as if she's made from the sun itself, and I may blind myself if I stare too long.

She sits in a chair at the same table as Messer, but she doesn't look at me. Hasn't in three days since we went to the dovecote. I pushed her too far. My own desires became blurred. I wanted to touch her, but I needed her to admit that she wanted it just as badly as I did. Telling her to lie to me was just to lure her into admitting the truth, that my hunger for her isn't one-sided. And if there's anything I know about Jovie, it's that her stubbornness will win every time. Then once she gave it to me, the words spilling from her beautiful mouth with resolve in her gaze, it only made me want more. Fueled by the lust funneling through the tether, I wanted those three little words to come next.

Most importantly, I wanted them to be true.

But maybe she was a little bit right. I did want to punish her, just not for the reasons she thinks. As much as her betrayal hurt, I now understand why she did it even if it's not what I would have done if our places were switched. And as much as I loathe the fact my friend knows what she tastes like, I don't blame her for doing the very same thing I attempted to do with Irina on my wedding night.

No, my frustration stems from something else entirely.

Like right now, as she offers Messer a smile when she refuses to look at me. "I returned home after training one day and you were gone," she says.

He nods. "Apparently the entire grove had been looking for me," he continues. "And Jovie had told Kai about the bird she was harboring. He was able to put the pieces together and he warned me against revealing my true self to her. It wasn't long after that when I sensed a change in their friendship."

My heart stops altogether before picking up pace.

Fredrich looks at Jovie, surprised. "Kai influenced you?"

"I don't know," she says, expression shuttered. "I want to think he wouldn't do that to me, but . . ." She trails off as she contemplates the likelihood that her childhood friend could have done that to her.

"And you . . . ?" I ask Messer. "What do you think?"

His expression is equally torn. "If he did, I'd like to believe it would have been by Wren's command."

"Kai had a way of making it seem like he was letting us in on all the secrets," she says, biting her cheek before releasing it. "I barely believed anything about magic was true, let alone that it could be used on me."

"Either way," Messer says, shrugging. "She seemed happier. And after being miserable for so long, how could I deny her that? So, I kept a close eye out just to make sure that if he was influencing her emotions in his favor, that he wasn't taking it too far."

Jovie offers Messer a pitying smile and it says everything without the need for words. She clearly forgave him a long time ago for never revealing what Kai was possibly doing to her. If she even considers it something in need of absolution.

"Why are we even discussing this?" she asks.

"Kai wants to meet," Messer explains.

Judging by the expression on Jovie's face when her gaze shoots in my direction, I'm going to go out on a limb and say she also doesn't think it's a good idea. It's the first time she's looked at me since the day I basically professed my undying love for her, and I have some pride left in me to pretend as though I'm unaffected by the weight of her gaze despite the way my heart stutters in my chest.

I return my attention to Messer. "But you know what his main demand is," I suggest.

"He wants an alliance," Messer says, "But only under the condition that Acker doesn't sit on a throne."

I'm unable to restrain my sudden burst of laughter at the sheer hilarity of his demand. "I'm going to take that as confirmation he did send men to kill me," I say between breaths.

Messer's expression reveals as much. "He didn't deny it."

I slide a curious look in Jovie's direction, eager to know what she thinks considering the alliance she holds with Chryse under the guise of sparing my life. But her expression is carefully placid. Not a single blink despite the spike of anger I feel down the tether. It's astonishing, her ability to mask her emotions. Her composure should be studied.

Fredrich throws up his hands in exasperation. "Why were you even willing to work with Wren's son if he's, please forgive me, such a piece of shit?" he asks to the room.

Messer's expression is contemplative as he considers. "He hates his father because it was his actions that led to Alaha's exile and what they've been subjected to for all these years. Deep down, Kai only wants to do what's right."

"How likely is he to divulge our plans?" I ask.

"He wants Chryse's land and his father dealt with," Messer says. "He's not going to risk either of them surviving this war. I think if we can eliminate Edmond as well as Wren, Kai will be much more trusting of a new alliance. Including one that involves you on the Kenta throne, Acker."

Fredrich and I trade glances. "What are you thinking?" I ask him.

"There're a lot of advantages to having him on our side. The men, the trolls, the inside knowledge of his father's maneuverings. But to ask you to give up on the throne . . ." He lifts a shoulder, leaving the rest his thoughts unspoken.

"It's not as if you have to follow through with the deal," Jovie says as if bored by the conversation. "You can always agree for the time being, then reevaluate once the war is over and the bodies are cleared from the battlefields."

"You're already planning to backstab one of our allies before an accord is even established?" Fredrich asks, incredulous.

Jovie shrugs, noncommittal.

But it's Messer who looks at Fredrich like he's dumb. "It's kind of her thing."

Fredrich and I share a pointed look, assessing the other's thoughts on the matter. Eventually, he offers a raised brow. "The least we can do is hear him out," he says.

I once swore that I'd kill Kai if I ever laid eyes on him again and, unlike my Match, I intend to keep the promises I make. Not that I need any more reasons to kill the fucker, considering everything Messer and Jovie just revealed. But as I look at Jovie and note the calculating look in her eyes, I have to consider the possibility that she's setting me up. It's the same easy stare she hid behind while making me fall in love with her. If I'd thought taking her from Maile would knock her off-kilter and give me the upper hand, I'd be sorely mistaken. She's plenty smart enough to find new, inventive ways to stab me in the back again, all while looking me right in my eyes.

"Messer," I say, swinging my gaze to the worn-out shifter. "Can you set up a meeting?"

And even though he's exhausted, he doesn't hesitate to nod. "Time and place?"

"A week from today, at the southern cottage. It's nearly due south from here on the coast. I can draw you a map."

Messer nods. "If I'm not too far behind, I should be able to find your trail, too."

"Don't you think that's a tad risky?" Fredrich asks.

I shake my head. "My father isn't going to leave the capital in my absence. It's not all that far from here, and we need to leave as soon as possible anyway. It's only a matter of time before someone puts together where the pigeons came from."

"Pigeons?" Messer asks, perplexed. "What do those flighty bastards have to do with anything?"

I grin, and when my gaze swings to Jovie, I'm pleasantly surprised by the conspiratorial hint of a smile behind her eyes.

Fredrich mutters a curse under his breath, knowing me well enough to not ask for any further explanation, before he says, "I'll go ready the horses."

Chapter 38

JO

The smell of salt water elicits such a profound sense of nostalgia that it makes my heart hurt.

I keep my eyes on the horizon, searching for a glimpse of the sea or cottage, whichever were to appear first. The view of the coast blocked only by gentle, rolling hills. Acker said we should reach our destination by midday, and while the temperature is blisteringly cold, we at least have clear skies, even if the sun's warmth barely touches my skin.

I suppose I should just be grateful that it's not snowing. That and the fact I've been granted the privilege of having my own horse for this trek, which *almost* makes up for having to follow behind the horse shared by Acker and his wife.

I've tried not to dwell on Irina's words from the day we arrived at the tavern, but they've been nagging at me. Her insistence that we're equals, somehow, as if what I have with Acker is on the same level as the tryst between her and Acker that left her heartbroken.

What I *had* with Acker, anyway.

I'm ashamed of how juvenile and petty my thoughts have become. It's not as if I need to prove anything to her, but I'd be lying if I said I hadn't thought of grabbing Acker by the front of his shirt just so I can plant my mouth on his and show her that we are not in the same boat. That I could have him if I wanted to . . . I'm just fairly sure that I *don't*. Not when he only wants to use me as a tool to further his ambitions.

If I was okay with being used, I would never have left Kai.

I don't know if he influenced me, but I firmly believe he thought I was going to play a pivotal role in getting him out of Alaha. I think it's the only reason he even revealed any of the information his father shared with him, especially regarding the truth of my identity. He heard his father speak of a prince who had searched for me at the Market the year before I was set to visit with my class of guards in training. While I humored Kai's belief that I was the lost princess of Maile, I was also desperate to get onto land, so I agreed to his ill-conceived plan to go to the Market together.

Neither of us, however, considered the possibility that the prince—*Acker*—would accuse me of thievery and threaten to cut off my hand when he saw me.

Just when I'm sure I've reached the limits of my sanity, I spot a glint in the distance. As we get closer, I'm able to distinguish the sunlight gleaming off the copper roof of the cottage, although *cottage* is a tame word to apply to the sprawling estate atop the hillside. The stone walls are white, bleached from the salt water and sun over the decades or centuries it's been standing. Arched glass windows stretch from the bottom to the top of the third floor. Gardens frame the structure with a variety of colorful plants that I'm positive aren't native to the area, and I figure they must be maintained by an earth elemental.

It's not long after when I'm able to make out the sound of waves crashing against the shoreline that must be just over the hill.

I squeeze my legs against my horse, urging him into a gallop toward the top. The wind bites at my face and ears, and whips my hair into knots, but I'm too eager to care. Once the horse's hooves meet stone instead of grass, I pull on the reins to slow him to a stop before the cottage's gate. The wrought-iron entrance stands open. The walkways through the gardens are limestone, the same stone as the cliffs at the

Market. A footman hurries out the front door and down the stone steps toward us, servants hot on his heels.

He greets Acker with a bow. "My apologies, your highness. We were not expecting you."

But it's not the grandiose property with accents of metal and glass that has my attention, but the booming sound of waves from over the hill.

I'm swinging myself down from the saddle just as Fredrich and Acker maneuver their horses to a stop beside mine. But I don't wait for them, my heart pounding in my chest as I follow the well-worn path leading beyond the cottage.

"Let her go," I hear Irina say behind me.

I venture underneath trellises of climbing roses, around the iron fence and the side of the estate. Cresting the hill, the ocean air slaps me across the face, the smell of salt like a balm for my tired soul. The water that crashes on the beach below is bright blue and gnarly. It's very different from the water found in the gulf off the coast of Maile, where the ocean mixes with the muddy water of the Yanka River, creating a murkier blue with a sweeter scent.

Messer, despising being landlocked, never understood my willingness to live in the palace, so far from the coastline, but it's because nothing could ever measure up to the sea that surrounded us in Alaha for the majority of our lives.

This is exactly what I've been missing.

Stairs are carved into the cliffside, and I eagerly head down them. They're uneven and broken in places, making the descent all the more treacherous, but my excitement is too great to slow down. Toward the bottom, they become pockmarked from erosion, showing just how high the water can get when the tide comes in, likely often swallowing the beach completely.

I sit on the second to last step to remove my boots and socks, then roll up my pant legs. My toes sink into the cool sand as I make my way toward the crashing waves. The ocean has carved and shaped the cliffside into a half circle, which causes the wind to whistle loudly against the limestone walls as it blows around the cove. My clothes plaster against my body and my hair is even more of a mess by the time I reach the point where the water rolls onto the flat of sand. I'm prepared for the surf to be cold, but even still, it surprises me enough that I suck in a sharp breath through my teeth.

As much as the cold water bites at my bare skin, I don't move as the water recedes and then rushes in again with a vengeance. I stare at the expanse of water laid out before me. Large and foreboding and so much like the view that I grew up resenting. Now, it offers me a semblance of home.

Alaha is out there.

Past the horizon and further away than most probably realize. Where majestic trees, larger than any that live here on land, rise from the water, their soaring canopies providing sanctuary to a forsaken people. It's not the Alaha way of life that I miss—the desperate existence carved out over the ocean—but a time when everything felt simpler. All Kai ever talked about was getting to land, and while doing so, it also subjected them to a life of violence and uncertainty. What if the cost is ultimately too great? Isn't that what Wren always warned Kai about?

I feel Acker's presence behind me. Looking over my shoulder, I spot him at the top of the hillside, his arms folded across his chest, standing like he's ready to fight the ocean if it decides to try to swallow me whole.

If the water was warmer, I'd probably let it.

I turn my gaze back to the ocean, hating that Acker can likely feel the barrage of turbulent emotions flooding through me. It's infuriating, considering all I've sacrificed in the name of preventing him from intruding into my mind and life, the shame I carried with the weight of stones around my neck as the leader of Maile, for my people to know my greatest weakness, only to find out that it was all for nothing.

Beau was right in her assessment that magic doesn't like being denied, but even more than that, I think Acker hates being denied even more.

I still remember the night Kai snuck up to my shiel, panicking, his face stricken as he made me swear to *never* let his father touch me. He explained that there's no chance of shielding the power of influence if there's direct contact. His ramblings sounded nonsensical, and it wouldn't be until the day at the Market, when I touched the stone cliff so much like the one Acker is standing on right now, that I truly understood why Kai was adamant about teaching me to shield my mind.

And I did.

For so long and so well that I think . . . I think I even hid the truth of who I am from myself.

My thoughts and feelings and magic. All of it shoved to the furthest reaches of my soul, as if I should be ashamed of being vulnerable instead of embracing the power it gives me.

Closing my eyes, I reach for the place where my magic resides. The tether to the Bond is there, but I ignore it as I implore my gift to respond to my calling. Like igniting a long wick, the heat spreads up the center of my chest, toward my neck, before moving to my right shoulder, down my arm and into my upturned hand. I open my eyes to the flicker of light building in my palm. Brighter than the wintery sunlight, it dances.

I think it's about time my gift and I become well acquainted.

Chapter 39

ACKER

She directs the beam of light from her hands into the waves cresting over her feet, turning the water from turquoise to liquid gold. The ripples bending and breaking on the surface send refracting shards of light back at Jovie, illuminating her in the same whirling glow.

She's breathtaking as she walks into the ocean, letting her gift warm the water enough for her to swim, which she's obviously missed deeply. I feel her joy through the Bond, the kind of happiness that aches a little.

The same kind I feel every time I look at her.

When she dives under an incoming wave and emerges on the other side, it's like a miniature sun darting through the turbulent waters. Concern has me rooted in place, watching avidly as she swims through the churning waves to reach calmer swells before turning onto her back with her arms outstretched at her sides. But as she floats, I don't need the Bond to reveal how her worries have eased as her body goes lax, cradled by the water. Still glowing like a sprite.

The iron in Fredrich's blood signifies his presence to me before I hear his footsteps along the pathway behind me.

"I sent the staff away with bonus pay," he says, coming to stand at my side.

"Enough for them to keep their mouths shut?" The last thing we need is one of the servants trying to curry favor with my father by exposing our presence here.

"Plenty," he says. "Plus, I may have hinted that we know where their families live."

"Good," I tell him, my tone clearly a dismissal; I want to observe my Match in peace.

But when he doesn't leave, I turn my head to look at him, sensing there's more he wants to say. His eyes are fixated on Jovie, and I have to quell the desire to demand he avert his eyes. She's not doing anything scandalous, but it's such a private moment for her, and I don't feel he deserves to witness it. Hell, I don't believe I do either.

"That look on her face," he says, voice somber. "When she heard the ocean . . . That was the same look she had when she heard of your arrival in Maile."

If his intention was to wound me, it works. There's a sharp, twisting pain in my gut as I process his words. The realization that she came to me on the wharf, hoping for the same comfort the ocean gives her, only to find disappointment and heartache instead.

"Ace, we don't know what the future holds." His gaze shifts to me, a sharpness in his eyes that I haven't seen for many years, not since we were the last from our camp to survive the surprise attack by Roison. "And you're wasting time."

Wasting time doing what? But even as I ponder it, I already know. We've yet to experience the worst of this war. I need to return to the palace and handle my father. Instead, I'm trying to score an alliance with a man I despise just to appease Jovie when I'd prefer to eliminate Kai from the entire situation. He'd be one less unknown variable in an ever-shifting war. But Jovie . . .

I want her by my side.

And if this is the compromise I need to make to ensure she fights with me and not against me, then I'll do it.

Fredrich heads back to the cottage and leaves with the warning hanging over my head, as I watch Jovie get reacquainted with something she used to resent. It's almost as if the water is embracing her with open arms after all this time apart, having missed her, too.

I understand what it's like to have despised something—or some*one*, rather—only to later recognize the error. Time does funny things to one's perspective. The four years following Jovie's betrayal have felt like a never-ending nightmare, but the sting of her betrayal is beginning to feel like a distant memory, as if simply being around Jovie again has lessened its potency.

I watch her for hours and its nearly nightfall when her light finally dims, magic spent. She all but crawls out of the water and lays on the sand, the surf licking at her ankles for a long while more. I know she's freezing and tired, and I also know any attempt to help her up the cliff-side steps would be met with hostility. So, instead, I head back to the cottage to prepare one of the spare bedrooms and fill the porcelain tub overlooking the ocean, ready for her return.

It's another hour until she pushes through the gate leading to the back of the house. She follows the limestone path to the rear entrance of the cottage, soaking wet and shivering. She barely takes in the plush furniture and rugs once inside, venturing out of the parlor toward the butler's quarters where I'm sitting at the base of the stairs watching her underneath the flickering sconces lining the wall of the stairwell.

I raise my bowl of soup. "The maidservants left a pot simmering on the stove before they went home."

She eyes my bowl, the steam billowing up invitingly, but doesn't move. "Poisoned?"

I smile despite her attempt at a joke falling flat, the deadened tone of her voice giving away just how exhausted she is. "You're welcome to take a bowl to your room if you'd like." I jerk my head in the direction of the stairs. "Bath is getting colder by the minute."

Lifting a singular brow, she pins me in place with her eyes, as if to warn me against making any hasty movements as she trudges forward. Her stomach rumbles loud enough for me to hear and I bite my lip in an effort to hide my smile. She sees it anyway and, before I can even blink, snatches the bowl from my hands with more agility than I thought her capable of, stomping around me and up the stairs without another word.

I yell at her retreating back, "Second door on the right."

Her *harrumph* sounds something like an acknowledgment, and then the slam of the door shutting behind her echoes down the stairs.

Leaning against the banister, I feel for the iron in the blood of Irina and Fredrich, each in their own respective rooms. Judging by the sharper pull of Fredrich's, I'd say he's at least a bottle deep into whatever liquor he swiped from my father's bar. But Irina's is slow and steady as she lies unmoving, having gone to bed hours ago. She didn't have a lot to say after stopping me from immediately following Jovie when she ran for the cliff's edge. But once we were inside, a smile graced Irina's face for the first time in a long time as she moved into the parlor at the back of the cottage where she observed Jovie swimming from the floor to ceilings windows overlooking the beach.

It takes some time before I feel Jovie's blood slow its pace, exhaustion giving way to contentment as she drifts off to sleep. She's been working herself to depletion, but her dreams are thankfully nonexistent. Her restlessness was keeping me up all night along with her.

I'm able to sense her more deeply than I ever have before. Four years ago, her emotions were little more than a trickling stream down the tether. Now, it's as deep and steady as a river. As if a dam broke at some point in the years we were apart and the current can't be tamed any longer. But instead of it crippling her, it's somehow made her stronger.

The next few days continue in exactly the same way.

Having stolen one of my father's swords from the mantle, Jovie spends her days down at the beach. She runs through drills and repetitions before moving on to exercising her magic. She uses it to warm the water around her as she swims, sometimes sending the flaming balls of light skimming over the water, into the cliffside, or straight into the air before releasing them into explosions of raining light. Others she'll direct into the sword, making the iron red hot as she works through her movements.

I like to pour a glass of dark liquor and take a seat in the parlor as the sun begins to set to watch the show. The steel in her hand sings to me from all the way down at the beach. I can practically feel the heat of her light through the metal, almost as if her magic is flowing through mine. It's incredible to witness.

I tell her as much when she comes inside on the fourth night when she attempts to take the bowl of stew from my hand and pass me on the stairs like she's done every night since we arrived at the cottage. But I don't let her get away with it tonight, pulling the food out of her reach.

Her glare is a threat all of itself.

Instead, I place the bowl on the step behind me before calling the sword in her hand to mine, jerking the weapon from her grasp. It's warm to the touch. Almost too warm, the hilt stinging the skin of my palm as I rotate it. "The last light wielder commanded each of the four main elements," I say, placing the sword over the bend of my knee. "It seems you already favor metal."

Jovie's gaze flicks over me, the sword in my lap, before sweeping up the stairs leading to the bedrooms upstairs, obviously debating how much she's willing to entertain me. I don't give her the option, impaling the sword at an angle into the tread of the stair beside me, blocking her ascent in the narrow stairwell.

Her expression is equal parts annoyance and exhaustion as she gives me her full attention, although begrudgingly. "What do you want, Acker?"

Standing, I move down a step, closing the last of the space separating us. The new position makes her tilt her head back to maintain eye contact with me. Her hair is plastered against the side of her neck, the dark strands escaping her braid are stark against her frigid skin. Water drips from the tendrils, coasting over her pulse, and my mouth is suddenly very dry.

"Do you remember our first kiss?" I ask her.

She's wary of my intentions, but nods. "Yes."

So very slowly, I reach up and unstick the unruly strands with the pinch of my fingers. Goosebumps spread across her exposed skin. Her gaze jumps between mine; hesitation combined with expectation shines back at me. Understandably, considering the kiss in the tavern, when I all but laid myself bare at her feet. Then the day in the dovecote when I tried to force her to admit that she loved me.

I've never been able to think straight when it comes to her.

But as she reaches between us, hands splaying across the expanse of my chest to brace herself, I think . . . maybe she can't think straight when it comes to me either.

I trail the tips of my fingers to the edge of her jaw, down to the point of her chin. "It was as if I could feel your light like it was my own."

She licks her lips. "I could sense the metal in the ground for miles," she says.

I angle her face up to mine, desperate to taste her lips. But I don't want to push her this time. I want her to come to me. And as her gaze lingers on my mouth, she leans in, barely an inch away when she stops. Neither of us move for a long beat, our breaths meeting between us in expectation before I accept that a kiss isn't going to happen. Not until she's ready.

"If Kai doesn't agree to the alliance," I ask, dragging my thumb up and over her bottom lip. "What will you do?"

My question seems to drag her out of a fog, eyes slowly gaining clarity. "You mean, who will I choose?" she asks, tone hardening. "As if I owe you my blind allegiance after you've literally kidnapped and held me hostage."

Then, in a move I'm unprepared for, she grabs the front of my shirt in a fist and yanks me toward her with all of her might. In an effort to save both of us from careening down the stairs, I latch onto the banister. It works, but I stumble back a step, and there's no chance of saving the bowl as it topples down the stairs, sending its contents splashing onto the floor below.

I've barely righted myself when I realize Jovie has maneuvered past the sword and is already halfway up the stairs. Turning, I lunge forward to snag her by an ankle and she falls forward, catching herself on her hands. She kicks out with her spare leg, and I jerk her toward me so her foot swings wide, just shy of my head.

"Stop," I tell her, crawling over her and covering her with my weight, pressing her more firmly into the steps.

She doesn't listen, grunting as she attempts to buck me off. Futile, considering the current level of her exhaustion. And, after a long moment, she seems to come to the same conclusion, and her body goes slack beneath mine.

I brace myself with hands on the tread of stairs on either side of her head, chest tight from exertion. "You can't honestly tell me that bastard deserves your loyalty more than I do." There's no disguising the disbelief in my voice, the anger simmering inside of me at the notion.

"You don't get it," she says, voice cracking.

The raw emotion stuns me, lancing through my chest like a wooden arrow straight from the tether. I hurry to lift my weight from her back, but she makes no attempt to escape.

My breath hitches. "Jovie . . ."

After a moment, she flips onto her back, and I'm relieved to see there's anger in her gaze and not tears when she looks up at me. "I think I knew I would fall in love with you before we even left Alaha, Acker," she says, frustration giving way to determination. "I've *always* chosen you."

Her words hurt just as much as they're soothing. Somehow painful and healing at the same time. There's a sense of relief muddled with the adrenaline of our scuffle. My heart rate is elevated; the blood flowing through my veins grows hot at the untamed look in her eyes, as if finally admitting the truth has allowed the desire she's been suppressing to break through.

The heat in my veins turns into a blazing fire. Slowly, I lower my body once again, and our synchronized intakes of air when my weight fully presses down on her are sharp in the empty stairwell. I take it as an invitation to push my knee between her thighs and she opens them willingly, letting me sink into the space.

I sink my face into the curve of her neck, running my mouth over her damp skin. "Gods, I've missed you."

I drag my mouth up to close the final gap, covering her mouth with mine. I groan as she immediately accepts my touch, mouth pliable and soft, her tongue eager to meet mine. Everything from the way her back arches from the stairs, chest pressed against mine, to the angle of her hips when she feels the hardness pressing between her legs tells me she's missed this just as much as I have.

Her warmth becomes all-encompassing. As we kiss, her hands rake across the skin exposed at the open collar of my shirt, the sensation echoing down the tether. Her gift radiates from within her, and when I somehow find it in me to pull back from her lips, I'm as in awe as I am desperate to feel the ethereal glow of her illuminated skin against mine.

Instantly, Jovie's fingers reach for the buttons of my shirt, pulling apart the material with hasty tugs at the fabric, and I realize she must have seen the thought in my mind through the Bond. Our kissing turns biting, hands working in tandem to take off each other's clothes, mouths separating just long enough to get the material of her shirt over her head. I wrap an arm around her middle and a pleased moan escapes her mouth when I pull her body flush to mine. The feeling of her body pressing flat against my bare chest seems to be her final undoing. Mine, when her hands shove insistently at the waistline of my pants. I reach between us to free myself, wanting to end the prolonged and agonizing suffering we've endured, when a voice comes from below.

"Well, what *do* we have here?"

Jovie and I both freeze, eyes wide as we realize we aren't alone, that Messer is here, having returned from his second visit to see Kai.

"This is an interesting development," he says, smugness evident in his tone of voice.

I sit back on my haunches and look over my shoulder at the shifter below. "You're back early."

Messer stands with a hip cocked against the bottom banister; a smirk firmly planted on his face. "I can come back later. How long do you need, Ace? Three minutes? Four, tops?"

Gritting my teeth, I return my gaze on Jovie as she pulls the front of her shirt closed, the light fading from her eyes . . . quite literally.

"*Messer*," she warns, exasperated.

His responding chuckle grates on my nerves, and I think of the multitude of ways I could murder her friend. She shakes her head at my internal musing as she begins to re-button her shirt. Or rather, do up the buttons that are left attached. I cuss at my painfully hard situation as I adjust myself. *Fucking Messer.*

But it's the sudden spike of emotion coming through the tether that has my eyes focusing on Jovie as I try to shove my cock back into my pants. Her gaze snaps up to meet mine, cheeks turning ruddy at having been caught watching me struggle. She tries to cover it by scowling at me, but all it serves to do is bring a grin to my face.

"There's no need to hide from me, Jovie. I can feel the want, hot in your veins," I tell her, planting a hand beside her head once again. "Let me show you."

I haven't pushed my emotions through, knowing the last time I exposed my inner self to her was too overwhelming. But, as I tilt her chin up with a finger to bring our mouths back together, I hold her gaze and silently ask for permission. She's skeptical at first, but nods her assent, and I let the flood of raging need funnel through the tether toward her. Her responding gasp only adds fuel to the fire, and my eyes fall closed at the potent feeling of her lust mixing with mine.

She melts underneath me. It's raw, reducing us to our basest level, and almost too much, with nothing aside from the two of us mattering. Inescapably honest in our truest form.

I angle her face to the side in a bid to swallow her moans whole. The need to be inside of her is all-consuming, dangerously so as she once again reaches for the front of my pants, hand coasting along my hastily covered cock and I'm moments away from pulling myself out again when Messer's voice interrupts us. *Again.*

I don't fully comprehend what he's said, and my voice comes out more like a growl when I snap, "*What?*"

"Listen, you can proceed with . . . all of this . . . as soon as I relay a message." While his tone is teasing, there's a serious note that has me listening intently. "I'm back early to warn you that Kai is also arriving early."

"How early?" I ask, eyes soaking in the beautiful blush on Jovie's cheeks as it mixes with the soft glow of her magic.

"Tomorrow," he says.

Mother. Fucker.

His words are instantly effective at cooling my blood and dimming Jovie's light, her face falling at the realization we don't have days before Kai's arrival, but mere hours. I don't want to read too much into her trepidation, but it's unmistakable through the Bond.

Messer's voice echoes back to us as he moves further down the corridor. "What's with the beef stew everywhere?"

Chapter 40

JO

It's pouring outside, freezing rain pelting the windows of the parlor. The ocean is at high tide and the swell angry. I turn my back to the view, taking in the somber mood in the main living quarters of the cottage. The fire pops in the hearth, but it's as if the weather has added an additional layer to the gravity in the room. No one has spoken in hours.

Messer reclines on a leather settee, eyes closed as he slips in and out of sleep, turning every so often. Propped on a stool at the bar, Fredrich draws a stone against the blade of a sword. The fifth he's sharpened so far, if I've counted correctly. And try as I might to stop myself, my eyes slide to Acker, who twirls a dagger between his fingers. He's facing the door, his back to the bar, feet crossed at the ankles.

From my vantage point by the windows, I only have a partial view of his features, but I don't need to see them in their entirety to know his expression is severe, intense. And not in the way I enjoyed when we were on the stairs last night; the kind that makes me uneasy.

I'm not sure he slept at all after Messer dropped the news of Kai's impending arrival. He and Fredrich were already down here when I awoke. They've been shifty all morning.

I feel off-kilter. My mind volleying between being anxious of Kai's arrival and reliving the incident on the stairs with Acker only hours ago. I folded. The honesty spilling from my mouth like a broken accord. But once it was out there, it felt too good to take it back. Especially once I saw the stunned expression on Acker's face, awestruck before it filled with the same longing I've been harboring. Then the way he kissed me, held me in his hands, as if it was with all of his being.

The threat of a blush begins to creep up my neck and I dare a glance in Acker's direction, only to find his gaze is already on me, a knowing glint in his eyes as he twirls the dagger in his hand, a grin tugging at his lips.

The silence is broken by the sound of Irina's heels clicking down the main staircase, drawing everyone's attention to her arrival. Dressed in a formal gown, her hair and make-up are done to perfection, and sparkling jewels hang from her ears.

Messer whistles, his sleep deprived gaze raking over Irina's svelte figure. "What's the special occasion?"

She pauses on the threshold, hands smoothing out the silk fabric of her skirts. "In Strou, it is customary to greet dignitaries in our best attire. If I am to represent my people, I'm going to uphold the traditions of my family."

"Where'd you find the dress?" Fredrich asks.

But it's Acker who answers. "It was my mother's." He gives her a nod of approval.

The flare of jealousy in my chest is nonsensical. I think it's safe to say Acker doesn't have any connection to her. Not like what he has with me.

I turn my attention back to the windows and the turbulent waves below. It's strange to feel as though I can relate to the ocean's uncontrollable madness.

I've just gotten my thoughts under control when I feel Irina's presence beside me. I can smell her, too, the florals of her perfume forming a sweet cloud in the air around her.

"The mood in here is abysmal," she says, conversationally. After a tense moment where I don't respond, she continues, "How much do you want to bet he kills him?"

I pivot my head to look at her. "What?"

She shrugs, a soft grin playing on her painted mouth. "I'd be willing to make a small wager."

"On . . . ?"

"Acker," she says, as if the answer is obvious. "On how likely he is to kill your ex-lover."

The term *lover* in reference to Kai makes me uncomfortable, and a quick glance back at the room's other occupants tells me everyone heard it. Fredrich is grinning to himself, and Messer, the same. Acker, however, remains stoic as ever.

I shake my head, keeping my opinion to myself.

If Acker is insistent on taking his father's throne, then I'd say the odds are in Kai's favor. Kai could be a valuable asset if we're to go against Edmond's and Wren's armies. But that doesn't mean the chances of Acker harming Kai today aren't *zero*; I'd say Kai's attitude once he arrives will determine the likelihood of his leaving this cottage alive.

"I'm sure everything is going to be fine," I say, instead.

Irina lifts a brow at my cavalier attitude. "You do lie an awful lot, don't you?"

Oh, for fucks' sake. I'm sick of this whole liar narrative.

"I kissed Acker last night," I say, equal parts ashamed and petty. "Is that honest enough for you?"

If I expected Irina to be shocked or appalled by my admission, I'm sorely mistaken. "Oh, I'm aware," she says, lips upturned. "Everyone in the cottage heard your quarrel on the stairs."

"I think that's putting it mildly," Messer interjects, from where he reclines on the settee.

I narrow my eyes at him. *Whose side is he even on?* He doesn't see my scowl from behind his closed eyes, but his smile only grows, undoubtedly feeling the heat of my glare.

Irina leans in closer, voice conspiratorial and barely above a whisper when she speaks. "The second night following our wedding, I waited up for him in one of my most daring lingerie sets." Her gaze is locked on the view outside, but smiles to herself with an almost pitying expression, like she's talking about someone else. "I waited in bed with champagne and chocolates for hours, and it was near midnight when a man I'd never met before walked through the door of the bedchamber. When I demanded to know who he was, he introduced himself as Wesley, and said that he was there under the prince's orders." Her eyes flick to the side to meet mine. "It was then that I realized Acker was offering me something he could not."

My heart thuds in my chest at the realization. That Acker refused to bed her, at least after the night of their wedding. I can't imagine how much that hurt. Her pride, her heart.

"I refused at first, of course," she says, a genuine smile returning to her face. "But, after an unhappy year went by, I finally accepted the sliver of happiness Wesley gave me. He was very persistent."

"I'm sorry," I say, at a loss for words.

She scrunches up her nose in distaste. "I gave Acker hell for it. Hated him for a long time. You too, and then myself, before I realized there's no one at fault here but the man on the Kenta throne who forced his son to marry a woman for political gain."

With those final words, she squeezes my elbow and leaves me to go and sit on the settee opposite Messer's.

I look at Acker, whose eyes briefly meet mine. A part of me hates that the truth of his relationship with Irina didn't come from him, but I think he always knew I would be suspicious if he tried to discredit the validity of his own marriage. Especially considering what I witnessed the night of their wedding, when I was forced to watch them. The memory of it has haunted me for years.

Acker stands to his full height. "Someone's coming," he says.

Fredrich and Messer react in turn, standing as they watch Acker still the blade in his hand, eyes closed as he concentrates.

"How close?" Fredrich asks.

"Within minutes," he replies, opening his eyes. "They're moving fast by carriage."

He strides to the fireplace, where he places his dagger on the edge of the mantle, the tip aimed at the doorway. It's then that I begin to notice the other weapons. Not hidden, but positioned with precision around the room, and I'm not sure betting against Irina regarding Kai's safety would be a good decision.

Acker turns toward me, using the tether to send an unspoken request for me to join him by the open doorway, a strong tug emanating from below my breastbone. I want to defy him, a stubborn part of me urging me to stand my ground, but there's a larger part of me that wants to be by his side when Kai walks through the front door.

The truth is . . . I'm nervous of being near Kai again.

If Kai did influence me, is it possible that I'll fall under the same spell the moment he walks through the door? The last time I saw him was on the dock in Alaha when Acker and I were making our "escape." It was a ruse meant to cover Kai's involvement in my leaving, but the words he spewed in those moments hit too close to home, felt too real. Humiliating, even.

I don't have to voice my shame or nerves out loud for Acker to sense it, his eyes turning soft in the glow of the fire. "Come here," he says with a gentle tip of his chin.

And I don't hesitate this time, weaving through the ornate furnishings toward him, slipping my hand onto his upturned palm.

He threads our fingers together, pulling me to his side. "You're the queen of Maile," he says, eyes holding mine. "You do not falter before anyone, remember?"

I nod, indeed remembering how he told me something similar when I was forced to kneel before his father that first day in Kenta's palace.

He dips his face into the crook of my neck, inhaling before placing a chaste kiss there. "Besides," he says, letting his lips drag along the skin as he pulls away, before speaking directly into my ear. "He's going to know exactly who you *do* and *do not* belong to."

There's no mistaking the blush flooding my cheeks, and at the same exact moment there's a knock at the front door, I realize that may have been his plan all along. To distract me just long enough for the evidence of my blush to be splashed across my face when Kai and his party arrive, knowing that Kai will draw his own conclusion. As if my hand in Acker's isn't telling enough.

Messer looks around the room at us, meeting each of our gazes one by one, checking to make sure we're ready before crossing the entrance hall to open the front door. My heart thunders in my chest, my hand like a vice around Acker's. I hear Kai's voice a moment before he steps inside. He pushes the blonde strands of his wet hair away from his face, his boots squeaking on the stone floor as he stands aside to make room for the person behind him to follow. I'm unprepared for the sight of Aurora when she comes through the front door. My eyes move to Messer, wondering why he didn't warn me, as he greets the two of them with an easy smile.

"You must be freezing," he says, holding out a hand toward them and gesturing to the room where the rest of us wait with the other. "Let me take your coats and I'll hang them by the fire to dry."

Aurora's gaze is sharp as she takes inventory of the room. The girl I trained with and sparred against in Alaha was already intimidating, her presence alone enough to make the boys in our class shake in their boots. But now? Her brown eyes are downright lethal. But as she looks at Kai—her *husband*—it's clear as day that she holds affection for him in the way her eyes soften just a little bit, just for him.

I don't want to be suspicious, but it feels like it's crawling up my back like a spider and I'm just trying to convince myself it's a figment of my imagination. Just because I never saw this type of reaction from Aurora during our time in Alaha doesn't mean she's incapable of it now. It's normal for someone to seek reassurance from their spouse in tough situations.

Kai's eyes sweep the room, assessing, before stopping on me. He holds my stare. The boy I grew up with is unmistakably a man now. Stubble coats his chin, sharper now, less round. He's the same, but different. Familiar, but not. It's been years since he's returned to land and in all of that time he's spent it at the front lines of a war.

"Brynn," he says, dipping his head in a customary Kenta greeting.

I'm prepared for Acker to correct him, but I'm surprised when it comes from Messer instead. "It's Jo now," he says, offering a congenial smile as he finishes hanging the coats on the mantle.

"My apologies," Kai says. "Jo." My name sounds awkward on his tongue.

I offer a small smile in return. "None needed."

Silence stretches out as Kai's eyes dip to my hand in Acker's, before he looks away. I didn't realize I was holding my breath until it hisses from me through clenched teeth.

There are too many emotions inside me to pinpoint if any are out of place, foreign, but I'm relieved to know I'm at least not instantly infatuated with him.

Messer, acting as our unofficial liaison, motions to the empty seating. "Please, sit," he says.

Kai and Aurora move in tandem to the settee Messer had abandoned. Aurora is shivering, and there's no missing the way Kai places a comforting hand on her thigh. It's a gratuitous show of affection coming from someone used to Alaha's conservative customs, and I'm convinced he's trying to bait one of us into a reaction. Which of us is yet to be determined.

But Messer doesn't react, his smile firmly fixed in place. "Would you like anything to drink? We have wine, spirits—"

"With respect, I'd like to skip the formalities," Kai cuts him off, tone serious. "Due to a high number of anonymous messages declaring my father as the rightful king of Kenta currently spreading throughout the territory and beyond, he's currently ensconced in a meeting with Edmond and his council, where they'll decide his fate. If they banish him from Kenta, he'll be forced to return to the Alaha camp, where he'll discover my absence."

In other words, we need to make this quick.

Everyone in our group turns toward Acker and me. Fredrich, from his place at the bar, Irina's as she continues to lounge on the other settee, and Messer, standing beside us.

No. Not in our direction, but *mine*. Acker looks at me with the same expectation as the others. "You're the only person here who actually wears a crown," he explains.

I don't so much as blink for long moments, as I come to the realization that they planned this. I let my eyes convey my vexation, darting to Messer and Fredrich, but conclude there's nothing I can do about it now. Not now everyone awaits my lead.

Letting my hand slip from Acker's, I sit in one of the high-backed chairs set to the side of the hearth, facing away from the fire and into the room. Acker takes the seat next to mine, posture relaxed as he sinks into the plush seat. Crossing an ankle over his knee, he retrieves a dagger from across the room, the hilt spinning in his hand in an obvious show of his gift. I give him a pointed look and he winks at me, and it somehow works to settle my nerves.

I'm not sure why they thought I have any chance of swaying Kai into an alliance, especially as I'm the person who didn't, couldn't, follow through with the first arrangement we had.

"I assume since you're here regardless of the circumstances with your father," I say, meeting Kai's eyes, once gray, but now blue after his return to land. "That means you have a vested interest in this alliance."

He leans forward, threading his fingers together over his bent knees. "I'm interested in an alliance with *you* and the princess of Strou," he clarifies.

I lift a brow at the boy I once thought I'd marry. "Messer said you want Acker's throne."

"That's correct," he says.

"Your condition is a little counterintuitive, don't you think?"

"Oh?" he asks, eyes narrowing slightly. "How so?"

I shrug, as if the answer is obvious. "Acker's my Match. If you're in an alliance with *me*, you're in an alliance with *him*. Or maybe you're unaware of how a true Matching Bond works."

There's no outward change to his expression, but I still know him well enough to see how little he likes his intelligence being questioned. "Last I heard, you two weren't on good terms. May I ask what changed?"

"Or is that just what we've led everyone to believe?" I can practically hear Irina's words from earlier about how much I lie. "Maybe you should be questioning who's been feeding you such information."

His eyes flick to Acker beside me, assessing. "I want the Kenta throne. Acker being your Match is of little consequence to me."

"And if I did concede my seat?" Acker asks, refusing to look at me when my head whips in his direction. "What would you do with it?"

Kai's focus moves to Acker for the first time. "Assuming my father is dealt with, I'd rule over Kenta and Roison as a whole."

Acker scoffs. "Is Chryse's territory not enough for you? Roison holds the majority of this entire landmass."

"My people have lived in the confines of a tree grove for decades. I didn't take them out of it just to turn around and cram them into whatever leftovers we can find of an already established territory."

"It's going to be difficult to integrate an entire population in with the Kenta," I interject. "You'd have better success negotiating new boundary lines."

Kai's gaze hardens. "So, we can have less housing and resources than those within the cities?"

I can practically hear Acker's molars grinding over the crackling fire.

Even Messer has lost some of his carefully constructed enthusiasm. He kicks off the mantle. "If you don't mind, I'm going to get myself a drink."

Behind Kai and Aurora's place on the settee, Fredrich reaches behind the bar and grabs a bottle of wine and a glass. His pour is heavy, but Messer doesn't let it go to waste, swallowing half the liquid in one gulp.

He lets out a sigh as he inspects the glass. "Is everyone *sure* they don't want a drink? I feel like it could be really beneficial for all of us."

Aurora darts a look over her shoulder at Messer before sharing a look with Kai. There's a twitch at the corner of his mouth, a smile threatening to peek through. It's the proof that I needed that this isn't a stranger sitting before me, but a friend I once knew. Someone who shared laughter at Messer's outlandish behavior.

"What if all of us agree to integrate your people across all territories,"

I say, drawing Kai's attention back to the task at hand. "More than a handful have already found their way to Maile."

Any lingering humor on his face vanishes. "Then where does that leave me?"

"Well, which is it?" Acker asks, fiddling with the dagger. "Is it power you seek, or a better life for your people?"

Kai doesn't shrink from Acker's assessment. If anything, it emboldens him. "As someone who refuses to relinquish their own throne, the same could be asked of you," he challenges. "Or is serving at your wife's side not enough for you?" To add injury to insult, Kai's gaze volleys between me and Irina. "Whoever it is you prefer."

His words are cutting and I'm fairly sure I feel them in the pit of my stomach.

A series of images flash across my mind. Acker's hand as he readies the dagger in his grip. Its release. The blade flying through the air toward Kai. It hits its mark, through one of his eye sockets. Blood spurts all over his wife at his side as she screams in terror before he slinks back against the couch. Dead.

Heart hammering in my chest, I blink away the scene, only to find nothing amiss. Kai remains seated and unharmed across from me, eyes intact, not a speck of blood in sight. I whip my head toward Acker who meets my gaze with a concerned pinch of his brow. As if I'm the one on the verge of killing someone and not him.

To anyone else in the room, he appears as calm and collected as he's been since the moment Kai stepped inside, but it's a farce. It's been a while since I got a glimpse inside Acker's mind, but I just got an unfettered view of his internal musings, and we're currently skating on very thin ice.

Steadying myself, I redirect Kai's attention back to me. "Acker's seat on Kenta's throne is not up for negotiation."

Kai doesn't waver. "That's my condition. Take it or leave it."

Messer circles around the settee, his easygoing grin slipping. "This alliance guarantees you a throne. Why risk not gaining one at all if this war doesn't play out in your favor?"

"That's only if we were to find a way to eliminate my father," Kai says. "Which I'm not sure is possible."

"But would you have your own seat?" Irina interjects, soft voice cutting through the tension, drawing all the attention to her. "Or are you content to exist under your father's thumb?"

Her words hit their mark. Kai's face reddens with anger.

I'm impressed by Irina's ability to read Kai so easily without ever having laid eyes on him before tonight.

"We can take care of your father," I tell Kai.

He shakes his head. "You don't have any idea what he's capable of."

"I can't be influenced," Fredrich says, laying his sword across his lap.

Kai shifts in place, eyeing my friend where he leans casually against the bar, seemingly without a concern for his well-being. "Are you sure about that?" Kai challenges.

Fredrich's answering smirk is pure brass. "Care to test me, princeling?" Calling Kai by an incorrect title works to further incense him.

"Stand up," Kai commands.

There's a long beat where Fredrich doesn't move, eyebrows arching high on his forehead as he smirks at Kai. "Is that all you've got?"

Kai's skepticism turns into determination as he stands from the settee. "Stop breathing," he says, voice echoing powerfully with the use of his full gift.

I'm alarmed by how quickly he escalated the severity of his command, the order leaving his mouth as if he's issued it all too often. Probably more times than I'd like to know, honestly.

And yet, Fredrich is unchanged, his chest rising and falling evenly without a hint of effort showing.

"How?" Kai asks, eyes widening, either in fear or amazement, I'm not sure. Maybe both.

"All you need to know is that he's fully capable of withstanding your father's influence," I say, not wanting to reveal too much about my friend's ability to shield.

It's obvious Kai is perturbed by Fredrich, even though he tries to hide it. He takes in the room again, then the rest of us, as he considers the revelation that someone may actually be capable of resisting his father.

His gaze stops on Acker. As if he can see through Acker's carefully put on façade and to the depraved thoughts hiding underneath. "Even so," he says. "My condition for an alliance remains the same."

Everyone is stunned by his decision, Aurora somehow the most of all. She rises from the settee, her face set in a fierce scowl that she aims at Kai. When he refuses to acknowledge her obvious displeasure, she turns her attention to Messer. Pleading isn't something I'd ever believed Aurora capable of. Demanding is more her style. Yet, despite her still-steely demeanor, I get the sense she's trying to convey a message to Messer, to implore him to act. He's helpless as he stares back at her, his anger plain as day, and as his eyes shift to his former best friend, I'm worried about what he might say or do if I don't intervene.

I stand from my chair. "The offer still stands on the off chance you change your mind."

Messer's helpless anger is now directed at me, but I subtly shake my head in warning. There's nothing we can do to change Kai's mind.

Begrudgingly, Messer moves to the hearth and lifts the coats off the mantle to hand them to Aurora as she's closest to him, but before she's able to take them, Kai is there to grab them from his hands.

I slowly step between them and usher our guests into the entrance hall in a show of diplomacy. The roar of the rain sweeps inside the cottage when I open the front door, along with a burst of freezing wind. Kai pauses at the threshold. At first, I believe it's to steel himself before venturing out into the weather, but then he turns to look at me.

"Chryse knows you plan to renege on your agreement. He's planning on seeking an alliance with Edmond if my father gets banned from court," he says, appearing apathetic as he delivers the news. "Just figured I'd give you fair warning."

Even though I suspected Chryse would likely go back on our deal, it still stings to hear.

I nod my thanks. "I hope you have a safe return."

I shut the door behind them, blocking out the wind and rain. While I had hoped to weaken Edmond and Wren's alliance with the messenger pigeons, I didn't ever consider that Chryse would join ranks with Edmond. They've been at odds on and off for decades. Then, when my mother killed Osiris, Chryse blamed Edmond for not stepping in to stop it, but I suppose anything is possible in this ever-evolving war.

The silence is loud as everyone comes to terms with our predicament.

That is, until a giggle erupts from Irina, cutting through the tension. When I look at her, there's a sheen of moisture in her eyes, and her giggles turn into a full-blown fit of laughter.

"What could possibly be funny right now?" Messer asks, as exasperated as he is intrigued by her amusement.

"It's just that—" She shakes her head as she struggles to catch her breath. "The look on Kai's face when Fredrich didn't stop breathing—" Sucking in another gasp of air, she continues, "He was so *offended*."

It takes a second, but then we're all snickering, tension finding release. It's effective in breaking us out of our melancholy. But as I watch the grin slowly fade from Acker's face, I have an unsettling feeling in the pit of my stomach.

Chapter 41

JO

I wake to the sound of footsteps in my room. It takes a long moment for my mind to clear of dreams of a fishing vessel and endless thirst. When I peel my eyes open, I find Acker rummaging through the dresser beside my bed. Early morning light filters through the frost covering the window, bathing the room in a soft warm glow.

"What's going on?" I ask, sitting up, scrubbing the sleep from my eyes with my fingertips.

Acker pulls out a handful of garments, shoving them into the open pack atop the dresser. "We need to move while the weather permits," he says.

I'm confused.

After Kai and Aurora's departure last night, we all agreed to take the night to rest, to wait and have discussions in the morning. But as my mind clears from the fog of sleep, I watch Acker as he continues to shove socks and underwear into the steadily growing pack, and surmise he's already decided on a plan of action. He's wearing the same clothes from last night; hair rumpled from running his hands through it.

I swing my legs over the side of the bed. "And where are we moving to?"

"It's about a two-day's ride to the nearest port. From there, we'll catch a ferry north to a port town called Claudine."

I reach for the pants I draped over the foot of the bed, sliding them on one foot at a time before standing, buttoning them at the waist. "What's in Claudine?" I ask, realizing he's yet to look at me.

"Wells's parents," he says, tying the pack closed. "I sent a message to them when we arrived, so they're expecting our arrival. They're good people. They'll take care of you and Irina."

They'll take care of you and Irina.

"You plan on returning to the palace by yourself," I say, putting the pieces together.

He drops the pack on the bed behind me. *My* pack, allegedly. His eyes finally meet mine as he stands before me. We're close enough that I have to tilt my head back to hold his stare and I can't help but think he's trying to distract me with his proximity, making me feel small on purpose.

"Fredrich will accompany me," he says.

"Even if you're able to kill your father on your own, there's still an army bearing down on Kenta's capital." Whether it'll be Wren's or Chryse's is yet to be determined.

He nods, just barely. "And that's not accounting for the army your mother is undoubtedly mobilizing to attack from the west."

I'm in disbelief at his cavalier attitude. "Why did you ask me to choose between you and Kai if you never intended on me fighting alongside you?" I ask, anger beginning to simmer inside my chest. "Why did you take me from Maile?"

His attention strays to the mess of hair I've yet to tame as he reaches up to tuck the unruly hairs behind my ear. "I took you because you were determined on getting yourself killed."

I jerk my head from his reach. "What are you talking about?"

"I saw you that day, when you and Fredrich ambushed the Strou in the cave," he says, losing the tight grip he has on his calm demeanor, expression pinching in frustration. "You were just going through the motions of battle, not because you wanted the victory, but because you couldn't have cared less if you lived or died."

"I was fighting for my people while you had another woman in your bed!" I'm immediately ashamed of the outburst of my admission as soon as it's out of my mouth. "You don't get to judge me."

Scrubbing a hand across his mouth, he turns his back to me, pacing before he stops in the middle of the room. "I mean, what was the fucking point, Jovie?" he asks, turning to face me once again.

"Point of *what*?"

"Of wrecking me," he all but shouts, the outrage flashing across his face. "What was the point of wrecking me, only to turn around and do it to yourself as well?" Then, as quick as his anger surfaced, it leaves him all at once. "Sometimes I think you didn't believe you deserved the love we had. Going through with whatever deal you made with Kai was just an easy excuse to leave me."

I stare at him for a long moment, letting the hurt of his words settle in. "I thought I was doing the right thing," I tell him, voice cracking.

It takes three strides for him to reach me, hands framing my face once he does. "You were," he says, regret in the depth of his eyes. "I'm sorry it took me so long to see it."

When he presses his lips to mine, it hurts. Not physically, but in a place I've been determined to keep buried, a wound I've refused to acknowledge until now. And as I pull Acker closer by the back of his neck with tears escaping down my cheeks, I feel it start to mend.

He breaks the kiss, pulling my hands between his against the flat of his chest. "I need you to do something very important, Jovie, and that is to *stay alive*."

Already knowing where this is going, I sigh. "Acker . . ."

"I need you alive, because I sent Messer to tell Kai that I accept his condition late last night."

My heart stops altogether. "Why would you ever agree to that? Your *throne*, Acker?"

"We have no chance without him, and it's the only thing I have to offer other than you."

"You can't forfeit your title."

His brows meet in the middle. "Why not? It's not like I earned it," he says, unashamed by his admission. "I've done a terrible job of navigating this war. It seems I'm better suited on the battlefield, to killing men. Hell, I'm asking him to attack my own soldiers."

"To protect me," I interject.

"Exactly, Jovie. My priority lies elsewhere." He grins, the smile half-defeated, but his gaze is filled with acceptance. "It's always been you." The kiss he places on my lips is tender before he says, "Help me end this war and I will happily serve at your feet."

I'm not sure why his offer makes me even more infuriated, but it does. I rip my hands from his hold. "I don't want that from you."

"Is there someone else you'd prefer?" he asks, teasing.

And I'm astonished at his ability to make light of the situation. All I can do is repeat myself: "I don't want it."

He takes a step closer. "There's no other place I'd rather be," he says. "In Maile, with you, serving as your right hand."

"And if I refuse?" I challenge.

"If you deny me, the only mercy you could offer would be death."

There're too many emotions for me articulate, so I kiss him instead, knowing he can feel everything without my having to voice it. But it doesn't take long for anger to win out over the others, and I break the kiss, shoving him away from me. "You're such an asshole."

Chapter 42

ACKER

"I know," I tell her, unable to contain my smirk.

She can be properly mad at me after the war is over and she's still alive.

Her hands clench the front of my shirt, and I brace myself for another sparring round, but I am unprepared when she brings her mouth back to me. The kiss is almost as punishing as it is hungry. When she sucks my tongue into her mouth, it's nearly my undoing.

Tearing my mouth from hers, I'm able to get a few words out. "This isn't going to change my mind," I warn her.

She moves her hands to the buttons of my shirt. "Stop talking," she orders, sliding her hands onto my skin as soon as there's a big enough gap in the fabric.

Her touch laces heat across my chest, and she must sense how much I love it because she moves her mouth to the hollow of my throat. "Jovie," I say, with an effort of willpower. "I mean it. Don't do this if—"

She shoves me off her, and I think she's finally come to her senses, only for her to slap me across the face.

The shock of it is short-lived as fire spreads across my cheek, into my blood, and straight to my cock. When I meet her gaze, her expression is wild. As if she's not entirely in control of herself. Underneath all of it, a craving unlike anything I've ever felt before filters through the tether. Anger and desire, but most importantly . . . *need.*

"I don't know why I did that," she breathes, cheeks tinting pink. "But I'm sure you deserve it."

My choked laughter is brief as I grab her by the face and kiss her. She instantly melts into me, pliable beneath my lips. But it doesn't last more than a moment before she's attempting to break the kiss again, words already forming on the tip of her tongue.

I cover her mouth with my hand, directing her back onto the bed. "Shut *your* fucking mouth and let me give you what you need." My words elicit a rush of desire down the tether and I groan as I get her underneath me. "You've been needing me," I say, rocking the hardness of my covered cock against her.

Pulling back, I reach for the waistband of her pants, undoing them and stripping them from her legs. I strip off my own shirt too and lift the hem of her linen nightshirt to get a better view of her spreading for me. Then I grab her panties and yank them down her legs, sensing the inferno of lust shooting down the tether.

"From the moment I arrived in Maile. Haven't you? That's the real reason you let Fredrich taste you, because you couldn't admit that it was *my* tongue you wanted."

I spread her wider and *devour* her.

As much as she needed this, I needed it more. Ever since she made me kneel before her on the wharf, in front of all those devoted soldiers, I knew I'd have my mouth on her cunt again. Tasting her, making sure she knows exactly who she commands in front of the world, but obeys here. Me, and *only* me, as I erase any memory of another man's mouth with every swipe of my tongue. I suck and taste every part of her until she begins to rock herself against my face.

Her eyes shoot open when I pull away, fire igniting behind her dazed expression. I don't give her time to chastise me as I tear open my pants, shoving them down past my hips. She tries to reach for me, to pull me down over her, but I flip her onto her stomach. My name flies from her mouth as a sharp warning, but I ignore her as I kick my pants off fully and then jerk her hips up just enough for me to push inside of her.

Any protests she had die as she gives a low and delicious moan, her pleasure mixing with mine through the Bond so potently that it has me nearly coming already. I'm deliberately slow as I pull out and slide back in, trailing my palms over her ass, so perfect in my hands, and up her spine and back down again. Her cheek is flat against the bed as she looks at me out of the corner of her eye.

This time when she says my name, it's a plea.

My fingers follow the dip of her hips to the curve of her waist. "*I* need this," I explain, awestruck and a bit breathless. After all this time . . . "Let me admire you."

Then she practically preens under my attention, becoming soft under my hands. Maybe I did deserve the slap because there's no way I deserve *this*.

I shove her shirt over her head, twisting it around her wrists to keep her stretched out underneath me as I sink all the way into her again. I cover her body with mine as I push in to the hilt with a punch of my hips. She doesn't have any leverage underneath me, and I relish the trust she has to have to allow me this privilege, to submit to me so wholly. I dig a steady pace until she's squirming beneath me, a desperate edge in her moans, in the way her hands fist the material of her shirt.

Then I finally relinquish control. Pulling out, I flip her onto her back again before jerking her into my lap. I've barely gotten situated when she's settling directly over my cock. I groan. She's needy and, *fuck*, the pulsing sensation down the tether is magnifying everything tenfold. It's almost too much and not enough at the same time as she cants her hips, breasts swaying with every shift.

She can only handle it this way for so long before she wraps her arms around me, holding me to her as her moans turn into whimpers. Burying my face in her neck, I inhale her scent, her taste as I scrape my teeth across her skin.

"Just like that, Jovie," I tell her, and a sharp cry leaves her mouth. "So fucking good."

I'm so close. Too close. It only takes a few more shifts before her expression contorts from sweet pleasure-pain to outright bliss, body locking tight around my cock, a moan of pure relief as her head falls back. And I thank the fucking gods as I fall back on the bed, pleasure shooting down my stomach and into my groin as I come harder than I ever have in my entire life.

Chapter 43

ACKER

My stomach tightens in knots as I watch Jovie get dressed. I don't regret anything that just happened by any means, but it's going to make our departure all the more difficult, and it's as if the Bond already knows, the tether strung tight between us.

Jovie slips her top over her head, shaking her hair from her face, skin still flushed with a rosy sort of glow. "You're staring," she says, eyes flicking to me before reaching for her discarded pants.

I grin, but it's short lived. "You're stunning," I tell her, the words leave me in a punch of air.

Her answering smile only deepens her blush, and it makes the painful sensation in my stomach tighten to the point of nausea.

Steps sound outside the closed door of her bedroom, and as if the reality of the situation is hitting her, Jovie's wide gaze swings to me. "You don't think they heard, do you?"

Shoving my head through my shirt, I bite my cheek, releasing it as I contemplate lying to her. "At this point, Fredrich's heard it all," I say, chuckling at the shade of red her cheeks are turning. "And I had to find new sleeping arrangements on many occasions due to Irina bringing her lover to our bed, so think of this as a little bit of poetic justice."

She makes a face but doesn't comment on it further. But a look of determination quickly paints her features, and I know I'm going in for another argument. "The second you step foot in the palace without Beau or Irina, your father will know you haven't been doing what he tried to influence you to do. He'll kill you and Fredrich both on the spot."

Sighing, I sit next to her on the haphazardly unmade bed, wrapping an arm across her waist and pulling her onto my chest as I lie back. "You underestimate me."

Propping herself up on an elbow, she looks down at me. "I think your arrogance will be your greatest detriment."

I sweep her hair over her shoulder, getting a peek of her exposed shoulder through the opening of her shirt, running my fingers over the bite marks across the tender skin. "I warned you that I wouldn't change my mind."

She gives me a smart look. "If there's anything your father understands, it's that he knows you'd never go to Maile and return without your Match."

That's . . . a fair assessment.

I love the idea of keeping her with me. It's why I went to get her in the first place, aside from just seeking an alliance. Even though I knew Fredrich was looking out for her, shielding her when possible, it never satisfied the anxiety of not being able to see her with my own two eyes. It's tempting, but I could never walk her into the palace, not now knowing the depravity my father's hiding behind its walls.

I shake my head. "It's too risky." Before her temper can spike again, I kiss her, my lips brushing against hers when I beg: "Please don't make this any more difficult than it already is."

After a long beat, I ever so slowly feel the tension melt from her body, her weight settling over me. "The message I sent my mother," she says, laying her chin on my chest. "After assuring her that I was alive and well, I gave her the orders to send the armada up the Yanka River to set up camp in the valley west of the capital."

I suck on my teeth as I think of an appropriate response, but all that comes out is: "I know."

"You know?" she asks, dubious.

"The quill had a metal nib inside of it," I explain.

Her mouth falls open. "You were able to decipher what I wrote just from the sliver of metal inside the spine of the feather?"

"It took a great deal of concentration, but I was able to get the gist."

Her astonishment doesn't last long. "Then I think you would agree it's best that I meet the Maile forces in the valley, to ensure they don't invade and further complicate your coup."

I open my mouth, but I'm unable formulate a sound argument against it. She'd likely be safer with her own militia, and she can command them far away from the palace and my father. She takes my hesitation as confirmation, already sitting up and making for the door before I can stop her.

"Wait," I yell, reaching for the pack that got knocked to the floor before following her out the door. She's already at the servants' stairwell when I emerge, "I never said yes."

She doesn't bother looking over her shoulder as we descend the narrow stairs. "The word you're looking for, Acker, is compromise."

Fredrich is the first to speak when we enter the parlor. "He's never heard of the concept," he remarks, sitting with his back to the bar.

I point at him. "Mind your business."

"It'll cut our travel time in half," he says, ignoring my warning. "And it makes the most sense, having Jovie lead the charge from the west rather than risk the wrath of Evelyn." He lifts a brow in my direction. "I promise you that."

Jovie retrieves my father's sword from the mantle once again, swinging her smug gaze at me. "Don't you trust me?"

I shake my head. "Not even a little."

Her answering smile is pure brass and I can't help the grin from spreading across my lips as I stride across the parlor, pulling her by the neck into a kiss. I've learned my lesson to never underestimate her again, and I just pray to the gods that she's on my side moving forward, or Mother help me otherwise.

If Jovie lays a trap from this point forward, I'm willing to walk into it with a fool's heart.

A grumbly noise of exertion draws our attention to the entrance hall where Irina heaves what appears to be a bundle of furs over the back of a settee. She swipes the fallen strands of hair from her face and straightens. "I found these in the coat closet. Should be enough for everyone, assuming Messer won't need one."

Jovie detangles herself from me, my hands slipping from her as she moves toward the woman I've called my wife the past four years; the girl I once courted in hopes of a successful union. Somethings flipped in Irina since we left Kenta. She's been less volatile. Happier, almost. And as she looks at my Match with a small, accepting smile, I wonder if I underestimated how miserable she was as my forced spouse, regardless of how I tried to cater to her.

She wades through the different furs before settling on a white and speckled coat, holding it up for Jovie to see. "I think this one may fit you," she says.

Jovie takes the coat from her hands, running her own over the soft fur, appreciation in her gaze when she looks up at Irina. "My armada is likely anchored at the mouth of the Yanka River. When we get to where the men are camped in the valley, I can make arrangements for a ship to take you across the gulf to Strou," she says, voice soft. "If you'd still like to return home, that is."

Irina's answering smile is small when she nods. "I'd like that very much."

The poignant moment is interrupted by the front door whipping open and a wind beaten and naked Messer trouncing inside, bringing forth a blast of icy cold with him. He stops at the entrance of the parlor, gaze swinging between the four of us. The man is entirely too comfortable with having his cock out at any given moment. Irina takes it upon herself to throw one of the furs at him and he thankfully wraps it around himself.

His gaze stops short on Jovie with a healthy amount of trepidation. Rightfully so, considering he went behind her back to secure the alliance with Kai under my command. I can't see her face, as her back is to me, but whatever Messer sees has him deploying the full effect of his puppy dog eyes.

"Would it make a difference if I said your Match threatened to pluck out my feathers if I didn't comply?"

I sneer at him. "You fucking snitch."

Jovie lifts a hand to stop whatever Messer was about to spout back. "Did Kai seem satisfied with the terms of the agreement?"

He dips his head in a nod. "Yes."

Jovie's gaze swings toward Fredrich as he tries and fails to slink away from the conversation, knowing he, too, was aware of the decision made behind her back. "Go get the horses ready," she says, giving him a pass.

He nods. "Will do."

Irina, uncomfortable with the turn of discussion, excuses herself, pulling on a fur coat as she follows Fredrich out the door.

Jovie's attention turns back to Messer, and I have a feeling his betrayal hurts just as bad as Fredrich's and mine combined. "Just say you're sorry so we can move on," she says, curtly.

If the poor bastard wouldn't have just ratted me out, I might actually feel bad for him as he spits the apology out quickly. "I'm sorry, B."

Although she demanded the apology, she doesn't immediately accept. There's a pinch between her shoulder blades that hasn't abated. The emotion from her end of the tether is sharp. Maneuvering closer, I place a hand against her back, rubbing the tension there.

The gesture diverts Messer's attention, a grin slowly overtaking his features. "This," he says, pointing a finger between us. "This is cute."

Jovie glares at him. "*This* is a serious discussion, Messer."

"Sure," he says with a halfhearted shrug. "After finally giving in to the sexual tension you two've been harboring for weeks now, it's actually quite adorable."

I narrow my eyes at him. "How are you able to discern that?"

"I've been thinking about it, actually, and I think it's an animal instinct," he says, expression turning contemplative, as if my question actually is worthy of a considered response. "Like, an additional sense I'm more attuned to because of my shifting."

Messer's musings are effective in knocking the wind out of Jovie's sails. "What am I going to do with you?"

Messer's answering smile is full, simply happy that Jovie has decidedly let the anger over his decision go.

I would love nothing more than to dim it a little. "You could roast him over a spit," I offer.

Chapter 44

JO

We're in a race against the storm billowing in from the west. A few inches of frozen rain already blankets the ground and the horses' hooves crunch over it with every step, ice clinging to their noses. We've been riding for days, but the valley west of the capital shouldn't be more than a half day away.

I look over at Irina as she rides nearby, keeping her head down. Bundled up as she is, the majority of her face and hair is hidden under the hood, with only her eyes visible. As much as it pains me to admit, I've been unfair to her. She's given me more understanding and grace than I deserve. Hopefully, helping her return home will work to atone for my wrongdoings.

I'm grateful for Acker's warmth at my back. He's kept a hand flat against my stomach underneath my fur, tucked his face into the crook of my neck to offer as much of his body heat as possible. The kisses he places against the skin there are totally self serving, but they heat me up nonetheless.

Irina's voice shouts over the wind. "Look," she says, pointing to the sky.

Like a black smudge against the gray blanket overhead, the winged creature battles against the vicious wind as he flies toward us. We slow our pace in preparation for his landing. Shifting midair, Messer lands on his human feet, a few loose feathers scattering to the ground in the process. His body is racked with shivers as he braces himself against the icy wind. We sent him to scout ahead this morning and he should have been back hours ago.

"Oh, thank gods," I mutter, dismounting.

But as I get closer, the look on Messer's face makes my stomach drop. "They have the valley surrounded on all sides," he says, shivering.

Acker appears with furs, throwing them around Messer's shoulders. "Who?" he asks. "My father's soldiers?"

Messer nods. "They're spread out for miles. All the way to the Yanka River, to the city's walls, and to the gulf in the north. Not close enough to provoke, but a boundary strong enough to defend the city in case Evelyn decides to invade."

Acker cusses, scrubbing a hand across his mouth. "I didn't think we had any men left to disperse."

"Were you able to get close enough to see Drake?" I ask.

He shakes his head. "I didn't want to risk it," he says, shuffling his feet in the freezing snow. "There're too many archers. It'd be better to wait for nightfall."

Fredrich stomps toward us, holding the reins to the horses. "We're sitting ducks if we stay here," he says. "Too close to the capital."

Messer shivers. "Even if we weren't, we can't outride this storm. It's too gnarly."

Acker's been staring into the distance, but when his eyes finally meet mine, he's already shaking his head. "No," he says, adamant. "We'll turn around and find shelter at one of the neighboring farms."

"You know that's a temporary solution," I say, fighting to speak past my chattering teeth. "After the storm passes, we'll still be stuck where we are now."

"We'll backtrack to the closest port and make our way to Wells's parents," he says.

"There's not enough time, Acker, and you know it."

His expression is shuttered, jaw tense as he holds my stare. "I will not march you into the walls of the palace with that—" he stops mid-sentence, mouth snapping shut as he struggles to get a hold of his anger. After taking a breath, he tries again. "Even if the oath would allow it, I can't control my father, and your gift is too valuable. There's no telling the price someone would pay to obtain it."

"He would have to know where my magic is, and your father won't touch me, not when he knows that you're tied to the oath to protect me." I don't need to go into further detail. He's fully aware that the cost would be at the price of his life as well as mine. I reach for him, grabbing him by the front of his coat. "Nothing is going to happen to me," I say, meeting the worry in his eyes with the assurance in my own. "Your father is not infallible. We've seen as much already. If anything were to go awry, we'd handle it. Together."

Everyone shifts in place, waiting for Acker's final decision.

He stares at me for long moments, eyes shifting between mine, over my face and neck and back again. Then he takes a deep breath, as if he was holding it the whole time before releasing it.

"Messer," he calls, eyes shifting over my shoulder. "Are you able to shift into anyone?"

Turning, I watch as Messer tries to put together a reason Acker would ask. "It depends. Who do you need me to be?"

"My father wanted me to retrieve my sister," Acker says, but Messer's already shaking his head.

"No. Not Beau. You could ask me to be just about anyone, but Beau isn't one of them."

I'm slightly taken aback by his refusal, but after a moment to think about it, I can surmise why it's a point of contention to him. She's a friend, but also *female.* Having Messer take on her form feels . . . violating.

Acker nods, understanding.

But it's Irina's voice that draws our attention. "I think I could," she says, pulling the furs from covering her mouth for us to hear her better from atop the horse. "Illusion myself enough to look like Beau, that is."

Acker shakes his head. "While I suspect my father plans on using Beau and her gift for reasons I'm not privy to, I don't know what he'll do if he discovers he's been deceived. I can't ask that of you, Irina."

She walks her horse closer to our grouping, dismounting and handing the reins to Fredrich. She removes her hood, and we collectively gasp at the image of Beau staring back at us. Dark hair, dark eyes, facial structure, all the complete opposite of Irina's petite features. She's shorter than Beau, but it might be passable.

She smirks and her resemblance to Beau is uncanny. "Well," she says, cocking her head to the side. "Am I convincing enough?"

Messer's the first to speak. "That's crazy."

Fredrich makes a face, eyes cutting to Messer. "It has nothing on your grotesque masquerade of my dear friend."

I interject before they can begin squabbling. "Acker?"

"I can't deny that it's good," he says, tilting his head as he watches her. "Almost too good."

"How would you explain the absence of your wife?" Fredrich asks.

"That I had a fit when I discovered Acker intended on bringing his Match back with him and ran off," Irina answers. When Acker looks at her with a flat expression, she gives it right back: it's odd to witness on Beau's typically expressive face. "Is it not believable?"

He doesn't refute her question.

And after a long stretch of silence, he turns to Fredrich and tells him, "Get the rope."

Fredrich wastes no time turning to dig in the pack tied to his horse and Acker removes his hood as he ventures to look through his own pack. I'm somehow as relieved as I am nervous. Irina, too, as a shaky breath leaves her.

I reach a hesitant hand out, touching her shoulder. "Just pretend every man you see is beneath you."

Messer shivers, obviously miserable in just his furs, but still manages an encouraging smile at Irina. "And that they're just dumb in general," he adds.

I'm rolling my eyes at his remark when Acker walks up to me. "Take off your cloak."

"What? Why?" I ask, gripping the fur around my shoulders with tight fists.

"I wouldn't care about a prisoner's comfort, even yours," he explains.

He stares at me expectantly and it's then that I notice the shackles in his hands. Not for Irina, but for me. When I meet his stare, he only lifts an impatient brow at me. I debate the merits of fighting him on this but then consider how his father will view the situation. Me, walking into the palace without safeguards in place. Gritting my teeth, I begrudgingly jerk the coat off, tossing it on the saddle of the horse. I hold out my hands for him to place the shackles back on my wrists, the locks clicking into place once again with a clang of metal.

"Not going to bind my hands this time?" I ask.

He doesn't find my attitude amusing. "If the scenario arises where you need to protect yourself, I want you to be able to call your blade."

Fredrich approaches Irina with a length of rope in his hands. "You can back out," he tells her.

She gives him a shaky smile. "Right now, my only concern is pulling off Beau's confidence."

"Just let me do the talking," Acker says, moving toward her as Fredrich ties her wrists in a vice. "But he's likely going to put you in the dungeons."

She nods, swallowing. "I can handle it," she says, but her voice betrays her by trembling slightly.

The lack of confidence in her response doesn't bode well, but no one calls it out. Fredrich leads her to one of the mares, head tilted close as he whispers to her. Irina is stoic as she absorbs whatever advice he's giving her before finally nodding. Then he hoists her onto the saddle and hands her the reins.

Acker walks with him back. "Go quickly. Enter the city by the northern gate. It's where the majority of traffic flows in and out of the city. If you get questioned, tell them you're meeting family that's already sought protection in the city's walls. Hasselback is a common name of some of the farmers in the area. Then shelter at Wells's smithy until I send for you."

Fredrich nods, then pulls Acker into an embrace. "Don't do anything reckless without me."

"Same to you," he says, patting his friend on the back.

Then, to my surprise—although pleasantly—Fredrich moves in to hug me. We don't speak, knowing nothing we say will fit just right. I don't believe there's a platitude that encompasses the complexity of our tenure as friends. He offers me a smile after and I watch him mount his horse, the weight of Acker's stare heavy on the side of my face.

Messer's voice cuts through the moment. "I need to shift or I'm in real danger of losing my toes," he says between chattering teeth.

Acker nods. "Lead Fredrich from above then come and find me after."

Messer doesn't need to be told twice, sliding off his fur off and handing it to me with a wink. "See you soon."

In the next moment, he leaps into the air, body folding in on itself, shrinking into the form of a snow owl. He hoots, beating his wings against the force of the wind until he finds his equilibrium. Then it's just Acker, Irina, and me as we watch them disappear into the night sky.

Chapter 45

ACKER

I crook my fingers at Jovie, motioning her to come over, and I can't help but smile at her displeasure over being cuffed and at my command once again. Grabbing her by the hips, I dip my head to the crook of her neck, breathing in her scent. "You chose this," I remind her.

I smile even wider at the hint of pink she can't hide as it fills her cheeks. "You're such a prick," she mutters.

I hoist her atop of my horse before pulling myself behind her. I pull the edges of my fur cloak forward as far as they will reach over her shoulders and it calms her shivering a little. Looking over, I make sure Irina is good to steer her horse, and she nods an affirmative. She's a skilled rider. It's the one extracurricular her parents gave to her that wasn't useless and will work in our favor to be convincing she's Beau.

I'm concerned about her mental fortitude if she is faced with the dungeons, but Jovie was right. We're stuck where we are. Unable to go west with my father's soldiers blocking the valley and unable to move east due to the front lines of the war. Our only options are forward or back, and backtracking would take entirely too long. Forward to the palace is somehow our only option.

The overcast sky limits our visibility. I keep a compass in my palm, feeling the needle to help us stay the course north. Jovie shutters in my arms and I tuck my face into her neck, hoping my breath can offer her some semblance of warmth. Plus, I know she likes it when I scrape my stubble against her skin.

Her pulse sings to me, her life source pumping a steady rhythm in the side of her neck. The desire to feel it beneath my lips and tongue has plagued me for years. Even now as I relish the flutter under my lips, my mouth waters.

Jovie's voice vibrates against my mouth. "Don't you dare."

"Dare what?"

"I can practically hear your thoughts, and I have no interest in becoming your meal before I freeze to death."

I hum, grinning at her responding shiver, knowing it has nothing to do with the cold.

Up ahead, a figure comes into view, like a ghostly shadow emerging from the night. Then another on horseback as the road leading to the city's gates becomes clearer.

I place my hand on the side of Jovie's neck, tilting her head back against my shoulder, angling her face up to mine. "Whatever I say or do, know it's to keep you safe."

She nods. "I understand."

I cover her mouth with mine, pouring as much reassurance as I can into the kiss, letting her feel the tenderness I have for her through the Bond as I taste her, melting into her warmth for long moments before letting her go.

There's a sharp pinch in my chest, and I can't distinguish if it's fear or the oath warning me from the city slowly coming into view.

Soldiers stand at the city gate, and many more on the battlements above. The roads become congested with people the closer we get to the walls, and I'm forced to steer our horse through the throngs of people, Irina right behind us. It doesn't take long for it to become obvious that we intend to enter. The largest of the men steps forward, yelling at us before we can reach the iron structure.

"Back of the line," he orders. When it becomes clear that we don't mean to comply, he steps forward again, hand on the hilt of his sword. "I told you to stop," he yells.

"Stand down, soldier." I pull back my hood, revealing my face. Even if they don't recognize it, my nose ring is well enough of a signifier, uncommon jewelry amongst royals, that they all freeze in place. "I'm simply returning home after a long trip," I tell them.

The soldier is skeptical. "We didn't receive word of your imminent arrival," he says. "The palace would have sent a carriage."

"Does it look like I'm in need of a carriage?" I ask.

A low murmur from one of the soldiers hovering behind the lead guard reaches our ears. "The king did say the prince was due any day."

I cock my head. "Is there a problem?"

The first soldier steps back. "No, your highness. Please, forgive me. I'll tell them to raise the gate."

He directs a whirling motion with his finger to one of the soldiers on the battlements and the loud drag of iron against iron starts up as the iron gate begins to rise. I turn and see Irina's uneasy tension slip from her shoulders as we pass underneath the battlements.

"I hope Fredrich got through," Jovie whispers.

Me too.

The city is full. Families from the farms nearby that have come inside the city walls for safety, dressed in plain clothes and tattered coats. We pass through the city's central plaza, where the statue of the Mother standing in the fountain remains barren of water, like she's revoked life's sustenance as penance for our transgressions in this war.

Little do these people know, the true danger lies within these walls with them.

The soldiers at the palace gates are laxer than their brethren guarding the city wall, clearly assuming the first point of defense did their due diligence to vet us properly. Either way, I recognize a few of their faces, and one of them nods at my return, almost reluctantly, and I wonder if he has an inkling as to who he serves.

"Please stay to the far left when you enter the courtyard," he says. "It's . . . seen better days."

As we pass underneath the gate, I can feel Irina practically sigh with relief.

"You're doing great," Jovie tells her quietly.

"We've barely made it onto the grounds," she replies.

I keep my gaze ahead, but say, "Which is a true testament to how well you're keeping up the facade. No one has stopped us yet."

The sound of the flies reaches us before the smell does. Decaying blood isn't a scent you forget after you've smelt it once, and I'm impressed by Irina's ability to remain stoic when we finally enter the main courtyard. The ground is coated in a churned mixture of old blood and ice, creating a muddy, lumpy texture. A few maidservants are toting buckets of water about as they attempt to wash it away. Soldiers stand around and watch as the women use brushes to scrub the stones clean.

It pisses me off, seeing them just standing there. "The fuck are you all doing?" I yell at them, and they startle at my presence. "Help them clean this shit up!"

They scatter like ants.

It's too cold for there to be any spectators on the veranda but there is a familiar face standing at the top of the stairs, waiting before the palace doors.

My voice sounds hollow to my own ears. "Hallis."

"Ace," he says, eyes taking in me and Jovie, then the woman on horseback beside us. "Beau?"

There's purpose behind each step he takes down the stairs toward her, and I hate that I'm unable to inform him of the truth, not while we're visible to others. His concern over my sister's arrival is evident. He's almost to the last step when he opens his mouth to say something but stops mid-stride as he scours Beau's features.

I dismount and hurry to reach him, placing a hand against his chest. "I'll explain later," I say under my breath, smiling as if I'm excited to see my friend safely returned from the warfront. Which I definitely am. I give him a pat on his cheek, partially to divert his focus to me, but also so he can see the authenticity in my eyes. "It's good to see you."

Slowly, his tension fades, but not entirely. He holds my stare. "I can't wait to swap stories over a few drinks," he says.

"Zion?" I ask.

"Alive," he says, eyes flitting to the other side of the courtyard. I don't need to look over my shoulder to know what he's referring to—the dungeons. "For now."

I bite my tongue, wanting to know why he's being held, but know it's not the time or place as I nod my understanding. "Where's my father?"

His teeth clench at the mere mention of him. "If he's not already in the dining hall, he'll be there soon. He spends most nights schmoozing his *guests*." The derision in his voice when he says the last word isn't missed.

I sense a soldier as they step out onto the veranda. "Let's get inside," I say.

I nod to Irina and move to help Jovie down from the horse. My chest feels as though it gets tighter and tighter with every step we take toward the palace. The memory of my mother's shrunken, wizened form back in Maile is a constant reminder of what my father can do.

Hallis's gaze lands on Jovie's bound wrists, his eyebrows tipping up, but he doesn't voice his thoughts on the matter. Then he eyes Beau again as he leads us through the palace doors. Our pace is brisk as we walk down the expanse of the great hallway, the gold ceiling above reflecting our movements. Petitioners congregate along the length of the corridor. Their eyes follow us as we pass; Hallis first, Irina right after, then Jovie and me. Her shackles clink with every step. Taking a right into a hallway under the stairs, Hallis pushes on the paneled door, and I owe the Mother all my praise for the empty storage room.

Once we cross the threshold and are alone, Hallis spins on us. "Who the fuck is this?" he demands, pointing at Beau's figure.

I motion for him to lower his voice. With everything that's transpired, there's no telling what anyone in this palace is capable of anymore, nor who could be listening at any time. I nod at Irina and she lets her illusion flicker just enough for Hallis to see through it, before quickly putting it back in place.

He tongues his cheek, closing his eyes. "He's going to see straight through that."

"*You* didn't," Irina challenges.

There's not enough time for this. It's only a matter of time before word spreads of our arrival and the last thing I want is to be caught hiding in the broom closet. "What happened with Zion?"

Hallis shakes his head, mouth clamped shut almost like he's too afraid to speak.

I bark his name. "Hallis."

He sighs. "When we returned, your father had reorganized the men on his council."

My heart drops. *No.*

"Your father threatened to kill whoever disagreed with the new alliance with Roison, and you know Tyreek." His gaze falls to the ground, as if he can't stomach looking at me as he continues. "He made a spectacle of their deaths in the courtyard and Zion went berserk when he found out, killed a bunch of soldiers."

Fuck. Fuck. *Fuck.*

I squeeze my eyes shut as I struggle to process his words, scrubbing a hand over the back of my neck. Zion is giftless. There's no reason to keep him alive. "Why would my father spare Zion?" I ask, opening my eyes.

He shakes his head like he's baffled. "Your guess is as good as mine. After the guards were finally able to get him under control, your father ordered him to the dungeons."

I suppose it doesn't matter. For whatever his reasonings, I'm grateful he's at least alive even if it's in the hellhole known as the dungeons.

"But Ace . . ." Hallis steps closer, eyes flitting between Jovie and me. "You shouldn't have come back."

There's not enough time to go into specifics on why I am. "Listen," I say, steeling myself. "Find my father and let him know I've returned with Beau, get him to meet me in his sitting room. I'll explain more later."

He looks at me with concern, and I'm not so sure he believes there'll be a later, but I give him a firm nod to go ahead with my directions.

"Trust me."

Chapter 46

JO

Edmond's just as I remember him. Less formidable-looking than he is in my nightmares, however, and that somehow settles my nerves. It's such a contradiction, because I'm aware that he's more powerful than ever. I suspect he likes it that way, appearing less threatening than he actually is.

"Well, well, *well*," he lilts, eyes roving over the lot of us. "This *is* interesting." He looks at Hallis who escorted him here. "Will you please excuse us?"

Hallis dips his head in the customary Kenta way before leaving, and it's then that I notice the two men who've entered the room in the king's wake. The man dressed in court attire smirks as he moves to the drink cart, the soldier with him following close behind. "Would you like a drink, Edmond?" he asks, pouring himself a glass.

The king declines, moving to the tufted chairs in front of the hearth. He flicks a hand at the half-charred logs, and they ignite with a whoosh of fire.

"Ace?" the man asks, turning his attention to Acker, unstoppered decanter still in hand.

"No, thank you," Acker replies.

The man then hands the glass to the soldier and, as the boy takes a sip, I realize with immense pleasure that the soldier must be a court taster. I bite my cheek to prevent myself from smiling.

"Son," the king says, folding his hands in his lap once he sits. "I was beginning to wonder if you'd left for good."

Acker pulls a blade from the strap across his chest. "Whatever gave you that impression?" he asks, twiddling the weapon in his hand. "It was your idea for me to retrieve my sister, was it not?"

Edmond lifts a curious brow. "When did you come to that conclusion?"

"About the time I was setting sail for Maile." Acker moves to sit in one of the other chairs. "As you can see," he says, pointing with the tip of his dagger at Irina. "I delivered."

With the courtier and soldier to our backs, I try with all of my might to give Irina my silent support when I look at her.

She is stoic in her response. "Hello, father."

It's not the best, but it could be worse.

The king dismisses his daughter, not even thinking to inspect her form for an illusion as his eyes slide to me. "And you brought the traitorous bitch with you."

"Watch it," Acker snipes, eyes cutting to his father before moving to me. "A traitorous bitch, yes, but she's no different than Greta. How many times did your Match try to kill you? Was it two or three times before you locked her in the library?"

What the fuck is he doing? I narrow my eyes at him, still standing awkwardly in the middle of the sitting room.

Edmond shows the first real hint of emotion since he walked in: a smile tugs at his mouth. "Three," he answers.

Acker crooks a finger at me, arrogance dancing across his features as I take tentative steps toward him. He proceeds to pat his thigh in a silent order for me to sit on his lap. There's no chance I'm able to disguise the disgust on my face and it serves to make a smirk spread across his face.

"Sit," he commands.

Biting my lip to keep from voicing what I'd really like to say, I perch on his thigh, posture stiff as I try to adjust my shackles, so they don't press painfully into my skin.

This pleases Edmond, his eyes crinkling at my obvious discomfort. "So, she's cooperative now," he says, gaze moving to his son. "How'd you manage that?"

"Cooperative is a stretch," Acker replies, placing a tight grip on my hip. "But she'll get there."

"And your wife?" Edmond inquires. "Where is she?"

Sucking his teeth, Acker lets the silence stretch before he pulls me fully into his lap. It's beyond inappropriate to sit like this in the presence of the king, but it reminds me of a time, very much like this, when I was in a similar position, and unseen by anyone in the room but my Match.

"If you want to have an honest conversation, father, then I need assurances you're going to give me the same regard in return." I go still as he twirls the blade in his hand and then drags the flat of the blade along the length of my arm. "I need to know you're not going to try to manipulate me with your gift of influence."

Edmond shifts in his chair, crossing one leg over the other. "Back then, I wasn't sure I could trust you. Having me followed wasn't really a good way to build confidence, now, was it?"

Acker stops the blade, lifting it from my skin as he twirls it in his hand, and I release a slow breath. "I knew you were keeping things from me." I see the flick of his wrist a second before he stabs the dagger into the wooden table beside us. "Things like how to siphon magic from another Heir with a slatstone."

Edmond leans forward, there's a hint of want in his eyes that tells me that I need to keep my wits about me. "How did you figure it out?"

Acker's breath fans over my skin. "Beau."

At the mention of her name, everyone looks at Irina, still standing where we left her. She appears scared for all of a second before she's able to pull the mask back in place. If you weren't aware of her true identity, you probably wouldn't have even noticed.

"Oops," she says, as if she's bored.

Edmond's eyebrows meet in the middle as he stares at her. "How did you know?"

"You didn't believe this whole time that I tried to kill you and your entire council just because I wasn't your favorite child, did you?" she smarts.

Her cadence is off. The delivery wasn't the best. But the words themselves? *Perfection.*

I doubt Edmond paid enough attention to his daughter to catch on to the missed nuances. "You were always too nosy for your own good," he says, gaze flicking to the courtier behind her. "Send for more men and have her escorted to the dungeons. Make sure there're no less than five guarding her at all times. She's sneaky."

The man opens the door, speaking to a soldier stationed outside before closing it again. "Are you not going to collar her?" the unnamed courtier asks.

Acker gives him a pointed look. "If you've seen what her gift does to her after being around too many people with heightened emotions, you'd know that just being in the dungeons will be plenty to keep her in line."

The king considers his son's answer before nodding his agreement to the courtier. "Her threat is mostly physical, not magical. Just make sure she's held in a cell."

"And not with anyone else," Acker adds. "She can manipulate anyone into doing her bidding."

The courtier looks Irina up and down. "Do you intend to use her?"

Edmond smirks. "She's correct that she was always my least favorite child, but she has proven to be useful from time to time."

"For what?" Acker asks.

His father looks at his son for a long moment, then says, "I'll explain more at a later time," he says, gaze sliding to me.

The soldier returns with more guards than the five that Edmond originally requested. They converge on Irina, but she's quick to jerk from their touch, her chin held high as she marches toward the door.

"I know where the dungeons are. I've put enough men in there to fill it ten times over," she declares, leading the men from the room instead of the other way around.

"What are the odds they make it there alive?" Acker ponders.

"I'd say half," Edmond replies with a smug smile. His eyes lingers on me, attention falling to the space below my chin, losing focus a moment and I suppress a shiver of revulsion. "I should have expected that you'd be unable to withstand the temptation of your Match if you went to Maile."

Acker runs his thumb along my hip. "Like you said, I am your son."

"That you are. But did you not once stop to think about the consequences of bringing the princess of Maile back with you?"

Taking a deep breath, his chest expanding against my back, Acker nods. "I did. And while there's an army of Maile soldiers headed toward us as we speak," he says, stroking a finger down the side of my face in a gesture that could be considered adoring as well as intimidating. "I'm hoping, with the growing cooperation of my Match here, that she can issue orders of their return to Maile in due time. Have you heard that Jovie holds the throne now?"

"Queen?" his father asks, surprise splashing across his face. "Since when?"

When Acker's finger reaches the base of my neck, he spreads his hand across the expanse of my throat, and I realize he means for me to answer. "A year and some months," I say on a swallow.

I'm not sure the king is convinced, judging by the way his gaze flicks back to Acker, dismissing me. "And what are Irina's parents, Joss and Urich, going to think when they find out that your wife is . . . where, exactly?"

"I can't say for certain, but there's a possibility she's alive." Acker continues to twirl the blade between his fingers. "Depending on her ability to swim."

Edmond sighs, as if his son murdering his own wife is an inconvenience and not a major concern. "There's no way to prove her death wasn't an accident, I guess. The worst they could do is point fingers, but it's not like they're going to join forces with Evelyn."

"Not after they've laid siege to the Maile borderlands for months now. I'm quite pleased with that move."

His father nods. "There's more to be discussed," he says, eyes shifting to me. "We'll talk in private. In the meantime, I'll have Stassia set up a guest room for your future wife—"

"Absolutely not," Acker says, cutting him off. "She'll stay with me."

"It'll be suspect if you move your Match into your bedchambers at exactly the same time we report your current wife missing."

Acker sits forward, forcing me to perch on his knee. "I don't care what it looks like. Hallis informed me of the guests you've accrued in my absence, and I don't trust a single one of them to be alone anywhere near my Match and the rarity of her gift."

Edmond's expression hardens. "We'll station soldiers outside her door."

"Then put them outside *my* door," Acker challenges. "She's much too valuable and too tempting."

His father stands, and telling by his posture, he's going to physically and metaphorically attempt to put his foot down. Acker jerks to his feet and it nearly slings me to the ground, but I'm able to find my footing.

"I am your son, yes," Acker says, tone a combination of passive and somehow unyielding at the same time. "But this is not negotiable. If you put her in a guest room, you know I'm just going to end up there anyway."

Edmond eyes his son. He's a few inches shorter than Acker, so seeing Acker's dominating presence measured up against his father's smaller stature creates an interesting dichotomy. But because of Edmond's title and the magic he has accumulated, he is the one who holds all of the power here.

After a long moment, Edmond finally relinquishes his control. "History loves to repeat itself, son." Grinning, he grabs Acker by the neck in a tight hold. "Collar her, make sure she's restrained, and don't let her best you again. There will be no leniency given. For either of you."

"Understood." Then Acker's cocky smile returns in full force. "And there's nothing to worry about. She won't be able to scheme when she's chained to my bed."

Chapter 47

JO

The weapons that used to adorn the wall above his bed are gone. Every surface is pockmarked. From the bedframe to the ceiling, there's not an inch of surface that remains unscathed. I can only surmise what caused the damage. Or rather—*who*.

Acker returns from speaking with the soldiers who have been assigned to stand outside his door, a mangi collar in his hands . . . and chains.

I raise a brow in question when he places the length of metal and collar on the table beside the bed.

"I figured you'd like to have an honest-to-gods bath before you have to wear it."

There's a beat where we simply stare at each other, partially in disbelief about the fact that Edmond bought Acker's lies so easily. That we've surpassed the first hurdle to get into the palace.

"Are you okay?" Acker asks.

He warned me, but I'd forgotten the mask of callousness he's so easily able to slip on. It's the same bravado I saw him wield when we were surrounded by soldiers in the woods of Roison. Cocky and put on for show. I can only hope his father well and truly bought his act and that I haven't walked myself into my own demise.

Acker dips his head, so his face is in my line of sight. "Jovie?"

"Uh, yes," I stutter, holding out my shackled wrists. "Can you . . . ?"

He steps forward tentatively, as if he's scared to spook me. His hands reach out to cradle my wrists, fingers encompassing the entirety of my metal cuffs. The metal locks clink open and I take a steadying breath.

Rubbing my wrists, I inspect the room once more. From the desk angled in the corner and the stacks of books overflowing onto the floor surrounding it, to the unlit hearth and the half-burned candles lining the mantle. The last thing I look at is the bed I saw Irina in.

I meet Acker's gaze with a lift of my brow. "I would have preferred my own bedchamber," I remark.

The strain around his mouth releases at the return of my attitude. "If you had a preference on sleeping arrangements, you should have agreed to stay with Wells's parents."

My eyes slide from his as I walk past him toward the bathroom. Inside, I marvel at the opulence that I, too, had forgotten about. Stone sinks with gold hardware, ornate mirrors, and a chandelier of brass hanging over the copper tub. Every metal is different and polished to perfection, yet somehow still cohesive in the space. I run my hand along the edge of the tub, turning the spigot for the water to fill the basin. A pedestal holds different soaps, and I imagine Irina soaking in the bath as she rifled through the array of oils. The image makes my stomach clench, and as much as I want to bathe, I need to know something first.

I stalk back into the bedchamber.

Acker sits shirtless at the end of the bed as he undoes the laces of his boots. His head snaps up at my sudden return.

I almost hate the words I'm about to say, but I have to say them. "I need to know—" I stop as I look from him to the floor, then to the balcony doors he must have opened while I was in the bathroom. "For the sake of knowing," I begin again, as I try to find my courage. "Irina said you . . . didn't . . . after, but your wedding night . . ."

Comprehending my jumbled words, he sits up, giving me his full attention. My heart thunders in my chest, the memory of her straddling his lap on one of the chairs in front of the fireplace at the forefront of my mind. The image of her in the very bed he sits on now.

Standing, Acker moves toward me, legs eating the space in a few strides. His eyes are soft as he inspects my face. "No, Jovie," he answers, sincerity plain across his features. "I tried, but I couldn't go through with it." He reaches up with a careful hand, cupping my cheek in his palm. "Not when I could feel every pulse of your pain through the tether."

I had spent the night drowning my sorrows in a bottle of wine. Then another, until the stabbing sensation in my chest abated to a dull throb. My mother spent the following morning holding my hair back as I chucked up every drop of the liquid from my guts.

"Was what I did with Fredrich more than . . ." I can't even find it in myself to finish the question.

"By far," he answers, a smile reaching his eyes. "Do you feel better now? Knowing I never touched my wife?"

Something about the way he says the words causes a low throb between my legs.

He tucks a few strands of my hair behind my ears, still smiling genuinely. "Go take a bath, Jovie."

For once, I do as I'm told.

In the bathroom, I strip from my dirty clothes and sink into the now-full basin. My skin prickles from the warmth of the water, and I spend an indulgent amount of time bathing, letting myself relax as I soak. That is, until I remember that Irina is in the dungeons. It's makes me feel guilty enough to propel me from the bath. I pull on the robe hanging from the rack beside the tub.

When I enter the bedchamber, Acker is lighting the candles on the mantle. An oil lamp is already lit on his desk, and, as he turns to look at me, there's a glint in the gold of his nose ring when his eyes rake over me. The robe I'm wearing is thin as it clings to my damp skin.

"Stassia is sending up a clean set of clothes along with some dinner," he says, averting his gaze as he extinguishes the match between his fingers with a flick of his wrist. "I'm going to go wash up. If she returns in the meantime, don't answer the door."

Then he disappears into the bathroom.

Sighing, I wander over to the bed before deciding I'm more interested in the work he left unfinished on his desk. The books range from historical records to straight folklore and every kind of genre and topic in between. The one open on his desk, however, is on alchemy. Notes are scrawled in the margins.

I grow bored and end up crawling on top of the bed anyway, fatigue hitting me harder than expected. Even though Acker's been away for weeks, the bedding smells exactly like him. It reminds me of the woods in Roison, where the air is rich with life, but masculine. Intoxicating.

I must have fallen asleep, because when I wake, Acker is leaning over me. It takes a moment for the sleep to dissipate, but when my mind clears, I note the heaviness of his gaze. He's bare-chested, with only a towel around his hips. Droplets of water cascade over his shoulders. In his hands, chains.

There's a knock at the door, and by its forceful nature, I'm assuming it's not the first summons.

"The staff will undoubtedly be given orders to spy on us to ensure I'm doing as I said I would," he says.

Sitting up, I hold out my hands before me. Acker unravels the thin links of iron, revealing a single cuff at the end. I slide my wrist inside the mechanism, and he closes the clasp, lock instantly snapping into place. I follow the length of chain to where it's weaved into the iron filigree on the headboard. Next, he holds up the collar, and I detest the stones around my throat, its heaviness smothering me once again.

Acker pinches my bottom lip between his fingers. "Don't pout."

I glare at his back as he makes his way to the door, adjusting the towel around his waist. Testing the length of the chain, I pull on it and find it's just long enough to reach the width of the bed.

Acker returns with a plate covered with a silver cloche and a pitcher of water. He sets the pitcher on the nightstand and uncovers the dish. "I'm not sure we should eat anything the kitchen sends us," he says, inspecting the plate of food. "Hallis will be by shortly and I'll get him to bring us something to eat."

It would only be fitting for Edmond to poison me as revenge. I recall the last time I ate anything, and it was before we left our makeshift camp the night before and it was little more than thin strips of dried meats and a few cubes of cheese. A far cry from the plate of what appears to be roasted hen and carrots. My stomach betrays me by grumbling in hunger from the smell permeating the air.

Acker's gaze flicks up at me, roving over my stomach in thought. Then he picks a carrot and shoves it in his mouth, followed by a torn piece of meat from the hen all before I comprehend what he's done.

"What are you doing?" I voice, incredulous.

He finishes chewing and swallows before picking up the pitcher of water by the handle. But I leap across the bed in time to stop him, grabbing the pitcher from him with both hands. Water sloshes over the side, soaking the front of my robe, and I look up at him from where I'm kneeling in astonishment.

"You just said we shouldn't eat anything," I say.

"You're hungry," he says, as if the answer is that simple. "And now I'm thirsty, so hand over the water." When I don't move, he lifts a brow. "Please."

"What if you keel over and die?"

"I made the suggestion under an abundance of caution, but I'm sure it's fine. My father wouldn't risk poisoning *both* of us." I slowly pass him the pitcher and watch as he takes a gulp, water spilling down his chin and onto his naked chest. He grins, having caught me obviously ogling, and sets the pitcher down. "Probably, anyway."

I shove him in the chest. "Ugh. You're the worst. If you die and I'm left chained to this bed, I'm going to eat the rest just to find you in the afterlife and kill you twice."

He smiles, catching me by the wrist. "All I heard is that you can't live without me."

"Don't flatter yourself. I've managed the last four years just fine."

Head cocking to the side, his expression turns less teasing, more earnest. "Is that so?" He towers over me as he comes closer, hand still trapped in his grasp, stopping me from pulling away. With his other hand, he fingers the panel of my dampened robe. "Tell me all the ways you were fine," he says.

I'm distracted as his finger coasts between the open material of my robe, across the swell of my breast, down over the raised scar between them from the time he carried me with an arrow lodged in my chest. "I lied," I say, a tad breathless.

His gaze flicks up to mine, lashes casting shadows across his cheeks. "I know," he says with a grin.

Then he wraps an arm around my waist and drops me onto my back. My robe falls further open and his heated gaze rakes down my body right before he presses his lips to mine. This kiss is unhurried and easy as I wrap my arms around his neck, enjoying his weight over me, his bare chest against my skin. It's the reminder I needed that this is the man I trust. With my body, my well-being, my—

Then, like a splash of cold water, I remember Irina's predicament, the sacrifice she made to buy us time, and I place my hands to Acker's chest before breaking the kiss.

"Irina," I say, letting her name hang between us.

He seems to come to the same realization, the moment crashing around us as reality filters back in. Sitting back on his knees, he looks down at me. My robe is rucked up. His towel hanging dangerously low on his hips. He scrubs a hand over his face and into his hair, blowing out a heavy breath.

A knock sounds at the door and his head swivels in its direction. "That must be Hallis." He leans forward, giving me a swift kiss against my mouth. "Go ahead and eat. I think we're in the clear."

I watch him leave the bed and a sense of loss hits me like a wave even though he's less than a room's width away. Yes, I may have survived the last four years without him, but it was not easy by any means, and I'm fairly sure it'd be worse if I had to ever do it again.

For the first time in as long as I can remember, fear takes root inside me.

Chapter 48

ACKER

A *ting* resonates from the glass door leading to the balcony. Pulling on a shirt, I peer through the frosted glass and spot a bird perched on the railing. I check that Jovie is covered under the bedding before I open the door. I'm quick to shut it after the hawk flies in through the gap.

Releasing a bundle from his talons, Messer shifts. "Good morning," he sings.

Jovie jerks awake, her disoriented gaze swinging around the room before her eyes land on Messer's bare backside. She makes sure her robe is properly closed right as Messer looks over his shoulder in her direction.

"To you, too, your royal highness."

She rolls her eyes. "You know how much I hate that."

I pick up the item he dropped, the pants unfolding from my grip. "Where'd you find these?" I ask, tossing them to him.

He catches them against his chest. "They were left on a clothesline to dry," he replies, rubbing the back of his head. "A lady whacked me a few times with a broom."

"I actually would have loved to see that," I tell him.

"I bet you would," he replies.

"Will you hurry up and put those on already?"

His mouth thins, but he acquiesces. "You're starting to give me a complex," he says, shoving one leg in at a time.

"Maybe you need one."

Straightening, he buttons the waistband and turns to Jovie. "You look like you slept well. I was—" He stops mid-sentence, eyes narrowing. "Is that—Are you chained to the bed?" His gaze swings back to me. "I thought we were past this."

"You and me both," Jovie mutters.

"It's an assurance I needed to give my father. I don't like it any more than either of you do."

Messer blinks at me. "Why do I feel like you're lying?"

"Because he secretly loves it," Jovie insists.

And I can't deny it. There is a part of me that loves knowing she can't go anywhere. By her own volition or otherwise. It's not something I'm proud of, but it settles something in me that I'm not ready to dissect.

Messer's eyebrows jump up on his forehead. "Interesting."

It's my turn to roll my eyes, calling a blade from the strap I hung on the end of the bedframe to my hand. "Did Fredrich make it to Wells's smithy?"

His expression turns serious as he nods. "Yes, but it was being occupied by some vagrants. They were less than . . . *welcoming* to any newcomers. We handled them, and their bodies are currently in a refuse bin near the city center. With the weather being what it is, they shouldn't start to smell for days."

I twirl the blade between my fingers. "If not weeks."

"Ideally," he agrees.

"I need to show my face at court," I tell them. "And I need to check on Irina in the dungeons."

"You want me to stay with B?"

"For the time being, yes. I'm not sure how long I'll be gone."

"I won't have any problems sneaking in if you want me to go tonight."

I shake my head. "I also have a friend I need to check on."

"Zion?" Jovie asks.

"Yes," I answer, moving to the other side of the bed. I look toward Messer. "As much as I prefer you clothed, it's best if you're a little more inconspicuous on the off chance anyone does try to come in while I'm absent. My father will likely send in maidservants to spy and report back to him."

"Not a problem," he says, undoing his new pants with a smirk. "I can be inconspicuous." He shoves his pants off with unnecessary flourish and I sigh, waiting for the sound of bones and cartilage cracking and moving to settle before looking back in his direction. Or rather, down at the floor, at the new four-legged creature standing in Messer's place.

"A housecat," I state flatly.

"Aww," Jovie coos.

She pats the bed for the small orange tabby to jump up. He stretches as she runs a hand down his back and I can't believe I'm jealous of the motherfucker. Pawing at the blanket, he settles on her lap.

"You do realize he's a grown man, right?" I ask, moving toward her.

"But he's so cute," she says, scratching behind his ears.

I swear his purring is extra loud just to spite me.

"What am I to do if I need to use the bathroom?" she asks.

Raising my hand, I unwind more filigree from the headboard, twisting the plated metal into additional length for the leash of chain.

Her eyes widen. "You could have given me that much leeway the whole time?"

I smile as she comes to the realization that I could have, but simply didn't want to. I liked having her body plastered against mine all night, and I can't stop my grin as I fasten the strap of daggers across my chest.

"You're such a prick," she says, but there's no heat behind her words.

I reach into my bedside table, producing a string of mangi stones. Jovie eyes me as I put them on, lips pursed, and I give her a look. Like, *see*, even I have to wear them.

Bracing a hand against the bed, I lean over to place a kiss on her mouth. I meant for it to be quick, but something about leaving her has me deepening the connection. A tiny yowl from Jovie's lap has me pulling away.

As sick as I felt at the thought of being separated from her when I intended to leave her at Wells's parents, it doesn't hold a candle to the way my stomach tightens leaving her in the worst place she can be, chained with a collar and no way to defend herself.

It's those thoughts alone that has me scratching the top of Messer's cat head with rough strokes. "Keep her safe," I tell him.

He swipes a paw at me but I jerk back in just the nick of time.

The soldiers stationed outside my door are the same as last night. I don't recognize either of them as being room guards I've had previously, undoubtedly a conscious choice on my father's part, but I nod my head at them in respect regardless.

"When is shift change?" I ask.

"Noon," the one on the right says.

Good to know. "Have a good day, boys."

As I leave my wing of the palace, the halls become more and more congested. People I've never laid eyes on before roam the halls. Dressed in their finest, they congregate, some already with drinks in their hands and its barely even breakfast. More soldiers loiter about, and I suppose I should find comfort in their presence, but somehow it just makes my unease grow.

In the dining hall, I finally see some familiar faces. Members of my father's council and their families, as well as neighboring lords who often frequented court before the Roison invasion. Some of them are less than pleased about my return to the palace, however. Paul and Draken are the most obvious about their opinion, turning away from my approach to their table.

"Gentlemen," I say, sliding into an open spot on the bench seat. "I must apologize for my extended absence. My father had me on a special errand."

"Oh, we've heard," Lord Furlough says. "Retrieving your sister, right?"

"That's right."

Paul all but sneers at me. "And your backstabbing whore, as well. Don't forget to mention *her*."

I reach for an apple from the fruit bowl on the table, rubbing it on my shirt before I take a bite. "Consider her mentioned," I say, pointing a finger at him. "But watch your fucking mouth."

His face reddens under the attention of his peers. "You can't talk to me like that, boy."

"I believe he just did." All of our heads turn toward my father, and his mere presence is effective in shutting Paul up. "Son," my father says. "There's someone I'd like you to meet."

I take another bite of the apple before depositing what's left of it on Paul's plate, then give one last look at the rest of them while standing up. "Lord Draken. Furlough," I say, nodding my farewell.

My father grabs me by the back of the neck as we step away and I do my best not to flinch under the touch. "I thought you were going to put a fork down his throat," he says, smiling once our backs are turned.

"Didn't want to upset the women," I say, waving to one of the councilmen's wives.

"I appreciate your restraint," he says, smiling at me. "You're in a particularly good mood this morning,"

"What can I say? I'm glad to be home."

"And with your Match," he beams. "I suspect you've had a good night?"

My smile isn't as forced. "The best I've had in a while."

"Good," he says, and I'm reminded of the man I used to look up to. The father who seemed interested in my well-being. It's the first time in a long time that I feel like he's not looking at me with a hidden agenda, which makes me all the more apprehensive. I feel for any stirrings from my magic, searching for a hint of my father's influence, but if he's attempting to persuade me, it's too subtle for me to notice. That or the small string of mangi around my neck is muddling his abilities when he's touching me. There's no telling just how powerful each of his gifts are, if some are stronger than others.

He leads me to someone I've never laid eyes on before. But the yellow emblem on his lapel reveals his identity before my father needs to say anything. I suppose Kai can be trusted after all. At least, to some degree.

"Chryse, this is my son, Acker," my father says, introducing us. "Son, this is the king of Roison."

The man who made a deal with my Match to exchange her life in payment for mine. The weight of every pair of eyes in the dining hall is on our backs.

I hold out my hand in greeting. "It's a pleasure to meet you."

He returns the gesture, but, unlike me, there's not even a hint of a smile on his face. "Likewise," he drawls. "It's nice to put a face to the man who's been sneaking into my territory and killing my men for years."

I release his hand, casually putting mine into my pockets. I could lay out all the reasons why it was self-defense when I had to sneak into his territory and kill his men, but it wouldn't make a difference. Not when I'm entirely unrepentant about any of those transgressions.

"Chryse," my father says with an air of chastisement. "I've secured the asset you specifically requested. Are you or are you not dedicated to making this alliance work?"

The king of Roison is a formidable man. His shoulders are broad, and he's taller than myself by at least a foot. He's not above using his physical presence to his advantage, letting his stature do the intimidating for him.

"An asset I've yet to lay eyes on," he says, drinking from the chalice in his hand.

"Soon," my father assures him. "He's secured in the dungeons."

After a few more minutes of idle chat about the battlefront being stalled to the east, Chryse departs the hall with a disinterested glare in my direction, taking his fellow Roison men with him.

I turn toward my father. "Why would we ever fucking align with Chryse?"

"He's agreed to join under a truce. The front lines have been stalled under a white flag he raised just hours ago. He wants to end this war as badly as the rest of us."

I ask under my breath. "Wren agreed to this? After the whole spiel about him wanting to take over Roison's territory?" My eyes scan the dining hall. "Where is the captain of the Alaha anyway?"

My father hushes me with a stern look as he guides me out of the dining hall and into the narrow servants' passage leading up from the kitchens. "I'm calling for a meeting tonight. A lot has happened in your absence, but right now is not the time to hash everything out."

I clench my teeth. There's a fine line between pushing back so I don't appear too agreeable and pointing out the fact he's the one who just introduced me to the ruler we've been in active opposition to for years in front of the entire Kenta court. Chryse is the very man who's pushed the front lines right up to the walls of our city. The only thing stopping him from invading in truth is some agreement that allows him to steal someone's magic. Even if I wasn't secretly aiming to topple the house of cards my father has precariously built, it doesn't take a genius to know all of this is flimsy, *at best*.

"I do have some regretful news to share," my father says, expression a pitiful show of sympathy. "Tyreek refused to see the benefit of the new order of things and was rousing some of the councilmen against me."

I dip my head in a nod in an effort to hide the rage wanting to surface. "Hallis told me," I say, meeting his stare when I feel I have my emotions under control. "Said Zion is being held in the dungeons. I'd like to go speak to him."

Once again, he clasps me by the neck, and I concentrate on not flinching under his touch. "Of course. I know how much you value your friendship with the boy, hence why I spared him." The next words out of his mouth sends a chill down my spine. "But don't get any wild ideas."

Chapter 49

ACKER

The dungeon is fucking atrocious. There's no light. The only sound is the prisoners stalking back and forth within the tiny confines of their cells, which shakes the chains bolted into the walls. There are only wails when the madness of their captivity becomes too great to bear. During the summers, it's usually as hot as an oven down here. In winter, it's bone-chillingly cold. No matter what season, it's always wet. Rain and melted ice seeps through the ground under the paved stones of the courtyard, and drips in steady rivulets down the walls of the dungeon.

And holy fuck, the *smell.*

Light from the oil lamp in my hand barely allows me to see more than a few feet ahead. The cells are laid out in rows, some of them have four and five men per cage. Their expletives bounce off the stone walls, creating a cacophony of hatred echoing all around me.

"—saw your father in here earlier . . ." one of the men taunts.

Another continues the jeering in the next cell. "Such a small man, it'd be such an easy kill."

Yeah, I'd like to see it.

But it's not the angry voices that bother me the most; it's the pointed stares of the quiet ones that bore into the side of my head that have me averting my gaze. The women and, *gods*, the children. None younger than their teens, but still too young to be subjected to this nightmare.

My stomach roils as I maintain my steady gait, focusing on my mission. I finally lay eyes on the woman I'm looking for; Irina sits in the corner of a cell by herself, arms banded around her bent knees, head tucked into them.

"Beau," I call, bending down to her level.

She peeks over her knees, eyes squinting against the little bit of light my lamp gives off before they're able to adjust. Setting down the lamp, I retrieve the apple from my pocket and extend my arm through the bars toward her. Leaning forward, she takes the fruit from my hand, still angling her head away from any onlookers from the cells beside hers. I want to tell her something encouraging, but some of the prisoners are here by my sister's hand, and they'd love to sell a lie if it awards them an inch of freedom. She bites into her apple, and I know without a doubt she won't last long if I don't find a way to get her out.

Taking my lamp, I continue down the row of cells until I reach the end, then I take the turn onto the next row. My father will know I came to speak with Zion regardless of his warning, so as I pass one of the guards making his rounds, I dip my chin at him in a show of respect.

I find Zion in a corner cell, shackled to the wall by all four limbs. He recognizes me instantly, sitting as far forward as the chains will let him. Dried blood has matted the hair around his temple and the gash over his eye looks like it's going to scar.

"Ace," he says, but there's an iciness to his voice.

Rightfully so. Guilt clogs my throat as I struggle to find the words to say. Just as I've done with Irina, I've royally fucked everything up when it comes to him. There's nothing I can say that will suffice. Not after I pleaded for his father to take a seat at the council. Tyreek was a good man, and that's the exact reason I petitioned so hard for him. It's the very same reason he's dead right now.

"I was away," I tell him, unable to voice the rest: that I would have prevented his father's death if I could have. I suspect my father waited for my departure on purpose.

He doesn't respond, eyes masked in shadow, but the anger in his gaze is felt nonetheless. I turn the dial on the lamp, lowering the wick and its flame with it. Removing the blade from the lowest strap on my chest, I slide it under the bars of the cell and sling it across the floor toward him. He's able to hide the weapon under the sole of his shoe.

I give him the same warning I did Irina. "Soon."

He's cautious, but gives a single nod, letting me know he understands.

He doesn't trust me, though. Not yet.

On my way out, I slip the apple I had originally intended for Zion to a young girl in one of the first cells I saw upon entering. He wouldn't eat it, with how little he trusts me, out of fear of it being poisoned. The girl is just as hesitant to take it, but the woman who I suspect is her mother grabs it quickly, hiding it from sight. She gives me her thanks with a clipped nod, understanding the transaction needs to be quick.

The sky is fading to dark when I ascend the stairs and come face to face with Hallis. "What are you doing?" he asks.

"Don't worry," I say, stepping into the courtyard. It's been cleaned, but the smell still lingers. My father always had a penchant for public executions but doing them en masse makes bile coat the back of my tongue. "My father already knows I intended to speak with Zion."

He lets out a breath. "And?" he asks.

I shake my head. "He doesn't trust me."

"Your father or Zion?"

"Both." He falls in step with me. "Were you looking for me?"

"Yes," he says. "Your father requests your presence in the sitting room."

Fantastic.

I stop him before the place doors. We didn't get to talk last night, not wanting to give the soldiers outside my room too much fodder when reporting back to my father, but I need to ask, "Are you good?"

He's taken off guard by my question before he sobers some. "I'm good, Ace. We'll figure it out, just as we always have."

Nodding, I slap him on the back as we part ways when we enter the palace doors. I cut under the stairs, taking the winding hall toward my father's sitting room, and I steel myself for what I'm walking into, stopping outside of the door when I near it. Nothing good is going to come from this meeting. I finger the string of mangi stones around my throat.

My father calls as soon as I step inside. "Ace."

He's standing among the members of the council in front of the fire. The majority of them, anyway, minus a few. Tyreek's absence was to be expected, but there are more missing. The last of the common-born men remaining on the council is Johannes, and he's pouring himself a drink from my father's bar cart. When I look at him and meet his eye, he's quick to look away.

My father waves me toward the seating area in front of the hearth. "Come, have a drink with us."

I accept the glass of dark liquor from the maidservant, taking a tentative sip as I sink into one of the empty chairs. My back is to the room, and I can't help but feel it was intentional. Chryse sits to the left of me and he barely spares me a passing glance.

There's one notable absence, however. "Are we all in attendance?" I ask.

"If you're inquiring about Wren," he father remarks, the glass in his hand already empty. "He has been asked to step back from court proceedings for the time being."

Lord Draken continues. "False messages were being spread across the territories that made his presence at court a little . . . uncomfortable."

I cross an ankle over my knee, balancing my glass on the arm of the chair. "What kind of messages?"

"The kind I don't take lightly," my father says. "And the council agreed it was best he took a leave of absence. At least, until the rumors die down."

"Is he still part of the alliance?" I ask.

"Of course," my father declares, as if my suggestion that he might not be was silly. "He's currently readying the battalions we have stationed closer to the city after we received reports of Evelyn and her men encroaching into our territory from the west."

Well, shit. "Not ideal," I say, noncommittally.

My father smirks, sharing looks with some of the other men, an inside joke passing between them that I'm not privy to.

"I actually have a present for you," my father announces, gathering everyone's attention.

"What is it?" I ask, deadpan. "A new crown for your *favorite* child?"

My father nods to Lord Draken, who stands. "You've gone above and beyond to help us secure Beau. She's an important asset, and because of that sacrifice, the majority of the territories will be united once again under one law."

This is interesting. "But . . ." I draw out the word, prompting my father to continue.

He grins. "But your return with your Match has set off an additional conflict in a war we were preparing to end, and that makes the council nervous."

"As well as my own council," Chryse interjects.

"Hm," I hum, watching Lord Draken cross the room to the door. "You said 'present,' but this kind of sounds like a reprimand." He knocks on the door—a signal.

"Oh, no," my father says, eyes alight with something I don't like. "You're going to like this gift, I promise."

Two soldiers carry a man through the door. Or more like drag, as he's unable to get his feet underneath him long enough to successfully walk. A bag has been placed over his head, his clothes nondescript and threadbare, and his hands tied before him. When the soldiers heave him to his knees in front of me, he groans in pain.

Planting my feet, I sit up, looking to my father for direction.

"Go ahead," he says with an encouraging nod.

I reach out and grip the burlap sack with my hand, yanking it from the man's head, and I'm met with the face of someone I've wanted dead since I was thirteen.

Vad.

The member of my training battalion who gave away our location to the Roison encampment. He's the very reason we were ambushed. All but six of us died. Myself and five other soldiers in training, not including Vad himself. He's also the man who put a wooden arrow through my Match's heart and nearly killed her.

"Well?" my father prompts.

Leaning back in my seat, I swallow the entirety of my drink. "Where'd you find him? He's evaded me for over a decade."

His eyes slide to the man to my right, and Chryse fidgets in his seat. "He is my contribution."

My father sees the question in my eyes. "Each of the leaders must provide a person of interest as a symbol of their loyalty to the new alliance. Chryse wanted a particular gift, and I wanted Vad. For you."

I don't like this. Either the way the room is eerily quiet as they watch me, or the way Vad is cowering before me. I've had enough run-ins with him to know the man is as arrogant as they come. But now, kneeling before me, his eyes are lifeless when he looks up at me, as if he's already accepted his fate.

"How gracious," I say, dismissing him with a wave of my hand. "Put him in the dungeons."

Chuckles sound from around the room, and my father smiles indulgently as he leans forward. "That's not how it works."

He crooks a finger and the soldiers jerk Vad away, pressing him across the low-lying table before us, making drinking glasses rattle across the surface. Only then does fear register on Vad's face, head hanging off the side of the table, eyes wide as he looks at me. He throws his gift at my mind and I startle at the unexpected pressure as he tries to get inside. He's weak. I've struggled to keep him out when he's tried in the past, but this is a pathetic whisper in comparison.

My father stands. "Millenia ago, Heirs were worshipped as gods," he says, striding toward the hearth. "The bloodlines were pure and crossbreeding with the giftless was considered a crime against Mother Nature." He lifts a hearthstone dagger from the mantle. A long blade with an ornate handle carved from an elk's antlers. "And the more diluted the blood became, the weaker the gifts when they awakened. As magic became more and more common, Heirs weren't held with the same regard as the rulers of the past." He turns and looks at me. "We've become so fixated on fighting among ourselves, we forgot who we are."

Vad's gift continues to slam into the barrier of my mind. "Heirs," I clarify.

"*Kings*," my father says.

I lift a brow. "Are queens not allowed?"

"Absolutely," he answers, as if my question is ridiculous. "Of our choosing, of course." He moves around the table toward Vad, sitting on the table beside him as a soldier keeps a hand on the back of Vad's neck. "You see, when Heirs reigned, their magic was the ultimate currency."

Someone hands my father a bowl and he places it beneath Vad's hunched form. Vad's magic claws at the outside of my mind, desperately digging to get inside.

"A trade of gifts," I say.

"Yes," my father answers, pleased by my deduction. "But by our design."

He produces a stone from his pocket that fits in his palm, a mineral I don't recognize. There's no metal in it that I can identify. Then the light hits it just right, and the green swirls luminate in the otherwise gray object. There's only one place I've seen the same colors and patterns before. It's the same mixture of green that was in the slab the healer in Roison forced me to hold Jovie to when she was bleeding out in the middle of her awakening. Somewhere deep in the forest of Roison, under the illusion of the healer's husband.

"This is a slatstone," my father says, rotating the rock in his hand. "The most valuable and rare stone found on this earth."

I'm careful to remain stoic. "Doesn't look like much."

My father's smile is wicked. "It can draw out someone's magic if you know where it's at."

No one would give up that information unless . . . "Torture?" I ask.

He nods. "Usually."

"He wouldn't give up that kind of information easily," I say, motioning to Vad with a tip of my chin.

"No, he wouldn't," my father agrees, holding the tip of the dark blade to the side of Vad's neck. "But thanks to your sister, she was able to tell me exactly where to look."

Horror settles in my bones at the realization of why, exactly, my father wanted Beau. Only she has the ability to identify the location of a person's magic, as evidenced when she told Jovie where to aim her own hearthstone blade during their betrayal.

But I didn't hand over Beau. I handed over Irina, and she has no such ability.

My heart skips a beat when my father pierces the skin of Vad's neck, the edge slicing across his jugular, sending blood spraying from the laceration. It splashes across my shins before the pressure reduces to a steady flow to the ground, pooling inside the bowl.

With a sickening horror, Vad continues to fight to get inside my mind, all the while knowing he's going to die. It terrifies me enough that I let him in. Not all the way, just enough to know what he's so adamant to tell me as he spends his dying breaths.

And it's an image.

Wait. A *memory*.

His own as he looks up at Beau. She's chained in the dungeons. But he, too, knows it's not my sister but Irina, his gift as an oracle able to see the truth inside her mind. The guard yells at her to hurry as my father stands to the side, watching. She flinches but doesn't look away from Vad's stare. In quick succession, her thoughts reveal our plans to him. Our intentions to kill them all. Which, apparently, was Vad's plan all along. He had seen the depravity in the mind of one of the commanders when we were children. When he escaped to Roison, he didn't mean to give away our location. It was an accident.

All the while he's projecting the truth to my mind, I watch as he struggles to breathe, the blood gurgling in his throat, and I know there's nothing I can do to stop it. I swallow the knot forming in my throat, the burn of emotion I work to keep down as I watch him struggle through his last breaths.

How did we get here? Why didn't you show me then? Why now? I ask him from my thoughts.

He answers my unspoken and pained questions with an image of me at camp. Standing next to my father who I was staring at in adoration. Then again, as an adult, in the wood with Jovie when I wouldn't let him into my mind. Then we're back in the dungeons, and it was there, on the soaked ground of the dungeons, that he made the decision to tell her the truth, knowing what would happen to her if he lied . . .

. . . and his hope that we can do what he's been unable to achieve, and that's kill every bastard in this room.

I promise him that I will. Swear it on my life from my mind to his. And it's as if he finally relents to his fate, shoulders caving into the flat of the table. But there's one more memory he sends me.

This time it's mine. The memory he had plucked from my mind years ago, when we met in the woods and he asked to have access to my thoughts in exchange for directions to a healer nearby to save Jovie. He chose a memory following my mother's death, or, rather, what I believed was her death. When my father called me into this very sitting room, having never done so before, and offered me my first drink.

It's that memory that flickers through my mind until Vad's heart begins to slow and he can no longer afford the energy to use his gift.

My father moves forward, motioning for the glass in my hand. I hand the glass to my father and he holds it underneath the flow of blood. Vad's eyes droop closed, each breath slower and longer than the last, and I never thought I'd feel sick to my stomach watching the death of a man I've wanted to kill for nearly half my life. It's not until my father holds the stone over the wound, the drops of blood slowing in the crystal of the glass, that I catch the glisten in the light. My breath catches at the beautiful tendril of essence flowing from the gash toward the stone like a living entity. It encases the stone, swirling and pulsating with life.

Vad's features begin to wither. Skin and muscle decaying and turning gray as the magic continues to be pulled from his body until there's nothing left. Only then does his chest finally still, never to expand with breath again, the last drops of blood fall into the glass.

My father holds up the writhing magic covering the stone in his hand. "This, my son, is what separates the ones who make the decisions from those who abide by them."

He drops the stone with the glistening flow of magic into the glass. He swishes the blood around before plucking the stone from the glass, now magicless. Then holds the glass out to me.

"I have no desire to hold the gift of an oracle," I say, panic-stricken, but somehow emotionless. "I'd rather gouge my eyes out than read people's minds."

"Like all things of this world, it just takes practice," he says, glass still suspended in his hand between us. "You'll master it in no time."

I don't move. I try to conjure any excuse or way out of this, but this is very obviously an initiation of sorts. Every man in this room is waiting for my decision. If I don't drink it, the consequences will be far-reaching. The tamest thing would be the dungeons. The worst . . . is chained to the bed in my godsdamn room.

Leaning forward, I take the glass from my father, and it's as if he releases the tension in his body with a sigh of relief. I inspect the glass, half a finger full of blood. "Was wine not sufficient?"

There're a few chuckles, my father's grin when he tells me the magic won't release from the stone without a host. The blood tricks it into letting go. I sniff it and my face contorts from the foul scent. More chuckles ignite around the room, the mood getting lighter as I accept the inevitable.

Fuck it.

Placing the rim of glass to my mouth, I toss the contents to the back of my throat and swallow, clenching my teeth to stop it from coming right back up. But after a few breaths, the same warmth that I'm used to accompanying my own magic makes my head spin.

They applaud.

They *fucking* applaud as they stand around to take turns patting me on the back, to congratulate me on my newfound power. Vad's body seems forgotten where it leans over the cocktail table. I'm off-kilter and my father tells me it's the effect of the magic entering my bloodstream. It's not long before they drag in another man. The source of Chryse's requested gift, I realize, and I watch as they hold the man to the same table beside Vad's body. I watch as Chryse digs the hearthstone dagger into the man's chest and uses the stone to remove his magic. It's the correct location and I surmise it must have been given under duress. I think I ask to be excused and somehow get my feet beneath me before I stagger out of the room.

The next thing I know, I'm puking behind a bust.

Chapter 50

JO

I awake to the sound of the bedchamber door shutting. Messer stretches out besides me on the bed, feline eyes reflecting green in the small amount of light from the oil lamp on the table.

Acker unbuckles the strap of daggers from his chest and lays it on the end of the bed. His eyes laze one glances at me, noticing I'm awake. "Go back to sleep," he says, working the buttons of his shirt through the holes.

It's then I notice the blood splattered across his waist and legs, and I jerk up. "Acker—"

"It's not mine," he hurries to assure me. "I'm just going to clean up."

He strips the shirt off his shoulders, balling the material in his hands and stalking into the bathroom. Messer looks at me, and I've learned all his expressions, even in animal form, so that I know he's asking if I want him to stay.

I shake my head. "You need to go check on Fredrich," I tell him.

He leaps from the bed gracefully before shifting back into himself. "I'll return first thing in the morning," he says, opening the terrace balcony door, looking over his shoulder at me.

He waits for my nod, assuring him I'm fine. Then he shifts again, this time into an owl, and launches himself through the opening. I adjust my leash of twisted filigree and slip out of bed, walking to shut the door behind him. It was barely open for a minute, but the draft of winter air has dropped the temperature in the room. I hear water running from the bathroom, and I make my way toward the door, but my leash stops me short. I look at the metal around my wrist, following the length of it to the bed. I've had plenty of slack all day, but as I tug on it again, it doesn't give, and I realize Acker's preventing me from going into the bathroom on purpose.

Worry has me frozen in place as I listen to him wash the blood from his body, the water splashing vigorously. He said it wasn't his, but then whose was it? My heart sinks as I hear him spit into the basin.

I crawl back into bed, and it feels like forever before he finally emerges. We don't speak as he sinks beneath the covers. His skin is chill to the touch, and he's dressed in only his underwear, but I don't complain as he pulls me in close. I let him wrap his arms around my middle, tucking his face into my neck. He breathes me in. A deep inhale that he releases slowly. I don't need to see inside his mind to feel the somberness of his mood. Whatever transpired tonight has shaken him, and that's what scares me the most.

I drift in and out of sleep, and every time I wake, I can sense Acker still has yet to drift off to sleep.

It's not until morning that I broach the subject of what transpired the night before and he recounts how his father killed Vad, and all that came after. He said it was a long time coming, but it was more difficult than he expected, given the circumstances. There was no dignity in it, he says. And as he explains how Vad pushed into his mind, then about the blood his father made him drink, my stomach becomes queasy.

Palm flat against his chest, I find comfort in the steady beat of his heart beneath his warm skin. "Do you think you can steal the stone?" I ask.

His fingers run through the length of my hair, hand skimming down my back. "Possibly."

We stay like that for a long while and I don't ask him if he can read my mind.

I don't think I want to know.

He kisses me slowly before he gets dressed and leaves, and that's the pattern for how the next series of days flow. Me, stuck in Acker's bedchamber, spending my time reading through one of the many books he's accumulated, while Messer keeps me company. Sometimes as a cat, other times as a mouse, or a tiny finch. I think it depends on what kind of head scratches he wants that day, but always small enough to scamper underneath the covers or behind a pillow when a maidservant enters. It's very reminiscent of our time in Alaha together. Hallis brings me food, but any time I try to get information out of him, he becomes mute and makes any excuse to leave.

I have so much time to think about nothing and everything all at the same time. Maidservants pop in, spying for the king and making sure I'm in my rightful place and chained to the bed. I worry and I pace, and I wait for his Acker's return. Sometimes it's early, before dinner even, but mostly it's not until after I've already fallen asleep that he sneaks into bed.

Acker holds me close, arms like a vice around me. It makes the desire flooding through the Bond nearly unbearable. But aside from the chaste kisses he places along my shoulder and neck, he doesn't touch me. Not in any way I secretly wish for. My resolve is weakening with each passing night, fear making me question if I'm wasting what little time we might have left. The weight of his father's ever-evolving power is heavy. Every day he leaves this room, I worry about what he may face in the walls of the palace.

One night I awake to muffled voices coming from out on the terrace balcony, Messer and Acker's shadows silhouettes visible through the glass. When I get out of bed to inquire what's going on, Acker blocks my view of the courtyard below, shortening the leash so I can't move closer.

"They're moving prisoners to the mines," he says, shutting the doors behind him. "Don't worry. Go back to sleep." So I do. A lot of sleeping, that is. It's as if my mind and body are catching up to the years I've spent running from my dreams, finally offering me peaceful rest in my Match's presence.

It's two days later when I awake to find him sitting in one of the armchairs across from the bed that I know something has changed. He's usually gone the moment the sun is up and it's evident he's been watching me for a while. Likely since he woke. His eyes are soft; an elbow balanced on the arm of the chair. It reminds me of the time I found him waiting beside my bed in the healer's house, after my awakening. When he knew we were a Match and I didn't.

It's then that I notice Messer leaning against the closed door to the terrace.

"What is it?" I ask, sitting up and adjusting the stretch of twisted metal still tying me to the damn bed.

"Messer has found a weak spot in the west wall of the city," he says, running his knuckles absently on the edge of his jaw. "Fredrich and you are going to cross the wall for you to reach the valley where your men are waiting."

"That sounds distinctly like an order." My humor vanishes quickly. "You don't want me to stay and fight with you," I say.

He shakes his head. "No," he says, sitting forward. "I need you to lead the charge from the west."

I'm surprised. "When?"

"My father has requested all of the heads of the alliance be present for a dinner tomorrow night. That's when we'll make our move."

"Because the last dinner when Jovie was in the palace went *so* well," Messer smarts. "One would think he'd have learned his lesson the first time."

Acker and I both glare at him, and he shrugs as if to say, *What?*

"Was Kai able to move his men into position?" I ask.

Messer slumps into one of the chairs in front of the hearth. "Wren is making it difficult, but he's been able to sneak a handful into the city each night."

I nod my acceptance. "Okay, but I'm not taking Fredrich," I say, laying my down my one condition.

Acker levels me with a look that any of his battle-hardened men would be scared to be on the receiving end of, but I refuse to back down. "Yes, you are."

I shrug, nonchalant. "Then I won't go."

"I'll have to wear the mangi stones at court, Jovie. I won't be able to feel if you need me."

"You can check in with me when you can," I argue. "You've done it for years."

A muscle ticks in his jaw. "Why do you have to make everything so difficult?"

"I don't know. Why do you have to be such an asshole?"

Messer dares to intervene. "I agree with her." He raises his hands in mock surrender in the face of Acker's cutting glare. "All I'm saying is you don't always think logically where B is concerned."

"You know, like when you drugged and kidnapped me?" I add, raising a brow at Acker when he turns his glare on me.

Judging by his expression, he doesn't find my comment humorous *or* necessary. Messer stills, mouth spreading into a massive grin as he observes our mirroring postures of defensiveness.

After a long beat, Acker releases a breath through his nose, and I already know I've won. "Messer, are you able to lead her across the city to the west gate?" he asks.

My friend drops any joking pretense when he meets Acker's gaze. "Not a problem. I can take her just before the scheduled dinner and circle back."

Acker nods, albeit a tad reluctantly. "Inform Fredrich of the change of plans."

Messer unfolds from his seat. "Not a problem."

Then, as if a thought occurs, Acker stands, stopping Messer from stripping out of his pants with a hand on his shoulder. "Wells likely has a stash of his own hearthstone weapons hidden. Tell Fredrich to look under the floorboards."

After we watch Messer leave, I do find myself wanting to make one last-ditch effort to convince Acker to let me stay and fight with him, but he's already shaking his head as he strides toward me, cradling my face in his hands.

"The best thing you can do is give me the peace of knowing you're not inside the walls of this palace when the time comes."

I hold on to his wrists. "I'll feel better knowing Fredrich is with you."

I can see the waver in his gaze a moment before he gives in, kissing me on the forehead. "Okay," he says, meeting my eyes.

Relief floods through me. "Thank you," I tell him.

His response is to place his mouth on mine, letting me know he has no intention of arguing with me anymore in the hours we have left, but instead means to enjoy me as much as he can, as he lays me down on the bed. I savor his body over mine and reassure myself this won't be the last time.

There's no hurry in his movements as he strips me bare. Every time I push for more, he refuses, slowing to the point of being nearly maddening. And I learn to give in to the languid pace of his kisses and his touch, and to the steady thrust of his hips. By the time he does allow me to tip over the edge, the pleasure stretches on for so long that I'm left exhausted once it's over.

After, we lay in bed for a long while. Not speaking as we ponder what the next set of days will be like for us. Apart, but working together toward a goal. The plan is decent. Good enough to work if all goes right.

But if there's anything I've learned, it's that nothing ever goes according to plan.

Chapter 51

JO

Jovie."

I open my eyes and find Acker leaning over me. I must have fallen asleep.

He brushes the hair from my face. "It's time."

Sitting up, I spot Messer standing by the balcony doors, noting the fading sun through the window. His expression is mildly more reassuring than Acker's, but there's a noticeable tension lining his body. He turns to give me some privacy as I slip from the bed. "I'll see you in a few," he says. Then I hear him shift, followed by the flap of his wings that signal his departure.

Acker releases me from the filigree leash and I hurry to get dressed. When I pull my shirt over my head, he's there with one of his coats and he helps me slip it on. It's thick, made of wool. I'm finishing buttoning the front when I notice Acker's holding something I haven't seen in many years. Beau's metal rope.

"You kept it," I say, gauging his shuttered expression. "Why?"

"I'm not sure," he says, draping the weight over one of my shoulders. "But I think she'd like it back."

I think we both know Beau's waiting in the valley with the Maile soldiers. She would never sit idly by knowing we're likely both in this fight, but I do wonder if she believes we're doing it together.

"You'll need to move quickly," he says, pulling on the hood of my coat. "Look for Messer atop the palace wall. The passage is hidden behind poisonous vines. Stay covered until you're underneath."

"Once I'm free of the city's walls, I'll wait for you," I say, repeating the plan.

He nods. "And if I don't come to you?"

I voice the least favorite scenarios, running a hand over his stately attire, the lapel of his shirt is pressed silk. "I fall back."

He kisses me swiftly then grabs the string of mangi stones as we leave his bedchamber and wraps it around his neck. The soldiers that were stationed outside his room are gone and I find out exactly where they are when we escape into the hidden pathway behind the wall, their bodies just visible before we close ourselves in. Acker has been busy while I was sleeping.

I create a small light in my hand for us to see by as we step over the dead soldiers and Acker leads me further into the secret maze of passages than I'd ever traveled when I was here years before. He stops before a door, sensing for any moving metals that would signify people beyond. Pushing a panel in the wall until it gives way, we enter the narrow stairwell that leads down to the kitchens, and I extinguish my glow.

Workers prepare dinner, servants moving hurriedly about. Their eyes linger on us, and news will undoubtedly spread of the prince sneaking through the castle with his Match, but I assume by the time the king finds out, I'll be long gone, and I don't need the Bond to tell me that's Acker's only concern right now. We continue past the butler's pantry and into another hall.

When we reach the end, Acker turns me toward him, hands framing my cheeks. "I love you," he whispers, the words unhurried despite the circumstance.

I can't find any words without feeling the threat of tears wanting to emerge.

Grabbing him by his strap of daggers, I yank his mouth toward mine. He kisses me with just enough bite to not feel like he's saying goodbye.

He smiles against my lips. "What's going to be your first command when I'm serving under your crown?" he asks.

I don't find his question amusing in the least, but I play along to stave off the tears. "Probably something that requires you to be on your knees."

His eyes dance between mine. "I'm looking forward to it."

Removing the rope from my shoulder, I twist the metal strands in my hands to create enough tension to prevent any rattling. He kisses me once more before he opens the door, ushering me out into the cold. The temperature shouldn't surprise me, but it sucks the air from my lungs, having been inside since we arrived almost a week ago, only experiencing the biting air when the balcony doors are open to admit Messer. A hawk sits atop the palace wall, and I check the portcullis for any soldiers. There are two standing at the nearest parapet, and I wait for them to turn their backs before I make a run for it.

One of the soldiers laughs, slapping the other on the back. Messer's head swivels from the men, to me, and back again. Vines cover the passage, but I'm not sure where it is exactly, and my eyes dart to the soldiers in a panic just as a hand reaches out from under the veil. Before I can touch it, a sword darts out, moving the vines away, and I dart under the foliage.

"Fredrich?" I whisper.

"Yes," he answers, voice low. "Take this."

I can't see what he shoves toward me, but I know what it is as soon as I touch it: a belt with a sheathed sword attached. I wind Beau's rope around my waist and pin it under the belt before buckling it tight to my hips.

A sharp trill from Messer—a warning—and Fredrich squeezes my arm in farewell before darting out from under the vines, heading in the direction I just came from back to the servants entrance. I listen carefully for any sign of trouble as he passes beneath the solders on the parapet, releasing a tense breath when I'm met with silence instead.

There's a gate on the other side of the wall, left with a gap open just wide enough for me to squeeze through so that I'm unsure how Fredrich managed. Once on the other side, I keep my back to the stone, following Messer's lead as he wheels overhead.

The sun is just beginning to dip as we move to the middle point between two parapets, at the place where the lanterns are the farthest apart and the light seem to fight back the dark shadows. Here, Messer lands on the roof of a nearby building, indicating the location of a cut-through to a main street. I can't see a single soldier from my position, so I blindly make a run for it and don't look back.

The alleyway is narrow, and I dart in between the buildings, skidding to a stop a few feet in to listen for any sound of pursuit. Looking up at Messer, he keeps watch from above, ensuring no one saw anything before taking flight again. Once we're free from sight of the palace, I breathe easier.

There're very few people out on the streets, the temperature steadily dropping along with the sun. I keep an eye on Messer as he swoops over the buildings, checking different paths of travel for potential dangers. Up one alley, down the next, over and over. I split my attention between my surroundings and the bird in the sky. Sometimes we have to back-track to avoid patrols, but it's not until we've had to do so twice in quick succession that I become concerned.

Messer swoops low into an alleyway and I freeze in my tracks.

Something doesn't feel right.

I turn in place, listening to the eerie silence of the city. The muted moonlight reflects off the frozen ground and for a moment I even consider the possibility that I'm dreaming. Then I shake my head to clear the strange, surreal feeling, and I continue around the corner.

I hear the whizz of the arrow a moment before I hear Messer's cry of pain.

The scream pierces the sky as the arrow knocks him down. He flops to the stone alleyway, blood from the arrow wound splattering across the icy ground. A black tipped arrow jutting from his body. Hearthstone.

"No!" I cry, scrambling toward his heaving body, only to be stopped by the hands of a man I don't recognize. Tears fill my eyes as I wail, my feet slipping, but I'm stopped from falling to my knees as I come face to face with Wren. And it's only now that I realize exactly how dire the situation is. Men surround me on all sides. I'm outnumbered twelve to one.

I reach for the tether, but I'm met with only the familiar weightlessness that indicates the mangi are smothering the Bond on Acker's end. I summon my magic, the heat of my light beginning to shine from my hands.

"That's enough," Wren demands, and my body begins to feel sluggish, my magic dulling. "There's no need for violence."

"Why?"

He stares at me for so long that I begin to think he's not going to elaborate, but then he heaves a sigh. "Edmond is trying to oust me from the alliance." He rolls his eyes. "As if I would ever want to be a part of his blasphemous party of magic suckers in the first place."

I'm as shocked by this revelation as I am confused. "I don't understand."

"It's the very same reason I tried to take control of all the territories before, to stop Edmond's polluted agenda before it went any further, and he spun it around to make it seem like I was the one hungry for power, warped their minds with the gift of influence," he says, shaking his head as if the mere idea is absurd. "But this time, I'm going to stop him from spreading his sickness once and for all."

My vision is blurring from the tears clinging to my lashes. "What do you want with me?"

I suppose it doesn't matter, because Wren's final words put an abrupt end to our conversation. "Go to sleep."

Chapter 52

ACKER

Stassia opens the door of her personal room, and her eyes grow to twice their size as she takes in the sight of me and the man at my side.

"Please," I say, eyes darting down the hall to the kitchens.

She motions for us to come in and Fredrich and I rush inside. The space is barely large enough for a bed and a small desk, let alone for the three adults to crowd in, but Stassia crowds against the wall to make room.

"Thank you," I tell her.

I suspect my father gave me an oracle's gift just because he knew how much I would despise it. My mother made me paranoid of people who read minds and made me train how to shield myself from their ability. Understandably, now, considering what my father was doing to her, but he made a grave mistake making me take on the gift.

During the days following, I struggled to control the influx of mental sound from the people around me, especially those who haven't been taught to shield their minds in the presence of Heirs. They projected their inner thoughts like a beacon, almost as if they were shouting them directly at me. And it was during one of those mind-splitting moments when Stassia's revulsion toward my father came through.

My father's most trusted maidservant despises everything about him, down to the way he breathes, and he has no fucking clue.

Fredrich pulls back his hood and shakes the ice from his shoulders before dropping the cache of swords and daggers on the neatly made bed. "They were right where you said they would be," he says.

I take in the numerous weapons carved from hearthstone. "I knew Wells was skimming off the top, but *godsdamn*."

"This isn't even all of it," Fredrich says, lifting a weapon of his liking. He runs his thumb along the flat of the double-edged sword. "Just all that I could carry."

Stassia watches the interaction with careful consideration, and I nod to the weapons. "Take one."

She lives only on the pay of a servant, which is basically nothing, and I know her family could never afford basic iron weapons or tools, let alone any made of hearthstone. She chooses the smallest of the daggers, tucking it carefully beneath the sleeve of her uniform.

Fredrich looks at Stassia, then at me and the stones around my neck. "How'd you convince Jo to leave?" he asks.

I look at him as if he's dumb. "You're here, aren't you?"

He at least has the decency to hide his grin, knowing the only thing Jovie would bargain for in return for leaving would be my safety, and having his shield here is the best thing to help with that. "So, how's this going to go?"

"We wait for Kai. He's organizing his men to ambush the dinner."

"What about Zion?" he asks, having been updated on our friend's imprisonment from Messer.

"I've been unsuccessful in getting a key to him all week. My father's paranoia has made him hide them. Not even the guards know of their location."

"I have a key." Both of our heads whip in Stassia's direction. "The kitchen sends gruel to the dungeons every night for dinner. I can make sure a key gets to . . . Zion, right?"

I nod. "That's right."

"Shouldn't be a problem," she says.

"Okay, that's good." I look at Fredrich. "Stay here."

"What's the signal?" he asks.

I find a couple of daggers in the pile of hearthstone weapons with metal hilts, shoving them in the waist of my pants and adjusting my shirt. "I'll send Hallis to come get you. If he doesn't show, then come when you hear the screaming."

"All right," he says with a sigh. "But if I don't hear anything in an hour, I'm coming anyway."

We embrace, and then I follow Stassia out of her room and into the hall.

She's quick to stop me with a touch to my elbow. "Your father has said tonight's dinner is about declaring the official end to the war, and the formal creation of the new alliance, but . . ." She looks both ways before leaning close. "Like you did with Jovie, he had Greta sent away."

Shock has me reeling back. I hadn't been able to find her and had come to the conclusion that he must have been keeping her in his bedchambers when I didn't find her in the library. I never even considered that he'd part with her. "Did he say where?"

She shakes her head. "No. It wasn't long before you arrived." She swallows before steeling herself to continue. "But I think he's scared."

"Of what?"

"I don't know, but I felt like I should warn you."

"Thank you, Stassia."

She dips her chin in a nod and excuses herself.

I continue toward the dining hall as I try to process what she just told me.

My father has never once taken Greta away from the palace. While he's pretty much ignored her for years, he hordes her like a prized possession. He wouldn't send her away unless he was truly concerned something might happen to her. Who would want to harm Greta? She's practically a saint.

By the time I reach the dining hall, my stomach is in knots. Everything appears as expected. Helmeted soldiers line the edges of the hall, keeping watch over the festivities. Each territory's ruler has a seat at the table on the dais. My father, Chryse, seats for Irina's parents—Joss and Ulrich—although only one is filled with Bru, their appointed regent since they're not in attendance, and Wren. Tonight, my seat will be among the rest of the council on the hall's floor.

Until dinner is served, however, everyone mingles, clustered into small groups in the spaces between dining tables. I make eye contact with Hallis and we circumvent the majority of the crowd to meet in an unobtrusive location.

"Where the fuck have you been?" he questions.

"Getting her out and Fredrich in," I say, keeping my answer vague.

But he understands, and it's enough to cool his temper. "And Z?" he asks, abbreviating Zion's name.

"I've got it handled."

He releases a breath of relief. I slide one of the daggers from my waist and hand it to him as stealthily as possible, keeping my gaze toward the crowded hall.

"You're my best friend, Hallis, but I wouldn't blame you if . . ." My words trail off, letting the silence fill in the gaps for me.

"Shut up," he smarts.

I don't reply verbally, just slap him on the shoulder and leave him to make my required social rounds. The families of the council members aren't at court any longer, having left when they heard the battlefront was headed straight for the city's walls, so the room is mostly filled with dignitaries. Men who are used to speaking to their subordinates and therefore who believe everything they say is golden.

After I've done my due diligence, I approach my father as he chats with Lord Draken. "Where's Wren?" I ask, interrupting.

He excuses himself from the conversation before turning his vexation on me. "He's likely to make an appearance when it suits him."

"And you're going to stand for that?"

He takes a drink of his wine, swallowing with a sharp breath. "As long as I hold the slatstone, he'll obey," he says, but his words lack their usual cockiness.

I've never seen him be so . . . *shifty*. Fingers drumming his chalice, pulse racing in his neck as his eyes study the room.

A servant passes and I swipe a glass of bubbly alcohol from the platter. "You know how much I despise these dinners," I say, forcing conversation.

He doesn't look at me when he replies. "It's important to show your face, son."

"Your face is slipping," I say, pinning him with my stare.

My forwardness seems to knock him out of his thoughts, face hardening at my attitude. "Your insolence is the least of my concerns tonight."

A servant comes to inform my father that dinner is ready to be served, and he leaves me to ascend the dais, where he directs the room to take their seats. Everyone disperses to their assigned tables, and the glaring emptiness of Wren's chair makes his absence all the more noticeable. The smell of food envelopes the hall as dish upon dish is delivered to the tables in a seemingly unending stream of indulgence. I force myself to fill my plate, all the while watching my father as he barely even picks at his meal.

Out of nowhere, the scent of wildflowers tickles my nose, only to be gone by the next inhale. But for a few split seconds, I'm convinced Jovie is behind me. I feel for the stones around my neck, half tempted to take them off despite being so visible. Just as I'm about to stand to find a private space where I can take them off unseen, the man of the hour finally makes his appearance.

Wren strides across the dining hall's floor, steps even and measured, as unhurried as if he were the one who owned the place. My head whips about to observe my father as he watches Wren approach the dais, the whole room falling silent.

"Edmond," Wren greets him. "I see you've begun without me."

My father rises from his seat. "You haven't missed anything, my friend," he says, waving to the empty chair beside him. "We saved you a place."

Wren's smile is empty. "I realize it's impolite to rush, but I'm sure a man as important as yourself understands the value in skipping pleasantries and moving straight to the task at hand when necessary."

The hair on the back of my neck stands up. Kai used almost the exact same words during our meeting.

There's an awkward beat where my father meets Wren's smile with an equally empty one of his own before he concedes. "Of course."

My father motions a nearby soldier over, speaking directly into the man's ear. The soldier accepts his directive with a nod before departing via the door to the side of the dais, taking the stairs toward the kitchens. Hushed whispers float around the room.

Wren's gaze tilts up toward the golden ceiling, to the chandeliers dripping with crystals, and the tapestries hanging between the stained glass windows. "You've spared no expense when it came to building your empire, Edmond." His gaze falls on my father. "Truly a masterpiece," he says for the entire hall to hear.

My father misses the condescension in the man's voice, or he chooses to ignore it. Either way, he dips his head in a proud nod. "I like a man who notices and appreciates the finer details in life," he says from the dais.

From my father's perspective, I can see how he may feel as though he has the upper hand. But from down here on the floor, it's obvious who holds all the cards, and I don't care for the disparity. Standing, I look at Hallis, giving him the signal as I make my way toward the dais. My father's eyes dart to me and there's no masking the sense of reassurance my approaching presence gives him.

Let's see how long that lasts.

Chapter 53

ACKER

The shackles around Irina's ankles force her to shuffle onto the dais. Her hood is pulled over her head, shielding her face from the congregation. She doesn't look up as she is navigated toward the stairs. She's covered in filth, and I can imagine how humiliating this must be for the princess of Strou. There's even a part of me ashamed I've put my own wife in this position. I'd do it again to protect my Match, but I never would have imagined I'd subject any woman I married to such neglect.

"With her gift, you can have any gift of your liking," my father says, holding his hand out in a flourish as Irina reaches the floor. As if she's dressed in finery and not excrement.

Wren looks over her malnourished body with a casual stare. "I was beginning to think you didn't have her at all," he says, moving closer to Irina. "Especially once you and the council voted me out of court."

"Wren," my father says, placating. "You know it was a decision not made lightly, but that's behind us now. You requested this dinner to facilitate the final step in our alliance. Please, let's proceed to my sitting room for some privacy."

Wren grins, and I don't like it.

"Just one thing," he says, removing Irina's hood.

I'm still impressed by the image of my sister. Irina's eyes don't falter as she looks up at Wren. Dark hair, dark eyes, and a full mouth that mirrors so much of my own features.

"The infamous and terrifying Beau," he lilts, the first genuine smile to grace his lips. "I've been eager to meet you after the stories of your ability to make the most ruthless of men cry reached me all the way across the sea."

Irina doesn't reply to his admiration and it's obvious Wren is disappointed by her lack of response. He removes the sword strapped to his waist and the entire congregation grows uneasy. I finger a dagger loose from my strap. My father's eyes slide to me; a stern and fierce shake of his head tells me not to interfere.

Wren leans close to Irina's ear, whispering for only her and the likes of us on the dais to hear. "Can you point to all the men and women in this room who have taken the magic of others?"

My father takes a step forward. "What are you doing?"

Wren cuts my father a look of warning. "I am ensuring you have been honest in your claims to have not given the knowledge to anyone outside the heads of the alliance." This seems to mollify my father and Wren turns back toward my sister's figure. "Beau?"

Irina holds his stare for a long moment before she shakes her head. "I can't," she says.

"Is it the shackles? They're bothersome, I know."

Snapping his fingers at my father's soldiers, the men step forward to remove the chains from her ankles. I look toward my father, silently asking him if he's going to allow another man to order his men, but he only shakes his head at me in response.

Irina practically sags in relief when she's released from her bonds. It doesn't last long, however, as Wren grabs her by the shoulders, positioning her in front of him as he faces the majority of the room, his back to the dais. A brave thing to do, as I flip the dagger in my hands.

"Now," he says. "All you need to do is point out to me who has partaken in the stealing of another's gift."

I can see the top of Irina's head as it turns side to side.

"Is it easier to point out the ones who have *not*?" he asks.

Still, she continues to shake her head, refusing.

He steps out from behind Irina, inspecting her. "Are you . . . not able?"

His eyes narrow on her, and there's no way to stop what's coming as he reaches up to touch her face. We can't see what causes the flurry of raised voices from the congregation, but I already know, as Wren's accusing stare shoots at my father.

"I thought you knew better than to fool me," he says, voice veiled in threat.

My father is confused. Wren grabs Irina by the face, turning her by the head toward the dais, and my father's confusion quickly morphs into rage as Irina's illusion falters to reveal her true identity. The entire congregation gasps. Bru, the Strou's regent, yells his displeasure toward my father's back.

But my father is too focused on me, outraged. "You bastard," my father spits.

I keep my posture lax, movements unhurried as I continue to manipulate the dagger in my hands. "I am your son after all," I say, repeating his own line back to him once again.

He never sees the sword coming.

Fredrich plunges the blade straight through his back, the tip of the dark hearthstone protruding from his chest. Blood gurgles from his open mouth, shock displayed across his face as he falls to his knees. Fredrich places a boot on his back, kicking my father forward and onto his face before ripping the blade free.

Not a word is spoken, not even a whisper as he swings the blade into the back of my father's neck in a final blow, severing his head from his body.

And for the first time since Greta's premonition, I breathe a sigh of relief.

The helmeted soldiers lining the room don't know what to do, hands on their swords. I motion for them to stand down with a shake of my head. They're anxious but submit to my instruction.

Wren is the first to speak. "Edmond always kept a messy house," he says, voice void of any emotion.

Fredrich wipes the blood from his sword on the front of his pant leg. "Consider it cleaned," he remarks.

Wren makes a face. "Not quite." He steps onto the bottom step of the dais as he looks up at me. "You see, I requested Beau for the purpose of cleaning house. Without her expertise, I'm left with no other option but to assume every person in this room is guilty."

"Guilty?" Chryse asks, standing from his seat at the table. "Of what? Ending the war?"

Irina takes the distraction as a chance to run to Bru, the regent of Strou shielding her from the rest of the room, from Wren with his body. They collectively try to make an escape into the stairwell, but Wren stops them with a point of his finger.

"Sit," he demands, the power of his gift ringing in the single word. They easily submit. He issues the same command to Chryse, but it doesn't require the force of influence for the king of Roison to acquiesce. "Claiming to have fixed the problem you created is a fallacy, Chryse."

"You began this war right alongside me," he protests, pounding a fist on the table.

"I was left with no choice," Wren says, taking another step higher. "I was fine living amongst my people over the ocean, but after being barred from the Market, we were going to starve unless I decided to join you in your efforts to supersede Edmond's control."

"He was getting too powerful," Chryse says.

Wren's upper lip curls, signaling the anger simmering underneath. "And yet, here you sit, on his dais like the leech that you are."

"Because of *you*," he yells, standing from his seat once again. The air begins to crack around him, electricity seeping from his person. "You went to strike a deal with him behind my back, and that was after your Match failed to honor our agreement." He ends that last bit with a finger in my direction.

I'm unbothered by the accusation, lifting a shoulder in indifference.

Wren isn't concerned either. "I was finding the root of the poison," he answers, reaching the last step. "I didn't tell you because I knew how fallible you were. The second Edmond pushed me out of the palace, you came running like the fucking dog that you are."

A bolt of lightning shoots from Chryse's hand toward Wren, but it's as if the captain was expecting it, and he shifts just in time for the snap of electricity to surge past him.

In the next instant, he speaks a command, his gift of influence booming across the stage. "Remove your dagger from its sheath and shove it through your temple."

Chryse's eyes widen in abject terror. His hands shake as he pulls the dagger from the sheath on his waist. The metal glinting underneath the light of the chandeliers as it vibrates in his hand. His muscles strain in the effort to stop what is already happening, but nothing aside from Wren's command will suffice.

And the captain stands with one foot on the stage, elbow draped over his bent knee, completely at ease as he watches the king of Roison position the tip to the soft spot behind his eye. "Do it," he says.

Irina covers her eyes at the exact moment Chryse plunges his own dagger into the side of his head, eyes wide open as he slumps forward, face meeting the table with a sickening crack.

Fredrich and I look at each other, astounded, but no less pleased by the turn of events. We couldn't have planned this any better ourselves. The rest of the congregation, however, has the direct opposite reaction as they all begin to make a run for the nearest exit.

Wren doesn't look away from me as he says, "No one leaves."

Holy hell.

His gift is un-*fucking*-matched.

Any doubts regarding the veracity of the tales about his capabilities to manipulate entire armies are dispelled as the entirety of the mass exodus comes to a standstill. Most of the soldiers abandon their posts, removing their helmets and standing amongst the council. The few who are loyal are shaking in their place.

I feel Fredrich move closer, and I've never been more grateful Jovie fought so hard for him to stay with me, because I wouldn't stand a chance against the man before me otherwise. A muffled scream sounds in the distance, somewhere outside the dining hall's doors. Zion releasing the prisoners. Where the fuck are Kai's men?

Wren speaks his next command with too much confidence. "Take a seat."

There's a beat where I hold his stare, and a slow smile pulls at my mouth at his obvious confusion when I don't obey. He eyes the stones around my neck, but he's plenty strong enough to overpower them, but so is Fredrich. I prepare the blade in my hand, ready to end this with a careful flick of my wrist.

A seedling of fear crosses Wren's face. "I have your Match."

I quit breathing. All of the air in my lungs refuses to budge as I come to a halt.

It's the only thing he could say that would make me hesitate. I immediately strip the stones from my neck as I feel for the tether. It snaps into place, the anchor tying me to the other side of the Bond. Not in the west where it should be, but here, in the palace. I don't have to leap through the Bond to find her, because she's being carted through the dining hall doors by two Alaha guards.

"Ace," Fredrich warns when I begin to move toward her.

"She's my security," Wren says, hands slipping into his pockets.

The congregation parts as the two guards carry her to the dais. As soon as they lay her down on the table, I have two daggers poised in the air and aimed at their throats. They back away with their hands raised, practically on their tiptoes to avoid the dip of the blades pressing against their jugular. I issue a third dagger angled at the back of Wren's neck, ready to sever his spine at a moment's notice.

He senses it, head tilting toward the weapon. "If you kill me or either one of my men, she'll never wake," he says.

I look at Fredrich who nods, letting me know he'll stay with me as we collectively move toward the table. Jovie's chest rises and falls on even breaths, as if she is indeed sleeping.

"Where the fuck is Messer?" I ask.

"Dead, most likely," Wren says, as though speaking of the weather.

No.

Hatred like I've never felt in my entire life has me seeing red. I hear Fredrich, but I can't make out what he says as I call two of three daggers to my hands. They're covered in blood and tissue, the two guards dropping like sacks of potatoes. But their deaths don't feel good enough. I want the life of the man who made the order.

I turn to Wren. "Wake her up right now," I say, surprisingly calm.

"No."

I stalk toward him, bloody daggers in each fist. "I will fucking kill you, then your wife, and your pathetic excuse for a son if you don't wake her up right the fuck now."

He doesn't flinch in the face of my rage. "You'll kill me anyway."

Every one of his breaths feels like a testament to my restraint, because he's right and he godsdamn knows it. I pivot in place, eyes snagging on Irina as she trembles in her seat, Bru next to her, doing his best to shield his princess from Wren's sight.

I point at them with a dagger. "Let them go." When I turn back to him, I search for his eyes. I want him to see my sincerity when I say, "Let them go or I'm severing your spine." It won't kill him, but it'll incapacitate him for a long while. "They've done no wrong."

His gaze flicks to them, and with a begrudging shift of his chin, he releases them. "You may go."

They scurry from their seats and toward the stairs leading to the kitchen. Irina's worried gaze lingers on Jovie, then me, and I nod my okay for her to leave.

Hallis appears at the top of the stairs just as they pass, his eyes taking in the room at rapid speed. "Evelyn is invading the city. What's your order?"

While I wanted Evelyn to do exactly as such, it was under the assumption Jovie would be leading the charge. Now, my father is dead, and Evelyn is undoubtedly out for blood. My men's blood. *My* blood.

Fredrich looks at Jovie's motionless body. "If she finds Jovie like this, we'll all be dead in the matter of seconds."

I shake my head in defeat, knowing the only hope I have is to surrender. "Tell the men to stand down–"

"That is not your call to make," Wren says, cutting me off.

I pin him beneath my stare. "Excuse me?"

The cocky son of a bitch shrugs. "According to the agreement you made with my son, you no longer hold claim to the throne."

That spineless motherfucker.

I knew better than to trust Kai, but I was hoping the hatred Messer swore his childhood friend held for his father trumped his hatred of me.

"You missed a vital part of that agreement," I say with a sneer. "Which included your death."

He grins. "Then it appears we have a battle on our hands, now doesn't it?"

Chapter 54

JO

A crown of wildflowers sits on top of the pail. Flowers in every shade of color. I pick it up, inspecting its delicate work before placing it atop my head. It falls over my forehead, more like a diadem than a crown. The tall grass catches on the end of my yellow dress as I march away from the cottage to go look for him. I cross the hillside until I get to the creek where I spot him. His back is to me, and I'm glad Hallis is nowhere to be seen. I have things I need to say to Acker without his friend making fun of me.

I march up to him. "I don't want to marry you when I'm older," I say, spitting the words out all at once.

He turns to look at me over his shoulder, eyes squinting against the sun. "I don't think you have much of a choice," he says, returning to his task.

I stomp closer, watching as he picks rocks from the creek bed. They're pretty. Blues and greens and pinks. The water is clear like glass and I can see the fish dart away when he reaches under.

"What are you doing?" I ask.

"Looking for gold."

I sink to my haunches beside him. "My mother said there's no gold in this creek because it dries up every summer."

"There's gold," he says, chin balanced on his knee.

"No, there's not."

"You'll see."

I hate it when he pretends to know everything. Mother said it's because he's a boy, but I think it's because he's a know-it-all. "Well, I just came down here to tell you I'm not going to marry you, even if I have to."

He grins but doesn't look at me as he continues to shift through the rocks on the creek bed. "What if I give you a gold ring?"

"Every king gives the queen a gold ring. That's hardly special."

"Wait," he says, holding up his palm from the water, pointing at the soil in the center. "Look."

Bending close, I squint at the blackish mush in his hand. "You're seeing things."

"Jovie, it's right there," he insists.

Then he shifts his hand just so, tiny flecks of . . . *something* . . . reflect in the sunlight. I can't hide my awe, and he gets more excited.

"The creek is full of it," he says, splaying a hand over the water.

"How would you know?"

He shrugs. "I just do."

I roll my eyes. "Great. Maybe you can find enough to make a gold ring for yourself to wear."

"Don't be silly, Jovie."

"I'm not," I say with a hand on my hip. "I don't want a ring, and I don't want to get married and especially not to you."

He looks at me in a way that makes me feel like I was too mean. I wanted to be, but now that I realize I may have hurt his feelings, I feel kind of bad.

"You don't even like me," I insist.

"Who said that I don't like you?" he asks.

"You and Hallis are always mean to me."

"Hallis is . . . *Hallis*," he explains. "But I don't want to be mean to you. That's why I made you another crown."

I'd forgotten about the flowers on my forehead. "It's too big." I take it off and place it on his head instead. Then I laugh, because it fits him just right. "Did you measure it on your head?"

Put out by my flippant attitude, he rips the flowers from his head and tosses them in the creek, and I realize once again that I hurt his feelings.

"Do you really want to marry me, Acker?"

He looks up at me. "Why wouldn't I? You're the prettiest girl I've ever seen."

I laugh, because it's the most absurd thing I've heard. "You've seen, like, seven girls."

He washes his hands in the creek. "Best out of seven ain't bad."

Sighing, I bend to look at him in the face. "I'll make you a deal." For a moment I forget what I'm even saying, too enamored by his long lashes before I find my words again. "I'll marry you, but only if you wear the gold ring instead."

His smile starts to make a reappearance.

"But you have to wear it on your nose," I say, poking him on the tip of his.

He swats my hand away. "Only nomads wear rings on their faces."

"Do nomads have betrothals?"

He huffs a laugh, splashing me with the water. A water fight ensues, because of course I can't let him get away with that. We both end up in the creek as we attempt to soak the other. It doesn't take long before we're both sopping wet and we relent, our argument forgotten as we begin our hunt for more gold. Acker shows me where to look, the place where the water collects the sediment between rocks and crevices. We scoop the silky mud in our hands and let the flow of water wash the heavier pieces of dirt and mud away until there are only tiny flecks of what looks like rust.

After a while, Acker stands, eyes turning toward the sky. "The sun's been out for a while," he says, then looks at me. "I think you should wake up."

It's nonsense, his words, but I shake my head. "Not yet."

We continue searching for what feels like forever. The sun never moves and it makes me happy. For some reason, I know I don't want the day to end. I want to stay here for as long as I can. We collect our findings, combining the specks of gold in my palm, just enough to pinch between two fingers as we stand knee deep in the stream of water.

"We need to go home," Acker says, inspecting the sky once again. "You need to wake up."

"We don't have nearly enough for a gold ring, though." But when I look up, Acker is no longer the boy from my dreams. Instead, he's the man I love.

His expression is stern. "You need to wake up, Jovie."

I shake my head. "I don't want to."

He grabs me by my arms, no longer the limbs of a child, but of an adult. "I need you to wake up. Right now, Jovie. Wake up." I shake my head, but he's adamant. The gold ring in his nostril glaringly obvious under the midday sun. This isn't real. Not anymore. "Wake up. Wake. Up. Wake–"

Breath fills my lungs as if I'm coming up for air after being underwater, and with a sharp gasp my eyes snap open. The golden ceiling above gives me a view of my reflection as I lie on the table of the dais. Fredrich cusses, and I can see Acker's relief. The slack in his shoulders, his breath leaving him as he leans over my form. It takes a moment for everything to come back to me.

I look to my right, at the man from my dreams, eyes dark and fanned with lashes. "Messer?" I ask.

Acker's crestfallen face should be all the answer I need, but it's not. I need him to say the words.

"Tell me," I demand.

He shakes his head. "I don't know, Jovie. I don't know. I'm sorry."

But I think I do know. The memory of his bird form flopping against the hard ground, chest racing as he struggled to breathe, and I crumble. As quickly as the tears fill my vision, they overflow. Acker cradles me to his chest, arms tight as though if he holds me hard enough, he will be able to keep me together.

It's not real. It can't be. Not Messer. But as the memory of his death flashes through my mind, I know it to be true, and the pain feels unbearable. The kind of heartache that can't be fixed, cleaving me in half.

"Listen to me," he says, moving the hair from my face with his hands, wiping the moisture from my cheeks. "Jovie, listen. I need you to fight with me, okay?"

I struggle to make sense of his words, feeling so lost as I look into his dark eyes. I reach for his face, trying to find something real. Anything to hold on to. He's coated in sweat, and I feel the moisture on the high of his cheekbone, to the dip underneath, then to the gold ring in his nostril.

His grin is fleeting, tinged with sadness as he kisses my palm. "You want this fight, Jovie." He wipes away a stray tear, holding my face in his hands so I can't look away. "You're going to get up and fight for Messer and for me and for this entire godsdamn land," he says, his voice growing with emotion, his own fight igniting behind his eyes. "You're not going to allow him to get the final blow."

Him. *Wren.*

I sit up. "Where is he?"

"He left," Acker says, bitter. "He knew I wouldn't kill him, *couldn't* without risking you never waking up."

Little does he know, this man has spent four years pushing himself past the boundaries of mangi stone to get to me. Nothing would've been able to keep him out.

Shame has Acker looking away. "And he knows your mother is coming," he says.

Hell.

"Kai sold us out to his father, so we need to stop your mother before she kills all of my men,"

I nod, but it's disjointed. It feels like my head isn't attached to my shoulders.

"Jovie," Acker says, leveling his eyes to meet mine. "Let's find the bastard and end this."

This time my nod feels steadier.

There's a sense of deadly promise radiating from him as he holds out his palm to help me from the height of the table. It's then that the room comes into focus. We're in the dining hall, but it's empty. No, not empty, I realize, as the bodies of the entire council are splayed on the floor. They lay haphazardly across the room as if they were running from something. I follow the line of splatters from each body leading back to the dais, to Acker's feet where he stands, the drips falling from the daggers in his sash. Then I notice the dried traces of blood around his nails, in the divots of his hands and wrists, such contrast to the paleness of my skin against his.

I meet Acker's gaze, understanding what transpired while I was sleeping. The fury he felt toward every man in this room who contributed to this moment. Power hungry and selfish and greedy.

"We need to go," Fredrich says, urging our attention.

"Wait," Acker says, walking toward a man dead on the ground.

His father, I realize in startling clarity, as I watch Acker dig through his pockets before finding what he was hunting. A gray stone the size of a child's fist, and he shoves the slatstone in his very own pocket.

Acker descends the steps of the dais and moves toward one of his fallen soldiers, no longer wearing a helmet, having met the same fate as the council. He holds a hand over the sword still in the soldier's hand and lifts it as if on an invisible string into his waiting palm. He inspects the weapon before holding a hand out toward another dead soldier, taking his weapon as well. With both swords in hand, he strides toward me, holding one toward me by the blade as an offering.

"Wren has declared war against my crown and Maile as your mother pushes her army into the city," he says. "No matter what happens, you do not leave Fredrich. Do you understand?" He doesn't bother waiting for my answer, eyes leveling on his friend as if the words were meant for him and not me.

"All three of us stay together," Fredrich says, pinning Acker with a hard stare.

He nods. "Yes." Then he hauls me to his mouth with a hand on the nape of my neck. When he pulls away, he says, "If you ever leave me again, I'm going to chain you to my bed permanently."

I push at his chest. "You were the one who insisted I'd be safer away from here."

"Since when do you listen to me?" he asks, a disbelieving smile pulling at his mouth as he turns toward the stairs.

"You . . ." I don't finish the insult, knowing he's just trying to goad me as I follow him into the kitchen.

Fredrich's chuckle echoes off the walls behind me. "We kill Wren the moment anyone lays eyes on him."

Ackner nods. "I suspect he'll be leading the charge. Keep your eyes peeled. He likes the control."

"And his son?" Fredrich asks.

Acker doesn't look at me when he replies, rotating the sword with his wrist. "He better pray to the gods I'm not the one who finds him."

Chapter 55

ACKER

Women and children from the dungeons huddle in the middle of the courtyard as the stronger of their counterparts push against the Kenta soldiers manning the gate. The rest of the soldiers along the battlement are fighting a battle unseen from the other side of the wall.

I stick my pointer finger and thumb in my mouth and whistle in succession three times, the signal familiar enough for the soldiers to halt. "Ceasefire," I yell as I cut through the yard. "Yield!"

The prisoners part for us and I spot Zion in front of the gate, two men lying on the ground at his feet, a third nestled in his arms. When he sees me approaching, he drops the unconscious soldier, the body hitting the ground in a wet heap.

"My word is the decree, I am telling my soldiers to stand down," I say, addressing the entirety of the court. But I don't look away from Zion. He is the greatest threat and liability to me, my men, and my Match. "My word is the decree; I am telling my soldiers to stand down."

A commander calls down from the parapet. "The king?"

"Dead," I announce. "I hold the crown."

Zion's eyes shift to the man beside me, Fredrich. "This true?"

"Killed him myself," Fredrich says. The cocky bastard.

There's not enough time to deal with the guilt of his father's death or to verbalize an apology. For now, I give him what I can. "I'm sorry. Your father was a good man."

His eyes shine under the torchlights. "The best," he agrees, gruffly.

I'm risking a lot when I grab him by the front of his shirt and jerk him into an embrace, and I'm both relieved and unworthy of the hug he gives me back.

It's brief, and we jump apart at the sound of arrows flying above the palace, followed by a moment of silence.

Then screams.

"What's your order?" the commander yells down. "We're still taking fire."

I glance at Fredrich, and he gives me an already exasperated nod, confirming he has Jovie secure as I ascend the stairs to the battlement. Arrows continue to rain down, thudding against the shields as soldiers line the battlements to protect themselves. Between the gaps, I take inventory of the fight happening within the city.

Maile has well and truly infiltrated. Their army outnumbers my men by two to one. They hold the rooftops as well as the streets, moving through the city blocks like ants on a hill, converging with the siege happening below. Their archers are proficient, hitting one of my men within feet of where I stand, the shaft of the arrow protruding from the man's eyeball.

I lean over the side of the parapet facing the courtyard and motion Jovie up with a crook of my fingers. Fredrich follows her up the stairs, but it's Zion's inclination to also accompany them that soothes a worry inside of me. He's with me. He's with *us*.

Jovie takes my hand when she reaches the top of the stairs, and I lead her and Fredrich to the nearest gap in the battlements, between the shields. She doesn't need direction, and uses my hand as leverage to pull herself onto the stone wall. She stands tall, without fear of the height or the arrows as they ricochet off Fredrich's shield.

"I am Jovinnia, Queen of Maile," she declares, voice clear in the winter air. "And I am ordering you to cease your attack."

The siege below stutters, but the attack doesn't let up. Lifting her sword high above her head, she ignites it in a blaze of white light. Only then do the arrows begin to slow, the honed sound of arrows hitting metal slowing as the news spreads of their queen's orders.

The last time she stood on this wall and wielded a sword of light, I thought she was stunning, and she's just as magnificent this time. Now, she's divine. Strong. Confident. *Angry.*

When she turns to look at me, I'm considering sinking to my knees in worship. She knows it too, a smile flashing before she's able to hide it.

The commander's face is ruddy with fear and adrenaline as he turns to me. "What's your order, my king?"

"Raise the gate."

He's taken aback by my command. "W-what?"

Fredrich answers. "He said raise the gate."

The sound of metal grinding against metal drowns out the silence as the gate begins to lift from the ground. There's a hesitant yet persistent surge from the prisoners as they filter out of the courtyard. Once on the other side, they make haste in their departure, fleeing into the city streets.

Turning to the west, I march to the farthest end of the battlement. The army in the distance is visible even to the naked eye, but nothing more than a smudge on the horizon. A soldier hands me his spyglass, and I raise it to my eye. The lens sharpens the image and my breath catches. *Holy . . .*

The enemy army dwarfs ours. Possibly by tens of thousands. They're equipped with catapults and battering rams, flanked by two ginormous trolls lumbering like mountains in motion.

Shit.

I return to relay the information to everyone, but Jovie is already brimming with energy. I don't get a word in before she's descending the stairs from the battlement, and Fredrich and I have to keep up.

"What the hell is this?" Zion asks from behind us. "Are you both fucking her or something?"

Fredrich erupts in laughter just as we reach the courtyard's ground, and I level Zion with a glare.

But it's Beau who intervenes. "Jealousy never suited you, Zion," she says, coiling the metal rope in her hands.

At the sight of my sister, Zion freezes in place. She is the only person on this earth to render the man speechless.

Jovie throws her arms around Beau, but the embrace is short-lived as she reaches out a hand toward the metal rope in Beau's hands.

"What is it?" Beau asks, eyes searching Jovie's.

She breathes out the words. "Messer? Did you find Messer?"

Beau shakes her head, confused. "A soldier found my rope and a belted sword, but that's it." Then she considers the last detail before saying, "And blood. He said he wasn't sure who's, but it wasn't a lot."

As hopeful as that tidbit of information sounds to me, it doesn't do a lot to ease Jovie's fears. "He can't shift when he's injured. And if no one removes the arrow . . ."

Putting the pieces together, Beau's facial features go slack. "*Messer*?"

Jovie's tears threaten to reemerge as she struggles to answer, simply nodding as she turns away from Beau to hide her emotion. She misses the look on my sister's face, but I do not. Beau's tanned features turn a ghostly white, eyes wide as she realizes Messer's likely fate.

"Fuck me," Fredrick mutters.

And we all swiftly look in the direction he's looking, toward the palace. Evelyn troops out of the front doors with a sword in hand, a handful of Maile soldiers in her wake. She'd obviously planned the ambush as a diversion from her real plan to sneak into the backside of the palace and steal her daughter from my–

Fuck.

Fredrich hits the snow a split second before I do, both of us choking.

"Mother!" Jovie yells. "Stop."

My soldiers take the defense, but there's nothing I can think or do, except fight for breath. It's futile, I know, but it doesn't eliminate the effort.

Falling to all fours, my hands slip on the wet ground, vision turning black around the edges.

Somewhere in my periphery, I hear Jovie's voice. "Where's Sam?" But it distorts as it begins to fade from existence.

This is it.

Dying by the hands of my own mother-in-law.

The Mother is laughing, I know it.

Then, right before I totally black out, air fills my lungs. It's as painful as it is blissful. I gasp, sucking in glorious, freezing air. Sitting back on my haunches, I look up at the former queen of Maile. The woman who issued me the dagger Jovie made with her father to keep on my travels. And I know, without a shadow of a doubt, she hates me.

I bow my head in subservience. "Forgive me."

Her tone is biting. "How can I forgive you for something you're not even sorry for?"

Well, she's got me there. I dare to look up at her. Dressed in armor, sword close enough to take my head. Jovie stands at her side, fingers gripping her mother's elbow.

I could lie. I *should* lie. "I'm only sorry for the danger I put Jovie in, but I did it under the intention of keeping her safe."

Evelyn sneers at me, disgust plain on her face. "You are nothing but a slave to the Bond, and that makes you weak."

"Mother," Jovie chastises.

I don't deny it. "I have pledged my loyalty to your daughter's crown. As long as she lives, I live at her mercy. My men are her men. My life is her life. She can do with them as she pleases."

This declaration makes Evelyn pause. Even Zion cusses, taking a step back from me. But I am not ashamed of the love I have for Jovie. It's the only decision that I've ever made that doesn't feel tainted by outside forces. She is mine and I am hers. There is nothing in this world or any other that could change either of those facts.

"Now that it's settled," I say, slowly coming to a stand. "There's an army five times the size of ours to the west, and I suggest we begin preparing for the bloodbath heading our way."

Chapter 56

JO

There's no escaping the inevitable.

All we can do is prepare.

The biggest concern is Wren taking command of our army. Sam doesn't believe Wren is strong enough to control our men as well as his own, but we want to prepare for any scenario. While small doses of mangi stones don't seem to affect his ability, we're hoping enough of it can at least deter him. Especially if he's weakened. We amass as much of it as we can, giving it to the soldiers who will be on the front lines.

There's little we can do against the trolls other than bear the brunt of their demolition. The only chance we have to stop them is by taking them out by the head. Not their heads, but the one that controls them, and I'm not sure exactly who that is. Messer said they were Kai's doing, but after realizing he double-crossed us, there's no telling what's true and what's not.

The city as a whole offers protection we'd otherwise be without on a battlefield. We have the element of surprise, but it is also packed with people, so we spend all night getting as many residents we can to evacuate. The rest we usher inside the palace walls. It's the most fortified area of the city, but as we deposit the smallest of babies within its halls, I'm afraid it won't be good enough. I pray it is though, with Beau and Hallis guarding the doors.

Height is our best advantage.

It gives us a clear view of their advance as the morning sun begins its ascent. We watch as they set their catapults. I wish I could feel the sun's warmth, but the overcast sky prevents it. I look up at the sky, heart stuttering when I find it empty of a black eyun. It hurts to breathe as I search anyway. I can't help it. Desperate to see his familiar figure cutting through the winds.

Acker's arms offer little warmth, but I cling to them anyway. He sways us side to side, keeping our muscles loose. Every so often he'll tuck his nose into the crook of my neck, breathing in deep.

His breath fans across my skin when he speaks. "What are the odds your mother offs me in the middle of battle and tries to claim it was enemy fire?"

I know he's trying to distract me, but I play along. "Sixty-Forty."

"Here I was thinking fifty-fifty was being conservative."

I smile, but it's momentary. "She'll come around."

He hums. "Like my mother will?" he asks.

"Uh, no. That woman has hated me since I was twelve," I say, thinking of the day I moved next to her on Urchin row. "You know what's strange? I don't remember her ever showing up in Alaha. It was like, one day she was there, and people acted as though she was always around."

"Probably Wren warping people's minds," he says.

"Maybe."

Then he spins me in his arms, tucking me close to his front as he looks down at me. "So we agree, then? No in-laws at our wedding?"

"Acker," I say, half in exasperation and half in warning.

He continues. "I mean, we can both agree our fathers are out of the question."

I slow our swaying. "I do have a father." His expression becomes serious as I tell him. "Sam is the man who raised me. Until I was seven, anyway."

"Sam?" he asks, perplexed. "The general? He's not who I remembered your father to be when we were children."

"My mother would bring me to visit with your family during the summers, but also in part to allow Osiris, my real father, to see me. Sam, or Leo as you know him, would stay in Maile."

"Did Sam know that you weren't . . ."

"Yes," I say, answering the rest of his unspoken question. "He was aware of my mother's mistakes when it came to her Match. It's why she despises the Bond so much. She feels like it strips people of their minds."

He doesn't comment on that last remark. Instead, he resumes our swaying. "Are they together now?" he asks. "Your mother and Sam?"

"They don't say. Before my mother killed Osiris, Edmond agreed to extract his magic for her in exchange for sparing his life, knowing she was planning to kill him next. She gave Osiris's magic to Sam in hopes the Bond would transfer along with the magic."

"It didn't work?" he asks.

I shake my head. "He gained Osiris's magic, as well as the stolen magic of others, but not the Bond. He changed his identity so no one would question how he came upon his newly acquired abilities."

"So, your father then," he says, a smile pulling at his lips. "He's invited to the wedding."

I roll my eyes. "Can we talk about this another day?" *If we're still alive.*

His eyes rove over my features, soft as they were on the boat when I watched him fall in love with me as I was doing the same in return. "I just want to hear you say yes," he says, a wry smile on his lips.

The dream of my memory has me reaching up to touch the piece of gold in his nose. "I suppose . . . if even nomads get married–"

Fredrich cuts us off. "It's begun."

We spin in place to look out toward the front line just as a boulder smashes into the city wall. It takes a moment for the sound to meet us where we stand on top of the roof of a furniture repair store. The second is already flying through the air, scoring the land as it comes up short. In the distance, they begin to reload.

"Why don't they send the trolls first?" Zion asks.

"You said they were difficult to keep in line, so maybe they're not being cooperative," I say.

Acker isn't so sure. "Or maybe they're waiting for an opportune moment."

"What the hell is that?" Zion asks, pointing the sword in his hand at the objects moving toward Wren's army.

"Those," I say with a small smile. "Are rabbits."

And they haven't been fed since they left Maile, so they're very, *very* hungry.

Even from this great of a distance, it's obvious the men on the front lines don't know what to make of the creatures scampering toward them . . . *at first*. Then they begin to thrash, swinging their weapons and falling out of formation as they run from the animals. Little by little, the men begin to meet their fate, dropping to their slow and painful deaths one at a time.

"What the fuck," Fredrich says, uncharacteristically troubled. "They're poisonous?"

"Venomous," I correct. "And, yes. Duh."

His furrowed brow and creased eyes turn on me. "You didn't think to tell me?"

"They're not a threat as long as they're fed." I shrug, turning back to the sight beyond the city walls.

"Dear gods," he mutters. "I almost died the night I snuck into your room."

"Which time?" I ask.

Acker throws up a hand. "Don't answer that. I don't care to know."

Zion looks between the three of us. "Me neither," he says.

The rabbits hinder the army's efforts to breach the walls, and it takes nearly half a day for them to make progress. It starts as a break just wide enough for a person to fit through. Then another, a tad bigger, as three and four soldiers at a time push through. The siege continues to swell, no longer a trickle of force, but a tsunami. By the third break, my mother makes the call.

We can't hear it from where we stand. She's on the battlement along the top of the wall of the front lines. When I insisted I fight alongside her, she refused. The steel in her voice contradicted the water in her eyes as she stood firm on her reasoning.

Mothers and daughters aren't meant to experience battle together.

We watch as a ripple of archers knock their arrows, getting into position. They release in the same wave, arrows cutting through the air with a collective whizz of sound. It's a sight to see as they arc into the sky, only to fall back toward the sea of men with stunning accuracy. They drop like flies.

But not nearly enough. It does about the same amount of damage as scooping a spoon of water out of a basin in a bid to empty it. My mother calls for another round of ammo, and the cycle carries on well into the afternoon. The goal was never to keep them back forever, but to slow their progression in hopes that Wren wouldn't be far behind. But as his men encircle the city from the east, there's yet to be a sighting.

More and more men begin to flood through the wall and into the streets. Our men on the ground work to cut them down. The siege at the city's wall becomes hundreds and hundreds of men deep and my mother deploys the last effort. Tar spills down the wall and over the men below. Their armor and uniforms are a mix of Roison and Alaha colors, and I can't help but think of the people I lived and trained with over the span of my life. Many of them down there as someone ignites a flame and sends a blaze of fire across the siege.

Somehow, out of all the battles I faced against the Strou, this makes me the sickest. Their screams can be heard from where we stand as their limbs flail in futile protest. Bile burns up my throat.

When fighting the Strou, I almost didn't find them human. With their scarred skin and faces, they more closely resembled monsters. Their violence felt inhuman. But now I understand with horrifying fear; we're all just humans, and all equally capable of cruel and depraved things. Myself included.

Acker reaches for me, but I step out of his hold. I can't hide from this any more than he can.

"Come on," Fredrich says under his breath. "Where is he?"

The front line collapses, and we watch as my mother issues the call for retreat. Like a rock jutting from a riverbank, the tide of people separate around her. Their attempt to avoid her ability is in vain as she siphons the air straight from their lungs. I also realize how lenient she was with Acker, because the men surrounding her die almost instantly. They crumble to the ground, their counterparts running over their bodies to get away. I keep my eyes on her, silently willing her to concede.

Then Sam appears like an apparition next to her. And I can breathe again as I watch him speak to her the same way he does to me when I'm being stubborn during battle. Posture firm, shoulders tense. Finally, she retreats. Sam covers her back as she crosses the battlement and she's within distance of a neighboring roof.

Metal against metal sounds from the streets below. The fight has well and truly overrun the city as archers continue to pick off anyone with yellow or blue insignias on their uniforms. The melee scrambles onto the rooftops as the enemy tries to eliminate their greatest threat–our archers.

The fight reaches us as three Roison soldiers leap from rooftop to rooftop, descending on our location. Zion cuts them down with quick work of his sword. It takes less than four moves before he's kicking them all off the side of the building, and I look toward Acker with raised eyebrows. His answering smile is brief, because another bout of soldiers are making their way up to our roof.

And the battle continues until there is no longer a front line at all, and only mayhem drowns the city. We maintain our position to keep an eye out for Wren or Kai. All the while Zion and Acker keep the fight from swamping our roof.

That is until the fight takes a turn for the absolute worst.

A thundering quake shakes the air, rattling the windows of the city's buildings, and it's enough for the entirety of the battle to go still. Another booming sounds, and we turn our attention to the west, at the giants running straight for us. One of them swings a flail, and each hit of the spiked ball into the side of a building brings forth a new quake.

"Holy shit," Fredrich murmurs. He pulls his blade from the chest of a soldier, pushing the body over the ledge as he keeps his sights on the incoming giant.

Acker readies his sword. "We stay together," he says, reiterating the plan.

Head peeking over the tallest of buildings in the city, the giant swoops his hand over the archers stationed there, squeezing them in his fist. Blood and guts ooze from his hand. And when he opens his palm, he holds out his tongue and licks the human residue from his skin.

I cover my mouth to stop the bile threatening to come up.

Chapter 57

JO

We're all distracted by the sight that we don't realize we're being ambushed until we're surrounded from all sides. Acker whips the sword in his hand as he would a blade, the weapon rotating in a wide arc, slicing across the faces and necks of the soldiers in front of us in one fell swoop. All but one drop to their demise. The one remaining is enraged, eyes bulging, nose sliced clean off as he storms toward us.

But as soon as the sword swings back into Acker's hand, he steadies it, takes a step forward, and plunges it through the man's chest. The sound of metal cutting through bone and tissue meets my ears at the exact moment Acker jerks the blade free.

Zion is contending with two soldiers, but their weapons catch my attention. Black.

"Hearthstone," Acker whispers.

There's no telling how many of the lethal weapons are within the hands of our enemy.

But it's the Alaha soldier Fredrich is grappling with mid-fight that makes my heart stop. The only way to surpass Fredrich's shield is by getting within reach of it without attacking. Once inside, it's very possible to inflict injury, precisely as I had when he threw me over his shoulder and kidnapped me. And it seems Lawson has managed to figure that out, sword discarded at his feet, arms locked tight around Fredrich's throat to cut off his air supply.

Acker pulls a blade from the strap across his chest.

"Wait!" I yell, hand outstretched toward Fredrich, toward my friend from Alaha. "Lawson, wait."

Fredrich gives me a look as if to ask me what the hell I'm doing, especially as his face is turning a scary shade of red.

I call him by name. "Lawson. *Please*. Let him go."

There's a flash of recognition behind his eyes when he looks at me before they harden further, taking a step back toward the ledge of the roof. "You traitor," he spits, anger unlike anything I remember seeing on his face. "You became one of them. The same fucking land dwellers that imprisoned us."

Acker doesn't look at me as he speaks. "There's not a scenario where they both live, Jovie. All you're doing is prolonging his death."

I can save him.

"You can't. His mind has been tampered with. Whether by influence or indoctrination, he will never see you as anything other than the enemy."

I step away from Acker, away from his unwanted voice. Holding Lawson's stare, I plead with him. "I cannot stop them from killing you if you don't let him go." His eyes flit to Acker, then to me, but he's missing Zion as he encroaches on Lawson's back. "Just let him go, Lawson," I beg.

Maybe he sees the sincerity in my eyes, or he senses the danger in Acker's slow advance, but he releases Fredrich with a heavy push before leaping to the rooftop on the other side of us. Zion moves toward him, but Acker issues a call for him to halt.

"We stay together," Acker repeats.

His friend isn't happy with the release of the man who threatened Fredrich's life, and he directs that anger toward me in a heated gaze that I refuse to back down from.

The building we're standing on shudders, sending us all to our hands and knees. Eyes the size of windsails stare over the lip of the roof at us, the black abyss of its pupils encircled in a murky green that seems fitting for his smell. Meaty fingers close over the side, crumbling the brick and stucco.

"Run," Acker yells.

And we all stumble to our feet, doing just that as the troll swipes a hand over the top of the building. It stirs enough wind to catapult us onto the next roof, the same path Lawson had taken, as I realize it wasn't us he was running from but the giant he knew was descending upon us. The troll bellows his displeasure, and the stench of its breath makes me gag. The giant takes off after us, hands pounding into the roof as he tries to grab us, each strike nearly knocking us off our feet.

On our next attempt, Acker spins, launching his sword at the troll's eye. It hits the target perfectly, the ball exploding with a loud pop, sending a spray of mucus-like substance over the lot of us and the soldiers on the ground below. The scream the creature emanates has all of us covering our ears.

"We need to move," Zion yells.

But it's too late as the other troll slams his hand down on top of us. Fredrich grunts as the force of his shield is tested underneath the giant's strength, the palm overhead making the air around us tremble as the shield struggles to hold. We collectively take our swords and stab the hand above us, and it only serves to make the troll angrier, bringing his fist down instead.

It sends Fredrich to his knees. "Run," he squeezes out between clenched teeth.

Acker shoves me out from under the weight of the troll's hand, and I slide to the other side of the roof when the first troll begins to help his friend reach the men trapped beneath his palm, fingers swiping at the invisible barrier blocking them.

"Hey," I yell, jumping to get their attention. "Over here!"

They turn their heads in my direction, and my eyes widen as they both abandon their mission, horrid faces and bodies moving toward me instead.

Acker yells for me to run, and I do, turning toward the metal ladder on the other side of the roof. I swing myself over the edge, missing the first few steps before I'm able to catch myself on a rung. A stroke of luck, as the troll's hand strikes the top of the ladder, crushing the metal under his fist. It sends me sprawling to the ground, hands grasping at nothing as I land on my back, a burst of air punching from my lungs.

I struggle to breathe, turning on my side in a bid to get my lungs to work, then to my hands and knees before the organs in my chest finally allow me to take a breath. I take in the fighting all around me. Bodies crammed between alleyways, swords and fists swinging too fast to keep up with, blood scoring the snow underneath me.

Someone falls over my back, a Kenta soldier, I realize and I watch the man's horrified expression as an Alaha guard stabs a blade through his chest. I look up at the same moment the guard's eyes fall on me and I fucking *can't* believe it as I come face to face with Lawson once again.

I scramble onto my feet. "Lawson," I say on a wheeze.

He yanks the sword free from the soldier's lifeless body, eyes unwavering as he advances on me.

I hold my hands up in a show of surrender. "You know me," I say, keeping my eyes steady on his. "We trained together and snuck away for midnight swims and laughed together when Messer got caught cheating at cards–"

"You mean the other traitor?" he snarls.

He swings his blade in an upward strike that I have to dodge, shoulder hitting the brick of the wall beside me. I catch sight of Acker at the end of the alley through the throng of people. His gaze is lethal as he downs men in his fight to get to me. Stabbing a man in the neck, steps steady as he flicks a blade to the next soldier, then the next, and the next. All the while, his gaze returns to me, to Lawson's back.

"Lawson, listen to me," I say in one last plea. "The man you fight for is not who you think he is."

His reply is to swipe the sword at my neck, blade hitting the brick as I duck, spinning away to gain distance. My eyes land on Acker, his position impossibly close since my last glance. And his intention is very clear, the words unspoken as his stare meets mine, recalling a bloody dagger to his hand.

He will not spare Lawson's life again.

"Are you willing to die for the man who was willing to subject you to a life without a Match on Urchin Row?"

That nearly gets him. I see the momentary waver behind his eyes before he steels himself against it. "Things are different on land," he disputes.

"You haven't known peace on land," I counter. "Come to Maile. I'll show you—" I don't get to finish my offer before I'm forced to leap from the tip of the jab of his sword.

"I don't need anything from you," he snarls. "Not after you left us."

My eyes move to Acker over his shoulder and the trail of bodies in his wake. Still, impossibly closer.

"Kai knew. He wanted me to kill the king," I say in a rush.

Acker is within throwing distance, and I know he could end Lawson's life with little more than a flick of his wrist, but he's giving me just enough time to bargain for a few moments longer.

"And look what you did with that freedom," Lawson says, upper lip curled in disdain. "Squandered it for a mediocre cock and a crown on your head."

And I know in an instant that it's not Lawson I'm speaking to . . . but Wren as his hateful eyes bore holes through me. My eyes flick to the windows of the buildings beside me, to the rooftops, but come up empty.

"That's enough," Acker says, blade poised at Lawson's neck.

If I had any doubts of Wren's control, they dissipate at the lack of fear in Lawson's honeyed eyes. "Do it," he says, a smile pulling at his mouth.

I shake my head, knowing Wren will only enjoy the fact I watched my Match kill my friend. "Wren's controlling him," I say low for only the three of us to hear. "He's in the city. Somewhere close."

Acker's anger wavers, mouth tightening before he releases the blade. Maintaining the weapon midair, he slams the hilt of his sword into the back of Lawson's skull with a loud crack, knocking him unconscious.

Acker's unhappy expression is aimed at me. "The list of men you have prevented me from killing is almost as long as the list of men I've actually killed."

"Don't be dramatic," I say, reaching for Lawson's abandoned sword.

It's then I notice Fredrich and Zion at either end of the alley, further protecting us from incoming threats. The vibration of the trolls' steps increase in severity as they get closer. Yells ring out across the city blocks and the smell of burning flesh fills my nose.

"We need to retreat." I meet Acker's eyes.

Acker takes in the bloodied alleyway and the overrun street beyond. He doesn't like the idea, but he also can't refute the need. "We can make a run for it," he says. "To the isles south of the continent. You and me."

And I smile at his love for me, that he's willing to abandon everyone and everything if it meant my safety. Because he'd fight in this battle to the end if it wasn't for me. He's not scared of death any more than he's scared of living.

I say, "I have a plan. Make the call."

Having already expected my answer, he shakes his head. Not in genuine protest, but in frustration. "We'll get slaughtered in the valley."

"It won't be pretty," I agree. It's our last resort for a reason, but . . . "I just need you to trust me."

Sighing, he looks down at Lawson's body. "Let me guess. You want me to bring this asshole with us."

I can't stop my grin.

Chapter 58

JO

The final horn signaling retreat sounds right as we make it to Maile's base camp in the valley west of the city. It's nearing dusk. Soldiers who were closer to the back line are already resting with food and water. Healers have a tent set up for casualties to be brought in, and that's where Acker goes to deposit the six-foot man draped over his shoulder. He heaves him onto a cot. When he tells one of the women to strap him down, he sends a look at me, daring me to say otherwise, and I keep my mouth firmly shut.

"Jo!"

I spin in place at the sound of Raina's voice. I spot her pinned hair a few cots down. The healer is tending to a soldier sitting on the cot before her, face contorted in pain as she places her hands where a sword must have went straight through his shoulder joint, sweat coating her brow.

She yells over the broken sounds of the injured and shouting from the other healers. "Your father was just in here looking for you!"

I nod my understanding and turn for the tent's opening. Fredrich and Zion both fall in step beside Acker and I when we emerge into the growing frenzy of the camp. Soldiers come and go, searching for something or somebody, the chaos of the battle still lingering in their expressions. There's no reprieve yet. We removed our siege ladders from the west walls, but the sound of the trolls tearing down the stone and iron barrier echoes down the valley toward us. It won't take long for Wren's army to reorganize and descend on us.

Through the throng of soldiers, my eyes land on General Samasu's, and within a split second he's standing before me. "Jovinnia," he says on an exhale.

And I'm unprepared for his embrace or the might at which he squeezes me.

My relationship with Sam has grown differently since my return to Maile, especially in comparison to mine and my mother's. It's been slower, but steady. While I've never doubted his care for me, his affection is typically displayed in the form of his guidance and acts of service. Protection, even. But if there was ever a seedling of doubt that he didn't love me as if I was his true daughter, it's dispelled in this instant.

Then it's over.

He pulls away, his expression calm as he returns to business. "The munitions are being moved as we speak."

"Where's mother?"

"Getting the new front line situated." His gaze skates over the men at my side, eyes locking on Fredrich, specifically, before moving over to Acker.

He holds out his hand in greeting.

Acker looks at Sam's outstretched hand, with puzzlement on his face at the Alaha greeting before he accepts the gesture. "It's a pleasure to meet you," he says, and I can practically see the wheels turning in his mind as he looks Sam in the eyes. "Although, I wish it were under better circumstances."

"In which aspect," Sam challenges, dropping Acker's hand. "The battle or the abduction of my daughter?"

I shoot him an exasperated glare, but Acker takes it in good nature. "You know what? You choose."

The stern set of Sam's features doesn't waver. "I'll decide after we win this battle. Why don't you go help Evelyn while I have a discussion with my daughter."

It's not a question, but an order, rather. And the last time Sam tried to take me from Acker's presence, Acker didn't take to it too kindly.

But any momentary worry I had dissipates at the feel of the kiss Acker places at my temple. "Come find me," he says, dipping a chin in farewell to Sam as he turns toward the city.

Zion is quick to follow, but Fredrich, on the other hand, hesitates. "General, if I could have a moment," he says with a remarkable amount of courage. "I'd like to make an apology."

Sam looks at Fredrich with cold indifference. "If my daughter is fine with you under her command, then so be it," he says. "But you will never serve under me again."

My jaw goes slack at the harshness of Sam's words, the finality of that statement after the years Fredrich spent under Sam's command, the comradery and trust they built. My head swivels to Fredrich, my friend, and watch as he accepts Sam's decision with a solemn nod.

"Understood," he says. His eyes flick over mine as he turns to meet Zion and Acker who stopped to wait for him.

When I look at Sam, he gives a single shake of his head. "Don't look at me like that. You'll understand one day that forgiveness doesn't come as easy when someone wrongs your children."

The ground rumbles underneath our feet, sending a wave of fret over the camp right before what sounds like an explosion like none other reaches us from the east. My gaze whips in the direction of the city, but I'm unable to actually see the devastation from where I am standing in the middle of camp.

"Jo, listen," Sam says, grabbing me by the shoulders until I look at him. "If I know anything about Wren, it's that he only pursues what he believes is a sure victory. He's going to move forward hard, and you're going to want to pull back, but don't. Not until I give you the signal, okay?"

I nod, letting out a shaky breath. "Can you go check on Beau at the palace?"

He lets me go. "Yes, but you need to go to your men. They're scared. Give them the strength they need to stare death in the face."

With that, he disappears.

Another rumble trembles underfoot and men dart past me, weapons in hand as they make toward the frontline. My hair floats around my face as I look back to the east once again, and I suddenly remember I'm supposed to be cold. Not that I feel it as the wind scores across the land, the tents around me rattling from the force. Something I know should hurt but feels featherlight and cool against my balmy cheeks. Tiny specks of white dance in the wind and I look up, watching as snow begins to fall.

Maybe this is the moment my mother told me would always come, when I would finally adapt to the cold.

I make my way through the camp and to the front line. Once outside the line of camp, I'm able to set my sights on the back line. The soldiers see me, shifting to make room, silence spreading through the horde of men. Torches are held intermittently, lighting the way. Their faces are set, hands clutching their swords and shields. Some of them have the stirrings of an eternal stare and I swallow from the realization that the men in front of me may not last long in the battle coming.

I'm reminded of Queen Asa. The battles she led, the men who died under her crown. She's depicted as a ruler who wanted total control, to knock the leaders from their neighboring thrones. The very same men who would later pass their titles to their children. To Edmond and Osiris, and I wonder if she was fighting the same fight I am right now, trying to defend—not just her own people—but all people. That maybe the strength of her gift as a Light Wielder only fed the narratives of the men who feared her, including her own lover.

I follow the tether, knowing it will lead me. And when the final mass of men part, I get a glimpse of Acker rallying the soldiers, Fredrich and Zion are doing the same, shaking the life back into the worn men. Physically and emotionally, offering words of encouragement. Straightening their shields, making sure they keep their bodies protected. Snowflakes land on the men's hair and shoulders, even coating their eyelashes.

Acker straightens, his gaze meeting mine. Fear like no other has my breath shuttering. I don't want to lose him when I've just gotten him back. I've already lost my best friend. Messer was my family before I even knew what it meant to have any. But there's still my mother, my father. My friends. Fredrich and Beau and even Zion. I didn't get enough time with any of them to lose them now. Wasn't my time in Alaha without them penance enough for my wrongdoings? Having to live without Messer's cocky grin and jubilant laughter?

And it's as if Acker can sense my thoughts because he places a hand against his chest, eyes soft as he watches me.

The men around him notice his shift in demeanor, heads swiveling as I step out of the crowd. And once free of the front line, I have a clear view of the city's destruction, the mass of army gearing up for another fight. Wren thinks this is going to be an easy win. In his eyes, he likely believes he already holds the keys to the territory.

The weight of the stares of the soldiers at my back has me readying my voice. "I'm tired," I say, the truth evident as I face them. "Today was brutal. As was yesterday, and the day before that. And I know many of you are tired, too."

My mother appears from the fray, a sword in her hand. I recognize it from her personal cache and she nods at me, an encouraging gesture. I already feel the stirrings of my magic awakening, heat spreading in my veins.

Taking a moment to look as many of them as I can in the eye, I continue, "I want you to know, you're not fighting for me and you're not fighting for Maile. You're not fighting for any territory for that matter. You are fighting for *yourselves*. For your families and your loved ones, so that they don't have to live under the rule of a man like Wren. Or Edmond. Or Chryse. Where magic exists without shame or control. Today, we fight for *us*."

I hold my sword high above my head, igniting it with my light, and shouts begin to erupt across the valley, a tidal wave of emotion that goes on for what feels like forever. I can feel their energy in my chest; in the air I breathe.

Chapter 59

ACKER

She *is* magic," Evelyns whispers, eyes alight as she watches her daughter next to me.

I wholeheartedly agree. "She is."

She did a better job than Fredrich and I ever could. Keeping the sword raised, I watch as she walks to the front of the line and the soldiers' frenzy follows down the line with her. I move to follow her, but Evelyn stops me with a hand on my arm.

But even as she speaks, she doesn't tear her eyes away from her daughter. "You need to spread the word to your men. On the count of ten, cover themselves with their shield or whatever they can find."

Fredrich speaks up. "What happens after the count?"

Evelyn's eyes slip to mine as she says, "Just make sure everyone knows to take cover."

My eyes dart to Zion's and he doesn't need further instructions, disappearing into the fray. When I look back at Evelyn, she, too, is merging with the soldiers, and I quickly lose sight of the gold sword strapped to her back.

A piercing sort of pain shoots through the Bond that has me looking for Jovie, feeling her through the tether. She's within view. Head tilted back to the sky, her eyes search the expanse of black above, looking for someone who won't be coming.

Even as I think it, I don't want to believe it, half convinced Messer will swoop in and save the day.

Eat a troll or something.

Jovie's pain is violent. And when she drops her gaze from the sky, there's a new kind of determination in her stature. I can see her fury mixing with grief, a dangerous combination, but powerful as she matches the rage-filled energy of her men. Eyes blazing with the need for blood, teeth barring as she shouts her orders for the men to ready themselves. Their war cries are deafening.

But on the wind, there's an answering call.

Looking to the city, the flickering firelight slowly creeps closer, the vibration in the land growing stronger.

I make to move toward Jovie, but Fredrich stops me with a hand on my shoulder. "I'll stay with Jo. Don't let your concern for her distract you," he says.

Impossible.

He gives me a pointed look. "I've got her."

Knowing he means it, I jerk him to me in a swift embrace. "Let's get this over with, yeah?"

He grins. "Let's."

Jovie is staring into the distance when I come upon her. Snow speckles her hair, little flakes of ice against her red locks. The sword in her hand radiating a steady light. I say her name and it almost feels like she's looking through me when her eyes meet mine. I cup her face in my hand, holding her stare until I see fissures begin to form in her icy exterior.

"Marry me," I tell her.

There she is.

Relief floods through me as her mouth thins. She's annoyed, yes, but there's also a flicker of humor down the tether. She opens her mouth and I hear the answer in her mind, and I cover her mouth with mine before she can speak it. The kiss is a promise from each of us to fight until tomorrow, when we can look back at this in memory.

Pulling away, I cradle her to my front, forearm across her chest. I breathe her in. Wildflowers mix with the smell of ice; chin tucked into her neck as I watch the pinpoints of firelight descending on our position.

I love you.

I'm stopped in my tracks, registering the words she projects toward my mind. The worry I've carried since I first heard her fears of me obtaining Vad's gift spikes before slowly melting into something completely opposite.

Placing my mouth against her temple, I send my own message back. *Tell me tomorrow.*

A quiet settles over the army and that's when I notice the disappearing fire in the distance. One after another, the fires extinguish in a move reminiscent to the time Jovie arrived in Kenta. It's a strategic move to make the incoming army invisible in the night air, swirling snow and clouded breaths creating a veil over their position.

"Put out your fires," Jovie commands.

The order gets passed through the crowd and the light steadily wanes until we're also cast in darkness. Jovie's sword is the last to remain lit before she pulls her gift back. Removing two daggers from the strap across my chest, I move to Jovie's side.

Other than the clank of swords against shields, shuffling feet, and heavy breaths, it's silent as we listen for the incoming horde. It's the calm before the storm.

Then, so very slowly, a vibration increases under our feet. Not the booming caused from trolls, but the kind from a flowing stampede. The yells of the men come next, their chorus coming in much quicker. We ready ourselves, anticipation coursing through the entire throng of soldiers.

It feels as if a wall of metal is coming for us. In their clothes, and weapons, and blood. So much iron that it makes my teeth hurt.

"Hundred paces," I warn Jovie, Fredrich by her side. I run the back of my knuckles against the fist she has her sword clutched in and I can nearly sense her building anticipation through the Bond. "Fifty."

Like an incoming thunder, the sound of thousands of men comes barreling down on us, their yells mixing with yells of our own right before the collision. The incoming men are barely visible in the night, their arrival bringing forth a gust of wind. My ears ring as metal bangs into metal, bodies into bodies.

Fredrich's shield cocoons us, but not entirely. Unperceived threats sneak past the barrier, like the man stumbling into my front. I can't tell who he's aligned with, and I don't want to kill our own men, but before I can react, Jovie ignites her sword.

Except, it's not just her sword.

It's every sword within fifty paces that ignites with light.

Fredrich cusses and there's a stunned moment where the fighting stutters, everyone stunned, some of our own men dropping their weapons in fear. I stare at Jovie in awe. But all she does is cut down the Roison soldier who found himself within our shield with a backswing of her sword. It doesn't take long for the fighting to resume, our men using the newly quired advantage of blinding light to strike down their adversaries.

I flick a dagger to my right, the blade arching back toward me, slicing the man coming toward us across the throat. *Been hiding that nifty trick, have you?*

There's a cocky edge in her expression when her eyes cut to me. I find myself smiling as I jab my dagger into an Alaha's ribs, using my magic to shove the weapon through the front of his chest, out the back, grabbing the sword in his poised hand right before he crumbles to the ground, recalling the bloodied dagger in my other.

I hold the front line with Jovie and Fredrich and have the vague sense of Zion nearby.

The killing is mindless. I can feel my heart beating in my chest, hear it in my ears, but everything seems to calm in the sea of rage. Instinct takes over, an endless sequence of motion. My vision locks in sporadic moments, time caught in the span of breaths, in the pause of a blink. I watch as my sword splits a man open ear to mouth, his tongue visible on a scream I can't hear. Swirling snow as I spin and throw my sword up against an incoming saber. Jovie's blade spearing through the man's chest. On and on it goes. Stumbling over the fallen, we don't stop. We don't slow.

Then, the ground judders.

A violent shake that has everyone freezing in place, even our opponents as the tremor comes again, except stronger. The roar of a troll vibrates the air and everyone looks toward the bellow, as a growing figure emerges from the swirling snow. It's the troll with one less eye and he's hurtling through the horde of battle, feet hitting the ground with violent force as he stumbles over his own men. Their deaths end in abrupt screams.

When a second set of steps sound in the distance, Zion's prayer is just about audible above the melee. "Mother help us."

We move in unison to avoid being crushed to death under the foot of the troll. But every man around us has the same idea, Roison, Alaha, Kenta, and Maile alike, all make for a congested escape out of the troll's path. We're not going to make it.

Jovie and Fredrich skid to a stop ahead of me, and I clutch the sleeve of Jovie's leathers and yank her in the opposite direction. Toward the troll rather than away. Zion catches on. Faster than Fredrich and I both, he sprints toward the giant, sword raised over his head, a cry leaving his mouth as he slides underneath the falling footfall of the troll. He scores the bottom of his sole, sliding across the ground as blood waterfalls from over his head. He barely escapes being smooshed as the troll screams. The sound is ear-piercing, but the giant stumbles to the side, creating an opening for the rest of us to get by.

He's angry. He growls as he bends over, swatting a hand across the ground and taking out anyone in his path. Bodies fly, screams fading into the night sky. The giants are either too hard to control, or Wren *really* doesn't give a fuck about his own men. Shoving Jovie ahead, I make sure she and Fredrich are clear of the troll's rampage, I fall back. Jovie screams my name, but I don't break concentration as I ready the sword in my hand like a javelin, squinting as I take aim. And when the troll bends to grab a handful of soldiers, I hurl the sword, pushing the metal through the air toward my target. His remaining eye explodes as soon as the sword pierces it.

I make a run for it.

Blood and ooze rain down from above; the giant cries as he struggles to stay upright. A fight he's going to lose, I realize, skidding to a stop. I meet Jovie's eyes and shake my head when she makes to move toward me. Fredrich stops her with a hand around her arm as I backtrack, my feet fighting for purchase across the wet ground. Blood and guts and trumpeting feet have created a muck of mud. The troll careens toward the earth, blocking my view of them as his body falls, the resulting crash shaking the earth and sending a burst of wind in every direction. Anyone within a hundred paces hits the ground.

Lifting myself up, I shake the gunk from my hands. I feel for Jovie, the tether leading me to her location on the other side of the fallen giant.

Men scramble toward the troll as he fails on the ground, taking their chance to put him down permanently.

A resounding scream has me looking over my shoulder, the other troll's anger evident as he roars into the night air, and this one unfortunately has both of his eyes. Both of which are set on me and he's already headed in my direction.

Fuck.

I run along the length of the fallen giant for cover, but it's quickly evident that I'm not going to be able to outrun this troll; the booms of his footfalls closer too fast, the ground quaking underneath my feet make my knees rattle. I trip over the fallen, sliding in the muck. Scrambling onto my back, I pick up every piece of metal I can sense on the ground around me and hurl it at the troll looming ahead.

A useless endeavor.

What little connects barely wounds. Most he's able to swat away. The giant makes a fist, and with his fallen brethren at my back, there's nowhere for me to go as I wait for when he brings it down onto my head.

But something stops him.

Someone.

I sense bitterness of the blood. I see Wren, standing amidst the fray of battle behind the giant. His focus isn't on me, but the troll, hand outstretched, brow furrowed in painful concentration. His attention is so wholly focused that he doesn't see his son. Like he's been waiting for this moment his whole life, he comes from behind and slices his father's neck in one swift motion, splitting his neck open.

I look up and the troll's eye is rolling back, the white of his eye only visible as he sways in place. I think he may be . . . falling asleep?

I don't wait to find out.

I turn toward the fallen troll. The tatters of his tunic hang from his form, and I wrap my hands around the material, using them to climb atop his body. There's a rush of air from behind me and when I turn around, the troll is on his side—snoring.

When I look back toward Wren, he's face down on the ground, and Kai is long gone. Chaos reigns as the fighting continues. The casualties litter the ground, getting smothered by mud as they're trampled over. It's messy and stomach souring. Out of all the battles I've witnessed, this is by far the most depraved.

Worst of all, I see most of our own in the fallen. We're being fucking slaughtered.

The snow has slowed, just a few tufts of white floating to and fro, the overcast sky thinning just enough for the sliver of moon to be visible through the clouds. It affords me just enough light to have an unfettered view of the battlefield, stretching as far as the eye can see in every direction.

My eyes lock on Jovie. Fredrich and Zion have their backs to her as they fight off any incoming threat. Her gaze is set on something in the distance and as I follow it, I see a flash of gold wings. The first of many. Like a flower blooming amidst death and horror, gold butterflies emerge. Their flight draws the attention of the sea of men, heads tilted back, mouths agape at the sight. Sam stands on the edge of the box he's just opened, mouth moving as he yells to men below. I can't hear it, but as our men below yell in unison, the message travels on the wind, barely a whisper as it reaches my ears.

Light Wielder.

My chest caves as I realize the chant is the count. When I look back at Jovie, she's already looking at me. And on the next count, I join, the chant proud on my lips.

Light Wielder.

It's as if the wind stills as the chant continues to grow in volume. Almost as if the Mother herself has stopped to listen.

Light Wielder.

I call for a discarded shield, catching the weight of metal in my hands.

Light Wielder.

The fight at temporary impasse, Fredrich drops his sword to his side, mouth moving in time with the chant.

Light Wielder.

And as the count grows to encompass the entire battleground, Jovie ignites her sword, eyes still locked on mine. I wasn't exaggerating when I said I'd serve at her feet. I'd bend my knees at this very moment if I was standing before her.

Light Wielder.

And as the count narrows down to the final three, she ignites her sword in a burning glow, rotating it with her wrist as she readies herself.

Light Wielder.

Then she aims her sword toward the butterflies fluttering.

Light Wielder.

There's a flurry of crashing metal sounds as all our men lift their shields over their heads to take cover, myself included.

Light Wielder.

I watch from beneath the armor across my back as Jovie unleashes her light toward the golden butterflies in a beam of pure brilliance. Its radiance hits their wings, and the light is immediately reflected back, compounding with each beat of their wings before being redirected toward the ground in a stunning view of dancing shafts of light. I can't help but think to myself in this moment that light burns brightest after the dark.

Wren's men don't know what hits them.

Not until the light scores their flesh do their cries begin. A chorus of anguish as they burn from the outside in, skin melting from their bones as the light continues to shift and dart across the battlefield. It scores the faces and heads of anyone who didn't know to keep cover. It dances over me, its heat searing over the plate of metal on my back. I close my eyes from the blinding light, covering my head, praying to the gods that a beam doesn't come at me at an unfortunate angle.

It goes on for what feels like an eternity but is likely no longer than a few minutes. The smell of burning flesh fills my lungs. By the time the heat abates, and I dare to open my eyes, there is just a handful of beams left. Carefully peeling away the shield over my head, I look out over the valley. Cleared of enemy forces, either by death or surrender. Heat rises from the scored flesh and earth and into the air, steam billows around us.

And in the center stands Jovie, chest heaving, sword down by her side as she takes in her doings with wide eyes.

I sling myself off the troll, staggering on my feet on the soiled ground. Our soldiers rise from their makeshift shelters, stunned and off-kilter as they take in the suddenly quiet battlefield. Bodies lay in waste, their flesh still bubbling and sizzling, some of their skin sloughing from their bones as I step over them in my haste to get to Jovie.

Sam is already with her. He tells her he's proud of her. That it had to be done. Evelyn pulls her close next, but I can tell she's overwhelmed. And when her eyes meet mine, I feel her calling me toward her, the Bond pulling at the tether. Once I'm within reaching distance, she yanks me to her, and I bury my face in her hair as I cradle her against me.

I feel her shock.

"It's over, Jovie," I tell her.

And she repeats after me. "It's over."

The sound of soldiers cheering erupts all around us and it seems to pull her out of her daze. The men throw their fists in the air, shouting to the sky. It lasts about as long as it takes to realize there's an enemy soldier who somehow managed to escape with his life. Their cheers die as they move out of the way as the one soldier in particular walks through the throng of men with his hands raised in surrender, blonde hair escaping in tendrils around his face as he comes closer.

Kai.

A soldier rushes over and kicks his legs out from behind him, sending him to his knees. He catches himself with a hand before straightening, expression unreadable.

Stepping from my embrace, the rage Jovie had depleted returns with a vengeance. "How dare you show your face," she sneers, the sword in her hand trembles, the metal still hot to the touch.

Her skin begins to glow.

"Jovie," I say, a touch of warning in my tone. "Easy."

She looks down, taking note of her radiating heat, but she continues. "Where's Messer?" she demands. "What did you do with him?"

"I don't know," he says.

She stomps forward and I'm impressed by his ability to not flinch in the face of her ire. "Did you know? What your father planned to do? Kill Messer? Nearly doing the same to me?"

He shakes his head once. "No," he says, voice sallow. "He found out I'd been moving men into the city, and he basically disowned me. Said I was a waste of an Heir."

Her light flashes across her body. "I don't believe you," she says, eerily calm.

"Jovie," I say, placing a soft touch to her shoulder, the warmth nearly painful as I gently turn her toward me. "He saved my life."

This gives her pause, brows furrowing as she struggles to make sense of the words. "What?"

I tilt my head toward him. "If he wouldn't have stepped in," I tell her. "I wouldn't be alive right now."

A soldier in the distance yells something, interrupting, but it's difficult to make out.

"What did he say?" Zion asks.

Fredrich responds, "It almost sounded like he said—"

"—the captain of the Alaha is dead!" the soldier yells again.

Jovie looks at Sam, not needing words to give him the order, and he disappears in an instant.

"It's true," I say, drawing their attention. "Wren is dead."

"How do you know?" Jovie asks me. When my gaze shifts to Kai, her eyes snap toward him. "You killed your own father?"

The first flicker of true emotion ignites behind Kai's eyes. "I did."

Chapter 60

JO

Acker braces his hands on either side of the veranda, and I lean back into his warmth. Winter just refuses to let go of its death grip. "Are you ready to go home?"

Home.

A place I once wasn't sure I believed in anymore, but now feels a lot like the person against my back.

I nod, head lolling against his chest. "Yes. What about you?" I ask, looking up at him, seeing the reflection from the fireplace dance in his eyes. "Are you ready to live in Maile?"

He nods. "It's a beautiful city."

That it is. "We're going to have to find our own place," I say.

"We're not going to live at the palace?"

"With my mother?"

He makes a clicking noise with his tongue. "We're going to have to find our own place," he echoes, and it makes me smile.

It's something I've found difficult to do in the weeks since the battle. Each smile reminds me of all the reasons I should, while also all the reasons I don't want to. Guilt is a strange notion. Wanting to find happiness, but not exactly knowing what to do with it when it finds you, even if it's just a little.

"How are you feeling?" he asks.

He does this every so often, checking in on me. Some days are easier than others. But tonight feels more difficult for some reason. If I try to explain why, the feelings become too much, too big to articulate, and then I'll just start crying.

I offer him what I can. "I'm okay."

He kisses me on my cheek. "Let's get inside before you start shivering."

I let him pull me into his bedchamber. I mentally correct myself, knowing how much he hates it when I call it that—*his*—since we've been at the palace for weeks now, but I am ready for our own place.

A low fire burns in the hearth with a mound of pillows and blankets before it. After the battle, I spent days in front of the fire. It was as if I was unable to get warm, the cold lived in my bones. The frigid sensation still hits me out of the blue sometimes. It's become a routine of ours, to spend nights in front of the fire.

When Acker turns to shut the doors leading to the veranda, I stop him with a hand on his arm. "Leave them open."

I don't have to explain why.

We settle onto the blankets. My head on his chest as he plays with my hair. "How long do you think it'll take before Beau is begging to return to Maile?"

"Oh, about three and a half days," he says. "You?"

"I don't know," I muse. Her insistence that she's more than capable to run the territory so strong that I'm tempted to believe her. Not that I ever doubted she could, just that I can't believe she volunteered. She hates Kenta.

"Hallis swore to keep an eye on her."

I smile, a real one. "Of course he did."

"You tease him too much," Acker says. "Beau has never looked at him twice."

"You never know. A lot can happen with just the two of them, alone in this giant palace. . . ."

I can hear the grin in his voice. "And keep a new council to acclimate and city to rebuild."

Placing my chin on his chest, I look up at him. "If we can fall in love in the middle of the ocean and amidst a war, they'll have plenty of opportunity while helping organize Greta's new catalog system."

He laughs, head tilting back.

While Greta has made it known she doesn't intend to stay forever, she wants to leave the library in the best condition possible before the next librarian and record keeper takes over. Plus, I suspect she wants to stay with Beau. She worries.

Kai and Aurora are staying here as well. The Alaha have dispersed into the city for the time being, and the couple will act as their liaisons for the council. At least, for the time being. And while Beau is adamant there's no deception in either of their auras, I still have my doubts. We never found Messer. We looked across the city. The territory and beyond, but there's too much ground to cover and not enough men to search it all. I'm just sad I can't bring his remains home to Alaha where I can give him the sea burial that I know he would have wanted.

After a while, Acker says, "We're going to need a place big enough for you to have a drawing room," he says.

I roll my eyes. We've been over this time and time again. "I don't draw anymore."

"I know," he says, hands playing with my hair. "But I think it's a good time to pick it back up."

My smile is sad. "I was never any good at it."

His hands still before he flips me onto my back, looking down at me on the pile of blankets we've pulled together in a makeshift bed. "You can't be serious."

"My sketches were terrible, Acker. Just admit it. I promise it won't hurt my feelings."

He stares at me in pure disbelief. "I will never admit that, because it's not true. I still have the picture you drew of a prized horse."

"That's embarrassing for you," I tell him.

He lifts a brow, smile tilting to one side. "Jokes on you, because Zion and Fredrich spent all afternoon packing your old art supplies in the carriage for departure tomorrow morning."

Sighing, I can't even be mad at him. "I suppose we have the extra room since Irina left for home earlier this week."

I can hear the smile in his voice. "She practically skipped out the palace doors."

I take his hand in mine, admiring it for all of its perfection. Long digits, strong, veins in all the right places. Not overly calloused, but just enough to give purchase to his grip. A working man's hands, but capable of minute tasks.

I bring his middle finger to my mouth, biting on the pad. I sigh, finding something so satisfying in being able to finally do what I've fantasized about. There's nothing overtly sexual about it, but heat ignites behind Acker's stare as I continue to the rest of his fingers, ending with his thumb.

I bite a little too hard and he jerks back on a hiss.

But he smiles, pure mischievousness, and I love how easy it looks on him. "Do you love me, Jovie?"

"What a ridiculous question," I say.

He shrugs. "Answer it anyway."

I can't help my smile. "Yes, I love you."

"Then say yes to marrying me." He runs his thumb over my lips, eyes stuck on the motion. "Lie to me if you have to. I just want to hear you say yes."

Leaning on an elbow, I sit up so we're at eye level. "Why is it so important to you?"

"Our union could ease any lingering doubts of uncertainty. It would give the people something to look forward to after all they've endured under my father's crown, help unify our two territories under one rule."

The people have already called for it in the streets, chanting our names as if we're already betrothed, but . . . "Are you sure this has nothing to do with finding another way to ensure I'm tied to you forever." My smile dims as I notice his serious expression.

He continues combing through my hair before meeting my eyes. "It's what normal people do when they love each other. I want to think . . . if we weren't Matched, that'd you still choose me anyway."

My tender heart breaks a little at his confession, and I try not to cry for the umpteenth time today. He's been more insistent the last few weeks and I've been avoiding his questioning. The thought of having a wedding without my best friend by my side is painful. A deep ache like the cold in my bones.

He feels it now, eyes softening. Or maybe he hears it in my thoughts, I can never tell anymore. "Messer would want you to be happy."

I swallow past the burning knot in my throat, nodding. "Okay," I say on a whim, knowing how much he needs this. "I will marry you."

"Thank you," he whispers against my mouth, laying me back down on the blankets. He pulls my shirt over my head, his voice like a caress over my skin. "Glow for me, Jovie."

I shake my head. "I've never been able to do it. It usually just happens when I feel out of control."

I hear the smile in his voice as he reaches for the waistband of my pants. "I can make that happen."

Epilogue

MESSER

The wind isn't ideal.

I stretch my wings as I teeter on the windowsill, and pain radiates through my chest. But I can't wait any longer. I heard the mother talking to her husband about the prince and his Match leaving for Maile today. People are gathering below, lining the streets to send them off in part in farewell and victory celebration for the end of the war.

Lindy's voice sounds on the stairs, and I know I'm on borrowed time. The young boy has taken it upon himself to nurse me back to health, much to his mother's chagrin. I owe him my life. I wouldn't have survived after being left in the freezing cold. He found me in the alley and brought me inside where he kept me snug by the fire, fed me his leftovers and gave me warm milk.

But the kid thinks I'm his new pet. Plans on training me to hunt mice. Which is admirable, but I have people who I know miss me. At least, they better miss me. I hope they're beside themselves in their grief and heartache. I'm talking real tears and everything.

". . . check on Goblin," Lindy yells down to his mother.

The kid named me fucking *Goblin*.

Here goes nothing.

I leap from the open window and a cry leaves my beak. Searing pain lances throughout my entire body as I flap my wings, furiously trying to catch the wind. I hear Lindy's shouts from behind me, but I can't give him my honest gratitude as I struggle to not plummet to my death for a second time.

I ascend, only to get battered by cross winds. Dropping lower, I find a decent draft and expand my wings. My right doesn't fully extend. The joint near my shoulder is still a mess, not fully healed. But it works well enough to let me steer on an updraft. I follow the cheers to the southern gate.

The streets become less congested as I near and then I see why. Three carriages parade out of the city's gate, one behind the other. If I would have chosen to shift into any other bird before I was wounded, I would be able to sense her, but hawks have a stupidly limited sense of smell.

I bend my wings just enough to dive toward them, but the air gives and I'm fumbling toward the last carriage's roof. I hit the surface, tumbling over the surface. I'm able to stop myself from going over the side and getting run over by the wheels by using my talons, the nails scraping across the roof.

"What the fuck was that?" asks a male's voice I don't recognize.

Then I hear her, the familiar cadence of B's voice in the very first carriage.

I wobble into a stance and gauge the distance to the middle carriage. The driver of this one, however, looks over his shoulder and sees me. He makes a shooing noise, flapping his hand at me, and I jump onto his arm. He screams, throwing me forward and sending the horses into a tizzy. It's not a graceful maneuver by any means, but I land on the carriage with stumbling legs.

Pain? Agonizing.

But a success is a success.

The door to the front carriage opens, Acker's head whipping in my direction. He must have felt the familiarity of my blood and I use the last bit of strength I have to launch myself through the opening, tucking in my wings. I land on the cushioned bench in a blunder. I'm wing over tail over head over talons as I come to stop on my back.

B gasps.

When I turn my head to look at her, my heart sinks. I take back everything I thought earlier about being upset over me being missing. I can see the pain in her face as tears immediately well in her eyes, spilling onto her cheeks as she stares at me in shock.

I haven't tempted to shift since being shot down from the sky with a hearthstone-tipped arrow, and probably shouldn't after my harrowing flight here, but I can't subject myself to just watching B cry as a hawk.

Shifting isn't painless at any given time, but this one is worse than my very first. As my bones and blood and muscle shift into human form, a new, excruciating pain ignites in my right shoulder, and a scream erupts from my throat the moment it's in place.

But immediately after, the pain dulls to an insistent ache, and I'm able to manage a smile through short breaths. "Hey B."

Her cries turn into full-blown sobs as she throws herself onto my chest. I grunt from the weight, patting her on the back with my good arm. My eyes catching Acker's from across the carriage. Which, albeit isn't far. We're packed in here like sardines.

"You know, if you were anyone else, you'd be looking down the sharp end of my blade," he says.

He shoulders out of his coat, throwing it over my exposed cock. But even as he gives me a droll look, there's no disguising the delight in his eyes.

"Just admit you're happy to see me," I tell him.

All he does is grin.

Eventually, B sits up and looks at me, hands feeling the mangled skin of my chest. "How—what? Where?"

I laugh at her nonsensical rambling, face snotty. "It took a while to heal," I say, smile dimming. "I'm sorry I missed all the fun."

She shakes her head, wiping her face with the back of her hands. "You need a healer."

"Gods, that'd be great," I say.

Finally, Jovie smiles. Her joy turning into laughter as she wipes away her tears.

I'm careful to keep myself covered as I sit up. "Where's Kai?"

Acker sits forward, interest piqued. "Why?"

I remember how Aurora found me injured in the snow. She was frantic as she snapped the arrow and yanked it out, which hurt like a *bitch*, but it's all she could manage before Kai called for her.

Leave him.

His command was to leave me to die.

The hurt has since passed. I had plenty of time to let the realization set in as I slowly healed behind a street bin. Now, all I feel is rage, because there's one thing I know to be true. Without a shadow of a doubt, Aurora would have never allowed for that to happen. She would never leave me to bleed out in the freezing cold as if I was no one to her. The only plausible explanation is . . . Kai was influencing her.

Looking at Acker, I say, "He's got my girl."

Acknowledgments

Once again, thank you to the readers who loved *Metal Slinger*. Whether you were with me from the beginning or just discovered my writing, I'm so appreciative of everyone's patience as you have waited for this book. I know I left you dangling off the side of the cliff in the first book, and I hope the ending of this one made up for it.

Thank you to my agent, Emily Forney. I tell you all the time that you're the best, but I can't stress how much I appreciate you. And a huge thanks to Layla, Sophie, and the team at BookEnds.

Thank you to Sara Goodman, as well as Amelia, J, Sarah, Meghan, and the entire team at Saturday Books. Thank you to Millie Prestidge, Hennah, Harry, and the entire team at Gollancz. It's been an exciting and eventful year, to say the least, and I'm so appreciative for all the love and hard work that's been poured into this book.

Thank you to Sara, Millie, Emily, Sarah P, and J for working with me through developmental edits, copyedits, and more. This was truly a group effort, and I'm so glad to have had you all on my team for this story.

Thank you to my cover designer, Murphy Rae, for the breathtaking and beautiful art that encompasses the vibes perfectly.

As always, thank you to my best friend, Alicia, for reading every first and worst draft with me. I would never survive without you. To my husband, Marlon, for being a place of rest and comfort when I'm in the depths of my delirium when writing. To my mom, Michelle, for continuing to be a shoulder to rely on, even as you continue to fight for yourself. I love y'all.

And to all the friends I've made along the way, thank you for everything and more.

About the Author

Sydnie Decou Photography

RACHEL SCHNEIDER lives in South Louisiana with her husband and daughter. She loves to write wherever her imagination takes her, which includes fantasy worlds, thrilling surprises, and complex romance with a touch of heat. When she's not writing down her daydreams, you can find her at a hockey game or enjoying a bubble bath with a good book.

Instagram: rachelschneiderauthor
TikTok: RachelBeeps